it
STARTED
With a
TWEET

Anna Bell lives in the South of France with her young family and energetic labrador. You can find our more about Anna on her website, www.annabellwrites.com or follow her on Twitter @annabell_writes.

Also by Anna Bell

The Bucket List to Mend a Broken Heart
Don't Tell the Groom
Don't Tell the Boss
Don't Tell the Brides-To-Be
The Good Girlfriend's Guide to Getting Even

It Started with a Tweet

Anna Bell

ZAFFRE

First published in Great Britain in 2017 by

ZAFFRE PUBLISHING
80-81 Wimpole St, London W1G 9RE
www.zaffrebooks.co.uk

A CIP catalogue record for this book is
available from the British Library.

ISBN: 978-1-78576-369-4

also available as an ebook

3 5 7 9 10 8 6 4 2

Typeset by IDSUK (Data Connection) Ltd
Printed and bound by Clays Ltd, St Ives Plc

Zaffre Publishing is an imprint of Bonnier Zaffre,
a Bonnier Publishing company
www.bonnierzaffre.co.uk
www.bonnierpublishing.co.uk

For Laura Pearse: Despite the weight of the world on your shoulders, you are one of the kindest and most thoughtful friends anyone could have. Thank you, you're an inspiration x

Chapter One

Time since last Internet usage: 32 seconds

'If you could just lift it up a little bit more,' I say, tugging at the poor man's shirt. 'That's perfect, just so we can see those pecs better.'

I turn back to my best friend Erica who's holding my phone ready.

I pout my lips ever so slightly and tilt my head up to minimise the risk of double chins, all the while praying that the lighting is dull enough to hide any traces of the fluorescent cocktails we've been supping all afternoon.

I do a last-minute adjustment of my top, causing my cleavage almost to go X-rated. I desperately try and wrangle my boobs back under control, which in turn exposes my midriff.

'Bloody dress code,' I mutter under my breath. Only Helen could have friends who would think that 'slutty' was a good theme for a hen do. It was very *her* though; when we used to live in a flat share at university she always went out in the skimpiest of outfits, but still, I'm not used to having so much flesh on display.

'OK, that's lovely,' shouts Erica as she snaps away.

I channel my inner model, turning my head multiple ways and pointing my hand at the poor man's chest, as if I'm advertising him as a prize in a game show.

Content that she must have at least one good photo, Erica hands the phone back to me and I thank the stranger whose chest I've been exposing. He skulks back to his friends, unsure of what's just gone on, but they make as much whooping and hollering as mine do. The poor man's just been *henned*.

'Oh my God!' says Erica. 'I do not believe you had the shame to do that.'

'What? It was only his six-pack, it's not like I asked him to get naked,' I say, shrugging and reviewing the footage. 'Ah, bingo.'

I select the one that shows not only his six-pack, but also my provocative pout, and I send it to the chief bridesmaid. I also post it to Twitter for our friend Amelie to see, and within seconds she's favourited it.

'I can't believe Amelie's missing out on these shenanigans,' I say, secretly thinking that she lucked out by being on a business trip in New York this week, so that she gets to witness the humiliation of skimpy outfits and ridiculous challenges from the comfort of her hotel room. She's definitely not facing the constant dilemma of whether or not she's going to have an involuntarily nip slip or thong flash whenever she moves.

'I think I'm the first one to complete that challenge,' I say, looking around at the other members of the party stalking their prey around the bar. 'Now perhaps we can work on yours, ladies.' Erica and Tess groan as they peruse the list of acceptable photos in the game:

Sexy six-pack
Separated at birth (celebrity lookalike)
Mutton dressed as lamb
Escaped from captivity
Most likely to vomit first

'What about him?' asks Erica, pointing at a man in the far corner. 'If you squint, he kind of looks like Ryan Gosling.'

'What, if Ryan Gosling was six-foot-ten and ginger?' replies Tess.

Erica tilts her head. 'OK, so perhaps he's more a ringer for that long jumper – you know, the Olympic one that was on *Strictly*.'

I quickly tap that into my phone. 'Greg Rutherford,' I say, thanking Google.

'That's him. Be right back,' she says, tottering off to snap a selfie.

I turn my attention back to Tess but she's off like a rocket in the other direction.

What is it about hen dos that sends you into a frenzy trying to do things you never would in your right mind? As I take a sip of my cocktail I get my answer: it's only 3 p.m. and I've already lost count of how much alcohol I've consumed today.

I look around the bar – which, for a Saturday afternoon, is buzzing – full of the hen-and-stag-do crowd, all high spirits and bravado, vying for the prize for most cackling. While the other girls are off humiliating themselves (and others) in the name of the hen, it's nice to actually sit down for a minute and have a bit of time to myself – it's been a full-on day of activities. We started off with a life-drawing class this morning

(#SeeingLotsOfWilliesAtBreakfast), followed by a pole-dancing class (#ChannellingMyInnerStripper), lunch at the OXO Tower (#NomNomNom), and now we're having late-afternoon cocktails (#TroubleWrittenAllOverIt) before we head onto a party boat tonight (#BringOnTheVomit).

My phone vibrates in my hand and I look down to see a message from my mum:

> Hi, Sweetie, don't forget it's Rosie's birthday today. Speak soon, Mum xx

Oh crap. How did I forget my sister's birthday?! Surely Facebook should have told me that! She's obviously one of those inconsiderate people who turn off their birthday notification. I mean, what do they expect us to do? Remember on our own? Last year I was working so hard that I would have forgotten mine, if I hadn't had notifications of birthday wishes from eager friends when the clock struck midnight.

I rub my temples as if to chide myself for forgetting. Of course it's her birthday; it was one of the first things I thought when the hen do was announced for today. But in all the military planning that Helen's chief bridesmaid Zoe has done, I'd been reprogrammed to think that nothing else was going on today.

> Hey, Sis, hope you're having a great birthday! Did my card arrive in time? I'll try and get up to see you soon – it's been ages. Daisy xx

I send the message before logging into Moonpig and ordering a quick birthday card, picking the first 'Sister' one I find that doesn't require a photo upload. By the time Erica makes it back to the table, I've written it and had it posted, and can now blame Royal Mail for her not receiving it on time, *cough*.

'Now, I tell you what, if I wasn't with Chris . . .' she says, winking at me. 'You should get yourself over there.'

'What, and incur the wrath of Zoe? Wasn't that against the rules – no diversions from the hen? Plus, he's not my type.'

'What, tall, handsome and here in real life?'

'Very funny. I do meet up with my dates, you know.'

'Uh-huh, then dismiss them for not living up to their online personas.'

'It's not my fault that people deliberately lie on their profiles. If only the men I spoke to on Tinder told the truth.'

Erica howls with laughter. 'Like you do? When was your profile photo taken?'

'It was taken at a temple at Chiang Mai and I use it because it shows I'm cultured.'

'Sure you do. It's not because it was taken four years ago when you had less wrinkles . . .'

'It's actually more about that awesome tan I had, rather than the wrinkles.'

'Ah, I've missed this,' says Erica. 'We haven't been out like this for ages. Hell, I haven't *seen* you for ages.'

'I know, work has been so crazy,' I say, nodding. 'It'll calm down soon.'

For the amount of time I see my best friend, you'd never believe that I was currently living in her spare room.

'Done it,' says Tess as she triumphantly walks back to the table. She shows us a picture on her phone.

'He definitely wins "Escaped from captivity",' I say, holding my handbag a little closer. 'He looks like he belongs on one of those photofits on *Crimewatch*.'

'Oh, he's harmless. I used to teach him; he's a gentle giant and an absolute whizz at algebra.'

Erica and I look over in surprise.

'Right, ladies,' says Zoe, storming up to the table. She's Helen's chief bridesmaid and BFF from home; she takes both roles very seriously. 'Thank you for your photo contributions, we'll be judging who won the challenge later on. But in the meantime, I've nabbed us a big sofa area so we can play the next game.'

She claps her hands together as if to hurry us along and the three of us plaster fake smiles on our faces.

'Great,' I say, feigning enthusiasm. Any actual enthusiasm was lost along with my dignity, which was around the same time as I put on the outfit that makes Julia Roberts's hooker costume in *Pretty Woman* look conservative.

'At least with all these games we're not spending that much money here,' says Tess as she struts off ahead of us. She's not wrong, which is good because the hen do practically warranted its own savings plan. Helen and her fiancé are eloping to Las Vegas so this is for all those who can't afford to attend the real wedding. Only, to be honest, I'm pretty sure that I could have flown to Vegas for less money than today's activities. I'm just counting my lucky stars that Helen wanted her hen do in London – at least Erica and I don't need a hotel for the night.

The area that Zoe's found for us sees two sofas facing each other, wedged into the corner of the room. Most of the other people on the hen do have nabbed the comfy bits already, so I find myself perching on a knobbly arm with Erica.

'OK, so I'm sure that everyone's played Cards Against Humanity before, right?' says Zoe. 'Well, I've made us a hen-do version. I'm going to give each of you six cards that have answers on them, then Helen will select and read a statement card from the deck and you have to put forward the answer card you think will fit best. The lovely Helen will then pick her favourite. OK?'

Before anyone can say anything, Zoe's started to deal the cards. No doubt because she's only allotted us a certain amount of time to play this game, as the whole hen do has been run to a strict time schedule.

I pick up the cards I've been dealt and read them over:

Keeping your toenails clipped
Owning a whip
A good right hook
The missionary position
Not giving a shit
Organisation and planning

I've only ever played the official Cards Against Humanity, and that was when I was pretty drunk, but this looks as if it's going to be less offensive and more risqué. Probably for the best, as I don't know many of Helen's other friends.

I pick up my phone and tap out a quick tweet.

Hang on to your hat @amelieMwah we're playing Cards
Against Humanity Hen Do style – be prepared!!!

'Right, then, first statement,' says Helen, turning over the card
with a cheeky glint in her eye that lets me know she's enjoying
every minute of this day. 'The secret to good sex is . . .'

There's a tittering amongst the hens as we all start rereading
our answer cards, looking at what's most suitable, e.g. the
funniest. To be honest, all mine are pretty apt – well, apart from
the missionary position one – unless that's what you're into.
I'm about to put down 'keeping your toenails clipped' when
I change my mind and put 'owning a whip'.

I tweet my response and a couple of the other responses too,
all for Amelie's benefit, of course, so that she doesn't feel she's
missing out. At university the five of us lived together and it
seems strange for her not to be here. With Helen having moved
back to her native York after uni, it's usually her that's missing
from our quintet.

'I think Erica's is the best,' says Helen, as Erica does a quick fist
bump in victory. 'The secret to good sex is being up for anything.'

'Nailed it,' she says, giving me a wink. She can be so competi-
tive but it makes me want to win the next round.

'The key to a good marriage is . . .' reads Helen, as she turns
over the next card.

'Damn it,' I say to Erica. 'Surely that should have been owning
a whip.'

'Ah, that's always a bugger when you play your trump card too early.'

I throw down my 'a good right hook' card and, of course, I'm not surprised when it's beaten by one of the other hens who has 'always being on top'.

I tweet the updates to Amelie, and to the rest of my one thousand, nine hundred and ninety-seven followers, who, I'm sure, are on the edge of their seats waiting for the next instalment.

'OK, next up: blank is a woman's worse enemy,' says Helen. 'So we're looking for the answer at the beginning of the sentence.'

'Too bad I don't have a card that says hen dos,' says Erica, nudging me.

I look down at my ever-escaping cleavage. 'If only,' I say, thinking that would hands down be a winner.

I scan my cards and select the only appropriate one left.

Helen peruses the answers before settling on mine. 'Here we are – the missionary position is a woman's worst enemy. Good job, Daisy!'

I beam, the cocktails making me feel like I've just won a Nobel Prize rather than a silly hen-do game.

I don't win any of the other rounds, and it doesn't take long for us to finish the game.

'Right, then, hens. We're leaving for the river cruise at sixteen forty, so that gives you fifteen minutes to drink up and go to the loo. We'll rendezvous by the door,' shouts Zoe.

I give her an *X-Factor* Cheryl salute and turn my attention back to my drink.

Erica shimmies off the sofa and joins the mass exodus with the other hens who run to the bar and the loos in equal numbers.

I glance at my Twitter responses before I scan my Twitter work account quickly. There doesn't seem to be anything that can't wait until Monday morning, or at least my hungover stupor tomorrow. I'm currently looking after the social networking for the marketing agency I work for, but I'd much rather tweet late than tweet drunk, I'm not a moron.

My phone buzzes with a text from my sister:

Thanks, Daisy. Having a quiet birthday as Rupert's away on business. Haven't got your card, maybe I'll get it on Monday. Looks like I'm going to be in London next week, do you fancy meeting for lunch or dinner on Wednesday or Thursday?

I feel a little guilty that not only did I forget her birthday, but also her husband isn't even there to take her to some fancy Michelin star restaurant or luxury spa, or whatever it is he usually does that involves spending copious amounts of money. But it sounds as if she's doing OK. And it's a bonus that I get to see her for lunch one day next week, which means I don't have to make the effort to go up to see her. We're not mega close sisters; we're more the type that catch up at Mum's at Christmas.

I know I should visit her more often, but I'm always slightly nervous that I'd get all the way there and we'd have nothing to talk about. When we were growing up, the three years between us seemed cavernous, and while the years between us don't matter so much anymore, our lives are still so different. She's a kept woman who's married and living happily ever after, whereas I'm more working girl and unlucky in love.

It's really busy at work at the moment so lunch would probably be best. Shall we try for Wednesday? xx

'Man alive, the queue for the bar was crazy. Here, get this down your grid before we go.'

I eye the glass suspiciously.

'Shots? Are we there yet, really? It's not even five o'clock.'

'Somewhere in the world it is, and, believe me, we're that desperate. I overheard the game that Zoe's got in mind for on the way to the boat. You're going to want this.'

Reluctantly, I take the glass from Erica and shudder as I sniff it. Tequila. I try and think of a time when something good happened after tequila, but most things that follow it are hazy. If the game that Zoe's going to have us play is as bad as Erica is making out, then maybe that's no bad thing.

Erica shakes a little sachet of salt onto her wrist before she pours some on mine.

'Three, two, one!' shouts Erica, before we both throw the shot back. And as I recoil at the putrid taste she thrusts a wedge of lime at me.

'Hold that pose,' says Erica as she snaps a photo of me. 'Adorable.'

'I bet that's my new Facebook profile picture right there,' I say laughing as I snatch her phone and see my gurning face.

'One more selfie for the road?' she asks and we both pick up our phones.

'Pose slutty,' I say, mocking the theme, and we both pout and push up our cleavage.

I hastily snap, then wince at how drunk we look when I see it. We've got hours to go yet; I dread to think what treasures I'll find on my phone tomorrow morning.

Chapter Two

Time since last Internet usage: 7 minutes and 13 seconds

I hear the ping of my phone and my ears turn towards it like a finely tuned sonar as my brain processes the noise. Instantly I know it's a Tinder message. I feel my stomach lurch slightly and my heart beat a little quicker in anticipation. Not that I can dive for my phone. I'm far too busy listening to one of my boring work colleagues rattle on about a pitch he's got next week. I'm feeling sluggish from the weekend and chronically overworked, so the melodic tones of his Scottish accent were almost sending me off to sleep. Luckily, the phone beep has re-energised me.

If I just lean a little more onto my elbow, I might be able to peek behind where he's perched on my desk, and be able to see my screen.

'So, you'll send it over to me, then?' he asks.

'Uh-huh,' I say, tearing my gaze away from his back and looking him firmly in the eye. 'Absolutely.'

I have no idea what I'm sending over to him, but I'm sure he'll remind me, he's not known as Marvellous Marcus in our office for nothing.

'Great. The Henderson report visuals, the FirstGroupFirst webmail campaign and the Honeybee report, all into the presentation file by tomorrow morning, OK?'

While relieved that at least I know what I've agreed to, I'm not particularly impressed by the timescale. My to-do list is already as long as my arm – and at five-foot-ten, I've got pretty long arms.

I stifle a yawn. I'm exhausted, but there's far too much to do before I leave for the night.

I look at the clock on my computer; it's already 6.30 p.m., and I'm supposed to finish at six. So much for me making it out of work on time tonight. Not that I'm particularly surprised. I rarely leave the office before seven on a good night, but right now, at our marketing agency, we're at our busiest time and I might as well work down a mine for all the daylight I see.

Any thoughts of me climbing into my snuggly bed and having a nice early night where I gently fall asleep are replaced by an image of me barely managing to take off my clothes before I pass out on top of the covers with exhaustion in the early hours.

I sigh out loud. It's not only my sleep that's been suffering because of my punishing work schedule, but also my wardrobe. I'm weeks behind on my washing. I was supposed to do it on Sunday, but I was so hungover after the hen do that the thought of the chugging noise of the washing machine was too much to bear. I wish I'd just taken the noise on the chin, as right now I'm sitting in the office wearing a silky top that's from a pyjama set, a misshapen cardigan with one arm longer than the other and a pair of leggings so threadbare that I'm pretty sure that if anyone looked at my crotch they'd be able to see the Snoopy that's emblazoned on the front of my knickers. I usually try my best to look reasonable when I leave the house, working hard to create an outfit that warrants a mirror selfie, but the only social media this outfit's destined for is a how-not-to-dress meme.

If I don't do any washing tonight, I'm going to be walking in tomorrow in my leopard-print onesie without underwear. Despite our office subscribing to casual Friday, that would push the acceptable boundaries of casual, and, besides, it's only Wednesday tomorrow.

I groan and turn back to my to-do list, and am about to start on Marvellous Marcus's work when I remember the Tinder ping and my fingers lunge for my phone instead.

Please, oh gods of Tinder, let it be the super-hot guy I swiped right to last week. I unlock my screen and my heart feels a little disappointed that it's not a message from him. It's from Dominic, another guy who I'm going on a date with. Clicking on his photo, I read the message:

Going to be a bit late. Can we make it 7.30?

I have to read the message again. Ugh, he must have sent it to the wrong person as I'm not meeting him until tomorrow. He's obviously playing the field and probably has dates every night of the week and has just got confused. I stare at his photo again and wrinkle my nose as I study him. He's cute, but do I really want to go on a date with a serial Tinder player? Granted, I don't expect declarations of exclusivity before we've even met in real life, but

I do at least want to pretend that I'm not one on a conveyor belt of dates.

I scroll back up through our conversation to remind myself why I'd decided to date him in the first place. Our brief messages are mainly flirty banter – mostly about work and where we live – nothing too deep, but, in scrolling through them, I read the message where we planned our date: Tuesday at seven. Today – in half an hour's time.

'Oh, shit,' I say out loud, having obviously written it down wrong in my diary. I'm supposed to be meeting him on the South Bank; it's going to take me at least half an hour to get there.

'What's up?' asks my desk neighbour, Sara, glancing up from her screen.

'I'd forgotten I've got a date tonight.' I stare again at my to-do list and check what's still outstanding. I wasn't planning to leave my desk for at least another hour, or more likely two. 'I'm going to have to cancel, I've got way too much to do.'

I hate letting people down, but there's no way I can go. And it's not only because of the work. I mean, look at me. As if it wasn't enough that my outfit's a complete shambles, I'm also rocking the panda look on my face with my pale skin and black eyes, and the closest my hair got to shampoo this morning was a can of Batiste. I'm so ridiculously tired that I'm pretty much struggling to remember what my own name is when I sign off emails, so how am I going to dazzle a stranger with witty and sophisticated conversation?

I glance down at the photo of Dominic, his floppy blond hair, and those sparkling green eyes. He *does* look cute. Imagine the babies we'd have, or, better yet, imagine the Instagram photos we could post: his blond hair polarised in a Valencia filter with his green eyes the colour of emeralds . . .

Plus, I even got Erica to track him down on LinkedIn to snoop at his CV, and he's a trader in the City, which means his credentials look good on paper. Not that that's a deal breaker, but it might mean that he'll at least pay for dinner.

'Is this the same guy you cancelled on last week?'

I hang my head in shame and she frowns at me. I don't dare tell her I cancelled with him two weeks before that too. I was surprised he rebooked after the second cancellation – I doubt I'd be so lucky third time around.

'If anyone can afford to sneak off a little early, it's you,' says Sara, rooting around in her in tray for something. 'You're the most organised person I know, with all your lists. Come on, one night's not going to hurt, Daisy.'

'But Marcus has just asked me to do some work for him and I've still got prep to do for tomorrow's meetings. But on the other hand, if I don't meet Dominic tonight, then I'm probably never going to meet him.'

'And what if he's the one?' says Sara, raising her eyebrows.

Sara's on an eternal hunt for *the one*, whereas I'd be content with *a* one right now. Being stuck in our office almost 24/7 for the last few weeks has meant that it's been slim pickings for both of us when it comes to finding a deep and meaningful relationship.

'You're right. I've really got to meet someone soon or else Marvellous Marcus and his quick reminders are going to start looking pretty attractive. Do you reckon he would give a recap before we had sex?' I say in a whisper as I lean over to her desk. I try and do my best Scottish accent: 'Now, I'm going to fondle you, you go down on me, and I'll do some finger work before we both orgasm, OK?'

Sara's eyes almost pop out of her head, and I wonder if I've crossed some sort of at-work boundary of what's appropriate to talk about, when I realise that she's looking over my shoulder.

I turn and see Marvellous Marcus standing there.

Sara pretends to be typing. I know she's pretending as she's doing about 600 wpm and not even The Flash could type that quickly.

'Marcus,' I say, wondering how I'm going to dig myself out of this hole.

'Um,' he looks between Sara and me and his cheeks flush red, 'I'll just get the pen I left and I'll leave you two to whatever you were planning.'

He practically runs off and I try and process what he said.

'Oh God, he didn't hear the whole thing, did he? Which, I guess, is good in a way,' I say, 'as at least he didn't know it was about him. But that means he thought I was propositioning you.'

'No, do you think?' says Sara, trying to hide her laughter. 'Surely, your fake accent must have given him a clue.'

'I don't know, I think it was pretty terrible. Do you think I sounded Scottish?' I say trying to recreate it.

'Actually,' she says, wincing, 'it was probably a bit more Irish.'

'Hmm, great, now Marcus thinks we're having an affair. Just the reputation I need in the office.'

'You could do a lot worse than me.'

'That's true,' I say to Sara, who looks as if she'd be more at home on a catwalk rather than a desk. 'If I was into women, you'd be top of my list.'

She smooths down her hair and smiles at the compliment.

'So this date of yours, you're going, then?'

'I guess so, as now I need to get a boyfriend to prove to Marcus I'm not a lesbian,' I say laughing.

I tap out a quick reply to Dominic to confirm the change of time, as I curse myself for stupidly agreeing to a date this week in the first place. I'm an account manager at a marketing agency, and the majority of my clients are City-based firms who all, very helpfully, seem to send their financial reports to their investors at the same time – which means that for the next month I'm busy chasing up designers, liaising with the Indian office, where we outsource most of the work to, and pinging drafts of glossy brochures or samples of digital campaigns across to our clients for feedback. Don't get me wrong, I love my job. It gives me a huge buzz to co-ordinate everything and deliver a successful project to a happy client. I just wish that they didn't all want to have their reports ready to go at the same time. And if that isn't enough at the moment, I'm also managing our company's Twitter feed while our social media exec is on holiday. Not that tweeting and getting paid for it is much of a chore.

I groan as I wonder if I've got time to squeeze any more work in before I leave. Maybe if I do my make-up on the train, I could do half an hour more. I scan the list and work out what's an absolute priority. I can always work late tomorrow night instead.

I'm just about to start finding the pieces Marvellous Marcus wanted when my phone beeps with a WhatsApp message from Erica.

What time are you going to be home tonight? Thinking of making a chilli if you are up to eating again! x

Scratch crawling into bed for an early night after doing the laundry, staying at work *or* going on a date with a super-hot guy. I'd much rather be sitting on the sofa with my bestie dissecting the hen do. Despite living together, we haven't seen each other since she grunted in her hungover state on Sunday morning that she was off to her boyfriend Chris's house.

I'm going on a date with Dominic, the Tinder guy. Maybe I won't be home at all . . .

I know that's a lie, I have the ultimate chastity belt on as the leggings are hiding a hairy forest. I can't remember the last time I shaved my legs.

Ooh, hope it goes well! In that case I'll stay at Chris's tonight. Don't forget to keep doing updates so we all know you're safe. I'm out tomorrow night, but catch up on Thursday if you make it back from work early enough? xx

I quickly reply:

Of course xx

It's funny, as I thought that living with Erica, I'd see her more, but in actual fact in the three months that I've been living in her flat I've seen her less. We're like ships that pass in the night. At least when we lived separately we used to make formal arrangements to see each other, now we're lucky if we bump into each other for long enough to gossip over a bowl of cornflakes.

Perhaps it's yet another reason to find my own place again. It's been on my to-do list for the last six months, ever since my previous landlord gave me notice that he was selling the flat I rented. I was so busy at work that I kept missing appointments to view other places and found myself homeless. Luckily for me, Erica has a spare room, or at least an estate agent conned her into thinking it was one. I'm more convinced it's a broom cupboard, but for all the time I've spent in it, I can cope with being Harry Potter. And, despite having to pay for storage of the majority of my belongings, the rent Erica's charging me is so low that I've actually been able to save. Which means that when I finally do get a chance to look for somewhere else, I might be able to afford something a bit better than my last mildew-infested basement flat.

But there's no time to dwell on that now. I put my phone down, turn my attention back to my work, and I soon start to feel the adrenaline pumping round my veins. I desperately try and achieve as much as possible and I'm actually on fire. I'm almost matching Sara's fake typing speed. If only I could keep this sort of a pace up all day, I would probably be able to leave work on time every day.

I email Marvellous Marcus his attachments and hastily shut down my computer. All that stands between me and my departure is a quick tweet from our work account to prove to my big bad boss Andrea that I'm still working, which I do on Tweetdeck on my phone. I quickly tap it out before shoving my phone into my bag and *voila*, Dominic, here I come.

'Are you going home to get changed?' asks Sara, looking me up and down.

'I haven't got time, and besides, nothing's clean. I was going to do my laundry tonight.'

Her eyes almost pop out in horror. Of course they would. She's dressed in a charcoal-grey shift dress and blazer, with neatly polished brogues on her feet. She's one of the few people I know who doesn't have to dress up specially for an Instagram outfit photo.

'You can't go like that,' she says horrified. She roots around in her office drawer and pulls out a scarf.

'Here,' she says, standing up and wrapping it elegantly round my neck. Without asking, she pulls off my cardigan, does up a couple of buttons, then hangs it round my shoulders like a middle-aged man stepping off a yacht.

She stands back to admire her handiwork. I can't be sure, but I think she's just caught sight of the Snoopy knickers situation, and so she pulls the scarf off and ties it round my waist like a belt, before knotting the arms of my cardigan to make it look scarf-like.

'There,' she says, smiling. 'It's not perfect, but I think it's making the best of a bad outfit.'

'Great, thanks, Sara.'

'Now all you'll need to do is hair and make-up.'

'Yep, going to do that on the tube.' I see her wincing but I don't have time for anything else; it's already ten past seven and I'm going to have to run to catch the train. 'See you tomorrow.'

'That's if you don't get swept off your feet and never return.'

I laugh sarcastically and give her a wave as I go.

I hurry down the metal staircase and pause briefly at the end that faces a mirror. I might not be able to take a full-length selfie with these clothes, but I can take an arty one of my new suede espadrille boots. I position half a foot down the final step, then take a photo of the reflection. I quickly apply a Mayfair filter and add the caption 'Hot date tonight' before posting it to my Instagram. Thank heavens for clean shoes, as there's no filter out there with the ability to turn the rest of my outfit into one worthy of getting those ego-boosting likes.

I jog out across the reception and make it out onto the street. I can't help feeling guilty that I'm leaving while it's still light outside, but I keep my fingers crossed that tonight will go so well with Dominic that we'll fall madly in love and it'll totally make my early departure seem worth it.

Chapter Three

Time since last Internet usage: 22 minutes

For once, the tube ride passes quickly, and I don't notice that for twenty minutes I'm cut off from the outside world. I've been far too busy trying to replicate a YouTube tutorial on contouring that I watched ages ago. I'm truly amazed at the results given the limited tools and compact mirror at my disposal.

I arrive at Waterloo and make my way out of the main entrance. It's a beautiful spring evening, and it seems that every man and his dog has decided to make the most of it and come out along the river. I jostle my way through the crowds, hurrying along to the South Bank, while trying to make sure that I don't perspire and ruin my hastily applied face.

I pull out my phone to check the time and I fist-pump as it's only 7.35. I don't even think that counts as being late when you're at the mercy of public transport.

I'm scanning an email from Marcus, thanking me for the work, when I spot Dominic already at the BFI Riverfront bar, nursing a drink.

I stop in my tracks in a slight fluster, causing a man to walk into the back of me.

'Sorry,' I mutter, as he gives me a look of death and walks on, shaking his head.

But I can't help but be stunned as I can't quite believe it – for once someone actually looks like their profile photo. He's like a Norse god: airy and fluffy blond hair that's truly magnificent and green eyes the exact colour of Bird's Eye frozen peas.

I scour the concrete landscape of the South Bank in search of sanctuary, somewhere where I can at least use a full-size mirror rather than my powder-splattered compact to fix my hair and make-up. I spot the National Theatre opposite and wonder if I can sneak past Dominic.

I figured that he'd be like the rest of them, guilty of choosing that one photo that makes him look a perfect ten, when on average he's only a 7.5. You know, like I did. There's no way that my roughly plaited hair and Sara's make-do-and-mend outfit are going to cut the mustard.

I'm stuck, not knowing what to do, so I pull out my phone and tap out a quick tweet. Mainly for Erica and Amelie's benefit as I know it'll make them laugh.

Sexy knickers £25, Brazilian £35, New outfit £170. When your Tinder date is hot as hell & you're going to f**k his brains out = #priceless

No one on Twitter needs to know the reality of the Snoopy pants, forest-like conditions or the threadbare leggings. The chances of me getting some might be pretty slim indeed, but a dull tweet about the real state of affairs isn't going to push me over the two thousand followers mark, is it?

I'm still debating about fixing myself up a bit, when I see him glance in my direction. He stares for a second, as if he's trying to work out if I'm the same girl in his photograph, but luckily – or unluckily – he decides I am and gives me a small wave.

I've got no choice but to go over. As I get up close, he stands up to meet me and I have to hold back a gasp.

I find myself looking down at him as he's at least six inches shorter than me – and I'm in flats. I falter for a second as my perfect specimen of a man *literally* doesn't quite measure up, but only for a second – what's in a few inches?

'Daisy?' he says as he leans up, presumably to kiss my cheek. I feel myself bend over as he grazes each cheek with his. 'We finally meet.'

I can rise above the whole height thing, literally and metaphorically. He doesn't appear to be that phased by my dragged-through-a-hedge-backwards look, so why should I care about his height? We know that size doesn't really matter in other arenas, so why does it matter standing up? So what, if he's shorter than me? Loads of women tower over their partners: Tina Fey, Sophie Dahl, Nicole Kidman. Plus, I've never dated a man shorter than me; maybe this is where I've been going so spectacularly wrong all these years.

Besides, I could totally hide his height in photos on Facebook if we're always sitting down in them.

'It's nice to finally meet you,' I say as I sit down.

'Great, well, what are you drinking?' he says, as he clicks his fingers and summons the waitress.

We sit there awkwardly for a moment while we wait for the summoned waitress, as if the click has killed any hope of a conversation. I quickly pick up a drinks menu, looking straight at the cocktail section. 'I'll have a Pornstar Martini,' I say, hoping it might be a bit of an icebreaker.

Dominic does not look impressed.

The waitress slinks away and Dominic opens his mouth to say something, but he's interrupted by the loud ping of my phone that I've still got in my hand.

'Sorry,' I mutter as I try and ignore the notification of yet another work email, and I slip it onto silent instead.

'Doesn't matter,' he says, despite him giving me the impression that it did. 'Why don't you tell me about yourself?'

'Um . . .' I falter, as he's looking at me so intently that I suddenly feel as if I'm at an interview and I slip into that mode. 'I'm thirty-one, I'm a marketing account manager, I live with my best friend Erica in Dulwich . . .'

'Yeah,' he says, nodding, as if I haven't told him anything noteworthy, 'and what else?'

'What do you mean?' I scrunch up my eyes as I look at him for direction for what he wants to hear. I thought I'd told him the main facts – my age (without lying) – that I'm gainfully employed and that I live in a trendy part of town. Surely that tells him most of what he needs to know.

'I mean, what are you about? What do you do for fun?' he asks in his peculiar accent, which is a mixture of posh British with a Transatlantic twang. It's as if he's doing a bad Lloyd Grossman impression.

'Oh, right, fun,' I say, trying to concentrate on what he said rather than how he said it. 'Well, let's see . . . I go out quite a lot with my friends – you know, bars, parties . . . Sometimes I go to the cinema, and the theatre now and then.' Even though I despise it, it looks good to check in every so often.

'So you don't have hobbies, then?' he says disappointedly.

'I'm sure I must have hobbies,' I say in my defence. 'I mean everyone has hobbies, don't they?' I just need to think what they are. I used to be fairly sporty when I was at university, I belonged to the trampolining club and I did street dancing. I'd always intended to do some form of sports in London but it was all so expensive when I first moved here, and then it's so hard to get back into it when you're out of the habit.

I think over what I do in my spare time, not that I've had much over the last few months. I can't remember the last time I cooked something for the enjoyment of it, and I've got a whole Pinterest board full of craft ideas that I'm intending to emulate when somehow I manage to have an abundance of time and/or realise that I have some crafting ability – neither of which are highly likely.

Surely I've got to have more to my life than that? I try and mentally run through my Instagram pictures, as if to trigger my memory, and that's when it hits me.

'I'm into photography,' I say, realising that I snap all day long. Dominic doesn't need to know that I don't own an actual camera.

'Oh, really? That's interesting,' he says nodding. 'I recently bought a new Digital SLR, I'm still getting used to it, mainly using the kit lenses – you know, while I'm a beginner. Perhaps you can give me some tips?'

I try and keep my smile from falling.

'Yes, I'm sure I could,' I say lying. The only tip I can give him is that the best Instagram filter to use when you're looking as rough as a dog is Valencia, and Mayfair makes your drinks look sharper. Probably not what he had in mind.

'I went to dinner up the Shard last week and I captured some fantastic shots with my wide-angle lens. The lights went all Bokeh in the distance and I had the perfect twilight photo. In fact, my boss was so impressed that we now have it printed on canvas on our office wall.'

'Oh, that's fantastic,' I say, wishing I'd picked a different hobby. 'I once had –'

'And then, there were some wedding shots' – he continues talking, not even acknowledging that I was starting to join in the conversation – 'that I took for my very good friend. They actually preferred them to the ones taken by the photographer they'd hired. They said I'd captured the more spontaneous moments of the day so they've used a lot of mine in their wedding album and in frames around their house.'

'That's excellent,' I say, nodding at his modesty.

The waitress comes over and places my cocktail in front of me; it looks delicious. I practically have to sit on my hands so as not to reach into my bag and pull out my phone to take a snap of it to share online. It's rare that I go out for food or drink these days and don't chronicle it, but I don't feel like I can after what Dominic has just been saying.

'So what other hobbies do you have, then?'

I'm guessing that if I say I play poker, meaning an app on my phone, he'll tell me that he's played at a Las Vegas tournament.

'I like to watch live music. I've got tickets to see the Foo Fighters at Wembley in the summer and'

'Who hasn't? Everyone always says they like the Foos.'

I open my mouth to tell him that I've actually seen them at all their UK live tours, but before I get the chance he's telling me about the time he got backstage tickets to see Dave Grohl's super group, Them Crooked Vultures.

'What about languages?' he asks, as he finishes his story. 'Do you speak any of those?'

I'm about to joke that I can totally speak Emoji; in fact, Erica and I sometimes have whole conversations in it. But I get the impression that Dominic, much like the rest of the population, wouldn't believe that it's a real language.

'No, other than my GCSE German, which I haven't used since I'

'Shame; I speak fluent French and conversational Italian and Spanish. Makes holidaying so much easier. I detest people who point and speak loudly in English.'

'Me too,' I say, nodding and pretending I'm not guilty of doing that.

'So what do your parents do?' he says, rolling on the inter-rogation at a rapid rate of knots.

'Um, my mum works as a receptionist at a dentist's.'

'Oh,' he says, 'and your dad?'

'He was an accountant, but he, um, died when I was young.' I get a bit flustered as I don't usually like to talk about my dad's death with strangers, and it tends to put a bit of a downer on first date conversation.

'Oh, he worked in the City, did he?'

'No, he worked in Fleet, in Hampshire. That's where I'm from.'

I think Dominic has to be the only person I've ever met who hasn't acknowledged my dad's passing with an 'I'm sorry', or who hasn't asked how it happened. Instead he's ploughed on as if he'd just retired.

'Hampshire,' he says, wrinkling up his nose as if I've told him that I've come from the back of beyond. 'Is that a home county?'

'No, but we border a few of them.'

He's stopped pretending to hide his disappointment on his face and I get the impression that I've failed the interview.

'Well, what do your parents do?' I ask, thinking that my parental heritage has not been called into question before on a date.

'My father is a hedge-fund manager and my mother was a barrister, but now she's a high court judge.'

'Right,' I say. It figures. 'And they live in the Home Counties?'

'Yes, in Sevenoaks.'

'Are they American?' I say, testing the water about his dodgy accent.

'No. Why?' he says a little gruffly.

'Oh, I thought I detected a little accent, I wondered if you'd lived there . . .' My voice trails off as there's a scowl descending over his brow.

'I do spend a lot of time there for work. It's always handy, I think, to get global work experience. I spent a year working in Hong Kong when I first graduated, and if I'd stayed with my company, I'm sure I would have been posted to a foreign office again. Have you worked abroad?'

'No, but I once had a client meeting in Dubai which –'

'Who hasn't,' he says, cutting me off as I was about to tell him a very amusing story about when I was nearly arrested for kissing Marvellous Marcus.

FYI – there was no actual kissing, just an eyelash stuck in my eye. Not that I have to clarify it to Dominic, as he's started to drone on about when he was flown business class to Singapore for an hour-long meeting.

The weird thing about Internet dating is that you build up an idea about a person in your head based on a few carefully curated images and heavily crafted messages. Usually, I suggest meeting fairly quickly after I start messaging, as I've found that the longer that goes on, the greater is the expectation that the person is a perfect match. Yet, despite the fact that I haven't built him up too much in my head, I'm still woefully disappointed that, in person, Dominic has failed to reach even the lowest of my expectations. We've already established that, in my head, he was a foot taller, but he wasn't a complete arsehole who didn't let me finish my sentences.

'I'm just going to go and have a smoke,' he says, getting up from the table as he finishes his story.

I've never been so thrilled to be on a date with a smoker. I'd usually be a bit offended that a date had sneaked off so quickly and left me alone, but, for once, I'm glad. I watch him walk onto South Bank to light up a cigarette, mentally wishing that he won't return.

I reach into my bag to find my phone, to quickly snap the photo of my Martini which I'd been dying to do earlier, only my battery has gone flat. I rustle in my bag to find my phone charger, before realising that we're sitting outside where there are no plugs. It makes me slightly panicky. What if there's an emergency? Or, more importantly, what if I need to fake an emergency to get away from this awful date?

I glance over at Dominic to try and distract myself. It looks like he's got no battery problems. I watch him on his phone and, if I'm not mistaken, he's swiping, occasionally pausing and squinting his eyes as he does so. I recognise that squint; he's blatantly checking people out on Tinder. He's obviously made up his mind about me too. He could have at least got through the whole evening with me before he started to look elsewhere. Surely that's common decency?

I take a sip of my Martini and it tastes pretty damn good. I start to drink more and more, bracing myself for the second onslaught of questions. Dominic comes back to the table and sits down. There's an awkward silence that hangs in the air along with the smell of stale tobacco.

I'm about to suggest that we both throw in the towel, when he clicks his fingers at the waitress and begins to order some food.

'Did you want anything, Daisy?'

The waitress has entered his order into her little machine and is looking expectantly at me, with a look that shows she doesn't have time for this. On the one hand, it would probably make my life easier to say that I don't want anything and to make my excuses and leave, but, unfortunately, I'm too British and polite and I can't leave him to eat alone. Plus, I haven't had anything to eat all day except a couple of stale Jaffa Cakes I found loitering at the bottom of my desk drawer. I barely have time to glance over the menu as the waitress taps her foot and looks over my shoulder at a new table that's just arrived.

'I'll have the naked hot dog,' I say, this time not even trying to be provocative; it's just the first thing I saw.

She nods and hurries away.

'So, do you like to travel other than for work?' he says resuming his line of questioning.

'Um, I do, but I haven't had a whole lot of time over the last few years; things have been pretty busy.'

'I recently went to Thailand,' he says, sipping his drink.

'I went there a few years ago,' I say, trying to find some common ground. 'To a little resort on Ko Samui and'

'Yes, but I went to the *real* Thailand,' he says with his weird drawl.

The entry visa in my passport made me think that I had too, but I don't have the energy to get into a debate with him. Instead I sip my drink.

'It was very spiritual. I went to a retreat, no phones, no Internet, no trappings of modern life.'

'Sounds . . .' *bloody awful.* 'Enlightening.'

'Oh it was. It really made me realise how I didn't want to work for The Man anymore. It's where I decided I wanted to be a private investor instead. It was at this fantastic Buddhist monastery up on this hillside outside of Chiang Rai . . .'

He launches into a story of his time and I do the only thing I can do to get myself through this awful date. I drink. I signal to the passing waitress for another one and I try and tune him out while also trying not to think of the one hundred and one things I'd rather have done with this evening.

An hour and a half later and we've finally finished dinner. Dominic has had his coffee, I've had three martinis, and it looks like this painful date is about to come to an end.

He summons the poor waitress once more with a cringe-worthy click, and she passes us the bill on a little metal tray. He reaches for it with such ferocity that I'm at once impressed with his chivalry of paying for the meal; I was about to reach for my debit card to pay my half but he's beaten me to it. If he hadn't been such an all-round vile man this might have gone some way to redeeming him.

'Right, then, so I had three beers, the ribs, a coffee and, oh, I had that side order of onion rings,' he says, pulling his phone out of his pocket and tapping the figures into it.

I watch in horror as he agonisingly itemises our bill and even adds on a shared tip. 'So you owe thirty-nine pounds.'

He smiles at me triumphantly, passing over the bill in case I want to see it. I give it a cursory glance and see that we wouldn't have been far off it if we'd just halved it, although this way at least I save myself £1.35!

The waitress comes over and takes our payment and then I'm finally free.

God, I can't believe I left work early for this torture. There aren't many days when I'd rather have been chained to my desk than be out and about in the real world, but this is definitely one of them.

'Which way are you headed?' he asks.

I glance at my watch and, based on the fact that it takes me a good minute to work out that it's half past nine, I decide that I'm too drunk to go back to the office, so I'm homeward bound.

'I'm going on the circle line to Victoria.'

'I'll catch it with you, then,' he says.

I look at him in horror, wishing that I'd said that I'd catch a bus instead.

We walk in awkward silence as we weave our way through the crowds on the bridge towards Embankment. He mutters under his breath as I fumble in my bag for my Oyster card and we soon find ourselves on the platform waiting for the train.

'Have you lived in Dulwich long?' he asks.

I groan internally. *Will the questioning never end?*

'Not too long, about three months, or maybe four.' It reminds me that I really need to start looking for a new place.

'Bit of a trek to get there, isn't it?' he says. 'I prefer being more central. West Kensington is perfect for me. Less than a half-hour commute to the City. Less of the pram brigade there too.'

I grit my teeth. Right now I'm glad that Dulwich is so far away – the further away from him the better.

A train pulls in and we climb on, and, wanting to signal my imminent departure, I shun the empty seats and instead stand holding the rail by the door so I can make a quick exit.

'I'm not a fan of north of the river,' I say, lying, as I was only thinking the other day how nice it would be to live closer to work. The hour-long commute is getting tedious, and even when the company pay for a taxi to take me home when I finish late at night, it still seems to take ages to get back.

'I don't think real Londoners live south of the river,' he says. 'I mean, I can walk to the City if I need to from where I am.'

'Um,' I say, biting my lip to stop myself getting into an argument with him. I'm feeling a little feisty after all those Martinis, but I keep telling myself that in just a few minutes the train will be pulling into Victoria and I can escape.

'Granted, things are a bit easier now with the Overground, but it isn't the same, is it? I mean, you might as well live out in Surbiton or Croydon for the time it takes you to get in.'

He rattles off more than a few reasons why I should be moving postcodes, all of which make me despise him more, so I tune him out. Instead, I start to wonder if Tinder needs to have an outlet to be able to leave Tripadvisor-style reviews. I can imagine what highlights – or lowlights – I'd mention now. *He might look great on the outside, but five minutes of interrogation – I mean conversation – and you'll be wishing you'd swiped left. Egotistical, self-absorbed and darn right dull. Wouldn't go back to his for coffee.* I'm just mentally awarding him one star (well, he was chivalrous enough to not let me pay that extra £1.35 that I would have done if we'd halved the bill), when we arrive at Victoria. Hallelujah.

'Well, thank you for, um . . .' I struggle to finish the sentence. I can't thank him for the food or drinks as I paid for them, and it's not like I can lie and say that we had a nice evening. 'For the company.' Though that's also a stretch.

'Right, well, thank you too,' he says, grabbing hold of my wrist to give me a kiss. I lean down to him as his lips brush my cheeks and it causes me to full on shiver.

'Thanks,' I manage to mutter. I'm about to turn to get off when I hear him speak.

'So I'll see you again?'

I look at him in disbelief. Were we on the same date? He was the one swiping potential dates during his smoke breaks.

'Um, I don't think so . . .' I'd usually leave it at that but the Martinis appear to have made me unusually feisty. 'I don't want another date, as I have to say that this was probably hands down the worst date I have ever been on.'

Oh good God. Why couldn't I have just channelled those super polite British manners that made me stick through the whole of dinner? I could have just said I'd see him another time then ignored his phone calls.

'What's wrong with me, then?' he says so loudly that not even the people in the carriage with noise-cancelling headphones fail to look up. 'Let me guess, you're too tall for me?'

'No, of course not,' I say, shaking my head as if the thought had never entered my mind. 'It's just that I don't think we've got any chemistry, do you?'

'Oh I see. What you're saying is, "it's not you, it's me",' he says rolling his eyes.

'Um, I never said that it's not *you*.'

I deliver the news still walking but looking at him, desperate to get off the train and bring this awful evening to a close. When I finish speaking I snap my head forward and go to get off the train, only to find that the doors have already closed and I smack straight into them.

'Wait,' I say, clutching my nose and jabbing at the doors, hoping they'll hear me and magically and swing open. Of course they don't, and the train lurches away. I grab on to a pole before I fall over. I'm well and truly trapped here with Dominic until the next stop.

By the time I make it home, I've got a raging headache. It might have only been a minute to the next underground station, but it felt as if the train I was on went all the way out to zone six and back, before we pulled into Sloane Square. I'm desperate to charge my phone up and tell Erica all about it, but even that is too much effort. Instead, I walk into my bedroom and collapse onto my bed fully clothed, pretty sure that the combination of the cocktails, headache and work exhaustion will knock me out any second . . .

Chapter Four

I sit down at my desk, careful to remove my sunglasses slowly to allow my eyes to adjust to the harsh fluorescent light. I take a deep breath and exhale.

My phone and its flat battery meant I missed my alarm this morning; I woke up in a panic with a blinding hangover. I had to scramble around trying to find some clean clothes to wear, and ended up raiding Erica's wardrobe. But I'm slightly impressed that I managed to make it to work only half an hour late, which I think is pretty good going considering. Short of hiring a Boris bike and riding like Chris Froome, there's no way I could have got here any quicker. I even sprinted from the Tube, so that's taken care of my weekly exercise too – bonus!

I reach under my desk, plug my phone into a charger and visibly relax as the charging symbol appears, knowing that my baby and I are about to be reunited. I can't remember the last time I went so long without my phone. I switch on my computer while I wait.

Sara strides across the office with a steaming cup of coffee in her hand and does a double take as she sees me.

'You're here,' she says, sitting down at her desk.

'Ha, I know what you're thinking, you don't recognise the clothes, but they're Erica's. I didn't run off with Dominic last night. He was definitely not the one.'

I bang my head on the desk as I stand up. If I weren't so late, I'd have filled her in on the details of the doomed date, but we'll have to wait until we have a natural lull in the afternoon.

'No, it's just . . .' she starts and then opens and closes her mouth.

'I'd better do some tweeting in the hope that Andrea won't notice what time I got in,' I say, thinking that my all-seeing, all-knowing boss probably isn't so easily fooled.

'You're going to do some tweeting,' says Sara, looking at me as if I've said I'm going to attempt brain surgery.

I generally tweet a few trivial things throughout the day to make it look like we're a young, dynamic company; it's no big deal, so why is she turning it into one?

'What?' I ask, narrowing my eyes.

'Um, I've got to, um . . .' She gets up from her desk and abandons the coffee. I'm not sure where she's off to in such a hurry, and as I watch her dart around the office, I'm not sure she does either.

'Weird,' I say, shrugging it off and loading up Twitter. I gasp as I see that we've got 2,879 notifications. Wowsers! One of our clients must have tagged us in something and they're having a really good day.

I click on the tab to see what's going on and instantly see the tweet I wrote last night about Dickhead Dominic, and I laugh at how I could ever have thought I'd want to sleep with him. I can't believe that I'd forgotten to log out of my personal twitter at work. I'm a little proud that so many people have liked and retweeted my tweet, and I seem to have loads of new followers, but I really shouldn't be looking at this at work. I go to click the profile picture to log out and I freeze. Our company logo is where my slutty photo from the hen do should be.

Uh-oh.

My blood starts to run cold. I feel the simultaneous urge to throw up and wee. Neither would be socially acceptable. But then again, neither was the tweet I'd posted.

What the hell have I done?

I panic as I click to view the profile, and there in black and blue is my tweet:

Sexy knickers £25, Brazilian £35, New outfit £170. When your Tinder date is hot as hell & you're going to f**k his brains out = #priceless

I reread it over and over again as the magnitude of what I've done hits me. Why did I have to make a joke out of the MasterCard ad? We have loads of financial clients, and one of them is a rival credit card – surely they're not going to be impressed with this.

The beads of sweat that were hangover related turn from mild perspiration to full-on drips as I try to come to terms with what I've done.

I attempt to force my wrist to work as I hastily try to remember how to delete a tweet. I'm not naive enough to think that's solved the problem – I saw the look of horror on Sara's face when I mentioned Twitter. I'm just wondering how I'm going to get rid of the evidence of those who have done the old-fashioned retweet using the words RT, but a shadow falls over my desk and I realise that I'm out of time.

'Daisy. So glad you can finally join us. My office, I think.'

And there it is. As I do the walk of shame behind Andrea to the other end of our office, people actually stop their work and stare at me as I go by like I'm a dead man walking – which, I'm guessing, after what I've done, I am.

I don't hear the voices at first, I'm too busy holding a Twitter vigil in my Harry Potteresque bedroom, but soon they are so loud that I can't ignore them.

'I don't know why it's such a big deal,' I hear Erica shout. 'It's not like she's here that much anyway. You stay over most of the time as it is. It's not going to be that different when you're living here.'

It takes me a minute or so to process what's been said, my mind still trying to process the fact that I got fired for the use of 140 ill-advised characters.

Chris is moving in?

It sounds like they're having quite a heated discussion about me, and I can't help but eavesdrop. I know that I should go out of the bedroom and let them know that I'm here, only I can't tear myself away from my screen.

'Of course it's going to be different,' he says sighing. 'I want to feel comfortable in my own home. I want to walk around naked. Hell, I want *you* to walk around naked. I don't want us to be constantly checking to see if Daisy's in before we strip off.' He sighs loudly. 'It's just not what I had in mind when we talked about moving in together. It's bad enough on the few nights I stay over having to remember to put boxers on in the middle of the night when I need a wee, let alone doing it every night. It's not like we need the money and have to have a lodger.'

I can't believe this, not only is Chris moving in, but he also wants to evict me!

Great, first I get fired, then I become homeless.

'It's not about the money,' says Erica. 'She needs a place to stay at the moment. It's not going to be forever. She's just under so much pressure. I can't add to that by telling her she's got to move out. She's my best friend and I know that she would do anything for me.'

And that, ladies and gentlemen, is why she's my bestie.

'I know she is,' says Chris. 'And I have nothing against her. You know I like her a lot, and really, as housemates go, she's perfect as we rarely see her, but it's not the same. I want it to be our place, just you and me.

'Think about it. I want to know that if I want to have you right here and right now on the sofa that I can, that you're not going to be panicking that Daisy will walk in while we're doing it.'

'But you know I can always check to see where she is on the Find My Friends app.'

Chris laughs. 'How romantic slash borderline stalker.'

'Well, I can promise you she'll be at work now. There's no fear she'll interrupt.'

Oh God. I can hear them kissing, and very soon I think I'm going to be hearing a whole lot more. I really wish I'd at least shut my door, but it has the worst creak on it, and they'd definitely have known I was here.

I stare at my bedroom window for a second and wonder if I can escape. But assuming I'd be able to fit through it, which is questionable with my hips, where do I think I'm going to go? We're on the top floor of a large Victorian town house, and unless I've got some previously undetected Spiderman skills, I'd be like a cat stuck on a roof.

I'll just have to hide out here and hope that they go to the bedroom after and I can sneak out of the flat.

I try to block out the smooching sounds and focus on what they'd been discussing. Even in my emotionally heightened state I can't blame Chris. If I was shacking up with someone I'd want the freedom he craves too; surely that's part of the appeal of living together. I know it's not really about me, it's about them taking the next step of their relationship and wanting it to be perfect, but it just couldn't have come at a worse time. Losing my job and where I'm living in one day: talk about brutal.

But this was only supposed to be a temporary arrangement and I know I've been here way longer than I should have been already, and in the grand scheme of things finding somewhere to live is going to be a lot less difficult than finding a new job.

'Hold that thought,' says Erica. 'I'm just nipping to the loo.'

For a second I'm relieved that they've stopped their sexy time before I realise that she's heading my way. My room's on the way to the bathroom and with the door wide open, and it being too small to swing a cat, I've got nowhere to hide. I launch myself off the bed in a bid to roll under it but she catches me mid-jump.

She shrieks at first before clasping her hand to her heart.

'Daisy, you scared the crap out of me! What are you doing here?'

I attempt to ignore the pain of landing in a heap on the floor and I stand up, trying to pretend that it's totally normal behaviour.

'I, um, finished work early,' I say. She looks up and down as I crawl back sheepishly onto the bed.

'You'll have to fill me in in a minute, I need a wee.'

I'm just refreshing my twitter stream again when Chris pokes his head round the door, presumably having heard the commotion as clearly as I heard their conversation.

'Hiya, Daisy, you all right? You're looking . . .' he says, squinting at me as if he's trying to find the right words.

'Like shit,' says Erica, walking in behind him. Trust her to say it like it is. Although, being my best friend, she can get away with it. She sits down on the bed beside me and Chris offers to go and make us a cup of tea.

'What's going on? Why do you look so bad? Are those my clothes?' she asks, pulling at the shirt I'm wearing.

'They are,' I say wincing. I'd hoped that I'd have been able to catch up on the much-needed laundry and hang them back up in her room without her noticing. 'Sorry. I was desperate, I had no clean clothes and you weren't here to ask.'

'It doesn't matter. So why did you leave work?'

'Because they made me,' I say, focusing on my computer screen rather than Erica.

'They made you . . . as in you got fired?'

'Uh-huh.'

'For what?'

'There was this tweet, and I thought I'd sent it from my personal account but I'd accidentally sent it from my work one.'

'A tweet? You got fired for a tweet? Surely they can't do that. I mean, how bad could it have been?'

I look up at her and pull a face and she gasps as if my expression tells her exactly how bad it could be.

'What did it say?'

I turn my laptop round and let Erica read it. It's still being retweeted, as even though it had been deleted, so many people had been talking about it that others have pulled off the screen shot of it. Not to mention the fact that people are taking the piss out of my tweet, and using the same hashtag, meaning priceless is currently trending in the UK.

'Holy shit, Daisy, did you actually write this?'

'It was meant to be a joke on my personal twitter, mainly for you and Amelie,' I say trailing off. 'It certainly wasn't supposed to come from my work account. I mean, I work in marketing, for God's sake. Who in their right mind is going to hire me now?

I've got no job, no hope of ever getting another one, and I'll be looking for a new place to live too.'

'Oh, you heard,' says Erica, giving Chris a scowl as he brings us in two cups of tea. He hangs his head a little sheepishly.

'You don't have to go anywhere,' he says. 'You know, what with you leaving your job. You can stay here as long as you need to sort yourself out.'

I see Erica's scowl disintegrate into a smile at his change of heart, and instantly I know I can't stay.

'Thanks. I just don't know what I'm going to do. I mean, how am I going to recover from this? This screen shot of my tweet has been retweeted over a thousand times, and the original tweet, before I deleted it, was retweeted over *two* thousand times. Everyone in the industry is going to know what I did.'

'Well, no one knows it's you, do they? I mean, it was your company feed. Maybe when you go to interviews no one will put two and two together,' says Erica, trying to exude positivity.

I sigh. 'Too late for that. Someone's done their homework and I've already been named and shamed.'

I look back at the Twitter stream.

'It's now about to hit one thousand five hundred. What are these people doing? Does everyone just spend all day on Twitter? Why aren't they doing actual work?'

I ignore the fact that if I was still gainfully employed I'd be keeping abreast of what was going on in social-media land.

'Look, it's bound to be bad today, but I'm sure in a day or two Twitter will be going nuts over something Donald Trump has tweeted. You'll be yesterday's news.'

I'm not so sure. I look at the columns of searches I've got on Tweetdeck, one for those that mention my old company's name, and the other for #priceless. Both are going crazy.

'First off, you've got to step away from the computer; it's not going to do you any favours staring at that all day. Why don't you go away for a few days? Have a break.'

'Go away? Where? And with whom?'

'You could go over to Vegas for Helen's wedding.'

'That's not for another three weeks and I couldn't afford to go before, let alone now I've just been fired.'

'Ah,' says Erica nodding. 'What about going to your mum's?'

'Oh, she'd do that disappointed-in-me voice that she does. I can't tell her that I've lost my job. I mean that would send her into overdrive: no husband and no job. Nu-uh, I can't tell her.' I try and take a deep breath to calm myself down, only it's not working. 'Why are you at home during the day anyway? You weren't fired too, were you?' I ask.

'Afraid not. Chris and I have tickets to a matinee; I'm just home to change before we go off. Of course, we'll cancel that and stay here with you,' she says hurriedly.

'You can't miss it for me. I'll be fine here on my own, I'll be –'

I drift off as I stare at the screen in disbelief at what's happening. My eyes are practically turning square at keeping up with the ever-changing stream. I shouldn't be watching. It's as if I'm rubbernecking at an accident, only the casualty is my life.

'I don't think this is good for you. Why don't you take Chris's ticket for the show? I'm sure *Les Mis* would cheer you right up.'

'Oh yes, because it's so known for its cheery theme. Thank you, but I can't. Even if it wasn't the most depressing musical ever, I'd have to switch off my phone and I'd never be able to concentrate as I'd be thinking about what was going on on Twitter.'

'Well, I don't want to leave you here. You look poised to have a meltdown.'

Before I can protest that I'll be fine, my phone rings and I flinch.

'You answer it,' I say, shoving it towards Erica, too scared to even see who's calling.

'It's Rosie,' she says handing it back to me. 'Surely you can talk to your sister.'

'Oh crap, I'm meant to be meeting her for lunch. She said she'd phone to arrange when and where. Speak to her and fob her off, will you.'

If my mum would be disappointed, then Rosie would be plain smug about the whole thing. I don't want my sister and her perfect life to get a whiff that I've monumentally fucked up mine.

'Hello, oh hi, Rosie, it's Erica. Yes, yes, Daisy's here home from work. There's been a bit of a situation. Uh-huh, uh-huh,' she says.

I wave my arms gesturing for her to wrap the call up, but Erica waves me away and walks out of the room as if I'm distracting her. I hear the odd word – *tweet*, *goggle eyed*, *worried* – and I know she's shared my shameful secret.

'OK, I'll text you the address,' she says walking back into the room. She hangs up the phone and starts tapping away a text on it.

'What's going on? I thought I told you to fob her off.'

'She wanted to come and check you were OK. She said she's at Clapham Junction so she'll catch an Uber and will be here in a bit.'

'What, coming here?' I screech. Could this day get any worse?

'Hopefully, she'll be able to stay with you until we get back,' she says, seemingly pleased with herself that she's solved the problem of leaving me here alone.

'My older sister babysitting me,' I say, almost laughing at how ridiculous my situation has become.

I sigh and think of all the people in the world who I'd want to see now, and my sister is not one of them.

Chapter Five

'Blimey,' says Rosie, as she walks into the tiny box room and spots me hunched over my laptop.

I see Erica out of the corner of my eye giving her an 'I told you so' look.

When Rosie arrived at the front door there were a lot of muffled whispers and I presume that Erica has brought her up to speed.

'Quite the predicament you've got yourself in, then,' she says, sitting down.

I feel myself tense up at the smug look she's got on her face. I knew she'd react like this; she's probably itching to get on the phone to Mum to share my misfortune.

'I'm sure it will all blow over in a day or two,' I say, not sounding very convincing.

'It's OK not to be OK,' she says, with the most compassion I've ever heard in her voice. She stretches out her hands as if I'm about to shatter into a million pieces and she's going to catch me.

It unnerves me and I almost burst into tears. I'd full on prepared myself for her scorn and self-righteousness.

'Look, Erica told me that you've been staring at that screen for hours now; it's not healthy. She said she'd suggested you go away.'

'Yeah, but I don't want to go anywhere on my own, and it's too short notice for people who still have their jobs!'

She nods her head and smiles. 'I'll go with you.'

'What?' I stare at her, my tears forgotten. 'Um, I think it might be better to stay here and sort out another job, and –'

'Nonsense, you need a break and I'm free. Let's go away somewhere.'

I do feel like running away from all of this, but Rosie and I haven't spent more than a day together since I was fifteen and she went off to uni. Back then we fought like cats and dogs. And despite us being older and wiser now, whenever we're together at Mum's, no matter how short the time, sibling rivalry always rears its ugly head.

'I thought you were staying down here for a couple of days?' I say, in desperation to find a way out.

'I came down to see Rupert as he's here on business, but . . . he's busier than expected. So I was going to head back to Manchester later this afternoon.'

'Well, don't let me keep you,' I say.

'Look, you're already exhausted from all that work and now this has happened, you can't stay holed up in this flat staring at the screen. Come back on the train with me and I can pack some stuff and we can go away from there.'

'Where would we go? Somewhere abroad?'

I slowly let the thought creep into my mind. I'm imagining myself on a desert island, somewhere with crystal-clear water and fluorescent cocktails. I'm reaching for my phone to take an Instagram snap, when it starts beeping with tweets on my Twitter stream.

I sigh.

Even if I run away, Twitter will follow me. When I close my eyes, I can see the words of my tweet in large letters, and I can almost hear the digital laughter of everyone reacting to it.

'No, I was thinking more of a staycation. In fact, on the way over here in the taxi, I had a brilliant idea. We should go on a detox.'

'A detox? What, some sort of spa retreat where we drink green shakes and lemongrass all day?'

'Um, no, a *digital* detox,' says Rosie, a glint appearing in her eyes that I haven't seen for a long time. That same glint that always got us into trouble when I followed one of her hairbrained ideas when we were kids.

'A digital detox?' I say, confused. 'Like no phones?'

'Yes . . . and no computers, tablets, kindles . . .'

I'm starting to hyperventilate at the thought as she practically reels off the usual contents of my handbag. 'Are you mad?'

Rosie laughs a little. 'Of course not. I think it would be good for you – good for us – to get away, and for you to have some space from all this.'

She waves her hand like she's waving a magic wand over my bed, which looks as if it's been lifted straight from an Apple Store catalogue with my MacBook, iPad and iPhone next to me.

'I am *not* going on a digital detox,' I say, folding my arms. At a push I'd consider going away with her, but this is one step too far. 'It's a terrible idea – see,' I say, pointing to the scared look on Erica's face.

'She can barely go one minute without checking her phone, let alone one day,' she says, backing me up.

'Oh, I can well imagine. When we were last at home together, she was commenting on *Britain's Got Talent*, based on the tweets she was watching, and she hadn't even realised we'd changed the channel ten minutes before.'

'Sometimes it's funnier reading about people's reactions to something. It's only like watching *Gogglebox*,' I say in my defence.

'OK, then what about when I had to Whatsapp you during Christmas dinner last year to get you to pass the gravy?'

Erica giggles and I fold my arms across my chest, I have no comeback to that.

'I could give up my phone, no problem. Yesterday, I went for a whole fourteen hours without checking it,' I say.

I'm still cursing my dead battery. If I'd just seen those notifications rolling in when I first tweeted I could have deleted it before it started trending.

'And how many of those fourteen hours were you asleep?' asks Rosie.

'About eight or nine,' I mumble. 'But I'm sure I could last a whole day.'

'I was thinking one week,' says Rosie.

'One week!' Erica and I scream in unison.

'As if,' says Erica. 'As much as I agree that Daisy needs to step away from the computer, I don't think she'd be able to do it.'

'You're right,' says Rosie, nodding. 'Silly me. I thought Daisy would have more willpower and determination than that. I must have got all those genes in our family –'

'Hang on,' I snap, my sister already getting under my skin. 'I'll have you know that if I wanted to do a digital detox, I'd be able to. I just don't *want* to do one.'

'OK,' says Rosie, nodding her head in a patronising way. 'Sure you would.'

'I would,' I say, standing up. 'I'm not addicted to my phone.'

At that exact moment it beeps, as if to test me and I pick it up without flinching.

'It's from Nan,' I say, scan reading it, 'she wants to know what a Brazilian is. Oh for fuck's sake, when did she start going on bloody Twitter?'

'Didn't you set it up for her?' says Rosie. There it is, the smug look that I knew would be all over her face if she came over. 'So what was it you were saying about not being addicted to your phone? You picked that up in a nanosecond.'

'Well, it could have been important. In case you haven't noticed I'm having a big life crisis at the moment and it's imperative that I keep up to date.'

'As I said, I was wrong. You'd never be able to digitally detox. It's a shame, as I had a great place in mind and everything.'

'You did?'

'Uh-huh, and I even gave them a ring when I was in the taxi to see if they had any last-minute availability.'

'And did they?' I ask, not sure I want to hear the answer.

'Yes, they do, but if you don't think you could do it . . .'

'Holy shit,' I say, ignoring Rosie and staring at the screen in disbelief as I read a tweet.

> Dominic Cutler @DomDomDom2434
> Apparently I'm hot as hell . . .
> WB_MARKETING Sexy knickers £25, Brazilian £35, New outfit £170. When your Tinder date is hot as hell & you're going to f**k his brains out = #priceless

'What?' asks Erica.

'Dickhead Dominic is getting in on the action.'

'Who's that?' asks Rosie.

'The Tinder date from last night, the one who the tweet was about.'

'Ah,' she says.

I scrunch my eyes up. I desperately want to look, but at the same time I don't want to.

'Daisy, this isn't good for you,' says Rosie in a calm voice. 'Why don't we pack a few things? All of this will have blown over by the time you get back.'

I watch in horror as my twitter search for '#priceless' has new notifications, and as I click on them, I see that other people are retweeting Dominic's tweet.

'I'll help pack,' says Erica, pulling open my drawers and seeing they're all empty.

'Washing. Haven't done. Nothing Clean,' I stutter, unable to string together a sentence.

'That's OK,' says Rosie. 'You can wash them at mine tonight and I've got a tumble dryer too.'

'What about booking the place? Maybe it's been booked up since you phoned,' I say clutching at straws.

Rosie pulls her phone out of her bag. 'I'll phone them right now,' she says, walking out of the room.

I'm vaguely aware of Erica packing me a suitcase full of my dirty washing.

'There,' she says, zipping it shut. 'You're all good to go.'

She pulls the suitcase off the bed and drags it down the corridor into the lounge before she comes back and gently removes my laptop from in front of me. I snatch my phone and clutch it to my chest before she can nab that too and I find myself escorted to the lounge.

'Great news!' says Rosie as she hangs up the phone. 'We're all booked in. I'll print all the paperwork off when we're back at my flat.'

I groan, wondering why I agreed to go. But at least we're not going until tomorrow, which means I've still got my phone and, hopefully, enough time to convince my sister to change her mind.

Chapter Six

Time since last Internet usage: 1 hour and 55 minutes

Bang!

My eyes fly open as the Land Rover hits a boulder as we pull over for a passing lorry, and my bum flies off my seat before crashing down again. Lorry past, we pull out onto the uneven and bumpy road, causing me to rock sideways. I must have nodded off. The last thing I remember was the concrete landscape of Manchester, and now we're way out in the country and all I can see are green fields and rolling hills. I barely got any sleep last night at Rosie's flat. I was too busy staring at my phone as #priceless continued to trend in the UK.

'Where are we?' I ask, rubbing my eyes.

I look out of the window and take in the grey slate walls that pepper the fields. I'm guessing we're somewhere like the Lake or Peak District.

'We're in Cumbria, Sleepyhead.'

I'm stare out of the window, admiring the scenery when it begins to dawn on me that we're on our way to a detox, and

I suddenly start to panic, wondering what I've missed while I've been sleeping.

I'm searching for my phone in my handbag, which is difficult because of the way Rosie is flying round the bends at almost break-neck speed. She seems to know which way to turn at every corner and I get the impression that she knows the roads well.

'I take it you come out this way a lot?'

'A fair bit. We should be there in a couple of minutes.'

'I don't know if that's exciting or not,' I say, wishing I'd asked more questions about where exactly we are off to before I agreed to it. 'Does this place have a hot tub or a spa or something?'

'It has something,' she says continuing her vagueness.

I finally pull the phone out of my bag, hoping that I can have one last look at Twitter and say my final goodbyes. I can't believe this will be my last phone contact for a week. I should have been making the most of our final minutes together rather than sleeping.

'There's no bloody signal,' I say shrieking. I start waving it around my head in a desperate attempt to find one. 'There's nothing.'

I can feel my heart race even faster than it has been over the past twenty-four hours watching the live Twitter stream. I'm about to hand over my phone for at least a week and I can't even check Twitter or Facebook beforehand. I haven't had time to say a proper goodbye to Siri; he doesn't like to speak to me unless he's connected to the Internet, he's fickle like that. I didn't even send Erica a hand wave Emoji and a heart, or put a holiday response on my email. Now it's going to look as if that ill-fated tweet has forced me offline.

'Don't look so freaked out, it's only a week, two weeks max,' says Rosie as if she knew that this was going to happen.

'Two weeks? I didn't agree to that . . . I need to be back and job hunting as soon as I can,' I say, wondering where the hell we are and whether I can walk back to civilisation and put myself on a train to London. This was an awful idea. A week was bad enough, but two weeks . . .

'It's just until you're free of your digital addiction,' she says calmly as if I'm a drug addict about to be checked into rehab.

I might have wanted to prove to Rosie that she was wrong, that I'm perfectly capable of doing this, but now, as we're approaching H-Hour, I'm beginning to have second thoughts. She's talking like I can't actually leave until I'm 'cured'. What if it's a cult that'll keep me prisoner, with my phone and link to the outside world ripped away from me so that I can't tell anyone I'm being held against my will? I stare at my sister, my own flesh and blood, and wonder where she's taking me . . .

I knew I shouldn't have binge watched *Broadchurch* – talk about making me paranoid.

I look out the window, desperately trying to take in the rise and fall of the landscape. I memorise the dry-stone walls and oak trees dotted over the rolling hills, the humpback bridges that the Land Rover bumps over, and the bends in the road. All in case I need to escape back to the main road. Back to civilisation.

We turn a bend and all of a sudden we're driving through a small village with the road sign declaring it to be Lullamby. The dark-bricked houses line the route as the road creeps round. A pub stands in the centre, its sign blowing in the wind, and a village-shop-cum-post-office is opposite. There's a small church on the outskirts and then we're back out into the countryside again. But at least there's hope, that's the first sign of people I've seen for ages. Maybe the pub even has WiFi.

We only drive a mile or two outside the village when Rosie turns sharply up a dirt track.

'Here we go, hold on to your handle,' she says, grinning manically with excitement.

I see that damn twinkle in her eyes and I wonder what I've let myself in for.

'Look out!' I shout as a dog runs out into our path.

She slams her brakes on and we go flying forward.

The springer spaniel bounds back to his owner, who doesn't look pleased to see us. Despite the blue skies and the fact that it's May, he's dressed like a yeti. Tatty old fleece over the top of another fleece, big boots, and a hat with flaps over his ears. Even his big beard's keeping him warm. I'm surprised, when he turns to give us a scowl, that he looks relatively young; I expect him to be older by the way he is dressed.

'Is this the welcoming committee?' I say laughing nervously.

Rosie gives him a cheery wave, which he ignores, as he walks after his dog up another track by a crumbling old building.

'No, no. He must be a neighbour,' she says putting the car into gear and carrying on up to the track.

I turn my nose up hoping that the neighbours aren't indicative of where we're going.

I hold on to the handle above the window as the Land Rover tilts from side to side up the drive. I'm glad that we're in this and not the nippy Audi she used to zip around in. I don't think much else would have made the journey, and I wouldn't have fancied walking up here with my suitcase.

'What is this place? And why haven't they got a proper road?' I say, thinking that it's hardly good for business.

We reach the top of a hill, and there, nestled in a dip just below, is what looks like an old farm.

Rosie screeches to a halt and yanks the handbrake on with two hands.

'Here we are,' she says excitedly, jumping out of the car.

I stay inside for a minute, trying to take in what I'm seeing. It's not what I had in mind.

The stone wall around the farm is crumbling, the barn nearest to us looks as if it was recently in use to house cows, and the main farmhouse is a bit fifty shades of grey – in a stone sense, rather than a kinky one, it looks so drab and cold.

'Come on,' says Rosie, opening my door.

I step out reluctantly, still clutching my phone. I look in desperation, hoping for a signal, but alas we're still out of range.

'You won't be needing that,' says Rosie, plying it out of my hand and switching it off. 'Come on.'

I'm still waiting for our welcoming committee to come and meet us, but Rosie marches up to the old front door.

The farmhouse looks like it's in a better state than the rest of the farm; the roof is tiled with dark slate that looks new and shiny, and the stone in the wall looks solid. But on close inspection, the windows and door tell a different story. The paintwork is still flaking on the windows, the wooden frames look rotten and the front door is broken at the bottom, leaving a hole the size of my foot. I get the impression that neither do a good job of keeping the elements out.

Rosie lifts a huge rock along one of the walls and retrieves a comically large iron key, which she uses to unlock the door. She gives it a good shove with her shoulder and it creaks open.

I follow her inside and we find ourselves in the kitchen of the house, if I can even call it that. The walls are covered in bare plaster with an assortment of mismatched cupboards along them, there's a sink with exposed pipes, a cooker that would look more at home in a museum and a large wooden table – heavily stained – and uncomfortable-looking chairs.

'So,' says Rosie, smiling. 'What do you think?'

'Um . . .' *Is she seriously asking me that question?* 'I'm thinking that you've gone bloody mad. Where the hell are we?'

'We're at your digital detox retreat,' she says, as if I'm the one who's lost the plot. 'We've got everything you need for it: lack of mobile signal, no technology, isolation . . .'

I blink rapidly before pinching myself; surely the past twenty-four hours has got to be one big bad dream.

'I thought we were going on some luxury retreat? This place doesn't even seem like it's got running water.'

'It does, look,' she says, running the tap. It splutters out in fits and starts and finally comes out in a small dribble.

'*Hot* water?' I ask, not knowing if I want the answer.

'I think so . . . probably.'

I shriek. 'Rosie, this is not what I had in mind when I agreed to this! I mean, why on earth have you brought me here? I wanted to go somewhere luxurious for a bit of pampering.'

'I brought some M and S Egyptian cotton bedding with me?' she says, hopefully. 'Look, appearances can be deceptive; this place isn't *that* bad.'

'What about the people running the detox? Aren't there supposed to be workshops and activities?'

'Uh-huh,' she says, nodding. 'There are. It's just a sort of low-key place where they send you a pack and you do it yourself.'

She pulls a wodge of paper from her handbag. 'Here, look, they emailed me directions and I printed them off at mine.'

She waves it so quickly that I can't see what's written on it, but I don't need to see what it says to know that I'm not impressed.

'Surely they can't rent out a place in this state? I know that we're supposed to be off the grid, but don't you think we're at risk of catching pneumonia or Weil's disease staying here?' I say, staring at what looks suspiciously like mice poo on the floor.

'It's part of the process, makes you really appreciate what you have in your life. Come on, it's not that bad,' she says, pushing open another door. It swings open and something flies straight into her face.

'Holy shit,' she says, screaming and waving her arms in the air as it heads in my direction. I quickly drop down under the table until I register the cooing noise and realise it's just a pigeon.

She runs over to the front door and leaves it wide open, letting in a cool breeze as she runs around scaring the bejesus out of the pigeon – and me, if I'm honest – until it gets the hint and flies out the front door.

She slams the door firmly before going into the room the pigeon has just vacated.

'Ta da!' she says, as if she's brought me to the Ritz.

I crawl out from under the table, uncertain of what other surprises lie in store for me.

While the room, which turns out to be a lounge, is in a better state than the kitchen, it's still a wreck. It might boast an exposed stone wall and open fireplace, and the rest of the walls look freshly plastered, but the concrete floor and shabby windows let it down. Not to mention the fact that everything has a fresh decoration of pigeon poo and the room smells mustier than wet towels in a gym bag.

'I hope the people you rented this place off aren't going to deduct money from the damage deposit for the pigeon crap everywhere,' I say, turning my nose up. Then again, I can't imagine anyone would even ask for a deposit, as how could we wreck it any more than it already has been?

'Don't worry about the details,' she says, going over to pull off an old white dustsheet to reveal two wooden rocking chairs.

'Huh?' she says, nodding as if she's shown me a top-of-the-range La-Z-Boy chair.

'Are there bedrooms?' I say, dreading what the answer will be.

'Uh-huh,' she says in a high-pitched voice that only comes out when she's trying to hide something. A childhood of playing Monopoly has taught me the clues.

I push past her and head up the stairs I saw in the corner of the kitchen.

To my dismay, the upstairs is in much the same state of disrepair as the downstairs. There's a long soulless hallway with four rooms off it and only one that has a door.

'Where are we supposed to sleep?' I shriek.

'There,' she says, pointing to a double airbed on the floor. 'I brought bedding, remember. And an extra air bed.'

'Is this some sort of joke?' I say looking at her.

'Of course not, you need to detox and here you are. There's absolutely nothing to distract you.'

'I'm pretty sure that they're only supposed to ban technology, not all basic comforts.'

I'm shaking my head. Maybe at a push, if I came somewhere like this with a boyfriend, it could be romantic and a bit of an adventure. But how am I going to cope, being here with Rosie who brings out my irritable side even when we're at Mum's clean and warm house and we're being force fed cake? Surely we're going to kill each other.

'But what are we supposed to do?' I say, the panic evident in my voice.

'We've got to do all the detoxing stuff. You've got to get in touch with your pre-digital self. You know, we'll do therapy sessions and stuff.'

'So there are actual people here to do that?'

'Not exactly, but I know what I'm doing.'

There were supposed to be staff and other detoxees to speak to. What the hell are Rosie and I going to talk about with no technology to bridge the silence?

'But what about the hot tub? You said there was a hot tub.'

'Well, there's this,' she says, opening up the only door to a room that has one of those old-fashioned Victorian roll-top baths with feet. It's the only nice feature in the whole house, but I don't think you'd even be able to enjoy it as the rest of the bathroom is mouldy and damp.

'And if that's not good enough, there's a stream at the bottom of the paddock; it's a bit cold, but I'm sure it would be refreshing.'

I blink rapidly as if trying to compute all of this.

'So aside from the detoxing sessions, what are we going to do? We're going to go crazy up here. Remember when we went on that family holiday to Devon and Mum took away our Gameboys and we nearly killed each other?'

'Yes, I still have the scar on my neck from your nails when you tried to strangle me.'

'Well, I can't imagine this is going to work out any better.'

I can't understand why Rosie is any happier about this situation than I am, it's not as if she's raced to come and stay with me in London over the years. Our sibling intolerance is pretty mutual.

'I guess we can enjoy the view,' she says looking out the window.

I follow her gaze expecting to be as underwhelmed with it as I have been with the rest of the place, but it takes my breath away.

'Wow, that's incredible,' I say, for the first time forgetting about my phone.

The view of the rolling hills from here is amazing, with all the different hues of green and brown. I eye up the highest point in the distance in particular – I bet I could get mobile signal up there.

'I know, isn't it breathtaking?'

She seems lost for a moment, before she sighs. 'So, now you're acquainted with the place,' she says, 'we should get going on the detox.'

'OK, I'm a bit peckish,' I say, patting my stomach. 'Perhaps we could get food first, then do some meditation or whatever else is on offer?'

'We've got to have the phone-locking-away ritual before we get started on anything else.'

I can't imagine where this crumbling farmhouse will have a safe, but she storms back down the rickety stairs on a mission and I follow. If I'm honest, I'm still a little creeped out by this place and I don't want to be on my own up here. With its sunken location and isolated feel, it's perfect for would-be axe murderers. And there was that Big Foot neighbour we saw on the drive in; he looks like he'd be a shoo-in for a role in the *Cumbrian Chainsaw Massacre*.

I'm reminded of when we were little kids, when Rosie and I still played with each other; she would always be the ringleader.

She'd usually lead me into mischief that would land me in trouble. It wasn't until I got to my teenage years that I stopped going along with her hare-brained schemes, and that's when we drifted apart.

As we walk down the creaky floorboards I'm wondering if I'm repeating a childhood pattern of following Rosie on another one of her foolhardy plans. After all, I'd expected her to bring me to something organised, with staff at our beck and call, and instead we've ended up in some dilapidated farmhouse that I'm sure is only days away from a full-scale spider takeover, if the cobwebs are anything to go by.

'Do you think we might be more comfortable in that pub in the village? I'm pretty sure it said on the sign that it had rooms,' I say, as we find ourselves back in the ramshackle kitchen. It looks even more depressing than when I first saw it.

'We'll be fine here. Where's your sense of adventure gone?' she says enthusiastically. 'You used to love camping when you were little.'

'Um, yes, I did, back when I didn't realise that en suites, feather duvets or fancy hotels existed.'

Rosie rolls her eyes at me and, seemingly ignoring my protests, picks up my phone and hers and drops them into Tupperware that she's pulled out of her bag.

'What are you going to do with them?' I ask.

She's still got that wild glint in her eye and that phone is worth quite a bit of money. I've pretty much accepted that I won't be able to use it while I'm here, but that doesn't mean I want her to burn it in some sacrificial ritual.

'Come on,' she says, pulling the old front door open and marching purposefully out.

'It's only a phone, it's only a phone,' I say over and over in order to remind myself that it's a small piece of plastic and not an actual living entity. Although it does nothing to ease my apprehension.

She comes to a halt beside a well.

'Oh no, you're not putting it down there,' I say shaking my head. 'That's full of water, it'll ruin the phone.'

'Relax, apparently the well's empty and the box is airtight – it'll protect it from the elements.'

Before I can stop her, she's put the Tupperware into a bucket that, with all the holes it's got, looks as though it should belong to Liza and Henry, and she starts to lower it down.

I go to yank her arm away from the handle but she pushes me away. I decide to bide my time instead. I'll come along and pull it up later on. In fact, this is infinitely better than a safe as at least I'll have access to it.

I chuckle to myself at my sister making such a rookie mistake. It's so unlike her. Perhaps the only reason her plans seemed brilliant when we were kids was because I was three years younger than her.

'Right,' says Rosie, pulling a penknife out of her pocket. 'It's time for you to cut the cord.'

I look at her in horror. *Surely not?*

'Your iPhone addiction is holding you back, it's time that you regained your life balance,' she says in a level-headed voice, despite the fact that she's suggesting something utterly ridiculous. 'In order to fully reconnect with yourself and fully embrace mindfulness, you've got to let go.'

'What?' I say, looking at her spouting all this claptrap.

'Come on, it's what the people who designed the detox said to do. Apparently, if you want to do this properly, you've got to empower yourself and let go. But think about it. That phone is the reason why your life is in such a mess. If you weren't so used to banging out social media updates every minute of the day, you'd probably have taken the time to consider *what* you were writing and *where*.'

The stupid thing is that I know she's right, but it doesn't make what she's suggesting any less painful.

'Now, are you going to cut or am I?'

She holds out the knife, which is a risky strategy as, right now, I'm pretty sure I value my phone more than my sister. 'But how will we ever get them out again?'

This is all going a bit *Lord of the Flies* for my liking.

'Ah, don't worry. The people have a plan for that. I'll be able to get it back out when the time is right, don't fret.'

I wonder just who these sadistic people are to have designed this. First we're staying in a falling-down wreck and then we're throwing away our lifelines down an abandoned well. It has all the hallmarks of being the opening to a horror movie.

I look deep into my sister's eyes, and for some reason, just as I did when I was a kid, I feel compelled to do what she says. Maybe the emotional turmoil of the day has taken its toll, but whatever it is, I take the knife from her and slowly cut the cord.

'I can't believe I'm doing this.'

I watch the strands snap one by one and I wince.

'You'll feel better when it's done. You'll be freeing yourself.'

'How do you know?'

'I just do. Trust me, in a week's time, you'll be begging me to keep your phone down the well.'

She says it in the all-knowing way she used to use when we were kids to prove her role of older sister.

'I doubt that,' I say, as the thought reaches my brain that this is actually happening, that my phone is going to be physically separated from me for one whole week, but before I can do anything about it, the last strand snaps and the bucket falls down the well and lands at the bottom with a big thud.

'Great job,' says Rosie, in a mock American accent. She takes the knife away from me, which is a pretty astute decision as the magnitude of what I've just done hits me.

'Are you sure the people have a plan of how I can get that back? It's got all my photos on it, all my music,' I say starting to hyperventilate.

'Don't worry,' she says. 'That'll be all backed up on your iCloud.'

That wasn't quite the reassurance I was after.

'I can't believe you did it,' she says.

'Did I have a choice?' I ask, almost lunging myself down the well to retrieve it.

Rosie pulls me back, 'No, but I thought you'd put up a fight. Maybe you won't have as much of a problem with this after all.'

She walks back towards the main house and I'm sure I hear a small giggle carrying in the wind, but I don't follow her. I'm adrift, staring into the darkness of the well, looking at my lost love. With my hand outstretched towards it, I start to wonder when a shiny bit of plastic became the closest thing I had to love?

Rosie's right, I do need to do this detox.

Chapter Seven

'I can totally cope,' I say, laughing a little manically. 'I'm unplugged, I'm free, and I'm totally fine.'

I try to pretend I'm A-OK that I've just thrown my life down a well, but as I shrug my shoulders, I find that they've practically lodged themselves at my earlobes. I now see why meditation and yoga feature so heavily in detoxes.

Rosie places a pan of water on one of the hobs on an ancient cooker that looks like it should be condemned.

'How long's it been?' I ask, thinking back to the well incident that seems like a lifetime ago.

'Seven minutes and thirty-two seconds,' says Rosie, glancing at her expensive watch.

'Oh,' I say a little deflated. Seven minutes is quite a long time in the world of Twitter; I'm sure that would equate to around a hundred tweets on my feed. God knows how many of those would be in relation to #priceless.

But hey, I might have only lasted seven minutes so far, yet in those seven minutes I've been all right. I haven't thrown myself down the well or run to the nearest village.

'I didn't even think to bring a watch, I always use my phone to tell the time,' I say, pointing at my sister's wrist. I don't want to be asking her what the time is every seven minutes.

'We'll pop it on the list, I'm going to have to go shopping tomorrow anyway.'

My heart starts to race a little. Shopping. The outside world. I know that I've been at this old farm for less than an hour, but already I feel desperate to get back to civilisation.

Rosie goes back to her cooking and I look around the kitchen trying to keep my mind occupied. I try and work out how many blocks of seven minutes there are in a day and, without a calculator – as we all know where mine is – I've concluded that it's a bloody long time.

I hear something and I immediately reach for my phone before I realise what I'm doing.

'What? Did you see something?' asks Rosie, who's still a little jumpy, presumably after the pigeon incident earlier.

'No, I just thought I heard my phone buzz,' I say straining my ears to hear.

I'm usually so switched on to the nuanced beeping of my phone that I keep expecting a ping to break out through the silence. I hear a creak from what sounds like up above and I look hesitantly up at the ceiling.

'It's probably the wind rattling the windows upstairs,' says Rosie, as she takes a seat at the table.

A shiver runs over my spine and I try to make my ears tune out from hearing noises, as my imagination runs wild at what each squeak and creak could be.

'So, what's next on the detox plan, then?'

Rosie glances at one of the pieces of paper she pulled out of her bag earlier and studies it.

'OK, so tonight, we've got, um, an evening of talking ahead of us. You know, just relaxing into the whole thing. Then, tomorrow morning, I thought I'd stock up on supplies and then perhaps we could go for a walk or something.'

'That sounds a bit vague,' I say. 'On the train to Manchester yesterday I googled digital detoxes and the ones I saw had every last minute timetabled, and there were reasons for everything.'

'Well, I'm going shopping so we can eat something, and the walk is so that you can reconnect with sodding nature without looking at it through a phone lens,' she says a little stroppily.

'Sorry,' I say in a mocking voice, like I would have done as a teenager. 'It's just this whole thing was *your* idea.'

'I know,' she says, exhaling loudly. 'Look, I thought you wouldn't be into the whole mumbo jumbo stuff, but if you are, here.'

She digs around in her bag and throws me out a floral-print notebook that looks like something straight out of a National Trust gift shop.

'What am I supposed to do with this?' I say, flicking through the empty pages.

'Start a journal. Get in touch with your feelings,' she says in an earthy tone as if she's taking the piss.

She's right, that isn't very me.

'Joking aside, I did bring that for you. I figured you'd miss writing things on social media and I thought this would be a good outlet. You always did write an interesting diary.'

I give her a scolding look as she knows as well as I do that I stopped writing one the minute I found out she'd been reading it.

It's funny how I got so mad that someone had read my personal thoughts, and yet now I broadcast them on a daily basis for the whole world to see.

I stare at the diary and pick up the pen.

My sister has kidnapped me and is holding me against my will in a crumbling old farmhouse.

Now, if I wrote that on Twitter, I'm pretty sure that it would go viral quicker than my #priceless tweet and I'd have the police helicopter hovering overhead before we knew it. But writing it in a journal when I'm the only person that's going to read it holds little appeal. Not even the little thumbs-up sign and shocked face that I draw next to it make me feel better.

'I'm starving, when do you think the food is going to be ready?' I ask, putting the notebook to one side.

Rosie jumps up, goes over to a box of food that she'd brought in from the car, and whips out a packet of Pasta 'n' Sauce, the type of thing we used to have when we camped as kids.

'You're not even going to cook proper food?' I say, my stomach growling, not from hunger, but from frustration.

'I will do, but not today as I only brought the basics up. I'll get better supplies tomorrow.'

'We could always go to the pub for dinner,' I say wistfully, imagining the cosy-looking pub with its hanging baskets and thatched roof that totally looked like the type of place that would serve big chunky chips and puff-pastry pies. I'm almost dribbling over the table as I daydream.

'We'll go there another night. I don't think it would be good for you so early on in your transition. I mean, how would you feel, seeing all those other people on their phones? I think it's best to keep you away.'

She's treating me like an alcoholic who can't set foot in a pub for fear of a relapse. 'I could totally handle seeing other people on their phones,' I say, imagining them swiping their fingers over those glossy screens and computing that rush of information . . . she's right, I couldn't cope. 'Pasta 'n' Sauce it is, then,' I say, sighing. 'So, did Rupert mind you coming away?'

I figure that we've been so focused on me and my problems that I haven't even asked my sister anything about what's going on in her life.

'No, not really,' she says stirring the saucepan. She's giving it the attention of a cordon bleu meal rather than a packet of dried pasta and sauce. I might not have spent a lot of time with her over the last few years, but I can still tell when something's wrong. Perhaps there's trouble in paradise.

'Is everything all right with you two?'

Her hand spasms a little and a chunk of pasta falls onto the white hob and blends in with the rusted patches where the paint has flaked off.

'We're fine,' she says, giving me the impression that they're anything but.

Interesting . . . I'm about to start digging but I decide I'll bide my time. We are here, distraction free, for a whole week after all.

'And what about work, are you looking for another job?'

My sister hasn't always been a kept woman. After graduating with a first she worked for various finance companies, never seeming to settle, and she got made redundant from the last one a year ago. I kept expecting to hear tales of a great new job from my mum, or to hear that she was pregnant, but it's been a year and neither a bump nor a new business card have been forthcoming.

'I've got projects on the go,' she says, not elaborating.

I'm about to ask her more about it when my bag starts to move across the floor. I jump up immediately, ecstatic that my phone is vibrating, and it's only when I pick up the bag and there's a squeak that *definitely* isn't electronic that I remember my phone is down a well.

I drop the bag down onto the floor and squeal as a little brown mouse goes scuttling under one of the cupboards.

Rosie's eyes follow it but she doesn't flinch. 'Mouse poison,' she says, nodding. 'I'll add it to the shopping list.'

I creep slowly back to my chair and balance my feet on the rung of another; I don't want anything running over my feet. I'm no stranger to mice, I once shared a flat in Clapham with a whole family of them, but I still don't want them anywhere near me.

Rosie places a steaming bowl of pasta down in front of me, and as I tuck into the food it takes me right back to my childhood holidays, which is apt as, although we technically have a roof over our head, we might as well be camping, for all the facilities on offer here.

My first thought is to take a photo for Instagram, with some witty caption about my old school dinner, but I can't, and instead I tuck straight in, getting my food hot for once.

'This is actually pretty good,' I say through a large mouthful.

'Well, it was this or pot noodles, and I ate too many of those as a student to stomach them again.'

'Oh God, yeah, those and cup-a-soups. Just the thought of that stodgy undissolved mixture at the bottom makes me retch.' We both laugh.

'I'm still quite partial to a tomato cup-a-soup though,' she says. 'Good job I didn't bring those out for tea, then.'

'*Very* good job, or I would have been walking down the hill to that pub.'

'Hmm, you'd struggle getting home. It's really dark up here at night without a torch.'

'I've got one on my phone – ah,' I say, realising the problem. 'So you've been here before, then? You seem to know what it's like when it's dark.'

She looks flustered for a second before she regains her composure. 'Well, not *here* here, but nearby. It's all the same up this part of the country. No streetlights but an amazing starlit sky.'

A normal person wouldn't have noticed the slip in composure, but I do. I played enough board games with her when I was a child to know when she's lying. There's something odd about this whole thing, and I can't quite figure out what it is.

'So tonight's plan,' she says, noticeably changing the subject, 'according to the people, is for meditation. Preferably in a candlelit environment.'

'Well, that shouldn't be too difficult,' I say, looking up at the ceiling and noticing that there's no bulb in the kitchen. Do you have candles?'

'They're in the cupboard,' she says, standing up and going over to the tall larder in the corner and pulling out a bag of tea lights and some matches.

'How did you know that?'

'Says so, in the notes for this place,' she says coughing and hovering in the doorway to the lounge. 'How about we go next door to light the candles and sit in the rocking chairs?'

'Don't you have to meditate sitting cross-legged on the floor?'

I've only ever done the type of meditation at the end of a yoga class where you lie down on your mat, and usually I fall straight to sleep only to be woken up by the prodding of the teacher.

'I'm sure this will be fine – besides, we'd probably end up with piles if we sat on the concrete floor.'

'I'm sure that's on old wives' tale Mum used to tell us,' I say rolling my eyes.

'Well, you're welcome to sit on it, if you want.'

I take one look at it as I follow Rosie into the pigeon poo-splattered lounge and opt for a rocking chair, just in case. It's going to be bad enough going to the toilet in such primitive conditions, let alone making it more difficult for myself with a new medical condition.

At least, since we've kept the door between the lounge and the kitchen open, it seems to have aired it slightly. I sit down in the rocking chair while she busily lights the tea lights around us. It's a good job, too, as the light outside is starting to fade.

I start to rock myself back and forth, and it's quite comforting, given my mental state. I try and think of things other than what might be going on online. Rosie climbs into her seat and closes her eyes almost instantly – she must be tired after the drive.

We sit in silence for a while, I don't know how long for, as I don't have a watch, but I'm guessing it's longer than seven minutes as the room has got progressively darker and the tea lights appear to be burning brighter.

'Whatcha' thinking?' asks Rosie, opening her eyes.

'Not a lot, just FOMO,' I say, shrugging.

Rosie looks at me like I've spoken a foreign language. 'What mo?'

'FOMO – you know, Fear Of Missing Out on something.'

'You're worried that someone's going to upload a picture of their dinner to Facebook and you're going to miss it?'

'No, believe me, I won't miss the food pictures. It's just that I don't like thinking that there's something going on in my friends' lives that I don't know about.'

I can feel my heart racing slightly at the thought. Right now, my friends are out and about interacting with each other, and I'm up here in the arse end of nowhere. I'm almost certain that everyone is having a better time than I am.

And it's not only that. It's not knowing whether people are contacting me. What if friends have seen the #priceless tweet and have guessed it's me? What if someone puts on Facebook that I got fired, and then everyone, including people I haven't seen since infant school, will know my shame? All I want is ten tiny seconds just to peek into my apps. Just to see what's going on.

'Are you OK?' asks Rosie, a look of concern spreading over her face.

'I'm wondering if everyone knows that I got fired.'

'I'm sure you are. But look, it's better not to know. By the time you're back online, everyone will have forgotten about it. Better to have a break than react to it.'

It doesn't do much to ease my apprehension. I'm still twitching. I'm almost planning a midnight raid on the well, but, given that I can barely see across the room, I doubt that would be successful.

I watch Rosie rocking back and forth and try to get into the same rhythm. She looks so relaxed and at ease and I will myself to calm down.

'Are you ready to start the meditation?' asks Rosie, in a quiet nasally voice. She sounds as if she's channelling our old RE teacher Mrs Molton. Her voice was so hypnotic that it practically sent you to sleep, or maybe that was just the boring subject matter.

'Don't laugh. This is very serious business,' Rosie says. 'Now, I don't have any music so we'll have to do it in silence. Close your eyes and empty your mind.'

I do as I'm told, trying to bite my tongue to stifle the giggles.

A pigeon coos loudly and both Rosie and I open an eye to check that it isn't in the room, but it appears to be perched outside on the window ledge. It coos away and it could almost be on one of those New Age soundtracks.

'Repeat these affirmations after me,' continues Rosie. 'I do not need my phone.'

'I do not need my phone,' I say, parroting it back and not meaning it.

'My phone does not drive my life; I am in control.'

I try and repeat it without laughing. *Where is she getting this claptrap from?*

Rosie starts to take long, deep breaths and I follow her, rocking back and forth. My eyelids are feeling heavy and I'm fighting the impulse to fall asleep.

'I don't need constant validation of my life from people I barely know.'

I try and parrot it back, but it's getting harder the sleepier I get.

'I will instead listen to those closest to me, especially my sister Rosie, who is wise beyond her years.'

My eyes fly open and I see Rosie grinning at me.

'Huh,' she says, nodding. 'My meditation's pretty good, right?'

'Only because I'm so tired,' I say laughing.

'OK,' she says, clearing her throat and going back to the rocking, and I get in sync with her again before closing my eyes.

'I will not be controlled by my phone . . . I will take time for myself . . . I will switch off.'

My eyelids are heavy once more, and I fight with the sleep to hear what Rosie is saying next.

I attempt to sit up straight but my neck creaks and my back aches. I try to work out where I am when I see Rosie in the rocking chair next to me, reading a magazine.

'Hello, sleepy,' she says smiling. 'I take it my meditation hit the right note for relaxing.'

'Sorry about that,' I say. 'Have I been asleep long?'

'About an hour. It's just before nine, but I'm pretty knackered, so I was thinking of heading up to bed.'

I yawn. 'Yeah, that's probably a good idea. I don't want to fall asleep in this chair again, it's bloody uncomfortable,' I say, trying to stand, but finding myself doubled over. I slowly try to straighten one vertebra at a time.

'We could do some yoga tomorrow for that, sort it out a little,' says Rosie. 'I think there's supposed to be a local class too, if you fancy that?'

She bends down and picks up a large torch and flips it on, before blowing out the tea lights.

I huddle behind her as we make our way back into the kitchen.

'I'll pop out to the car and get the bedding,' she says tugging the heavy front door open.

'You're not leaving me in here by myself,' I say clinging on to her.

'You're not on your own, your little mouse buddy is here,' she laughs.

That makes me jump out of the door even quicker and I grab hold of her arm as I go.

'It's just like when we used to go to Grandma's,' she says.

'I'd forgotten about that.'

My grandma never believed in lights at night, so if we needed to go and use the loo – the outside loo at that – we used to go out together with a torch.

'Do you remember how it always smelt of lemons?'

'Lemons with a hint of lavender,' I say nodding. 'Lemons were her answer to any cleaning situation.'

'Ha, yes,' says Rosie laughing.

Weirdly, it's lighter outside than in because of the full moon, and I don't feel the need to cling on to her as tightly.

I take a look up at the night sky and gasp. 'Oh, wow, that's incredible.'

I can't remember the last time I saw stars like this; in fact, I can barely remember the last time I saw stars. London isn't the best place for astronomy.

'It's quite something, isn't it?' says Rosie, as she opens up the boot of the Land Rover and puts her hands on her hips. 'Some nights, if you're really lucky, you can even see the Northern Lights.'

'What, really?'

'Uh-huh.'

'I didn't think it was possible that this place could be more beautiful at night than it was in the day.'

'Welcome to the Eden Valley,' says Rosie, turning her attention back to the car as she roots through it and pulls out a bag of bedding. 'Here we are.'

'Do we have to blow up the other bed tonight?' I say, staring at it all folded up. I've barely got the energy to talk, let alone blow that thing up.

'We can share the airbed that's already there tonight, if you like? Then it will really be like staying at Grandma's house, sharing a bed.'

'As long as you don't fidget like you used to.'

I used to wake up black and blue.

'I think all those years of sharing a bed with Ru have meant that I'm a lot stiller than I used to be.'

'OK, then fine,' I say secretly pleased. I didn't want to admit to Rosie that I was a little bit scared about sleeping in a bedroom on my own in the creepy house.

'Right, then, let's get sorted,' she says, slamming the boot shut and taking charge once more.

I look over to the well in the corner of the courtyard, its tiled roof dappled with pale moonlight. My heart aches for the phone lying in the holey bucket at the bottom, yet I'm too exhausted to do anything about it.

'I'll get you back soon,' I whisper, before I head back inside.

Chapter Eight

Time since last Internet usage: 20 hours, 5 minutes and 11 seconds

'Ooh that tickles,' I say, giggling, as Aidan Turner's curls fall over my toes. The tickles continue up my leg as his head moves higher, and I'm longing for him to reach his destination.

'Are you finally awake?' shouts Rosie.

I snap my eyes open and find myself alone. I momentarily wonder where Aidan's disappeared to before I take in the hideous Artex ceiling and peeling wallpaper. It seems my love affair with Aidan was the stuff of dreams, and unfortunately for me this dilapidated farmhouse wasn't some awful nightmare.

The memory and shame of how I ended up here comes flooding back and I close my eyes wishing I could just go back to my dream.

Rosie pokes her head through the door, her hair wet presumably from a shower.

'I thought you were never going to wake up, it's gone eleven,' she says, leaning against the doorframe. 'I'd forgotten how much of a lazybones you are.'

I rub my eyes, a little miffed to have been woken up from my dream, before the tickling commences again.

I check under the cover for Aidan just in case, and I'm met, not by his brown eyes, but by the eyes of something else.

'Ahh!' I scream as I throw the covers back and go running across the threadbare carpet to hide behind Rosie.

I watch as another little mouse, or maybe the same one I saw yesterday, scuttles out from my blanket and across the floor and into one of the large holes along the skirting board.

'I think he likes you,' she says laughing.

I give her a look to let her know that I'm not amused.

'Right, mouse poison – it's on the list,' she says shrugging. 'I was going to go out earlier to get the shopping but I thought you'd freak out if you woke up here alone. But I need to go now or else we'll be eating cup-a-soup for lunch.'

'I'll get dressed and come with you.'

'I think it would be best if you stayed here. I mean, I think you need time to be by yourself without temptation.'

'But I'm fine. Look, it's not like I'm a drug addict, I don't have the shakes. And it's not as if I'm going to scratch someone's eyes out to see what's going on with Twitter.'

She gives me a look that suggests she's not so sure.

'I haven't even thought about my phone since I woke up.'

Mainly because I had more pressing matters, like a rodent crawling up my leg. But now that I've realised my phone is missing, I'm not going as crazy as I thought I would. I might be intrigued to know how many people have retweeted my awful tweet, and I might want to see if my boss has emailed me to say they've realised it isn't such a big deal and I can have my job back. But it's not like I'm going to be climbing down the well to rescue it or anything . . . at least not yet.

'Why don't you jump in the shower and have some breakfast, and I'll be as quick as I can? Now, apart from mouse poison, I'm getting light bulbs, an extra torch, a cheap watch, enough food for two or three days – any special requests?'

'Chocolate and wine. I'm allowed wine on the detox, right?' I think the only way I'm going to get through spending so much time with my sister is by drinking.

'I bloody hope so. Right, wine and chocolate, done. See you later on.'

As she pounds down the stairs I head as instructed towards the shower, desperate to wash off the intimate encounter with my rodent friend.

Surprisingly, after the events of the last two days, I slept pretty well. We went to bed around 9ish and I don't remember waking up in the night. I expected to replay what happened with my job over and over in my mind, but I must have been truly exhausted.

I walk into the bathroom, trying to ignore the mould on the wall, and the windows, which look opaque from dirt rather than frosted glass, and run the shower. At least the bath looks clean and the shower curtain looks new. I peel off my clothes and step into the bath as the water splutters out in a chaotic fashion, just as it did downstairs.

I put a hand under it, and to my amazement it's hot! What a bonus. I put my whole body under it and immediately start to feel refreshed. I pick up a bottle of expensive shampoo, which Rosie must have left in here, and lather it all up, when all of a sudden the water starts to go lukewarm.

'Oh no you don't.'

I start desperately turning the hot up and the cold down, but nothing seems to be happening. The water temperature is dropping by the second and I can feel it getting colder and colder.

'Stay with me, hot water,' I say to the taps, as if I'm a doctor pleading with a dying patient I'm trying to resuscitate, but it's no use. I'm forced to jump back to the other end of the bath and I shiver as I assess my options. I know that I have to wash the shampoo out of my hair. I take a deep breath and lean my head in, my teeth chattering as the water makes contact. I do it as quickly as I can while I freeze my arse off and goosebumps prickle up my arms. Finally, I rejoice as I see the water running clear between my toes and I turn off the taps. I have the ultimate brain freeze, which is bad enough when you've been eating ice cream, but so much worse when you haven't even had frozen-chocolate pleasure beforehand.

I grab at a towel from the rack – at least that's clean and oh so soft. Rosie wasn't joking when she said she'd brought a little luxury from home.

I towel myself down as quickly as I can to get warm and dry. At least it's May and not the middle of January. I think my hair would have turned to icicles if it had been any colder.

I wander back into the bedroom I shared with Rosie and give my suitcase a prod around before I open it, just in case any of Mickey's friends have decided to set up home in it.

Deciding that it's not moving on its own, I open it up and pull on a fresh pair of jeans and T-shirt, followed by a nice fitted cardigan. It's great to have clean clothes again. I slip my feet into my suede espadrille boots and tie a scarf around my neck. I rub my hair as dry as I can, before plaiting it quickly to the side. I might not have a mirror, but I can tell I've pulled off the ultimate country chic look. If only I were able to snap a selfie. I'm sure it would look impressively arty taken up against one of the crumbling stone walls outside. It makes me pine for my phone, thinking how perfect this place is for Instagram.

I hear a thud above my head and I freeze. What the hell was that? It sounded too big for a mouse.

I wish that I'd gone with Rosie. I could quite happily have camped out in her car; she could even have locked me in. At least then I wouldn't be bait for the monsters that live in the attic.

'Hello?' I call.

It's quiet again and I reassure myself that it must have been the wind. I can hear it rattling around the windows. I'm sure that something just blew over.

I hurry downstairs and find myself in the big kitchen. It's draughtier today; the big hole in the bottom of the door is doing nothing to keep the chill out.

The noises are freaking me out and I figure that staying inside will only remind me of all the go-to gadgets I'm missing. I decide instead to go out and explore. It takes me three attempts to pull the heavy door open and it almost knocks me back as I set off. I'm met with a grey sky that matches the boulders in the walls and I instinctively fold my arms to stay warm. *Why didn't I bring a coat with me?*

I scan the horizon wondering which way to head, when I spot the well. I try not to look at it at first, but it's as if my phone is calling for me. I listen out for the sound of Rosie's car, but all I can hear is the wind.

I might have gone along with the plan of detoxing when we were in London, when I felt as if I had to escape the Twitter backlash, but now, after a proper night's sleep, I've realised that it was a mad thing to do – surrendering my lifeline to a *well* for all eternity . . . well, a week.

If I got it out, I could hide it in one of the derelict barns and then check on it occasionally. It's not like I'm addicted and can't live without it, it's just that I could be harming my career prospects by not being connected. I'd obviously only check my emails to see if Andrea was begging for me to come back, or if I was being headhunted now people knew I'd gone. I'd probably send Erica the odd little message too – I miss my bestie. But that would be it. I would be really good and wouldn't do any general surfing and I'd even forgo looking at Facebook.

I stride purposefully up to the well and look down.

I can't really see anything other than the fact that it's gloomy. If only I had a torch, but it's on my bloody phone . . .

I bend down and pick up a loose stone from the ground and throw it down the well. Am I supposed to make a wish, or does that only work with a coin? I wish for my phone back just to be on the safe side. It takes a couple of seconds before it hits the bottom.

What the hell does that mean? That it's quite far down?

On the plus side it didn't make a splash, so at least Rosie was right; there's no water.

I look around for something to help me and I see a big stick propped up against a barn. Maybe I can hook it round the end of the bucket and somehow pull it up?

It takes a little bit of angling to get the stick in, and as I lower it down, I have to lean myself in.

'Bloody hell,' I shout, as my scarf gets tangled in the side of the well and it tugs around my throat. I try and hold on to my precious stick in one hand and loosen the scarf with the other without strangling myself. It comes free from my neck so I lean back over the well, this time digging my elbows in so that I don't fall in too. Although, at least if I did, I'd be reunited with my phone . . . I weigh up the broken bones and pain caused by said fall versus the relief of my reunification with my iPhone. In the end, I pull myself back out, as I wouldn't get any signal down there anyway.

'Don't worry, phone,' I say down to it. 'I'll get you soon.'

I'll have to wait and think of a better plan to get it out of its resting place.

In the meantime, Rosie said she'd be at least an hour, which might just give me time to get to the village before she returns.

Now that I've been thinking about logging on, I can't seem to think of anything else, and now I'm desperate to go online. The village looked far too small to have an Internet cafe, but maybe there's a B. & B. with a computer terminal or someone might lend me a phone. I'm clutching at straws, but I feel as if I have to at least try.

I shove my ruined scarf in my pocket, deciding that perhaps a crumbly old farm in Cumbria is not the best place to wear it, and I set off up the drive.

Despite it being dry today, it's pretty muddy underfoot, and I have to concentrate to see where I'm putting my feet. The espadrilles are doing a pretty rubbish job at stopping the stones from wedging themselves right into the soles of my feet. Not to mention the fact that they're getting really dirty. I bend down and try to scuff a bit of mud off the pink suede.

'Bugger it,' I say, wishing I'd picked more practical footwear. I don't think there's any amount of suede cleaner that is going to get these back to their baby-pink hue. Damn Rosie. Messing with my phone is one thing, but my shoes are quite another.

I'm just coming up to standing when I hear a rumble growing louder, and it takes me a second to realise what's making it. I jump out of the way as a quad bike comes flying over a hill in my direction, splattering my jeans with mud.

'For goodness' sake,' I shriek. First my scarf, then my espadrilles, and now my 7 For All Mankind jeans. It's a bloody good job that I don't have my phone for this; there'd be no #blessed words written about this outfit.

'Sorry,' says the man, stopping in front of me.

He might have a helmet on but I'd recognise that beard anywhere – it's Big Foot from yesterday.

'I don't expect people to be walking up here. Got lost, have you?'

'No, I know exactly where I'm going,' I say snappily.

'Right,' he says looking me and my mud splatters up and down. I can see a slight smirk on his face as if he's pleased with his handiwork. 'I'll leave you to it, then.'

He puts his hands back on the handlebars and goes to pull away when I realise that I'm shooting myself in the foot – if he's off out, perhaps he can take me with him.

I look at the quad. I'm not entirely sure if you can ride on it pillion like a motorbike, but I'm sure I could perch somewhere.

'Wait! Can you take me to the village? I need to get there urgently,' I say.

'Not going that way.' He shakes his head, revs the engine and he's off, leaving me to jump out of the way as mud flies in his wake.

'How bloody rude was that,' I say out loud.

I start to reach into my pocket to rant about him in a tweet to make myself feel better, but my phone's not bloody there.

'For fuck's sodding sake,' I shout as loud as I can, but I know that no one other than me will hear it, as the wind seems to be swirling around me.

I look down at myself and know that I can't walk to the village like this, so I turn round admitting defeat.

'Who the bloody hell does he think he is. *I'm not going that way*,' I say, mimicking his gruff voice.

The horn of a car beeps behind me and scares the life out of me as I jump into a verge.

For a minute I think it's the yeti come to have another try at knocking me over, before I see that it's Rosie and her beat-up Land Rover.

'Hey, sis,' she bellows out the window. 'Want a lift?'

I sigh; she's got back quicker than expected. Any hope of reaching the village is now thwarted and only the phoneless farm awaits.

'What's wrong with you?' she asks as I climb in.

'What's wrong with me?' I say as she starts moving. 'Hmm, now that is a good question. Let's see: we've fallen victim to some sort of digital detox scam that should be featured on *Holiday Watchdog*, with a holiday let that is so disgusting it should be condemned; in the space of ten minutes I've ruined a Biba scarf, a pair of Solilla's espadrilles and my ridiculously expensive jeans have been splattered with mud; and if all that wasn't enough, I've been without Internet for at least twenty hours. *Anything* could have happened by now,' I shriek.

'Oh, boy,' says Rosie, pulling up into the farmyard and cranking up the handbrake. 'It's just like when I cut out caffeine, you're all grumpy.'

She pats me on the leg, like that'll make it all better, and jumps out of the car to open the boot. I get out, slamming the door with such ferocity that it's in danger of coming off its hinges.

'We'll start doing a few meditation sessions, maybe some yoga,' she says calmly.

'But that's my point,' I shout. '*You* can't lead yoga sessions, *you* can't even lead a conga line at a family party. This whole thing is wrong. Let's just admit that this was a mistake and go and check ourselves into a nice hotel. One where we won't be sharing a room with the cast of *Ratatouille* and where I won't go through more outfit changes than Lady GaGa in concert. Let's just abandon this place and leave it to rot like it was doing before we got here.'

'We can't go anywhere,' says Rosie, shaking her head.

God, my sister is so infuriating. Just because this was *her* idea.

'Come on, Rosie, we gave it a good go, but enough's enough,' I say pleading. 'These people, whoever they are, aren't going to care, are they? Unless it's like some creepy cult, in which case that's even more reason to leave.'

'We're not going anywhere,' she says again, firmly.

'But we can't stay here. I mean, look what it did to my outfit – it's ruined.'

'Then we'll get you some more appropriate clothes,' says Rosie, picking bags out of the back of the car as if she's listening but not hearing what I'm saying.

'Look, if you're worried because these people are friends of yours, we can pretend to stay here; they don't even have to know we've moved to a hotel.'

'There are no bloody people,' says Rosie, dropping the bags at her feet.

'What do you mean, there are no people?' I say, slowly.

'I made them up. I made this whole thing up,' she says turning to look at me. Her cheeks are flushed and her eyes look wild. 'The whole digital detox was to try and get you here.'

'You made it up?'

I'm trying not to panic that I let my sister throw my phone down a well on the advice of someone who apparently doesn't exist.

'Surprise,' she says.

Once I get over the shock, I'll bloody kill her.

Chapter Nine

*Time since last Internet usage: 21 hours, 10 minutes and
36 seconds*

I try to breathe in and out as I slowly consider my options. If
I kill my sister and bury her body here, it would be days, or
maybe even weeks, before anyone found her. I could totally
make it to Venezuela or somewhere else without a UK extradi-
tion treaty by then.

I take a deep breath, muttering a quick 'I love you' to Siri down
the well before heading back to the cottage, following Rosie.

I need to find out what she's talking about.

Besides, my earlier attempt to leave the drive proved that I'm
not going to make it out without her Land Rover.

'What the hell is going on?' I shout at her as I storm into the
farmhouse. My sister is calmly unpacking the shopping into the
cupboards as if she didn't just make a huge revelation minutes
earlier. 'What do you mean, you made the whole thing up? What
about my digital addiction?' I say, all high-pitched and squeaky.

'Oh, *that* is totally real,' she says, pulling a packet of pasta out
of the bag. 'You really needed to go on a detox, and by putting

your phone down the well, you effectively have. I just can't pretend anymore that this is an organised thing.'

'But the ritual at the well and the meditation, it all sounded like you knew what you were doing.'

'The power of the Internet,' she says winking, 'but I'm sort of relieved to have told you before we got to the whole self-awareness and mindfulness sessions. I don't think deep down that's really you.'

'It could have been, if we'd gone to a bloody spa instead of this place,' I say prodding at a wall, a lump of plaster crumbling into my hand. 'Why are we here?'

'Because I've bought it.'

'I know you've bought this holiday, but I'm quite happy to pay for something else.'

'No, Daisy, you don't understand. I've bought this *place*. The whole of it.'

I stare at my sister in shock for a second. She can't possibly mean she's bought a farm. What would she want with that?

'What are you talking about?' I say, wondering if my lack of phone is clouding my mind from being able to think clearly.

'I'm talking about a property purchase. I bought the house, the barns, the land – all of it. Ta da!' she says, doing jazz hands as if that's going to make it better. On this occasion, it would take the whole cast of *Chicago* doing jazz hands to make this place look any better.

'I'm so lost,' I say, my head spinning. I let her con me into coming here and putting my phone down a well . . . I'm starting to have palpitations.

'Come and sit down,' she says, realising that I'm no longer a violent threat, and she leads me into the lounge. She forces me down into one of the rocking chairs and instinctively I start rocking back and forth.

'It's a bit dark, can you switch the light on?' I say, thinking.

'Much better to use candles,' she says, bending down to light them again. It looks like we're about to have some kind of supernatural séance. It might have been fine for the meditation, but now I know that that was all a lie, it feels wrong.

'It's a bit creepy,' I say, thinking that it feels scarier here in the day than at night.

'Nonsense, it's totally hygee,' she says confidently.

'Hmm, are you sure you're not just trying to cover up the fact that this place doesn't have any lights?' I say, pointing to the ceiling where a bare wire is hanging down from the ceiling in lieu of a light bulb.

'Maybe – is it working?' she asks as she sits down.

'No,' I say coldly. 'So do you want to explain to me why you brought me to this place and threw my only lifeline down a well?'

'OK,' she says, taking a deep breath. 'I bought this farm a couple of months ago at an auction. It was a great bargain, I got it for peanuts.'

'Can't imagine why,' I say sarcastically.

She ignores me and carries on.

'I thought that Rupert and I could turn it into a holiday-cottage business and live up here, as he's been working so much lately that I've barely seen him. I thought this way, if we had another business opportunity, I could tempt him away.'

It's all starting to make sense now. Why she flinches whenever I mention her husband's name. 'I take it he didn't share your dream?'

'No, it turned out he was furious,' she says shaking her head. 'He thinks I'm totally out of my depth. I'd imagined us coming up here on weekends and painting and fixing away, but what I thought was going to be a fun project, one that was going to bring us closer together, has actually driven us apart.'

I get the impression she's trying not to cry. I don't think I've ever seen my sister properly upset before; she usually has an emotional fortress around her as strong as the Tower of London, but she seems to have sent the Beefeaters off for the day.

'So why don't you sell it and be done with it? Surely your marriage is more important.'

'That's what Rupert wants me to do but I can't. I mean, look at it, it's got so much potential.'

I raise a sceptical eyebrow.

'I can't explain why, but I feel drawn to this place, and I want to convince him that I'm right. I've already had builders in to do the roof and some of the plastering, and they totally get my vision.'

'Probably because you're paying them. Are you still thinking of moving up here?'

'No, I don't think Rupert would come, or at least not for the foreseeable future. He made that abundantly clear. What I want to do is turn it into holiday lets, so he'll see that it was a wise investment. That's why I need to get it done quickly. All the while it's standing here empty it's not making any money and it's a failure.'

'Do you think you've been watching too much *Homes Under the Hammer* while you've not been working?'

Rosie laughs. 'I did watch that a lot in the early days. It's why I started buying properties. I bought a few terraced houses and "flipped them" as they say in America. You know, bought them as a wreck, got the builders in, then I did the cosmetic bits and pieces and sold them on for a healthy profit. Which is how I ended up with the money for this place.'

Huh. I vaguely remember her saying she was buying a small terraced house to rent out one Christmas, but I never heard anything more about it. And there was me thinking she swanned around after her redundancy being a lady that lunched.

I stop rocking. 'As great as this all sounds, I still don't understand what it's got to do with me. How does my detox fit in?'

'Well, I'd been planning to come up here and start working on the house, and when I saw what a state you were in and how you didn't have anything to do after being fired, I thought you could come and help me.'

'So why didn't you ask me?'

'Because I knew you'd say no.'

'That's not true,' I say, lying.

'Of course it is. I could barely get you to make the two-hour train ride to Manchester where you'd get to stay in our luxury penthouse. Do you think I'd honestly have been able to convince you to willingly come here?'

I purse my lips. She's right.

'But helping me aside, I genuinely believe this is the best place for you with everything that's going on at the moment. It's perfect for your detox, there's no mobile signal around here at all.'

'*What?*' I snap. 'Then why is my phone lying ten metres down the bottom of a well?'

'So that you're not tempted to go hiking up the fells to find a signal. Believe me, it's in the best place. We'll get it out in a week or two.'

'How are you going to get it out? I cut the sodding rope and there's no International Rescue Team to save it like I'd been led to believe.'

And fishing with a stick doesn't work.

'Relax, I've got a plan.'

'You and your bloody plans are what got me into this mess in the first place.'

'Look,' says Rosie, who's stopped rocking and is leaning towards me. She grabs my chair and stills it. 'This hasn't changed anything. We're still on a digital detox. You're still getting away from modern life. It's just that there'll be less pretend meditation and more helping to pick out paint colours and curtain samples.'

I gaze around the bare room. 'I think it's going to take a bit more than a lick of paint and some curtains.'

'I know, but it's all under control,' she says.

I hate to side with her husband, but I get the impression that this project is far too big for her. A small terraced house is one thing, but a run-down farmhouse and barns is quite another.

'Rosie, there's way too much work for the two of us, even if we knew what we were doing.'

'Ah, well, I've got builders coming, and then I've got a French help-exchange coming to give us a hand next week too.'

'A help-exchange?'

'Yeah, I provide food and somewhere to live and in return they work. She's called Alexis, seems very polite and formal in her emails.'

'Um, are you sure that you can class this place as somewhere to live?'

'I know it's a dump now, but I've got a week to sort out one of the bedrooms so that it looks habitable. You'll soon see that everything looks a lot worse than it actually is once we get stuck in.'

All the way up here I thought I was the broken one who needed to be fixed, but having listened to my sister, I get the impression that this trip is just as much about her fixing the farm, or, more accurately, her marriage.

It suddenly puts my phone addiction into perspective. Unlike me not being able to snapchat a photo of myself with cat ears to Erica, this is real life-changing stuff for Rosie. And there was me thinking she had the perfect life. For once my sister is the vulnerable one, and having seen a chink in her armour, I've realised that she might need me.

I guess a week off from my phone isn't going to kill me, and it might let the dust settle after my tweet. As Erica kept saying, it will probably all have blown over by then. Meaning that I'll get my phone back, contact some agencies, and will be sure to have a few interviews lined up for the week after.

'It's going to take a hell of a lot of work,' I say to her, shaking my head.

'But you're going to stay and help for a bit, aren't you?' she asks, looking at me as if I'm her last hope.

'Of course I am. I can't go anywhere until I figure out how to get my phone out of that sodding well.'

Without thinking, Rosie hugs me with relief, and I hug her awkwardly back. I'm reminded of the times that Mum used to force us to hug goodbye when we visited her at uni, and the thought of hugging my sister in public was more embarrassing than the hand-me-downs she forced me to wear.

'This time next week you're going to have forgotten all about it. I may have made up that this was a real-life retreat, but I'm still going to take your digital detox very seriously indeed.'

'Unfortunately, I don't doubt that for a second.'

Chapter Ten

Time since last phone usage: 24 hours, 8 minutes and 19 seconds

I'm definitely going to have to be more careful what I wish for. First, I wished for sleep and I ended up losing my job, and then I wished for direction in my life and my sister presented me with a DIY project that would have Nick Knowles running for the hills.

'And with a separating wall here,' she says, flinging her arms out wide down the centre of the barn, 'we could turn these two into self-contained lets.'

Since my sister told me the truth about her homestead she's been animated in a way that I haven't seen for years. Probably not since she was in her early teens. The sparkle that used to dance in her eyes has taken up residence once again, and she's positively glowing.

'But,' she says shrugging, 'we need to get the main house done first. I can rent that out and then do this up in the background.'

I follow her back out into the courtyard, turning my back on the well. It's too painful to think about what lurks at the bottom of it.

It's been a little over twenty-four hours since I last logged on, and while I haven't spontaneously combusted, I have felt like I've had a limb cut off. I've even experienced the phantom-limb effect by imagining my phone vibrating and making noises all day, and most of the time it has nothing to do with the mice.

'How are you doing?' asks Rosie, sensing that I'm floundering.

'OK, I think. I just feel a bit lost. Like now, if I had my phone, I'd be snapping away, taking photos of your project and posting them on Instagram. I really miss taking photos. Not to mention I've never gone this long without speaking to Erica before. It's not right.'

'Well, why don't you write her a letter, or a postcard?'

I look at my sister as if she's really lost the plot this time.

'A postcard? Are we on holiday in 1985? It'll take ages to get to her.'

'We're in Cumbria, not darkest Peru. If you post it today, she'll probably get it tomorrow, or Monday at the latest.'

I yelp. I find it bad enough when I have to wait a minute for a WhatsApp reply from her.

'Why don't we go to the post office now? I'm sure they'll sell postcards.'

'Really? You'll let me leave the farm?' I say, as if we're headed to some vast metropolis and not the sleepy village of Lullamby.

'Uh-huh. I double checked with the pub earlier and they don't have WiFi, so there's nowhere you can sneak off to for your fix.'

My shoulders sink; she knows me better than I thought.

'At least we're going out,' I say, as I bound over to the Land Rover like a dog who's just been told he's going for walkies.

Rosie follows me to the car, climbs in, and starts the engine. As we bump down the drive, I can't see why I had such a problem with the terrain; it doesn't seem that bad or muddy from up here. The drive to the village only takes a few minutes and Rosie pulls up in a small car park behind the pub.

'Here we are,' she says as she hops out.

I step out and peer at the buildings as if we really are in some far and exotic land. The main street is lined with terraced houses, all made up of the same type of brown and grey bricks. It looks completely different under today's inky sky to how it looked when we drove through yesterday, when the stone looked yellower.

The post office sticks out from the other houses quite literally, with a bright green, latticed bay window poking out into the street, causing the narrow pavement to get even tighter. We push open the door and the bell over the top of it jangles noisily.

I expect to cross the threshold and step back in time, but the inside is surprisingly modern and fresh. There's a small post-office partition on the left-hand side, and the rest of the space is given over to the shop. Amongst the usual corner-shop staples of tinned goods, bread and magazines, is a large stand selling local produce of delicious-looking cakes and handmade pots of jam and chutney. Behind the counter is an eclectic mix of everything else from warm woolly hats to needles and thread. This really is a general store.

The three people in the shop stop talking as we walk in. They give us a look confirming what we already know –we're strangers in the village. One of the women, who clearly works there, starts to tidy the display in front of her. Yet, she continues to eye us suspiciously as she does so.

'This is a bit awkward,' I hiss at Rosie.

'Well, you wanted to get out. Afternoon,' says my sister to the shop women with a jolly lilt to her voice.

'Afternoon,' echoes the woman standing behind the counter, and the three of them go back to their conversation, albeit in more hushed tones than before.

'Ah, there you go,' says Rosie, locating a swivelling rack of postcards that all essentially offer the same scene – a sheep or a cow in front of a big hill. She pushes me in that direction before she heads over to look at the cakes.

I pick a few postcards at random before spotting writing stationery. If Rosie is really serious about me digitally detoxing, then maybe I could go proper old-school and write Erica a letter too. Although, what I'd fill a whole piece of paper with I don't know.

I find a pretty writing pad with matching envelopes, and some gel pens. I reconvene with Rosie at the counter, who, much to my delight, has selected a big fat chocolate cake, some cookies, and some lovely bright pink raspberry jam.

The other customer, who had clearly come in as much for a gossip as the loaf of bread tucked under her arm, says her goodbyes and leaves as Rosie and I spread our goods onto the counter.

'Did you have a good ratch about at the back?' asks the women as she rings the items through the till. 'We're just in the middle of a sort out.'

'Um . . .' I say, unsure.

'Yes, we found everything,' says Rosie.

Get her, knowing the lingo. She's practically one of the locals already.

'That's good. Got quite the correspondence planned, have you? Got a man to write some love letters to?'

I blush as my shopping is perused.

'No, just a friend,' I say, suddenly wishing for the anonymity of Tesco.

'Oh, but lovely paper all the same. Terribly popular. Although, not that many people write these days. Awful shame that is. But, luckily for Gerry here, everyone's selling things on eBay and sending back stuff they've bought on the Internet. Keeps her in a job,' the woman says laughing.

'Last post goes at four,' says Gerry, chipping in and pointing sternly at the clock, which says that it's ten to. I nod, thinking I'd better get scribbling.

'Now, this is a good choice in jam,' continues the woman as she picks it up. 'Goes best with those crumpets from Mill House farm. Those ones there on the end of the shelf,' she says pointing.

Rosie hesitates for a second before she goes over and picks up a packet, as if that was what was being asked of her.

'That's better. Proper supper that is. So you two up for a holiday, then?'

'Actually, my sister's bought a place up here,' I say quickly, catching a look of annoyance on Rosie's face. Perhaps she was trying to keep that quiet.

'Oh, have you? What place have you bought? Where's been for sale, Gerry?'

'I don't know, Liz. Mr Tompkins's place was sold, but that couple from Lazonby bought that. What about the Smiths' house?'

'No, they took it back off the market in the end. I think he was threatened with redundancy and thought better of it.'

'His job at the garage?' asks Gerry, carrying on as if we're not even there. You wouldn't get this kind of conversation in the M&S Food Hall in Dulwich.

'That's right. Got taken over by some big firm. Where did you say the house was?'

'It's Upper Gables Farm, off the old road,' says Rosie.

'Oh,' say the women together. They're silent for a moment as they consider it.

'You never bought that wreck, love? How much did you pay for it?'

My sister stutters for a second, too shocked at the bluntness to reply.

'She got a good deal at auction,' I say, filling in the blanks.

'You'd need to have done,' says Gerry. 'That's a big old farm. What do you plan to do with it?'

'I was thinking of doing holiday lets,' she says wincing.

'Oh, more holiday lets,' says Liz. 'But, it's better than nought for the community. It's worse when they're left a crumbling wreck on the landscape.'

'And the tourists always spend well in the village,' says Gerry.

'That they do. And your husband's helping, is he?' says Liz, pointing at Rosie's wedding ring.

'Um, he will when he can. We live in Manchester and he works during the week,' she starts muttering under her breath about weekends and I know that she's desperate to change the subject.

'So there are a few holiday lets in the area, then, are there?' I say, taking the focus off Rosie and Rupert.

'Oh aye,' says Gerry. 'People want to come here mainly for the walking, it's ideal with the Lakes and the Pennines so close. There's all sorts of accommodation here already; Lodges, B&Bs. You name it, we've got it.'

I nod. In all the talking with Rosie about her vision she hadn't mentioned her target market – who she wants to attract. Looks like we'll have to suss out the competition too. This project is getting bigger by the second.

'Have you seen much of Jack up at Lower Gables?'

'No, not yet,' says Rosie. 'We did run into someone with a cocker spaniel yesterday, though, who had a big hairy beard.'

I think back to his rudeness with me this morning and I feel a wave of anger.

'That would be him,' says Liz, her eyes lighting up. 'On his own, was he?'

'Just him and his dog,' I say, thinking we already said that.

'Bet he won't be happy, Liz, with the tourists,' says Gerry.

Liz nods wisely. To be honest, I get the impression that he wouldn't be happy with anyone.

I see Gerry's eyebrow hovering, as if she's waiting for us to say something more, but instead Rosie sees the silence as our bid to escape.

'So, how much do we owe you, then?'

'Oh, let's see,' says Liz, pressing a button on the till. 'Twenty-seven pounds seventy-five, then, please.'

'Can I have a stamp as well, for the postcard? Do I have to buy that over there?' I ask, pointing at the post-office counter.

'I'll run and get you one,' says Gerry. 'Liz will ring it through her till.'

Liz adjusts the balance and Rosie pays.

'I'll just quickly write this,' I say, getting one of my pens out of the packet.

Yo Erica,

Check this out – written by my own fair hand and everything. So Rosie and I are in Cumbria. Turns out that she conned me into coming to this old farmhouse that's riddled with mice and is falling down around us, as she's gone and bought the bloody place.

I do my best to draw a shocked face.

I'm coping like a trooper without the Internet. I've not missed it in the slightest *lying heavily*.

Hope all is well with you and Chris and now that I have departed there has been much –

I start to draw an aubergine but it looks way too rude to leave on a postcard. I'm not sure if Royal Mail have censors for decency, but, either way, I scribble it out and decide to write it instead.

– 'Aubergine' – wink. Righto. Miss you lots. Will update you soon.

Not entirely sure of our address, but I'm sure if you write 'Upper Gables Farm, Lullamby' it'll find us. The postwomen seem very helpful.

Love ya

Daisy xx

I stick the stamp on and hand it over, knowing full well that it's going to be read by Liz and Gerry, but I need it to catch the post. We say our goodbyes to our new friends in the village shop.

'See you again,' calls Liz over the bell.

'Ooh riddled with mice,' I hear Gerry say.

Blimey, she could at least have waited for me to leave before she read it!

'Talk about the Spanish inquisition,' I say as we reach the car.

'Don't forget you're used to being down South. Everyone's much friendlier up here.'

'Are you sure that it's not more about the gossip than being friendly?'

Rosie shrugs her shoulders. 'Same, same.'

She opens up the boot and puts in the bag of shopping before we climb back in.

The clouds that before were drab and grey seem to have become darker, as if rain is threatening, so we hurry back to the house.

I'm starting to wish I'd brought warmer clothes with me. I'm eyeing up Rosie's North Face fleece like it's a Stella McCartney sweatshirt. Hopefully, she was serious about sorting out my wardrobe issues as, despite the clean clothes, I don't have much that is suited to the conditions.

By the time we make it down the bumpy track back to the farm, it's started to drizzle, and as we're heading to the front door, shopping in hand, Rosie stops mid-stride.

'I can't have closed the barn door,' she says as she walks over and slides across the bolt. 'Don't want any more pigeons setting up home in there.'

I walk over to the farmhouse and wait for Rosie to unlock it with the old key. She pushes the door open like a pro and unpacks the shopping, leaving the cookies on the table and I can't resist helping myself to one.

'Oh, these are really good,' I say, spilling crumbs out of my mouth.

Rosie picks one up as well. 'Mmm,' she agrees.

'Do you think we should get started on dinner? I say, prodding at the worktop. 'Do you think it's safe to prepare food on here?'

'I bought a couple of pizzas we can put in the oven tonight as that's clean enough. I don't think it was ever used. But you're right about the rest of it, it could do with a deep clean and then it'll be fine.'

I don't share her optimism that a little elbow grease is all that's needed, but at the very least it might stop us from getting E.coli.

Suddenly, there's a large bang from outside and both of us jump.

'What was that?' I ask, peering nervously out of the window. The rain is really coming down now and the clouds are almost shrouding the big hills in the distance in mist.

'Probably the wind catching something,' says Rosie, opening the fridge to hunt for the pizza.

We hear a banging and this time it's more rhythmic.

'That doesn't sound like the wind, that sounds like something's trapped in the barn,' I say, gulping. 'Perhaps it wasn't you who left the door open.'

We open the kitchen door and can hear shouting too. Rosie and I look nervously at each other.

'Looks like you've caught more than a pigeon. What do we do?' I say, my heart racing.

'I don't know,' says Rosie, shaking her head.

Again I curse the fact that we're alone here without our phones. We could have totally skyped someone as we went to investigate, safe in the knowledge that someone could have at least called the police for us if it turned out to be a crazy axe murderer. Whereas now, no one, except maybe Liz and Gerry and perhaps, at a push, the grumpy Big Foot Jack, would know where we were, and even then none of them would know we'd gone missing.

'Perhaps we should go back to the village and get reinforcements?' I say, wondering if there's a village bobby as well as a pub.

'No,' says Rosie, 'if we're going to stay here, we're going to have to deal with things like this. It's probably just a neighbour with some scones or something.'

Listening to the thumping it doesn't sound like they're likely to have baked goods on their person.

Rosie takes a deep breath before jogging towards the noise. Being the supportive sister or, more accurately, the scaredy cat one who doesn't want to be left on her own, I follow her over.

She looks at me as she takes a deep breath and slides the door across.

A man with his arms outstretched flies at us.

I scream and cling onto Rosie, using her as a human shield. If I'm going down, then at least she's going first; after all, she's the one who got us into this mess.

Chapter Eleven

Time since last Internet usage: 1 day, 2 hours, 22 minutes and 43 seconds

The man staggers forward and just about manages to keep himself from falling into the muddy puddles that are popping up all over the courtyard.

He turns round to face us, and fearing that he's going to lunge at us again, I hold my position behind my sister. Well, she is the oldest and therefore it's only right that she should protect me.

But instead of lunging at us, he smiles and pats himself down. Clearly he'd only been going to knock as we opened the door.

Instantly I relax and pull myself out from behind Rosie's shadow. With his wavy dark hair and glossy chestnut eyes he doesn't look like much of a threat. Although, I guess what watching five series of *Dexter* should have taught me was you can never tell what a serial killer looks like.

'Ah, thank goodness,' he says with a heavy French accent. 'I thought I was stuck.'

I look between the man and Rosie. He doesn't sound like he's one of the neighbours.

'I came earlier and you were not 'ere. I look for you in the barn,' he says shrugging, 'and then the door was closed.'

I'm nodding along with his story, which sounds so much better in his sing-song accent. It doesn't occur to me to ask what he's doing here.

'I am Alexi,' he says, jutting out his hand and looking between Rosie and me.

I nudge Rosie. Seeing as it's her farm, she should welcome him.

'Oh, um,' she says shaking his hand.

'It is wet, no? Perhaps we talk in the 'ouse.'

He gestures towards the farmhouse, but my sister seems rooted to the spot – too confused to move.

'Yes, good idea,' I say, walking forward and ushering him inside.

Rosie follows us and we stand like shaggy wet dogs in the kitchen. I pat down my hair, cursing the weather for sending my straight hair into a frizzy mess just as an attractive man shows up.

'So, you are Rosie?' he says to me.

'Ah, no, I'm her sister, Daisy. This is Rosie,' I say, slapping her on the back.

'*Enchanté*,' he says to us both, and for a minute I'm wondering if I should step forward and get all the kisses. Isn't that what you do to be polite in France? I'm all for embracing other customs, especially when it involves hot men.

'What did you say your name was?' I say, realising that Rosie looks like she's in shock.

'Alexi,' he says.

'But you can't be,' pipes up Rosie. 'You're a *he*.'

He looks at her and squints as if he doesn't understand what she's saying.

'I'm expecting Alex*is*,' she says in a shaky voice, emphasising the s. 'Not Alex*i*. My advert expressly asked for a woman on the help-exchange website and your photo was of a man and a woman so I assumed you were the woman.'

It slowly dawns on me what's going on and why Rosie is so confused. This is the help-exchange worker she was expecting next week.

'I do not understand. You speak so quickly. I am a woman?'

'No, you are a man,' says Rosie. 'I was *expecting* a woman. I saw the photo of you and the woman or girl, whoever she was, and I thought she was you.'

'Ah. You thought the girl in the photo was who was writing to you? That was my girlfriend. But I do not understand. You thought she was Alexi?' he says in a tone that suggests Rosie is quite strange. 'It is a boy's name.'

'Yes, well, in English, Alex*is* can be a girl's name. You know, like Alexis Carrington.'

My mum would be so proud of her citing *Dynasty*; she adored that show in the eighties.

'I think she was actually Alexis Colby,' I add.

Rosie gives me a look that suggests I'm not helping. She's lucky I don't have my phone as I'd totally be googling it by now to find out which one of us was right. All I can remember is that she was played by Joan Collins.

'We do not pronounce the s. A-lex-i,' he says, breaking it down for us, so that we're in no doubt how it's said. 'But now I am 'ere, I will work,' he says, looking around the kitchen and nodding his head.

I want to point out that, in my book, he's totally welcome, merely because he's not a woman, but I've already had one death stare so I'm keeping out of it.

Rosie sighs. I know it's a bit of a shock that he is a he rather than a she, but I don't understand why she's getting so het up. He looks very fit and healthy, and his arms look like they'd be very strong . . . you know, for all the lifting and carrying needed for working on the house, obviously. I totally wasn't looking at them thinking they'd be great for picking me up and throwing me onto the hay bales in the barn.

'Well, you're going to be here with just me and Daisy, so I understand if you aren't comfortable with it being just the three of us.'

'I am very comfortable with girls,' he says smiling. 'I 'ave three sisters.'

'Of course you do,' says Rosie. 'But, um, you know, we weren't expecting you until next week.'

'No, no, this week. Today, in fact. I send you an email yesterday to say my plans change. I 'ad been in Portsmouth, but I thought I arrive early.'

Rosie looks like she could cry.

'Oh,' she says nodding. 'We don't have Internet here.'

'It is not a problem, I am 'ere now.'

'But we aren't ready for you. Your room isn't done, I don't have a bed for you; I don't even have a spare towel.'

Rosie's head looks like it's going to explode.

'I understand this is, 'ow do you say it, "a work in progress"?' he says with air quotes. 'I 'ave my sleeping bag and mat.'

He walks around the kitchen, having decided he is staying no matter how hard Rosie tries to convince him otherwise.

'So, this is the 'ouse,' he says, looking around and nodding in approval. 'It is run down but looks OK.'

He's knocking on the walls and rubbing his hand along the parts Rosie's already had plastered.

'Can I look around? Let me see the work I will be making?'

'Sure,' says Rosie, 'go ahead.'

He walks into the lounge and I sidle up to her.

'Well, this is interesting,' I whisper, my eyes wild at the unexpected turn of events. 'At least now I won't be scared at night any more, or if I am, I sure know where I can take refuge.'

'There'll be no funny business under my roof, thank you very much. Especially as we've got no doors. Oh God,' she says, clapping her hand over her mouth. 'We've got no doors on any of the bedrooms. I was going to get a carpenter in to hang them before she, I mean he, arrived.'

'I'm sure that he won't mind, he doesn't seem to be the shy, foreboding type,' I say staring at his bum in his tight jeans as he pokes his head up the fireplace to check out the chimney.

'I can't believe he's a *he*,' she says shaking her head.

I don't understand what the big deal is. If anything, I think it's a comfort he's a man. As much as it grates on my feminist ideals to admit it, the fact that he's going to be sleeping here makes me feel that little bit safer. 'Surely that doesn't matter?' I say, still thinking that it's an unexpected bonus.

'I specifically wanted a woman,' she says shaking her head. 'Don't forget I hadn't planned to have you come here with me, I thought that I was going to be here on my own. If I'm really honest, the help-exchange was as much about keeping me company as doing work on the house. I thought I'd get a bit lonely rattling round here on my own.'

'Well, that's OK. Now you'll have me *and* Alexis.'

'But what about when you go? It'll just be me and him.'

'And what's wrong with that?'

'I'm a married woman,' says Rosie, almost a little too loudly, and we both snap our heads round to check that Alexis hasn't heard.

'So what? It's not 1950 anymore, I don't think anyone will care.'

'You don't think Liz and Gerry will mention it?'

Point taken. I forgot that people up here probably take a bit more interest in that kind of thing.

'But to be honest, I don't care what everyone else thinks, I care what Rupert will think. I mean we're barely on speaking terms as it is. What's he going to say when he finds out that I'm up here on a secluded farm with a Frenchman?'

'A sexy Frenchman. Sexy Alexis,' I say, making sure I pronounce his name like he does.

I get the death stare again.

'And no doors on the bedrooms,' I add helpfully.

Rosie sighs.

'Thank you for reminding me. My marriage is already on choppy water, I don't want it hitting the rocks over this.'

'Just don't mention it to him. It's not like you're able to talk to him at the moment, anyway – I mean you don't have your phone.'

'No . . . but I'm going to have to use the payphone in the village sometimes. Alexis is supposed to be staying for a month, and maybe it will be longer – you saw what he's like, changing his plans. I can't not mention a help-ex being here all that time. And what if he comes to visit? I've asked him to come several times, what if he takes me up on the offer?'

'Then cross that bridge when you come to it. Besides, I'm here now, and I'm quite happy to take any hits for the team if it makes it look better in your husband's eyes.'

'Down, girl. There'll be no need for that. If he's staying here he's working on the house, not on you. You are supposed to be concentrating on your digital detox and finding yourself, not some Frenchman.'

I pout a little, but she's right. I think perhaps having zero personal life over the last couple of months has turned me into the desperate version of myself I usually reserve for when a slow song comes on at a wedding and I've drunk copious amounts of wine. I've got to remember the fact that Marvellous Marcus and his quick reminders were beginning to seem attractive to me last week.

'Besides, remember he said he had a girlfriend? The one in the photo.'

'Ah yes, how could we forget Alex*is*,' I say using Rosie's original pronunciation.

Rosie punches me playfully on the arm and I push her back, but before it can escalate, Alexis walks up to us.

'I go upstairs,' he says, more of a statement than question.

'OK,' says Rosie, 'but remember it's a bit of a work in progress,' she calls up the stairs, but we can already hear him stomping across the floorboards above us.

'You might need some insulation between the floors,' I say helpfully.

'Another thing to add to the list.'

Poor Rosie. This afternoon she'd almost come alive talking about her plans for this place and yet now she looks down in the dumps.

'I can't believe I'm about to say this,' I say, 'but I'll stay as long as Alexis does. That way it won't be awkward for you and Rupert.'

'You'd do that for me?' she says, wrinkling her nose in confusion.

'Uh-huh, but only if you give me my phone back from the well.'

'No deal,' she says sighing, as if I'd got her hopes up. 'I'd rather take my chances with Rupert. You're doing so well, one day in, you can't give up now. Your fingers have only just stopped twitching.'

I examine my hand and wonder if my fingers were moving without me noticing.

'OK, fine,' I say. 'I'll stay here without my phone.'

It's not as if I've got anything to rush back to in my ordinary life.

'Thank you.' Rosie hugs me for the second time today. This time it's not an awkward embrace but more a genuine hold.

I hear footsteps coming back down the stairs.

'But I'm going to have to find something to do without a phone. I need a distraction,' I say, whispering as Alexis comes back into the kitchen.

'Luckily, there's more than enough for you to do work wise, without looking at him,' she whispers. 'In fact, seeing as you're going to be here for so long, why don't you help me with the project management?'

'Me? Project manage a building site?'

I try the title on in my head and I quite like it. I've seen more than enough Grand Designs, I know that it's about good organisation and the ability to sweet-talk builders and contractors with tea and biscuits, and I *am* the queen of making tea. It would also put me on a more equal footing with Rosie, and be less like I'm just her little sister.

'Yes, help me sort out a plan of what we're going to do and when. I imagine you'd be all over a Gantt Chart and working out the critical path.'

'Now you're talking my language,' I say, thinking that's much more my cup of tea than getting my hands dirty.

'There is much work,' says Alexis. 'We start tomorrow.'

Rosie nods. 'So, your photo on the help-ex site,' she says, as she unplugs the kettle and fills it up with water, 'it was of you and your girlfriend?'

She looks a lot calmer now that I've agreed to stay, and it's as if she's thawed in her attitude towards Alexis.

'My girlfriend,' he says nodding as he pulls out a chair and makes himself at home. 'Or, how do you say it, my old girl-friend?'

'Ex-girlfriend,' I chip in helpfully, nodding at the nugget of information, much to Rosie's disdain.

'Yes, that's it. We travel together in Spain, and when I come here, alone, I forgot to change the photo.'

I notice that I'm sitting up a little straighter and tucking my hair behind my ear. I'm sort of glad that I'm not wearing a shape-less fleece, despite being chilly in my light cardigan.

I realise that I'm falling in lust mainly due to that sexy accent he speaks in. Although he is attractive in the conventional tall, dark and handsome way, I still don't really know him yet. For all we know he might turn out to have a personality reminiscent of Dickhead Dominic. But unlike Dickhead Dominic, whose words, I imagine, if you closed your eyes, would still wound your soul, Alexis could be telling me how he murders kittens and it would still make my insides stand to attention.

'So, you said there's no Internet at the farm?' He pulls his phone out of his pocket and I almost make a lunge for it. He stares down at it. 'This does not work also.' He looks at it sadly.

Welcome to my digital detox world, Alexis.

He shrugs his shoulders and pops the phone on the table. 'No matter,' he says.

Why is everyone else coping with the lack of mobile signal and Internet so well? If anything, Rosie's been relieved since her phone's been down the well, yet I can't stop thinking about mine.

While I've stopped hearing phone sounds, mainly because I'm trying to tune out noise for fear of it being rodents, I am still reaching for it all the time. Like now, I'm desperate to text Erica to tell her about the arrival of Alexis. He'd so get the flexed arm Emoji in his description. I'd also be trying to take a sneaky snap of him for Instagram – you know, to make it look as if I'm having the best time up on this lovely farm with my sister and a sexy, suave French dude. I'd look proper cosmopolitan.

'Right, are you hungry? We were just about to make tea,' says Rosie, standing up.

'I don't like tea,' he says. 'I'll just have water.'

'OK,' says Rosie, biting her tongue. It must be hard for non-native speakers to understand all the little nuances of our funny language. 'Would you like some food, for dinner?'

She gets out two pizzas from the fridge and switches on the oven.

'Food, now? It's only just after five.' He looks at us like we're weird.

'Of course,' says Rosie, switching the oven back off, 'we'll eat later.'

She must be able to hear my stomach growling as she automatically goes over to the toaster and pops in a couple of crumpets.

'This 'ouse, then,' says Alexis, 'there is a lot to do.'

I'm not sure if that's a question or a statement.

'There is,' says Rosie. 'I'm getting builders in to do the big things, but then I guess there'll be a lot for us to get stuck in to. Of course, you won't have to work all the time.'

I see a look of fear in her eyes as if she doesn't want to scare him off.

'Yes, I think there is much to explore here,' he says.

'Lots. There are lots of walks and climbs; the Lakes are, of course, outstanding and not very far. Scotland's only half an hour away and Newcastle's pretty close too,' says Rosie, turning into the local tourist information office.

He nods. 'Yes, lots to explore.'

He looks at me and I turn into a total teenager wishing he would explore *me*.

The crumpets pop up and Rosie puts them and the jam on the table, and I tuck in. Alexis looks dubiously at one before following suit and tucking into one, I can tell he's pleasantly surprised.

'So what are we going to do first?' he asks.

'I thought perhaps we'd start on the bathroom. It needs new laminate on the floor and the tiles all need to come off, and the wallpaper stripped. I've got a local plumber who can come and check things out and put in new units, and then I'm going to tile it.'

'*You're* going to tile it?' I say, almost choking.

'Uh-huh, I'm actually pretty good at it.'

I'm learning so much about my sister.

'Right, well, why don't I start a list?' I say, picking up my new journal. It'll be much better used for renovation planning than it would be for mindfulness. 'OK, so bathroom first,' I say. 'And then what's next?'

'Then kitchen, I guess.' And as she goes on to tell me exactly what needs to be done, I try and keep up, marking things with stars that need external contractors, and putting initials by the side when Alexis and Rosie volunteer to do things. After half an hour, the list has stretched over seven pages, and I get the impression that this is probably just the tip of the iceberg – after all, these are only the jobs that come instantly to mind, and once each room is started I'm sure there'll be loads more.

'This's some project. We can't get it all done in a month,' I say, shaking my head in disbelief.

'You'd be surprised,' says Rosie. 'But no, it'll probably take longer than that, but at least this will be a good start. I'm just glad that the previous owner did all the damp-proofing before they sold it, as at least now we can crack on with the painting and things.'

'I hadn't really thought about who was here before,' I say, realising that I hadn't considered who'd used the archaic kitchen, but presumably they left this place a long time ago.

'There was an old man living here until he went into a home about two years ago. His son considered doing the renovations, he'd pulled out everything in the lounge and had the damp-proofing done, but I think he balked at the project when he realised how much else needed doing: the re-wiring, the plumbing, the plastering . . . If you think it's a wreck now, you should have seen it when I first bought it. Over the last few weeks I've had the builders in to do the first fix.'

'A good start,' says Alexis.

'I think this calls for more than tea and crumpets, and now it's after five o'clock, let's open the wine.'

'After five o'clock?' says Alexis. 'You do not drink until after five?' He mutters something about the British under his breath as I open a bottle of red and pour it into three mismatched glasses.

I hand them out to everyone and raise it up.

'To the project,' I say, chinking glasses with Rosie and then Alexis.

As I look at the three of us I wonder what we've got ourselves into, but at least with the renovation, and now Alexis, I should have plenty to take my mind off the digital detox.

Siri who . . .?

Chapter Twelve

Time since last Internet usage: 1 day, 19 hours, 35 minutes and 2 seconds

Who knew that the secret to a good night's sleep was sleeping on a half-deflated airbed next to my sister in a crumbling farmhouse where the wind constantly rattles the windows. I don't know whether it's still the exhaustion or if it's the good old Cumbrian air, but for whatever reason, I've had a great night's sleep and I'm the last one up.

I can hear noisy chatter in the kitchen as I shove a large hoodie over my flimsy pyjama top. I hesitate for a second, wondering if I should shower first and get dressed, seeing as Alexis is here, but then I stop myself. We're all going to be living together, I'm sure at some point he's going to see me for the dishevelled mess I am in the mornings.

'Ah, you're up,' says Rosie, flicking on the kettle as I walk down the stairs. 'There's some porridge on the hob if you want some.'

'Yes, please,' I say, going over and helping myself.

'Not to put you to shame, Daisy, but Alexis has been out for a hike already this morning.'

I look over at the Frenchman and take a deep breath. He's got a little stubble on his face making him looking even more roguish.

'It was very nice. The sun over the 'ills was beautiful.'

And that accent. Resist, Daisy, resist.

'I'll have to get up early one day,' I say, trying to ignore Rosie's sniggers. I may not be a natural early riser, but I reckon I could make an exception one morning if Alexis was leading the way.

'Well, we're going to go and hit-up the local builders' merchants and then go to B&Q,' says Rosie, fussing around the kitchen.

'OK, well, I can hop into the shower and come too,' I say, rising out of my chair.

'Actually, it would be easier if you stayed here.'

'Oh,' I say, feeling a bit put out.

'It's just that we're going to put the seats down in the back of the car so we can fit the bathroom suite in, plus all the other bits and bobs we need to buy. And it will be easier for Alexis to do the lifting and shifting.'

'That's fine,' I say, trying not to feel too left out. I gaze around the kitchen wondering what I'm going to do by myself while they're away.

Alexis flashes me a smile as he and Rosie head towards the door.

'We'll see you later on,' Rosie says.

'OK, see you,' I say, waving and putting on a brave face.

I stare around the room wondering what I'm going to do with myself, then decide to clean the kitchen. Rosie would probably be really grateful, and it would ease my apprehension that we're all going to get sick from it. I stand up, a woman on a mission, and go in search of cleaning supplies under the sink, but there's nothing aside from a half-rusted can of furniture polish and a bottle of Jif disinfectant, which must be *really* old as I'm sure they changed that brand name at least ten years ago.

I'll just text Rosie and see if they can get some more supplies, I pat around the table, then stop myself. Bloody phone.

I look out of the window, just in case they haven't left yet, but the courtyard is empty. I suddenly feel lonely here in the house. Not to mention cut off. What if there's an emergency? What if we run out of milk and I need Rosie to pick up a pint on her way home? Or worse, what if the spiders cocoon me in one of their webs and start to eat me?

I stare suspiciously at a web in the corner of the stairs and remind myself not to walk under it.

I tap my fingers idly on the table and wonder what it was people did in the old days. It's not only my phone that I miss, but it's the TV, the radio, the noise of modern life. Even the old fridge in the corner doesn't have the right hum.

I can't stay in the house, the silence is going to drive me nuts. And with nothing to distract me, all my thoughts turn to the Twitter implosion and the mess my life is in.

I stare at the hills and figure that if Alexis went for a quick walk, then there's nothing to stop me from doing the same. It might even impress him – not that I'm trying to impress him, of course . . . The rolling hills around the farm look gentle enough.

I'm sure I can follow one of the crumbling walls and walk straight along it so that I don't get lost.

I go into the bathroom for a quick shower and, realising that it's on our list as needing to be gutted in the next couple of days, I spend a little longer making sure that my hair is fully washed and that I'm properly shaved, exfoliated and buffed, despite the fact that I've ended up in freezing cold water again.

I attempt to dress more practically, finding a Fat Face hoodie to go with some jeans, and as I slip on my espadrille boots it reminds me to pester Rosie about me going in search of more Cumbrian-friendly attire.

I pad back downstairs, having a quick glass of water to make sure I'm fully hydrated before I go, and I'm just about to leave when I spot Alexis's phone on the table.

What an idiot. They're off on an excursion where there'll probably be a phone signal and he's left it behind.

I shake my head, fighting every temptation to pick it up, and tug open the front door. I'm across the threshold when I peer back over my shoulder at the phone. It's as if it's calling me, telling me it wants to be held and cradled in my palm.

'Don't do it, Daisy,' I chide myself. 'You're stronger than this.'

I try to tell myself I don't need a phone to complete me. It's not even like I'd be able to use it; Alexis probably has it locked.

I go to walk out the door but before I've even got a foot over the threshold, I've turned back and picked up the phone, if only to prove to myself that it's locked. But, to my amazement, it isn't.

Now I know what Alice felt like standing at the top of the rabbit hole.

Who doesn't lock their phone? They're leaving it wide open to addicts like me to come along and steal it.

Of course I'm going to have to take it now.

I feel a ripple of excitement flow through my veins as I try to think about what I'll log in to first. Obviously, I won't be able to sign him out of any of his apps, so WhatsApp is out, but I can still access Twitter and my emails. Of course, I'm only checking from a professional point of view to see how bad Tweetgate has got, but even with that dim proposition, I'm still positively giddy with anticipation.

I peer at the screen and there are no bars of signal. But, luckily, I'm going for a walk up a hill, and didn't Rosie say that there was a signal higher up? It really would be like striking gold in the hills.

I slip the phone into the large front pocket in my hoody and triumphantly set off.

For the first hundred metres or so I have a real spring to my step. The weather is better than yesterday, it's dry and the sky is a dirty blue colour with only patchy cloud, and the wind that's been rustling all night has died down. Aside from the cool temperature, it's a pleasant spring day.

It's not until I get to the boundary of the farm, where I have to go cross-country, that the spring in my step disappears, largely due to the depth of the mud. It seems that yesterday's rain has turned the surrounding fields into a scene reminiscent of a festival.

I stare hard at the space between the quagmire in front of me and the hill on the horizon. I could stay here, where I'm standing upright without problem, albeit with no phone signal, or I could run the gauntlet of falling in the mud and be rewarded with a sneaky look at Facebook.

I take a deep breath and close my eyes as I step forward. The soles of my boots slide as they squelch into the mud. If my boots weren't ruined before, they certainly are now. With reed soles and baby-pink suede, this wasn't what the designers had in mind, but the lure of the Internet is too strong for me to resist.

I squelch along trying to keep myself upright, and after a while I get used to it. As long as I keep my arms outstretched for balance, I've got the stone wall running along to my right to grab on to if I need to cling on. Luckily, it's that really sticky mud that makes your foot slide slowly so I'll have time to react if I feel myself going over.

My calf muscles start to ache at the effort, my cheeks feel simultaneously cold and warm, and my lungs feel fuller from the fresh air. This must be quite the workout – almost as good as the military fitness class I see happening on the common near where I live, which I aspire to go to. I'm sure that I'm burning just as many calories.

Just think, if we had a mobile phone signal in the house, I'd be missing out on all this fresh air and exercise. I feel healthier than I have felt in years. It's also giving me plenty of time to think about more important things, like what I'm going to do with my life now that I don't have a job. Which is, of course, what I'm thinking about. I'm *absolutely* not making a list in my head of all the things I've got to tell Erica when I log on to Facebook . . . *ahem*.

I'm pretty proud at how much better I'm faring today than yesterday. The hill in front of me doesn't appear to be getting any closer, but I've been walking for a fair while so I'm sure I've got somewhere.

I spin round to see how far away the farmhouse is, but it causes me to lose my footing. Instinctively, I grab for the wall with my left hand, but now that I've spun round, it's on the wrong side of me and I end up on my bum.

'Bugger,' I shout, as I find myself wedged in. I try to stand up but instead I wedge my bum further into the mud. There's only one thing for it – I'm going to have to roll onto all fours and push myself up. I take a deep breath and roll over, sinking my hands into the slimy mud. I manage to force myself upright, wiping my hands as best I can down my jeans. I must look as if I've been on one of those Tough Mudder runs. Not that it matters; no one's going to see me up here anyway. I can't believe I endured that freezing cold shower this morning only to have ended up like this. All I can hope is that I make it back to the farm before Rosie and Alexis start tearing the bathroom to pieces.

Making sure I'm holding firmly on to the wall, I turn and look at the farmhouse and wonder if I should give up on my walk and go straight to the shower instead. But I feel the weight of the phone in my hoodie and I know that I've got to get to the hill. If I don't try now, who knows when I'll get another chance? Alexis might not leave it lying around again, or Rosie might not leave me unattended for so long.

I quicken my pace and I'm practically jogging through the mud, finding that the slippery nature of it is propelling me along quicker.

I've been so focused on not falling over that when I reach the bottom of the hill I notice my surroundings for the first time. I turn around and I almost gasp at the beauty of it. I've been walking uphill without realising it and I'm now looking down on the farmhouse in the dip below. I can see for miles. I can't imagine how incredible the view is going to be from the top.

I look over to the village, which looks quite big from here; its terraced houses huddled together. I think of Gerry and Liz and wonder who they're gossiping with – or about. Judging by the grilling that Rosie and I got yesterday, I bet we're the hot topic of conversation at the moment. Those crazy city dwellers who bought that wreck of a farm. But look at me now, that city dweller's tramped across a muddy field, and despite the story my jeans suggest, has fought with the mud and won.

Now all I've got to do is get to the top.

I turn round to face the hill and eye it up like my nemesis. It does look a little steep for my liking. In fact, in front of me is not so much a hill, but a cliff face of imposing rock with shrubs growing out of it. There seems to be a small path that goes up diagonally, but it's fairly narrow.

I pull the phone out of my hoodie and double-check to see whether or not I can access the Internet from here – after all, we are pretty high up.

I yelp and do a fist pump in celebration when I see that there's one bar of signal on the phone. But there's no 3G or 4G where that symbol should be; there's just the dreaded E. Error? Emergency? Evil? I'm not sure what it actually stands for, but I know from previous experience that it's a bad omen. I wait for what feels like forever while it thinks about loading a page on Chrome before it tells me the Internet can't be reached.

'Right you are, Mount Everest,' I say as I channel my inner mountaineer and start my ascent.

I begin to walk up the narrow path, holding the cliff for support, and at first it goes well. I get fairly high fairly quickly and I pull out the phone to check if I've got 3G yet.

'Yes!' I shout with a little too much gusto, and I feel my foot move and the ground crumble underneath me. I grab at a shrub growing out of the side of the rock face, and as I save myself from falling I drop the phone.

'Noooooo!' I shout as I try to grab it, but I can feel myself falling so I cling back onto the rock face.

It lands a metre down the hill in a bush and I sigh with relief that at least it looks intact.

Phew. All I need to do is reach down and grab it.

I bend down and edge forward. It might only be a metre away, but a metre's a long way when you're hanging off the side of a rock face. Plus, it seems that the phone has come to rest on the top of a thistly bush, and if I don't grab it carefully, I risk sending it toppling into the middle of it.

I try to work out my options. I could a) go down the path and try and reach it from below, b) reach down and risk pushing the phone further into the bush, or c) go back to the farmhouse without the phone and pretend none of this ever happened.

I pause for a minute. Option c is looking pretty attractive, and I'm almost tempted until I realise that Rosie's going to twig if Alexis declares his phone is missing. Alarm bells will ring that

I've been home alone, coping with my digital addiction, and she'll instantly point the finger at me.

I take a deep breath and slowly lean over, trying to grab on to a tree root as I do so. I reach my hand out and try to grasp my fingers round the phone, and the tips manage to tickle the touch screen.

'Just a little bit more,' I say, wincing as I stretch my limbs into an extreme yoga pose. I'm pretty sure I could see it catching on – the smartphone lunge – as it works all your upper body and your core. My hands finally grasp around the phone, 'Gotcha!' I cry, but as I go to pull myself upright, the tree root I'm holding on to bends, throwing me off balance. I tumble sideways and manage to ground myself over a boulder as I cling on with one hand to the prickly bush the phone was in.

I may be hanging off a cliff face, but at least I've recovered the phone.

I don't want to move too much in case I dislodge myself, but a quick peek over my shoulder confirms what I already know: the only way back, other than to fall down the hill, is to climb up. I give it a go but my upper body is still in spasm from the smartphone lunge and I don't move an inch.

'Fine pickle you've got yourself into, Daisy,' I say out loud.

I look at the phone, which now appears to have no mobile or Internet coverage. It just says *Appels d'urgence*, which I'm guessing is the French equivalent of Emergency calls only.

Oh no, nuh-uh. I'm not being that person you hear about on the news who calls the mountain rescue at a cost of thousands. I can imagine the *Daily Mail* story now: Thousands of taxpayer's pounds wasted as woman scrambles uphill trying to satisfy smartphone addiction. They'd totally nab my Facebook profile and pad the article out with psychologists reporting on how our digital addiction is killing us. I'd be like one of those stupid people risking their lives to catch bloody Pokémon.

The only trouble is, I'm out of options. If I don't call the emergency services, then I have no idea how the hell I'm going to get off this sodding hill.

Chapter Thirteen

Time since last Internet usage: 1 day, 21 hours, 1 minute and 11 seconds

I can't believe that I'm going to be mortified in front of the emergency services *again*. The last time, they showed up at my flat after I experienced the hottest night of my life. Let's just say, I was on a date with a professional fire-eater that took an interesting turn when he decided to give me a private show in the bedroom.

Looking back, it was probably no great surprise that my former landlord didn't give me back my damage deposit. I'm sure those scorch marks were really hard to get off the bedroom ceiling.

The only saving grace in that situation was that I didn't have to call the emergency services myself; luckily for me, the little old lady from the flat above did that for me. Whereas now I get the double whammy of feeling like an idiot when I call them *and* when they turn up.

It's frustrating as I can see the farm from here. If only they could see me. But judging how small it looks on the landscape,

I won't even look like a dot from where they are. Not that I want Rosie to find me when I've got Alexis's phone. I need to get out of here and return it to the kitchen table before he catches me and I look like some sort of stalker-slash-thief.

I look around, hoping to see salvation, but all I can see are the sheep munching away in the field below. They don't seem the tiniest bit bothered and none of them are exhibiting the slightest interest in morphing into a rescue animal like Lassie.

A cool breeze blows over me and I feel myself shiver. I've never known a place where the weather changes so quickly. One minute I'm enjoying blue skies and sunshine, and the next the clouds have gone an inky grey colour and the sun has disappeared leaving it bitter and dark. The winds pick up again and if I'm not mistaken, it feels as if it's about to snow. In *May*. Good job I'm wearing jeans that are soaked with mud and shoes that are made for walking in hot French summers, then. Even the hoodie, which I thought was the most practical item of clothing I owned, isn't doing a particularly good job for the near Arctic wind that has descended.

'Help!' I shout as loud as I can. 'Help!'

Not even the sheep look up.

Even if I was close enough to any form of civilisation, I doubt my voice would carry far enough in this wind.

I'm starting to get cramp in my hand as I cling on to a branch, and I'm wondering how long I'm going to be able to hold on.

'Help, I'm stuck,' I shout in desperation, as I know that, realistically, I'm going to have to call the emergency services. Yes, it's embarrassing, but it's also a matter of life or death.

'Dear Lord, I know that I only ever talk to you in times of crisis, and we haven't had a chat since last year when I broke my flip-flops during that torrential downpour at the Notting Hill carnival and I asked for me not to get dysentery as I walked the streets barefoot – by the way, thank you for listening – but I really need some help now,' I mutter under my breath.

'What seems to be the problem?' comes a voice, and I'm so surprised that I drop Alexis's phone again.

'Oh, bugger,' I shout, watching it tumble down the hill, bouncing off rocks as it goes. It's got to be broken now, surely.

'Are you OK?' comes the voice again.

'God?' I say, wondering if I've actually died of cold already.

'Um, I tend to go by the name of Jack.'

I look up, straining to see where the voice is coming from, but all I can see from this angle is the big thistly bush above me.

'I'm down here and I'm stuck,' I say, relieved that I'm going to be rescued, and I don't care whether it's by apparition or a real-life person. A few minutes ago I wanted a sheep to help me – I'm clearly not fussy.

'Hang on a second,' says the voice. 'I'll come on down.'

Immediately I'm struck by a giggle, as he sounds like he's a cheesy game-show host. *Hang on there, Daisy, I'll come on down.* What game show was that the catchphrase from? I rack my brain to think, but I'm stuck. If only I could ask my friend Google, he never lets me down.

'Oh, dear,' says the guy whose voice comes from behind me.

I look down over my shoulder and I recognise the thick woolly hat as that belonging to Big Foot. His eyes are still cold, like the weather, and although his face is contorted into a small smile, it's of the smirking variety, not a friendly one.

Of all the sodding people to come and find me.

'Can you help me? It's a bit uncomfortable like this,' I say swallowing my pride. As much as I'm loathe to get Mr Grumpy to help me, it's still better than phoning the emergency services.

'OK, I'm going to have to grab you,' he says with as much enthusiasm as if he were about to pick up dog poo.

He sighs and I feel his hands making contact with my bum.

'Oi, watch it,' I say, 'this isn't the time to cop a feel.'

I feel his hands let go. 'Fine, if you don't want any help, I'll leave you there. It's just that with the angle of the rock and the way your bum's hanging over it, it's the biggest thing for me to grab to be able to lower you down.'

'Oh great, so you're saying that my bum's big. Thanks very much.'

I'm pretty sure mountain rescue would have been a whole lot more polite and wouldn't have pointed out my gym failings.

'It's not that it's big, it just looks it from this angle.'

'Oh, that's much better,' I say sarcastically as I wiggle, trying to reduce my ginormous arse, only I think I've probably given him more of a view.

'Look, I was perfectly happy climbing on the other side of the hill when I heard you shouting for help, and I'd be perfectly happy leaving you and your bum hanging here. But I should warn you that there is a very black cloud over there, and that's usually the direction the bad weather comes from, and you're not really dressed for a storm, are you?'

I sigh loudly. 'Oh, go on, then. Grab my large bum.'

He places his hands back on me. 'OK, let go of whatever you're holding on to and I'll try to lower you down gently.'

'Are you sure? What if I flatten you? You know, me and my big bum.'

'Just let go.'

I do as he says and I scrabble with my hands as I find myself sliding over the rock.

True to his word, Jack lowers my bum until my feet are practically touching the ground.

'Oh thank goodness. Thank you so much,' I say, breathing out in relief.

'You're welcome. But you really should be more careful. Look at what you're wearing. You're dressed like a teenager hanging around the Co-op.'

'Now, hang on –'

'No, this is serious. You're on a hill dressed in – what are they, canvas?'

'Suede espadrilles.'

He shakes his head. 'Suede espadrilles, whatever the hell they are. You should be in walking boots, hiking trainers at a push, but something with a grip on them. You should also be wearing layers. The weather changes like that here,' he says snapping his fingers. 'If I hadn't come along when I did, you'd probably have died of exposure.'

'Actually, I was going to phone the emergency services,' I say, wincing slightly.

'Oh, even better, just what they want to do with their time. Rescue someone like you who wakes up one morning and decides to go hiking without any equipment, dressed inappropriately. Bloody tourists,' he says shaking his head.

I take in his outfit of sturdy-looking boots, grey trousers with reinforced black bits over the knees and thighs and a snuggly fleece. He's even carrying a harness round his waist, with a helmet clipped to his belt and extra rope slung over one shoulder. I take his point.

'I'm sorry,' is about all I can manage. 'Is the lecture over? Only me and my impractical clothing are cold, and if you've quite finished, I'd like to go and get a warm shower before my sister gets back and rips it out.'

Jack stares at me for a second before shaking his head like I'm a lost cause, and stands to one side.

I brush down my trousers as if I'm dusting off a little bit of light mud, which only reminds me how caked they are from my earlier fall. I shake my hair back and hold my head up, trying to give myself a little bit more dignity.

I walk about three steps before I feel my feet go out from under me, and I find myself on my bum for the second time today.

I hear Jack mutter under his breath and I'm pretty sure it was something along the lines of 'for fuck's sake'. I hear him stomp down behind me and, instead of making a fuss, I hold my hand out for him to pull me up.

'You are a liability,' he says looking at me like I'm a moron as he helps me to get upright. 'What did you think you were doing up here anyway?'

'I thought I might get a phone signal up here. Oh, God, the phone.' I look further down the hill and see where it's come to rest.

'A *phone*? You came up here to use your phone.'

'Well, not *my* phone, Alexis's, but . . .' I'm not making it any better; he's still looking at me like I'm a moron. 'Well, I won't take up any more of your time.' I go to walk and he grabs hold of my hand.

'Hang on, you're going to be sliding all the way home in those things.' He pulls his rope off his arm. 'Here.'

He hands me the end of the rope and starts to walk in front of me.

'You're going to walk me along like a dog?'

'It's either that or we hold hands,' he says with almost a growl.

'Rope it is, then,' I say, thinking that at least this way I might stay vertical. We start descending in silence until we get to the mobile phone.

Jack watches as I bend down and pick it up. I give it a quick blow to get the dirt off and, miraculously, not only is it not broken, but it also has 3G.

'Three G,' I squeal.

Jack doesn't look impressed and I get the impression that he's not about to stand there and wait for me while I log in to Facebook. Which is a pity, as I could totally send Erica an Emoji message with the lion head, as Jack with that beard looks just like one; well, at least he would if he dyed his hair orange.

'Good to know,' I say, coughing and shoving the phone back into my pocket, hoping that Alexis will leave it around another day, when he just happens to be going out for hours at a time and I'm the proud owner of walking boots and polar fleece layers.

'We'd better pick up the pace a little, that storm is getting closer,' Jack says pointing.

'Righto,' I say nodding.

We get down the hill and it starts to rain slightly. Jack turns to me as if to silently ask for the rope back and I look at him.

'Um, would you mind walking with me back to the farm? It's just it took me ages to get here and I slipped over,' I say, as if he wouldn't have noticed that I'm caked in mud if I hadn't pointed it out to him.

'Sure, why not? It's not like I was doing anything else,' he says sarcastically.

'I thought you would have been heading home anyway, what with the storm and everything. You know, with you being such an expert in the changes of the weather.'

Jack merely grunts and I can't help but smile. He knows as well as I do that he was homeward bound.

We start walking along in complete silence, apart from the sound of him stomping and my shoes squishing into the mud.

I try and distract myself from the awkwardness, concentrating on trying to think of the game show with that catchphrase. We get all of about a hundred metres before I can't take the silence any longer.

'I don't suppose you remember who said "come on down", do you? It's from one of those eighties game shows I used to watch, but I can't for the life of me remember which, and I can't google it.'

I'm expecting Jack to growl, but to my amazement he answers me.

'*The Price is Right*,' he says as if it pains him to join in the conversation.

'That's it,' I say, clapping my hand excitedly. 'Come on down, the price is right,' I say in a mock American accent. 'Bruce Forsyth presented it, didn't he?'

'No, I don't think so. He did that one about higher or lower, and the *Generation Game*, but I don't think he did *The Price is Right*.'

'Hmm, it wasn't Nicky Campbell, was it?'

'No, that was *Wheel of Fortune*.'

'Oh, yes, *Wheel of Fortune*.' I make the noise that the wheel used to make when it wiped out the contestant's money.

I detect the smallest hint of a smile on Jack's face. He tries to cough to cover it up, but I'm sure it was there.

'So who did *The Price is Right*, then?' I try to go through my head with all the familiar faces of childhood: Bob Monkhouse, Michael Barrymore, Paul Daniels. But the more game shows and presenters, the more frustrated I get that I can't remember.

'What about Roy Walker?' I say, clutching at straws.

'No, he did *Catchphrase*.'

The walk back towards the farm seems a lot quicker as we pass the time chatting eighties and nineties game shows. It turns out we were both big fans of *The Krypton Factor* and *Blockbusters*. By the time we make it back onto the field that is officially the start of Rosie's land, I've had three laughs.

'You are allowed to smile, you know, I won't tell anyone. Not even Liz or Gerry in the post office. Although I'm sure it would make their day.'

'Oh, so you've already met them, then? No doubt I'll get a full report next time I pop in there. Something to look forward to.'

I giggle. I can just imagine the reaction they'd get from him as they witter on about the village. 'Yes, they were quite excited about Rosie doing up the farm, and a little pleased that they might have some tourists to sell their jams to.'

'At least someone's pleased.'

'What have you got against tourists? It's not like you're a born-and-bred local, is it? Through all that growling and grunting, I can quite clearly hear a southern accent.'

I'm expecting a hint of bared teeth, like a dog issuing a warning, but instead I'm rewarded with a smile – a fleeting one – but a smile all the same.

'You're very right, I'm not from here – as Liz and Gerry will be the first to point out. I'm a newcomer, even though I've been living here for over ten years.'

'So, what is it you have against others coming here? It's a bit greedy for you to want it all for yourself.'

'I don't want it all for myself. I'm all for people coming to enjoy this part of the country, it's just that I get a bit fed up with people coming and going. If you lived here, you'd know what I'm talking about. It's bad enough when you get stuck in a traffic jam caused by a herd of cows, let alone when you are trying to get through a village in the Lakes that's bunged full of cars, making it seem like you're driving through Central London during rush hour.

'And then there's the fact that a lot of them don't respect the land, and end up putting themselves, and others, in danger when they go off with their GPS-enabled mobile phones thinking they can call Mountain Rescue like they would an Uber taxi.'

I bite my lip and hang my head a little lower in shame, but out of the corner of my eye I can see that his frosty exterior has softened a little.

'I mean, they do this stupid stuff like walking for miles to get a phone signal,' he says laughing.

'It's not funny. Have you ever been separated from your phone for three consecutive days?'

'I don't have one.'

I look at him like he's a Martian. 'What do you mean you don't have one? *Everybody* has a phone.'

He shrugs before conceding. 'OK, I have one somewhere,' he says, 'probably lurking in the glove compartment in my car. A pay-as-you-go one.'

I shudder in horror.

'As you found out today, the signal's so hit and miss that it's almost a hindrance having a phone when you're out climbing and what not. You almost rely on it, and then if you were to get into trouble, chances are you'd be somewhere where you couldn't use it. I prefer to use old-fashioned fail-safes, like I'll usually tell Rodney from the farm over the valley if I'm climbing, and I'll radio him when I get back safely. If ever I didn't, then he'd pop over on his quad to see if all was well.'

'I guess that's smart. But what about the Internet, how do you cope?'

'I don't live in the Dark Ages, you know. I've got dial-up on the farm.'

'Dial-up? Isn't that *from* the Dark Ages?' I try and recreate the squeaky noise that you used to hear in the days before broadband.

'It's more like this,' he says, squeaking along in exactly the right pitch.

'Oh my God, that's it!'

'I hear it a lot.'

'Don't you mind being somewhere so remote and cut off?'

'Not really. I enjoy my own company, and I've got my work to keep me busy.'

'What is it you do?' I ask, but I trail off, as, bounding down the road, is Rosie's green Land Rover.

'Oh shit,' I say, rubbing the phone against my hoodie like it's a lamp with a genie inside. But I fear that as much as I rub it, there's no one to answer my wish to magically teleport it back onto the kitchen table before they arrive.

Chapter Fourteen

Time since last Internet usage: 1 day, 21 hours, 21 minutes and 48 seconds

'What's wrong?' asks Jack as he follows my gaze.

'I borrowed Alexis's phone and now he's coming back and I don't know how I'm going to put it back without him knowing.'

The bumpy road is no match for the off-roader, and Rosie's going to be back at the farm in no time.

'When you say "borrow", you mean, you stole it,' he says, his scowl back on his face.

'You say "steal", I say "borrow". It's all semantics.'

'Why did you need to take someone's phone? What happened to yours?'

'My sister threw it down a well, along with her own.'

He looks at me like I'm quite barmy.

'Don't worry, it was in Tupperware so it won't get wet, and the well's dry.'

'Oh right, because that makes it much more normal.'

'My sister's making me do a digital detox; she thinks I'm addicted, but I'm totally not.'

'And half an hour ago you were hanging off the side of a hill-side trying to get a mobile signal. No, not addicted at all.'

Just when I was starting to warm to him . . .

I can't believe I'm wasting precious time trying to explain myself when I should be trying to beat them back to the house. I start moving again, hurrying along, and I find myself acciden-tally dragging Jack along too, who's still attached to the rope.

'Hey, what are you doing?' he says almost jogging to keep up. 'You're never going to get there in time.'

'But what am I going to do?' I say, power-walking the best I can in my stupid shoes. I stop in frustration, wondering if I should just throw the phone into the bushes rather than get caught red-handed.

Jack sighs again. 'Bloody tourists, they're always getting themselves into trouble. Come on.'

He drops the rope, seeing as we're now walking on the gravel path that, as far as I can tell, connects Rosie's farm to his. I try to keep up and we make it into the courtyard of Upper Gables at the same time as the Land Rover.

'Hello, hello,' says Rosie jumping out of the car at the sight of us. 'What the bloody hell happened to you? Go for a mud bath, did we?'

I can see her eyeing my appearance and carefully looking at Jack to see what role he's played in all this.

'Very funny. Just went for a little walk and it's a tad muddy.'

'Just a tad,' she echoes, laughing. 'I'm Rosie, by the way. I gather we're neighbours.'

'Jack,' he says, shaking the hand she's holding out for him.

'Nice to meet you. Liz and Gerry were telling us all about you.'

For a moment I wonder if he's going to abandon me and skulk off at the mention of the village gossips.

'So I gather.'

Rosie walks round to the back of the Land Rover and opens the boot, revealing the extent of their shopping trip.

'Oh wow, how many bathrooms are you renovating?' I say, marvelling at the contents.

'Daisy,' says Alexis, rushing over and looking at my front in horror as he gets out of the car.

For a second I'm worried that he knows I've got his phone in my pocket, but then I realise that he's looking at the mud.

'Oh, I'm fine, just a little slip when I was out hiking.'

'It is good? You are all right?'

'Fine.'

'Then, this is for you. A treat,' he says handing me a Boost, my all-time favourite chocolate bar.

'Thanks, my favourite. How did you know?' I ask, looking at Rosie, but she shrugs her shoulders. 'Thank you.'

I stare at it for a second, as if he's just given me the crown jewels, but Jack coughs and reminds me of his presence.

Alexis looks him up and down as if unsure how he fits into all this, and I notice that he's a bit slow to acknowledge him properly.

'Alexis,' he says thrusting his hand out.

'Jack.'

'Alexis is our help-ex worker,' I say, before he thinks he's Rosie's husband.

I notice that he doesn't say *enchanté* to him like he purred at us yesterday.

'Do you want me to give you a hand? Perhaps Alexis and I can take this in?' says Jack.

'I should be able to manage,' says Rosie, being more polite than actually protesting at the offer of help.

'I insist,' he says through gritted teeth.

Alexis leans into the boot, and as Jack follows suit he raises an eyebrow at me and I realise that that's my cue. I scuttle over to the front door, throwing my shoulder to it with such ferocity that I'm like a human ramrod. I go flying through into the kitchen and manage to shove the phone back on the table just as Rosie follows me in, carrying bright orange carrier bags.

She dumps them onto the table before heading out to get some more.

'You can help, you know,' she calls over her shoulder.

'Be right there,' I say, double-checking the phone is in the same position that I found it in.

Alexis and Jack walk in carrying a toilet awkwardly between them, with Rosie shouting orders.

'Let's keep it down here in the living room until we rip out the old suite.'

I go to the back of the car and pick up a collection of boxed taps and some paint. Even that's a struggle; my fingers still haven't straightened themselves out since they were clutching the rock. The wind did change when I was up there. What if they're going to stay like that forever?

Jack, much to his disdain, helps unpack the whole car. He scowls at me each time he passes, just in case I was in any doubt that he was doing me a big favour.

I go over to the kettle while everyone else goes back to the car to do the final run.

When Rosie comes in and shuts the door I look up at her in surprise.

'Where are the boys?' I say, thinking that after commandeering so much of his day the least I could do was to make Jack a cup of tea and offer him some of the handmade cake we bought yesterday.

'Jack said he had to go to the village, and Alexis asked if he could go with him. Don't worry, I asked him to pick up some more of those cookies.'

'Oh, good,' I say, suddenly feeling awful that I didn't get a chance to thank Jack for everything he's done for me – both the dramatic rescue and him covering up the phone theft. Normally, I'd send someone a text to say thanks, but it's a bit tricky with neither of us being in possession of a phone.

'I can't wait to get started on the bathroom,' says Rosie, clapping her hands in delight, the same way I do when I'm excited about something. It seems funny to be watching someone with the same mannerisms. 'Now, do you want to use the shower before we rip it out? It's going to be a few days before it's plumbed in and ready to use.'

'What are we supposed to do in the mean time?' I haven't asked before, too fearful of the reply.

'Ah, now I did think of that when we were at the shops.' She roots around in the bags until she finds what she's looking for. 'Ta da,' she says, holding up a solar-powered shower, the type you use if you're camping and desperate.

Having spent so much time with Jack this morning, I've got his frown down to a tee and I glare at her.

'You want me to use that? *Outside?*'

'Not exactly. I thought we could hang it outside to warm it up then pop it up in the barn, where it might be a bit warmer.'

'And a bit more private.'

'Oh, yes, there's that too. I'll get Alexis to whip up something this afternoon. I bought some value shower curtains, I'm sure he'll be able to do something.'

I'm starting to appreciate how easy my life was this time last week. Sure, I was slaving away, working all hours to the point of exhaustion, but at least I knew I'd always have hot showers, a warm and cosy bed, and my beloved phone. I chide myself because there are people that live in these conditions every day, even for their whole lives. I suddenly feel awful about the private pity party I'm holding just for me. If this was a Facebook post, I'd totally follow with #firstworldproblems, as that's exactly what this is.

'I'll be fine,' I say, instantly manning up. 'It'll be like one giant adventure.'

'Won't it?' says Rosie. 'You know it's so exciting actually living on-site and doing a refurb. Usually I'm just popping in and out, supervising the contractors before going home. Oh, I forgot, I bought this earlier.'

She picks up a Boots bag, pulls out a bottle of dry shampoo and gives me a nod as if to tell me that it's going to solve all our problems.

I take the bottle and plant a fake smile on my face, 'Great.'

'And . . .' she says, pulling out a bright blue box that appears to have an old-fashioned camera in it. It takes me a moment to register that it's a disposable one.

'What's this for?' I say, thinking that it looks like the type of thing that would look more at home on a wedding table.

'You said you missed taking photos, and this way you'll be able to snap away on your walks.'

I look at it and try and remember the last time I used a camera with real film in it. Was it the nineties? Just after? I scratch my head.

I take it out of the packet and smile at the faux snakeskin that gives it a vintage feel, which is in keeping for its surroundings.

'Thanks, Rosie, that's really thoughtful,' I say, almost in surprise that my sister would do something so nice for me.

I run my thumb over the wheel to wind it on so that it's ready to use. There's something so satisfying about the physicality of it.

'I bought a few,' she says, pulling out pink and cream boxes too. 'Thought it would be nice to have some in-progress photos as we do up the house.'

'Great idea,' I say, sitting down at the table, which is a bad move, I realise, as my wet jeans spread even more over my thighs.

'So, what was Jack like, then? He seemed a bit less frosty than he was when we met him on the road the other day.'

'You mean, when we almost ran over his dog.'

'I didn't almost run over his dog. His dog just did a very spirited run near my car.'

'Uh-huh.'

'Anyway, so, what is he like? He seems very helpful.'

Her eyebrow is raised in a way that I recognise; it's so much like our mother it's uncanny. I only need to pass within three feet of a man who's vaguely my age and unmarried for my mum to get her fishing rod out for information, and it appears Rosie is the same.

'Yes, it was nice of him to unload the car.'

'Wasn't it,' she says nodding and staring at me as if I'm supposed to elaborate. But I don't. I carry on trying to pick the mud off my jeans in big lumps. It's fairly satisfying when you get a big crusty bit off intact, and it's fulfilling my need to fidget now that I don't have a phone to occupy my fingers.

'So, did you just bump into him on your walk?'

I think my sister is going to strain her eyes with that eyebrow raising if she's not careful.

'Uh-huh. Now I'd better go and have this shower. Make the most of the luxury while I still can.'

My sister's face falls in disappointment. It's as if she could sniff there was more going on than a simple stroll in the country. Of course, she'd be right, but I'd rather she keep up the fantasy that I was attracted to our neighbour, rather than know the truth that I was trying to log on with Alexis's phone.

As I walk up the stairs and head into the bathroom, I almost laugh at the state of it. I can't believe I called this a luxury. I run the water and peel my clothes off slowly. The mud having dried makes the jeans more rigid, and it's even harder than usual to pull them off. I finally succeed and step into the warm water. I close my eyes and try to appreciate the warmth, thinking how I'm going to miss it over the next few days. Hair washed in record time, I get out of the shower reluctantly, as I know that if I don't, I will soon be reliving my ice-bucket challenge.

I dry myself off quickly and walk, in my towel, back to my bedroom and start rooting around in my suitcase, wondering what the hell I'm going to wear. I settle for the tracksuit bottoms that I slob around in at the weekends, and I team it up with a long-sleeve Gap T-shirt and a big woolly cardigan. It will have to do. I also decide to put on my smelly gym trainers too. They're not the type of trainers that Jack was talking about, but I guess they've got to be more practical than the espadrille boots, which are now only fit for the bin.

I'm about to walk out of the bedroom when I catch sight of my writing stationery. I must write Erica a letter; yesterday's postcard is already out of date, thanks to Alexis's arrival and my near-death experience this morning.

I pick it up and an idea hits me – I could write Jack a thank-you note and leave it in his mailbox at the end of the road. I feel as if I need to thank him, and a note is far less invasive than heading round to his house to do it in person. An old-fashioned equivalent of a text message.

I pop back downstairs and see that Rosie is bent down at the oven.

'Just shoving some jacket potatoes in for lunch. Are you hungry?'

'Starving,' I say, thinking that I worked up quite the appetite this morning.

'They'll be about forty minutes as I started them off in the microwave. I figure we'll wait for lunch before we get stuck into any work.'

'OK, I might go for a little walk, take a few snaps while I wait.'

Rosie nods and starts taking the bathroom supplies upstairs.

I lean over the table and write my note.

Jack,

Thank you for your knight-in-shining-armour impression – on both counts. Alexis didn't seem to notice the adventure his phone went on this morning, and my hands are slowly starting to relax out of the claw pose that they'd been stuck in from clinging on to that rock for dear life.

You'll be pleased to know I've thrown my espadrilles (those stupid bloody boots) in the bin.

I'll try and be less touristy in the future.

Thanks again,

Daisy

I'm deliberating whether to add a kiss or not when Rosie walks back downstairs.

'Hey, do you remember who used to present *The Price is Right*?'

She stops and leans on the banister. 'Hmm, Bob Monkhouse?' she says, wrinkling her face as if she's not sure that's the right answer.

'No, I don't think it was him.'

This really is frustrating. It's the kind of question that would be answered in a nanosecond if we had the sodding Internet.

'What about Des O'Connor?'

I do have a memory of Des presenting something with a shiny model.

'Could be.'

P.S. What about Des O'Connor?

'I'm just going to test out the camera,' I say, as I fold the note over and give Rosie a quick wave. I shut the door and I hope this time I have more luck on one of my walks.

Chapter Fifteen

Time since last Internet usage: 4 days, 21 hours, 37 minutes and 21 seconds

'It's day four in the *Big Brother* house, all of the housemates are going slightly mad. They've locked themselves in the world's smallest bathroom and have taken to ripping the tiles and wallpaper off the wall to entertain themselves,' I say in my best Geordie accent, which sounds more like I'm from Liverpool.

Rosie smiles a little and Alexis looks at me with confusion. It's probably the accent. I have enough trouble understanding it, let alone a non-native English speaker.

The more I think about it, the more I think I have in common with the *Big Brother* housemates. Trapped away from the outside world; no TV, phones or Internet; forced to cook on random rations – my sister doesn't appear to be a very practical shopper – and to make polite conversations with strangers – Alexis, and, to a lesser extent, Rosie. The only real difference that I can see, aside from millions of people watching their plight, is that they have a shower. What I wouldn't give for a shower now . . . I wouldn't even mind the millions of people watching me have one.

I've been steaming wallpaper off the wall for two days. Not only is it tedious, but it's also hot. I'm a right stinky mess, and I know that I'm edging ever closer to the barn shower.

True to her word, Rosie got Alexis to whip up a shower cubicle outside. I think she thought putting it in the barn would provide an element of privacy. Only, with the light flooding in from the holes in the roof and the use of a white shower curtain, I'm pretty sure that there would be some naked shadow puppetry going on.

I've been putting it off, but I'm slightly conscious that the three of us are working in such close proximity, and both Alexis and Rosie have braved the cubicle, so if I don't go soon, they're going to realise that the funky smell in here has nothing to do with the old toilet.

The only thing I'm glad of right now is that Rosie didn't get Alexis to whip up a toilet too. Instead, she's ordered a Portaloo, saying that it will be useful for when contractors are on site anyway, as when the bathroom is all finished, she's not going to want any muddy boots ruining it again.

So far, the project itself is going well. I've covered a wall of the sitting room in Post-it notes with all the work that needs to be done. Not only does the room require a much-needed boost of colour, but it also meticulously plots the path of outstanding work. Rosie went to the village and stood in the phone box for over an hour making phone calls to various builders, and we now have the next few weeks planned solidly.

As for the three of us living and working together, so far we are getting on quite well. But I think that's mainly because Alexis can only understand what we say if he concentrates, and the rest of the time he seems to zone out. I can't say I blame him. To make conversation, Rosie's been filling me in on the last few years of *EastEnders* episodes that I've missed. To give Alexis credit, he did try to stay with the plot lines, saying that it helped with his English, but then Rosie told me that Kathy came back from the dead and we lost him. Since I'm now fully up to date, things have gone pretty quiet and we're struggling to find a replacement topic.

'Finished,' says Alexis, doing a fist pump as he pulls the last tile off the wall.

'Blimey,' I say, taking a step back and admiring his handiwork.

The smashed avocado tiles litter the floor as he stands in the cast-iron bath that's covered in a towel. Rosie didn't want to make it any worse before the restorer comes to recoat the enamel next week.

It's hard to say it looks great, as now the wall's bumpy and uneven, but it looks a whole lot better now that it doesn't look as if someone's thrown up on it after a heavy night of tequila.

'All I've got to do now is sand it off,' she says, 'and then I can start tiling again tomorrow. Great work, Alexis. Why don't you take the rest of the afternoon off?'

'Thanks, I go for a walk up the hill. Daisy, you like to come too?'

'No, thank you,' I say, thinking back to my last walk and how badly that ended. I promised myself I wouldn't try that again until I was properly kitted out.

'You should have gone with him,' says Rosie as he leaves. 'It's probably easier if you're out of the way when I sand the plaster back. It's going to get really dusty.'

'Nah, I really should take a shower, and if he's out, I'll probably feel a little bit more comfortable in the barn.'

'It's really not that bad. I mean, he's put some Perspex on the top of it so that the pigeons can't poop on you while you're in there.'

'You're really selling it to me.'

I blow a bit of sweaty hair away from my face as I finish off the bit of wall I'm working on. I step back, feeling proud at my handiwork. I'm probably going to feel more exhausted than proud by the time I've stripped the wallpaper off all four bedrooms too, but for the moment I'm feeling accomplished.

'It's a good feeling, isn't it?' says Rosie, raising an eyebrow. 'If I'm honest, I find it quite addictive.'

'I can see that. It's nice to actually make an immediate difference to something.'

'That's it exactly,' she says, nodding so enthusiastically that she chips out part of the wall as she scrapes a bit of paper. 'I think that's why I couldn't go back to an office job.'

I look carefully at the wall, tilting my head; I'm not quite at that point yet. 'It's a nice break, but I can't see that I'd like to do it full-time. Every muscle in my body is aching, for starters.'

'Yeah, it's a lot more physical. But maybe it will tempt you away from going back to marketing.'

I start to collect the discarded wallpaper that's strewn all over the floor and place it into a bin liner. 'That's if the marketing industry will have me back. The more I think about what happened, the more it worries me that no one is going to give me a job ever again.'

I'm thankful that at least with the house renovations there's a lot to keep my mind occupied so I don't have to think about it, as I'm not qualified for anything else.

'I don't know what else I'd do, or if I want to do anything else. I did really love my job. OK, so it was maybe a bit too full-on and busy, but I'd love to do the same sort of thing with a smaller company.'

'It's hard, isn't it?' says Rosie, perching on the side of the bath. 'We're told that we're supposed to want these great jobs and then when we get them, we realise that it's to the detriment of our lives. I don't think I really noticed it when I was working, but since I left and I see Ru – or I don't see Ru – during the week, I see how much of our life he's missing out on.'

She looks a little lost and it's interesting getting a glimpse into her life. It's funny, as I'd always been so envious of her life with Rupert and their beautiful flat, but it seems as if it's not all as perfect as it looked.

'It's a shame that you don't like doing this, though. We could have gone into business together,' she says, laughing.

'Oh, yes, I'm sure Mum would be well impressed if we both became professional strippers.'

'Watch it. I'm managing a property portfolio, I'll have you know.'

'That's fair enough. I just don't think it's really me. I wish I was one of those people who harboured a secret dream to run their own company, like baking cupcakes or running a little country cafe, but I liked my job.'

I shake my head. It was nicer not thinking about the future and just mindlessly pulling off wallpaper.

'I think I'm going to take that shower now,' I say, picking up the last of the rubbish on the floor. 'I'll take this down on my way.'

I peer out the window on the landing and I see the tiny spec of Alexis walking on the horizon. Pleased that the coast is well and truly clear, I grab some toiletries and clean clothes and hurry to the barn before I can change my mind.

I slide the door open, leaving it slightly ajar, as the last thing I want to do is get stuck in here like Alexis did that time. Rosie would probably struggle to hear me over the sander and I've got no desire to be shouting again for someone to rescue me.

Pecking around the floor between me and the shower are half a dozen pigeons cooing away. I'm not usually bothered by them in parks when I'm eating a sandwich, but there's something about being in an enclosed space with them that makes me feel a bit uneasy. I feel as if I'm starring in Hitchcock's *The Birds*.

'Coo, coo,' I say, doing my best impression as I walk through them, trying not to make eye contact in case it sets them off.

I take a deep breath outside the makeshift cubicle Alexis has cobbled together. There are four old stepladders of varying heights, with brooms and shower curtains hanging off them, woven through the steps. He's then hooked the solar powered shower to the top of the tallest ladder, and the bottom of the cubicle appears to be an old baby bath, which I'm supposed to empty outside when I'm finished. If it were not me who had to use it, I'd be slightly impressed by the ingenuity, but as I strip off my clothes, I wonder again what I've got myself into.

I climb into the mini bathtub and I stand behind the bright white curtain. Forget *The Birds*, I now feel like I'm in *Psycho*.

I take a deep breath, bracing my shoulders, as I pull the shower cord. The water drips out in a warmish dribble, reminiscent of the inside shower. This isn't actually that bad; my bum barely has goosebumps on it. I'm just starting to relax when I hear the pigeons cooing loudly, followed by a bark.

'What the –?' I shout, desperately trying to rub the shampoo out of my eyes and hair in a race to finish quickly.

The barking gets louder and a pigeon flies into the curtain, making the brooms start to wobble.

'Buster!' shouts a voice.

I see the spritely springer spaniel dart around the back of the shower, yapping away as he goes.

I lunge for my towel, realising exactly whose dog it is, when a pigeon flies overhead and Buster decides to use the shower as a shortcut to get to it. Barging under a curtain and jumping over the baby bath as if he were a horse jumping a water fence, he bursts through the gap on the other side. For a second, I think that I've got away with it, that the shower is going to remain intact, but then I see the solar shower bag start to wobble and the next thing I know the cubicle starts to fall down around me. I instinctively crouch down, and fling my arms over my head and scream as I brace myself for impact. The ladders and brooms hit the ground noisily. I realise that I've escaped more or less unscathed; that is, until I open my eyes to assess the damage and see Jack standing in front of me.

'I'm not looking,' he says, shielding his eyes with his arm and desperately hissing at his dog to come to him.

I'm glad that I'm at least hunched up behind my knees so that Jack can't see anything. The only trouble is, if I make a lunge for my towel, I risk exposing a boob or a buttock. Neither of which I'm too happy about.

'Um, are you going to catch Buster anytime soon?' I say, my teeth starting to chatter.

'Absolutely. Come here, Buster, you're not getting away from me that easily.'

'What the bloody hell's going on?' says Rosie, running in and gasping as she sees the ladders and the tangled mess of shower curtains.

She picks up my towel, and for a moment I think she's going to run off with it, as she would have done when we were kids, but instead she wraps me up in it.

'Are you OK? Are you hurt?' she asks, looking a little nervous.

'No, I'm fine. Luckily everything fell away from me.'

'Gotcha!' shouts Jack as he grabs him with both hands and slips a lead on.

'Um, sorry about that. I'll leave you to whatever you were doing,' he says, his cheeks colouring.

He practically runs out, dragging Buster along behind him, and I wonder what he was doing here in the first place.

'What happened?' asks Rosie giggling, as I sigh with relief that he's gone.

'I was having a shower when his bloody dog came bounding in chasing pigeons. He leaped right over the baby bath and the step ladders collapsed like dominoes.'

'You could have been killed. I'm so sorry, this is all my fault,' she says shaking her head.

I start rubbing myself dry and dressing before I get any colder.

'It wasn't your fault. You didn't make Alexis build it to withstand attacks from springer spaniels, did you?'

'No, but I should have perhaps made sure it was a little safer. I feel awful.'

I think Rosie is more in shock than I am. 'I'm fine, really,' I say, towel-drying my hair.

'So apart from letting his dog run riot, what was Jack doing here?'

'I'm not sure,' I say, 'but I'm guessing by the way that he followed Buster in, that he was looking for him, that's all. I probably scared him more than he scared me.'

What with my giant bottom being naked and all that.

'Well, I guess that it's back to the drawing board with the shower. Hopefully, the plumber will at least have put the sink in tomorrow, and then we can do a good old strip wash.'

'Now you're even *sounding* like Grandma. You'll be pulling out those funny things she used to have on those taps. The ones that went separately from the hot and cold tap to mix them.'

'Oh my, I'd forgotten about them. You'd have one end and I'd have the other, then we'd both scream down them, "I am a mole and I live in a hole".'

We both start to laugh at the shared memory.

'Where did that come from anyway?' I ask, thinking how random it sounded.

'I think it was from an old song from the fifties that Grandma used to play.'

Rosie starts to sing it, and I laugh even more.

I honestly don't think I've laughed this much in ages. I'm doing that proper, infectious bellyache stuff, not the hashtag lols that I usually pretend I'm doing to make it seem like I'm having a good time.

'It used to be fun when we'd stay there, you know, before we hated each other,' says Rosie as she starts to sort out the mess of tangled curtains.

'I didn't hate you,' I say getting dressed under my towel. 'You were the one who never wanted me to touch your stuff or talk to you.'

'Didn't I? I just remember you whining all the time.'

'And I just remember you shouting all the time.'

'Huh, I don't remember that at all.' She shrugs. 'At least you're not such a whiner now. I thought you would have been whinging all day long about the lack of phone. I've been impressed.'

'See. I told you I could do it.'

I'm not going to tell her that I've already been out twice in search of the Internet.

Rosie doesn't even attempt to resurrect the cubicle; we'll have to take our chances with the dry shampoo in the meantime.

'Now that I know you're safe, I'd better get back to the sanding. The plumber's coming first thing tomorrow.'

'Are you sure you don't need help? I don't have a whole lot else to do.'

'Why don't you go for a walk? You could catch Alexis up?'

I stutter a laugh. He must have been gone at least an hour by now.

'Um, no, I might just have a stroll around the farm, take some photos. Then maybe I can get them developed to send to Erica next week.'

'That's a nice idea. While you're there, will you check the post?' she asks, handing me the keys. 'I'm waiting on some paperwork from the land registry and I don't want it getting all damp in the box.'

She marches back off to the house and I set off, scraping my hair into a messy bun as I go.

It's so much more enjoyable walking in shoes that keep me upright naturally, rather than mimicking walking on an ice rink. I can't believe I didn't think to wear my trainers before. I wonder if I could make that walk to the village in them.

Now that I'm not cursing the mud, I can appreciate the views as I walk. I'm enjoying the quietness of the surroundings when a sheep baas, scaring the living daylights out of me.

I look around to make sure no one's watching and I hop over the wall. I position myself between two sheep and, planting a silly smile on my face, I take a selfie. I spin the camera round and sigh before remembering it's not digital, and I wonder if I should take some more just in case.

'You all right there?' says a voice.

I look up and see an old man who's presumably the farmer.

'Oh, yes, perfectly fine,' I say, pretending that it's normal to be squatted down in a field next to a sheep with a camera held far out in the air. 'I wanted to take a photo of myself with the sheep,' I say tailing off in embarrassment.

'I'll take it,' he says, marching over and grabbing the camera. 'Say cheese,' he says, smiling and raising his eyebrows, which are bushy like caterpillars, and it causes me to laugh.

'Thank you, that's very kind of you.'

'No problem. I hear that you're our new neighbour.'

He's giving me the exact same look of suspicion that Gerry and Liz gave us in the shop.

'Not so much me; that's my sister. I'm just here temporarily.'

'That's a shame,' he says with a twinkle in his eye, sounding a little bit flirtatious. 'I live over there.'

He points across the main road at a white-painted cottage halfway up a hill.

'If you need owt, come and see me, I'll sort you.' He gives me a wink and leaves me in no doubt that his other comment was flirtatious. 'You're lucky with the weather. Blue skies,' he says very chuffed, despite the fact that really you'd expect it at this time of year. 'I must be going, though, I'm bidding on a hay bayler on eBay and it's ending in twenty minutes so I've gotta get back.'

'Did you say eBay? You've got Internet?' I say, scouring the landscape for telephone poles.

'Oh aye, I've got broadband,' he says in a voice as proud as mine was earlier, when I was inspecting my wallpaper stripping. 'Downloads my videos ever so fast.'

I'm too jealous to be curious as to what type of videos he's downloading.

'I'll see you around. Pop in for a brew, if you're passing,' he says, like he lives right off the main road and not what looks like a twenty-minute hike up a steep hill. Two minutes ago I would have politely smiled, but that was before he muttered the magic word: broadband.

'I might just do that.'

I look as if I've made his day and he goes bounding off across the field.

I climb back over the fence as best I can and I reach the end of the lane. If only I'd picked up my bag, I could have totally made it to the village.

I sigh and turn on my heels, thinking I'll head back to the farm to take photos, when I catch the mailbox out of the corner of my eye and remember what Rosie said about checking it.

I try not to look at Jack's box and cringe at the note I put in there a couple of days ago. He didn't mention it when I saw him this morning, but then again, me being naked meant that he didn't really mention a lot.

I turn the key in the lock and realise that Rosie's got quite a bit of mail, including a big brown envelope which might just be what she's after. I pick it all up without really paying much attention, until I see a bright pink piece of paper that has a note to me on it.

DAISY,

I DIDN'T MIND RESCUING YOU ONCE – FIRST TIME IS FREE, SECOND TIME I CHARGE. JUST BE THANKFUL THAT IT WAS ME AND NOT RODNEY WHO FOUND YOU – THAT WHOLE BUM THING WOULD HAVE TURNED OUT VERY DIFFERENTLY. HAVE YOU MET HIM YET? OLD FELLOW, FLAT CAP, DROOLS A LOT AT WOMEN (AND COWS WITH GLOSSY COATS).

ANYWAY, IT'S ME WHO SHOULD BE APOLOGIS-ING ABOUT WALKING IN ON YOU WHEN YOU WERE HANGING OUT NAKED IN YOUR BARN. BUSTER ISN'T REALLY A PERVY DOG, HE JUST HAS A THING FOR PIGEONS AND WHEN HE SAW THE BARN HE MADE A BEELINE FOR IT. I WAS COMING OVER TO THANK YOU FOR THE NOTE, AS THIS WHOLE WRIT-ING THING (AS YOU CAN TELL BY THE MESS I'M MAKING) ISN'T ME. PLEASE KNOW THAT I DIDN'T SEE ANY OF YOU OR YOUR GIANT BUM. I KNOW I SHOULDN'T JOKE ABOUT THINGS LIKE THAT AS WOMEN CAN BE SENSITIVE ABOUT THAT STUFF, BUT YOU ACTUALLY HAVE A NORMAL-SIZED BUM (NOT THAT I'VE BEEN LOOKING, BUT FROM WHEN I GRABBED IT.) AND, YES, I KNOW I'M DIGGING THE HOLE DEEPER. SEE, PROOF THAT I'M PRETTY CRAP AT THIS WRITING THING.

I'LL PROBABLY SEE YOU AROUND.

JACK.

P.S. HAVE GOOGLED PRICE IS RIGHT AND TO
PUT YOU OUT OF YOUR MISERY IT'S NOT DES
O'CONNOR

I flip the paper over and see that it's a flyer for a local barn
dance, and I picture him here picking up his post not long ago,
hastily scribbling it in his block capitals.

I can't believe he's left me hanging about *The Price is Right*
though.

I'm smiling as I walk back down to the farm and I make sure
that I hide the note in my pocket so that Rosie doesn't see it.
She reminded me far too much of Mum the other day, with her
eyebrow twitching at my walk with Jack, and, no doubt, she'd
be matchmaking the instant she found out about the notes. I'd
much rather keep this to myself, and if she wants to direct her
matchmaking attention to me, Alexis is a much better candidate; so easy on the eye.

Chapter Sixteen

Time since last Internet usage: 5 days, 3 hours, 10 minutes and 58 seconds

'I haven't forgotten you,' I say almost in a whisper to my phone, but it still echoes noisily around the shaft of the well. 'I'm still working on a plan to get you out.'

I look down to where the light disappears and imagine my phone being all alone at the bottom. The poor thing. It's been down there five whole days now. *Five.*

I think back to my earlier conversation with Rodney and wonder if I could pop over to his farm. I know he was a little amorous for his age, and Jack may have warned me about him in his note, but I'm sure he can't be *that* bad. I mean, I only want to check my emails for a few minutes, I'd even forgo checking Twitter as long as I could satisfy my curiosity that my boss hasn't come to her senses and rehired me.

I know that I could go and ask Jack, even a dial-up connection is better than no connection, but I wouldn't want him to think I'm stalking him after the note writing.

It's also not even the fact that I want to check anything, it's that I miss having something to do. The thought of another evening stretching out in front of me is daunting; they're definitely the worst. During the day I can at least kid myself that I'm busy with the house renovation; after all, I was used to not being able to monitor my phone when I was at work. But in the evenings, there was nothing to come between me and my blossoming relationship with my iPhone. Here, the only thing I have to look forward to is sitting around on uncomfortable chairs either under a harsh bright light, now that Rosie's hung a single bulb from the ceiling in the lounge, or by candlelight, which is a bit weird now that Alexis has joined us. And I have to make conversation with Rosie, of course. Although it's getting easier, we're still a long way from being bosom buddies.

'What are you doing?'

Alexis's sing-song tones carry across the courtyard and I try not to bang my head on the well roof as I stand back upright.

'You look like you are going to jump down it.'

He's wrinkling his forehead in confusion, which he does a lot. It's mostly reserved for when he's trying to understand what Rosie and I are talking about, either if we're talking too quickly for him to keep up, or if we're using words that don't make any sense.

'No, no, just making a wish,' I say, shrugging my shoulders.

I'm met with more brow wrinkles.

'Um, it's tradition that you make a wish in a well – that's why they're sometimes called wishing wells. You know, like when you throw a coin into a fountain.'

'Ah,' he says nodding, the brow unfurrowing. 'You threw a coin down there.'

'Uh-huh,' I say pretending. That's much simpler to explain than what I was actually doing.

He looks wistfully down the well. 'Any time I make a wish, I wish that my dad was still alive,' he says, closing his eyes for a second.

'Your dad died? Mine too,' I say. 'How old were you?'

'I was fifteen, and you?'

'I was only four, but fifteen, that must have been so hard. You would have known him so well.'

In some ways, I'm jealous that he has more than the few fleeting memories that I have of my own, but in other ways, I can't imagine the pain of loss that comes from losing a parent when you're old enough to understand it fully.

'It was, but my older brother is very good, very like my father.'

'And your sisters, they're a help too?'

'Um, yes, yes, my sisters. But I don't speak of it too often. Painful.'

I rub Alexis's arm as I watch him blink back a tear.

We stand there looking into the emptiness of the well, silent for a few minutes, presumably both thinking of our dads.

'How was your walk?' I ask, thinking it best to change the subject.

'It was good,' he says. 'How do you say – enlightening.'

'Good. Perhaps I should go on one.'

'Not now, it looks like it is going to rain,' he says, pointing up to a dark cloud rising over the hill.

FFS. This bloody weather. I'll have to go and see Rodney another day.

Alexis starts to kick his boots noisily against the barn wall to shake off the loose mud. He'd better be careful; I'm worried that it might fall down.

'You want to play cards?' he asks as he turns to walk to the farmhouse. Any hint of grief having disappeared. 'I am an expert at poker.'

My interest is piqued. Poker with sexy Alexis: I know what type of poker could make that more interesting.

'Absolutely, I'm a bit of a shark too.'

'A shark?'

'Oh, a card shark, it's an expression . . . I'll be there in a second and I'll whip your butt.'

'You'll whip me?' his face lights up and I close my eyes. I forget how confusing the English language is.

I choose my words carefully so that I don't insinuate any more BDSM habits. 'I meant, I'm going to win.'

'No chance,' he says.

He turns and walks away and I follow him. At least now I've got poker to look forward to. I play a lot on my iPhone, so I'm sure that it's no different in person.

Alexis sits down at the kitchen table and fills Rosie in on his walk while she stirs the casserole in the slow cooker.

'You're just in time,' says Rosie, as she starts to spoon out ladles of food onto plates.

'Great.'

I head over to take the plates and give one to Alexis before sitting down myself at the table.

For a moment, the three of us are silent as we devour our food. All this fresh air and hard work is a powerful combination that results in extreme hunger most days. We practically inhaled the homemade cake during our coffee break this morning.

'Well, that was really good,' I say as I polish off the last dregs on my plate.

'Thanks. I even impressed myself. So, Alexis, you missed all the excitement here earlier,' she says, raising an eyebrow in his direction. 'Daisy was having a shower and Jack's dog came running in and knocked the cubicle over.'

'*Mon Dieu*, my shower is broken?'

'I'm afraid so. It's back to the drawing board on that one.'

She stands up and goes over to the slow cooker. 'Anyone want any more?'

Alexis nods and holds his plate up and she spoons on another ladle full.

'I'm fine, by the way,' I say, smiling that he was only concerned about his handiwork.

'I can see that already.' He gives me a wink and I smile, satisfied at the attention.

'Poor old Jack, he practically ran off in embarrassment,' says Rosie, laughing.

'Jack was there too? When you were in the shower?'

I can't tell whether his brow is furrowing again in confusion or whether there's a flicker of annoyance there now too.

Maybe it's just wishful thinking on my part that he's the tiniest bit jealous.

'He wasn't in the shower with me,' I say for clarification. 'He came to retrieve Buster and he arrived just as the curtain went down.'

'And he saw you naked?' he smirks in the way that only a man could.

'I'd bent down to shield myself from the falling poles, so I don't think he could get a good view. Can we stop talking about this,' I say, my cheeks colouring at all this talk of me with no clothes on. Trust Rosie to want to embarrass me by telling it.

'What about the plan for tomorrow,' asks Alexis, 'what will we do while the plumber is in the bathroom?'

I'm desperately hoping that Rosie says we can take a day off. I could do with hitting the shops. I'm starting to covet hiking boots like I used to Louboutins.

'I thought we could start stripping some wallpaper in the upstairs bedrooms, before the carpenter comes to install the windows next week. Once that's done, we'll be able to the get the plasterer in there.'

Alexis nods his head thoughtfully. He puts his knife and fork down onto the plate before standing up and putting it in the sink and starting on the washing-up. Luckily, as dinner was prepared in the slow cooker, there's very little to do. So I stand up to give him a hand drying.

'So, Alexis suggested that we play cards tonight,' I say to Rosie.

'Great idea. Do you have any with you?'

Alexis shakes his head. 'I just assumed . . .'

I sigh, another boring evening to look forward to, then. Maybe I can use it as a way to get to know Alexis better; Rosie could have an early night, I could blow the bulb in the lounge, forcing me and him to sit in candlelight . . .

'I think in that case I'm going to go out,' he says, ruining my fantasies.

'Out? Are you going for another hike?'

I shudder at the thought. I couldn't stand up right in the day when I could see, let alone in the dark. I know he likes to go on sunrise walks so maybe he likes to go on starlit ones too.

'No, I am going to the pub,' he says matter-of-factly.

'Ah,' I say nodding. That makes a whole lot more sense. I wait for him to invite Rosie and me but the invitation is not forthcoming.

He puts the last of the washed plates on the draining board and drains the water before patting his wet hands on his jeans.

'Now, I get ready,' he says, giving us a smile and walking upstairs.

'I quite fancy going to the pub,' I say, flipping the kettle on instead.

'Me too, although I think at the moment it's better for you to stay here. Too much temptation.'

I'm not entirely sure if she means me with all those people with mobiles, or drinking with Alexis.

I pull two mugs off the decrepit mug tree and start to make Rosie and myself a cup of tea.

'It would have been nice to have been asked, though,' I say a little sulkily. I mean, one minute we were playing cards, the next he's off.

'Oh well, he's young, free and single, isn't he? He probably wants to go and sow some wild oats.'

'I'm young, free and single too,' I say in protest.

'Hmm, yes, I guess you are. Perhaps you could sow your wild oats next week. That way it won't seem like we're gate-crashing his evening. Don't forget, he's been with us for three days now, and for most of that we've been holed up in a bathroom boring him to death with our chattering.'

'Come on, our conversation was scintillating, and I'm sure we were helping with his English.'

'We spent most of the time talking about *EastEnders* and TOWIE; I'm not entirely sure it's widening his vocabulary that much.'

'Come on, we taught him what "Well jel" and "vajazzled" mean.' I can still picture his face as Rosie mentioned the diamantes.

'But do you think it's safe for him to walk on his own down the dark country lane? I could –'

'He'll be fine. We bought some head torches in B&Q the other day.'

He walks back down the stairs in a fresh checked shirt and even skinnier jeans than the ones he was in before. He slings a leather jacket on and I actually have to stop myself from swooning.

'*Bonne soirée.*'

'Have fun,' says Rosie cheerily.

'Are you sure that we can't go to the pub tonight?' I say as he slams the door.

'No,' says Rosie. 'We've got a very busy evening planned.'

I sigh. If she thinks I'm doing any more work tonight, then she is very much mistaken. I can barely lift my arms above my head, what with the claw fingers from hanging off the side of a cliff and then the stripping of the wallpaper in the bathroom. I know that I'm getting a free stay here, but I'm her sister, not her slave.

'I'm not doing any more work, my arms won't allow it.' I demonstrate how it's near enough impossible to even lift them off the table that I'm leaning on.

'Oh, I've got something else in mind,' she says standing up.

I groan, I can just tell this is going to end in me chanting round the candles again. So much for me thinking that she'd forgotten all about that mindfulness bollocks.

She digs around in the fridge and pulls out a bottle of Baileys and a packet of chocolate fingers.

'Girls' night in,' she says.

I breathe out with relief. 'Phew, now that I can do.'

I watch Rosie as she pours two large glasses and slides one across the table to me.

'I see you've got no trouble with your arms now,' says Rosie, raising an eyebrow at me.

I hesitate with the glass halfway to my lips. 'This is medicinal.'

'Uh-huh, sure.'

The Baileys slips down so nicely, and all thoughts of the pub go out the window. Who needs a room full of strangers who would no doubt stare at us as the odd ones out all night – or worse, be like Gerry and Liz and interrogate us instead.

'I wish we could put a rom-com on and chill out,' I say, as I wriggle my bum trying to get comfy on the wooden kitchen chair. I've been worked to the bone, and there's no bath in operation or a soft sofa to ease my aching muscles.

Rosie scrunches up her face. 'Yeah, I thought I was doing really well with this whole digital detox, but do you know what, I bloody miss the TV,' she says sipping her drink.

'Ha, I knew it,' I say, pointing at her and almost whooping with delight. It makes me feel better that I'm not the only one pining after modern life.

My ears start to tune into a buzzing in the room. 'I must be going doolally,' I say, looking around the room. It sounds so convincing, 'I'm sure I can hear a phone buzzing. Must be all the talk of technology.'

'Oh fuck it,' says Rosie, jumping up and heading towards the door, and for a second my heart starts to race as I imagine that she's going to go over to the well to get out the phones. I'm starting to fidget with excitement, but she reaches into a cupboard by the front door which I hadn't even noticed.

'I found this, this afternoon when I was looking for an Allen key. I was going to save it until we really needed it.'

My heart sinks as she pulls out a small radio. I don't know what I was expecting when she opened the door, it's not as if it's big enough to hold a secret TV or anything, but I can't help but feel disappointed.

'It's not even digital,' I say sighing, as if it's the end of the world.

'Then that makes it perfect with your *digital* detox.'

She's grinning as she switches it on, and she turns the aerial round as she twists the dial to get a station. It's so obvious that she's not going to pick anything up, as that's just our luck out here, but the static gives way to a tiny bit of music.

'Go back,' I shout, and Rosie turns the dial slowly and then moves it back and forth until she tunes it in.

Take That's 'Pray' comes on and I almost weep with delight. Not only is it my favourite old school Take That song, but we've also got music and something to drown out the creaks and squeaks of the windows and the imaginary buzzing.

'I love this song, I haven't heard it in ages,' says Rosie.

She puts the radio in the centre of the table and we both stare at it in wonder. I bet this is just what it felt like back in the day to hear something on the wireless. Our attention captivated by the tinny and crackly sound of music coming from this little machine.

I rip open the box of chocolate fingers and we both dig in. Despite the aches and pains, I seem to be doing a pretty good job of bobbing along in my chair to the music.

The song comes to an end and the DJ comes on with a real local-radio DJ voice, a Cumbrian version of Alan Partridge. I'm expecting him to call us pop pickers at any moment.

'*Time to give it large. Up next on the ultimate nineties and noughties is "Do You Really Like It" by D J Pied Piper and the Master of Ceremonies.*'

'Oh yes,' says Rosie, seeing my shoulder bob and raising it with a head nod. 'This was one of my uni songs.'

'It reminds me of my leavers' ball at school,' I say.

It's funny, as I often forget when I'm with Rosie that she's three years older than me. It doesn't make much of a difference now, but the gap felt as wide as the Grand Canyon when we were younger.

'Did you have yours in the school hall like us?'

'Yes, I think we had a sit-down dinner in the dining room first, and then a disco after.'

'I bet it's not like that now. It's all prom dresses and limos.'

'I know, and I thought I'd been indulgent having my hair done at the hairdresser's.'

'Wow, Mum let you have your hair done?' She shakes her head. 'Youngest children are always the spoilt ones.'

'She probably would have done that for you too, but don't forget you dyed it bright red after school finished and she was mad at you.'

'Oh God, I did. It was supposed to be crimson but it looked like I'd been tangoed. It took months to grow out. It was still a pale pink when I started at sixth form. It would be real trendy now though, the faded-colour look.'

'It would.'

I giggle at the memory of my mum going nuts about Rosie's hair. I remember her being grounded for weeks over it, as she'd not only, to quote Mum, 'ruined her hair', but she'd also ruined one of Mum's precious M&S white towels that had flowers embroidered on it.

'I think I've got to start dying my hair again,' she says, pulling at her dirty blond ends. 'I'm starting to go grey.'

'Only starting to? I've had grey for years now.'

She looks up at my head and I'm sure she's starting to spot them. 'I hadn't noticed.'

'That's because I rip them out when I see them, but the buggers keep coming back. Oh my God,' I say, clapping my hand to my mouth as Enrique Iglesias's 'Hero' comes on the radio. My cheeks immediately flush red at the memory.

'Why have you turned beetroot?'

'I slow danced to this with Russell Barns.'

If I close my eyes I can still feeling him grabbing my bum as we shuffled awkwardly around the community centre where my friends were having their birthday party.

'Ooh I remember him, he was the one with the really long curtains,' she says, shrieking with laughter.

'Yeah, and the undercut. He was one of the most popular boys in our year,' I say proudly.

'Did you snog him?'

'No, I wish. He later got off with Amy Johnson.'

'The one who had all those coloured braids in her hair?'

'Oh, yeah, she did. Those friendship-bracelet-type things.'

We're both lost in our thoughts of nineties nostalgia before Rosie interrupts to give me a top up. 'More Baileys?' she asks, holding up the bottle, and I look down in surprise to see that my glass is empty.

'Yes, please. You see, even back then my love life was a mess. I couldn't even seal the deal with Russell Barns.'

'Everyone's love life was a mess back then, that's the whole point of being a teenager.'

'Then if that's true, why has everyone else sorted theirs out and I haven't?'

Rosie nudges the box of chocolate fingers towards me as if it's going to make it all better. I bite into one, and for a second I think she might be on to something.

'Not everyone's sorted. They might seem it on the outside, but just because they've had their happy ending doesn't mean they're living happily ever after.'

Rosie looks sad, and I don't think it's helping that 'Wind of Change' has started playing, seemingly echoing our mood of melancholy.

'Yes, but at least they've had the happy ending and have something to work with. I haven't had a date with anyone that I wasn't introduced to by my phone for years. I have to find men using an app. I mean, I'm not ordering a bloody pizza, I'm trying to find a soulmate.'

'I'm married and I can't remember the last time Rupert and I went on a date. Sure, we go to client dinners and dinner parties with friends, but I don't know when we last went out just the two of us, where he didn't cancel because he was working.'

'But at least you get to share a bed with someone at night. I haven't slept in the same bed as someone in over two years.'

'You haven't had sex in over two years?'

'Of course I have,' I say, looking at my sister like she's an idiot. 'My love life's not that much of a disaster. I just mean I didn't stay overnight and didn't have the whole fall-asleep-in each-other's-arms-until-your-limbs-go-numb experience.'

'Then I don't think I've done that for years either. Rupert is definitely not a cuddly sleeper.'

'I don't understand how I can live in a city of eight and a half million people and still be desperately lonely.'

'I don't understand how I can live in a flat with the love of my life and still be lonely.'

I look up at Rosie and see her blink back some tears.

'I don't understand how our girls' night in got so depressing so suddenly,' I say, trying and failing to lighten the mood. One minute we were up and now we're so far down that I'm afraid if they play 'Everybody Hurts', we'll be throwing ourselves into the well, and not to retrieve our phones.

'Is it really that bad between you and Rupert? I thought he was just mad at you for buying the house?'

'It's worse than that. I mean, we still love each other, it's just . . . When I was working I wouldn't even have noticed that there was a problem; we'd be out at the crack of dawn and back after sunset, we'd grab a ready meal, collapse in front of the telly for an hour or so and head off to bed. It didn't matter if he worked late as I'd probably be doing the same. We'd both just update our joint Google Calendar with plans with friends without consulting each other, just assuming that if we were free we'd go along with it. But, somehow with me leaving my job and having time for myself, I've realised how little time we actually made for each other.'

'And that's why this house is so important?'

'If I could just make him see that we could run a business where he wouldn't have to work all the hours, then we could have a real life. One where I'd be happy to have children.'

'I've never wanted to ask,' I say, treading carefully, as I'd often wondered if they'd had problems conceiving, 'but do you want children?'

'Rupert really does, but I don't, at least not yet. I don't want to be a single parent, which is effectively what I would be if Ru carried on as he is. He wouldn't get home in time to see the kids go to bed; he'd be like a weekend dad. I want us to be parents together.'

I try to picture Ru being the kind of dad who'd do nappy runs and push a baby in a pram, but it's hard to imagine.

'Have you told him this?'

'I've tried, but he doesn't really understand.'

'Maybe it was him who you should have brought on your digital detox and not me.'

She smiles. 'Maybe you're right. When did you get so wise?'

'I have always been very wise; you always just ignored what I had to say because I'm your annoying little sister.'

'Oh yeah,' she says nodding.

I fill up our glasses without asking. It feels like too deep a conversation to be having with our glasses empty.

'I think the problem with your generation,' she says, as if there's a bigger gap than three years, 'is that you're too reliant on technology. I mean, I met Rupert in the students' union. I pinched him on the bum, thinking he was one of my flatmates, and when he turned round all confused we started chatting. If you'd shown me a photo of him beforehand I would have told you that he wasn't my type. He was practically bald even then. But after an hour of chatting I was smitten. You need to go out and meet a man in real life.'

'In real life,' I say, repeating it and laughing. 'If only it were that bloody simple. No one talks to anyone in London, it's not like I could strike up a conversation with a hot guy on the tube.'

'But what about at work or meeting someone through a friend of a friend?'

I shake my head. I didn't fancy any of my work colleagues and I know most of my friends' friends. My social circle gets smaller every year as people start moving out to the suburbs or commuter towns and start having kids. House parties have become a thing of the past, now it's afternoon barbecues where nearly everyone goes with their partners and offspring, and I'm usually left feeling like Bridget Jones.

'I just find the whole idea of apps creepy. It's like you're buying a man off Amazon.'

'Oh, I *wish* you could buy a man off Amazon. How great would that be, being able to customise the different bits and then return him if he wasn't right? Ooh and you could read reviews before you ordered.'

Rosie shakes her head at me. 'I just think dating was easier back in the day. We didn't really use our phones as much when we lived in halls, so Rupert used to slip notes under my door and that's how we'd arrange to meet each other.'

I see that her cheeks have started to go pink.

'Now who's the one going beetroot?'

She laughs a little before coughing. 'Just remembering one of his notes that really made me, um, laugh. I know that people text these days, but I don't think it's the same as seeing pen on paper.'

I pat the pocket on my jeans under the table, feeling the paper under the fabric. I actually know what she means. Getting that note from Jack was the highlight of my day, and he was been funny and just a little flirty with me, wasn't he? And he is cute, in that rugged, outdoorsy, dressed-like-a-yeti type of way. If Alexis is going to go off to the pub and not invite me, maybe Jack would be more interested.

'You'll meet someone,' she says, finishing the rest of her drink. 'Who knows, when you go back to London and start a new job, you might meet someone at work.'

'Maybe . . .'

'Ah,' she screams, jumping up. 'We have to dance to this.'

The violin intro to Steps' '5, 6, 7, 8' starts to play, and I watch Rosie start line dancing around the kitchen. I stand up with ease – the Baileys has been medicinal after all, I barely have any pain in my muscles now. I start shimmying around and lassoing as I try and copy Rosie's moves.

'Oh God,' she says, laughing as the song comes to an end. 'I've gotta pee so badly. What stupid idiot thought it would be a good idea to get drunk and to have a Portaloo outside instead of an actual toilet?' She grabs a head torch from the table and slips it on over her head. 'I'll be back,' she says in an Arnold Schwarzenegger voice.

I watch her go and sit back at the table. I can't help but pull Jack's note out of my pocket and read it again. Rosie's right, there is something about seeing it handwritten in pen.

Without thinking, I shove it back in my pocket and grab my notepad and pen, which are still on the table.

Dear Jack,

    No need to apologise about seeing me naked. Tons of guys have already.

I rip the paper from the pad and screw it up. That's not quite the impression of myself I want to give him.

Dear Jack,

    No need to apologise about seeing me naked, you've already groped my arse, so what's a little flesh between neighbours (or friends, hopefully)? Thanks to Buster, we now have no shower, so likely you'll smell me before you see me. Rosie says there's a stream nearby, so if the weather ever improves maybe I can go for a skinny dip – FYI, just in case Buster likes to go pigeon hunting there too . . .

I can hear the Portaloo door squeak outside, before the sound of footsteps coming across the courtyard and I know I've got to hurry.

Anyway, see you around, neighbour. Maybe I'll be over some day for some sugar.

    Daisy x

    P.S. I don't know what's worse, the fact that you won't tell me who presented The Price is Right or that you googled it in the first place.

I shove the letter hastily into my hoodie pocket, along with the scrunched-up ball, just as Rosie pushes the door open.

'I've got an idea,' I say, before she can step inside. 'Let's go for a walk.'

'Are you mad? It's pitch-black out there.'

'I just want to see the stars.'

'We can do that standing outside; we don't need to go for a walk.'

'Please,' I say, 'we can have a wander down the drive. You never know, we might bump into Alexis on the way.'

Rosie rolls her eyes at me. 'I see what's going on. We get all deep and meaningful and now you think he's going to be the man for you. Don't you think he's a bit young?'

I can't tell her that right now I've got another man in my sights, as she'd start meddling all over the place.

'I don't want to see him in *that* way. I just thought it would be fun going for a walk. Like going for an adventure.'

Rosie rolls her eyes again and sways a little. I step outside and slam the door so that she has no choice but to join me.

She's right, it is bloody dark, but thankfully her head torch is surprisingly powerful.

I loop my arm through hers and we start to walk up the small hill to the drive.

'The stars really are incredible,' I say, tipping my head back and appreciating them. Even though I've been marvelling at them over the last few nights, they still take my breath away. Even when I grumpily went for a wee in the Portaloo during the night, my mood improved as soon as I set foot outside and saw them.

'I know, I love it here, I really do. I just wish Rupert would see it.'

'He will, he's a good egg, that one. Why don't you write him a letter, tell him how you feel, or make it jokey like the ones you wrote at uni?'

'I don't know if that's really us anymore . . .'

'Then maybe you need to remind him what you once were.'

Rosie and I sway a little as we walk up the drive, and I realise I'm a lot drunker than I thought. I see a flash of light in front of us and my first thought is that it's a UFO. I jump behind Rosie.

'What the hell are you doing?' she screams. 'You scared the crap out of me.'

'Look, there's a tiny light dancing.'

'You muppet,' she says giggling. 'That'll be Alexis's head torch, that's why it looks like it's in the air.'

I don't need to be able to see her to know that she's shaking her head at me.

I creep back round to the front of her and, sure enough, Alexis is just coming into the beam of Rosie's torch.

'*Bonsoir*,' he says, slightly staggering too. 'What are you doing 'ere?'

'Just having a moonlit stroll,' she says, despite the fact that's there's only the tiniest sliver of moon, which is doing nothing to illuminate our walk. 'Did you have a good time?'

While we're standing still chatting I seize my opportunity to post the letter through Jack's box. I stumble slightly as it's bloody dark. I feel around for the box and I have a slight panic as I try and remember which is his and which is ours. His was on the left. Or was it the right? I don't want Rosie finding the letter if I accidentally put it in ours by mistake. I'm pretty sure it was the left.

'Daisy,' says Rosie.

I slip the letter in, hoping it was the right one.

I see the torch beam coming at me.

'What are you doing?' she calls.

'Um, I was trying to find somewhere for a wee, but it's a bit dark. I'll wait until we're at home.'

'Come on, then,' she says, lighting the way, and I walk back to her and loop my arm through hers once more, and I take the opportunity to loop my arm through Alexis's too.

'Let's go and introduce Alexis to the nineties. Do you like to bust a move?'

'Buster like the dog?' he says confused.

'Ha – like dance. Bust a move, spin a groove,' she says animatedly.

Poor old Alexis, he has no idea what he's just come back to.

Chapter Seventeen

I was so wrong yesterday, when I thought that wallpaper stripping couldn't get any worse. If only my problems today were limited to getting hot and sweaty from the steamer, with only the prospect of a dribbly shower in a makeshift cubicle in a barn to make it all better later. Today, I'm still hot and sweaty, have no prospect of a shower, and I have the added bonus of the hangover from hell, and muscles that have seized up from trying to teach a Frenchman the dance moves to S Club 7. I'm practically passing out from the heat, sweating Baileys from every orifice and trying not to gag at the smell of old wallpaper being soaked off the wall. I'm pretty sure MI5 could use this as a new form of torture.

As if all that wasn't bad enough, the plumber Rosie hired has the audacity to whistle as he works, and he's clunking around and banging metal pipes as if he's auditioning for Guns N' Roses.

'Here you go,' says Rosie, plonking a cup of tea down on the windowsill next to me.

I blow my fringe out of my face for the billionth time, and for the billionth time I mentally add: 'Get Alice band' to my list of things to buy.

'Thanks,' I say, taking that as a sign to down tools. I balance myself against the ladder and exhale loudly.

'You look like shit,' she says.

The only good thing about the bathroom currently being ripped apart is that the only mirror in the house is gone; at least we can't see how bad we look. Although, if Rosie's anything to go by, I must look pretty horrendous.

Alexis is not fairing much better either. He's currently slumped on the floor, supposedly trying to pull off the old rotting skirting board, but I haven't seen him move for at least five minutes so I suspect he's having a sneaky snooze.

'I'm not exactly feeling my best,' I say, wincing as I pick up the hot tea, scalding my fingers, which seems to take my mind off the rest of my hangover.

'Me neither. Do you think the boss would let us play hooky for the rest of the day?'

I shake my head. 'We've got to at least strip two walls or we'll be behind when the window man comes tomorrow.'

'Remind me again why I put you in charge of organising the work flow?' she says, sighing and picking up the wallpaper steamer.

'Because you're an idiot.'

I'm cursing myself for my organisation. If only I'd had the foresight to have scheduled in the hangover.

'But at least it was fun last night, eh? Totally took your mind off the whole lack of phone thing, didn't it?'

'I guess it did,' I say, realising that, for the first time, I hadn't missed my phone in the evening, and I've barely noticed its absence today, although that's mostly because my eyes hurt at the thought of peering at a screen.

But still, it's progress.

Perhaps all I need to do is drink my way through my digital detox, but my stomach lurches at the thought, telling me that's a bad idea. I try desperately to keep my stomach at bay, remembering that with the lack of a toilet, I'm going to be retching into a Portaloo or a corner of the garden, neither of which is appealing.

I watch Rosie pick up a broom and subtly poke Alexis in his side. He doesn't even flinch, and the only noise that comes out is a brief snore.

'Seriously, we can't go on like this,' says Rosie. 'How about we pop into the village for a fry-up or something? The pub must have something greasy on their menu.'

I take a look at the half-steamed wall. I guess it makes no difference whether we're doing it now or at ten o'clock tonight, it's not like we've got any pressing social engagements.

'Let's do it,' I say, desperately excited about getting off the farm. 'I'll go and change.'

I hurry into the bedroom, and quickly change behind the cardboard screen we've erected due to our lack of doors. I spray deodorant on liberally, followed by a spritz of Jimmy Choo perfume, which I instantly regret, as it smells sickly sweet with my hangover-heightened sense of smell, and I towel dry my clammy face. Then I throw on some clean jeans, a T-shirt and a red hoodie. It feels funny to wear tight jeans again after my last few days in tracksuit bottoms, and I do a few power lunges to loosen up the denim as my body adjusts to being restricted.

'You ready?' asks Rosie, as she strolls into the bedroom, merely changing into a slightly cleaner fleece than the one she was wearing. 'Meh,' she says in response to my raised eyebrow. 'I'm too hungover to care what I look like.'

'Do you think we should wake Alexis before we go?'

'Nah, he seems dead to the world. We'll bring him back a sausage roll.'

We walk out of the house and the cold air almost knocks me out. It's ridiculously clichéd to say, but the air here is so fresh, it almost takes my breath away each time I breathe it in. Not that I'm complaining after the stale air of London. I'm sure it will do wonders to cure my hangover. That and the biting wind.

'Are you OK to drive?'

'I think so. It's eleven now, so I've had over twelve hours since my last drink.'

'It's eleven already? We've been stripping wallpaper for two hours?'

'Uh-huh.'

My heart sinks as I realise how little we've done. We should have stayed in bed, at least that way we might have slept off the hangover.

I climb into the car with her and as we bump along I wonder if the question was not 'Is Rosie OK to drive?', but 'Are we OK to be in a car?' I rub my stomach, willing its contents to stay put as we make our way down the drive.

As we approach the end of it, we see the post van drive off.

'Ooh, I wonder if we've got any post,' she says, pulling up alongside it.

I look at the mailbox and suddenly a hope surges that I'll have a reply from Erica, before something starts to niggle at me. A memory of me stumbling along and clinging on to the mailbox in the dark pops into my head. I try to make it clearer, but it's hazy, like a dream I'm trying to recall.

'Did we go to the mailbox last night?' I ask Rosie as I squint at it. I touch the tips of my fingers as they remember the memory of the cold metallic box.

'No, we walked up to meet Alexis, remember?'

She walks over to the mailbox and pulls out envelopes, and as she flips through them I see a folded piece of paper which she looks at quizzically, and I lunge for the door handle and fling myself out.

'I'll take that, thanks,' I say, pulling the piece of paper out of her hand without needing to see my name written in neat capital letters on the front.

'What's that?' asks Rosie.

'It's just from Jack, directions for a good walk I'd asked him about,' I say as I open up the letter to read, while she's distracted reading a wad of official-looking papers that came in an A4 brown envelope.

DAISY

ALWAYS GOOD TO KNOW WHEN NEIGHBOURS OR FRIENDS ARE GOING TO GET NAKED IN PUBLIC. BUSTER DOES LIKE A DIP THERE HIMSELF SO I'LL MAKE SURE I KEEP HIM AWAY FROM THERE FOR THE TIME BEING AS WE DON'T WANT TO ADD TO HIS REPUTATION OF NUMBER ONE PERVE IN THE AREA. THAT'S OBVIOUSLY RESERVED FOR ROD-NEY. FYI – HE LISTENS TO THE ARCHERS WITHOUT FAIL AT 2 P.M., SO A SAFE BET TO HAVE A DIP WITH-OUT AN AUDIENCE.

BUSTER AND I WILL BE PLEASED TO SEE IF YOU COME ROUND FOR SOME SUGAR, ALTHOUGH I SHOULD WARN YOU THAT I'M MORE OF A CANDEREL MAN. YOU'RE ALSO MORE THAN WELCOME TO HAVE A SHOWER HERE IF YOU LIKE; WE HAVE A DOOR ON THE BATHROOM AND EVERYTHING.

JACK

P.S. I WOULDN'T HAVE GOOGLED THE PRICE IS RIGHT IF YOU HADN'T KEPT ON MENTIONING IT, BUT IT LED ME DOWN A SURPRISING RABBIT HOLE ON WIKIPEDIA. BET YOU'D NEVER GUESS THE LINK BETWEEN THE PRICE IS RIGHT AND JOHN MAJOR???

Oh my days. What did I write in my letter? You see, this is what's wrong with actual letter writing. Where's the archive of what I wrote when I need it? At least with a text message or an email, you've left digital footprints of what you said.

I try and force my mind to remember writing it, but it's all foggy. I remember perching at the table while Rosie was in the loo, and I remember giggling as if I was being terribly witty.

I reread what he's put, with the words 'getting naked' and 'coming round for sugar' jumping out. I cringe at what the original note could have contained. Perhaps I should be glad that I don't remember.

I shove it quickly in my pocket as Rosie stuffs the pages back into the envelope and looks at the rest of the post.

'Here,' she says passing me an envelope with a stamp and a postmark. One I can read without fear of cringing. There's only one person who knows my address and I immediately beam as I tear open the envelope.

I barely notice as Rosie pulls away and heads towards the village.

Daisy!!!

I've missed you so much! So you're surviving up North, then? Sounds . . . rustic. I'm so glad that you are making a go of it. I bet if it were me, I'd have been on the first train back down to London.

So, Chris has now officially moved in. The flat smells like boys and we have ridiculous amounts of gadgets for stuff and extra remote controls for who knows what. But the upside is there's more . . . I'd try to draw a camel or some rabbits here, but it would be no better than your aubergine attempt – I'm sure you get the idea . . .

The only problem is we've both got so much stuff that it's mega cramped. So, guess what? We've taken the big step of making an appointment for an estate agent to come and value the flat and we're going to buy somewhere together. Somewhere slightly bigger to fit in the remote controls, with enough room for guests so that they can actually stand up.

Other than that, work is busy. I've been given a new account, but there's talk of me getting promoted as early as next year!

I saw Amelie last night for a quick drink after work. We toasted your adventure – which you won't have seen as we Snapchatted it – but at least you'll see it when you next log on, if Rosie ever gives you back your phone.

Have you figured out what you're going to do work wise? Are you going crazy not checking Twitter?

All my love (and more!)

Erica xxxx

My heart sinks as I read the letter. I've only been away a week and already my best friend's life is transforming before my eyes. I'm sure her London flat will be snapped up within days, if not hours, of it going on sale. She'll be living her suburban life before I know it.

I fold it over and close my eyes as I try to stop myself from crying. Just as my life is spiralling out of control – nowhere to live, no job to go back to – my best friend's is going from strength to strength with her big promotion on the horizon and buying a house with a boyfriend who adores her. I'm happy for her, I really am, but I can't help wishing I had reason to be that happy myself. That's not being selfish, is it? It's not like I want her to be going through the same crap as me, I just want to be going through the same good stuff as her.

'Everything OK?' asks Rosie as we pull into the car park in the village.

I open my eyes and look around at the grey stone buildings in front of me.

'Fine,' I say nodding. 'It's just that Erica and Chris are selling her flat and buying somewhere together and she might get promoted in her job.'

Rosie nods her head as if she understands what the problem is.

'I can't believe I haven't been a part of any of it. It's happened so quickly. I know that this whole digital detox is supposed to make me feel less anxious, but I still feel as if I'm missing out on things. After all, Erica's just one person in the whole world and her life has completely changed. What's going on with everyone else? Something huge could have happened in the news and we wouldn't know.'

'I'm sure if something had then we'd have heard it on the radio.'

I sigh. Listening to the news for two minutes every hour is hardly the same as having it at your fingertips whenever you want it.

'You could always buy a newspaper,' she says cheerily as she gets out of the car.

'A newspaper? I can't remember the last time I bought one; probably when I last moved house. A newspaper,' I say, running it over in my mind. 'Retro.'

'Come on, we'll pick one up on the way over to the pub. Give us something to do while we wait for our breakfast.'

We walk out of the car park and cross over the street to the post office and Liz and Gerry smile and give us a wave as we walk in.

'You're still here, then?' says Gerry, raising her eyebrow and laughing with almost a cackle.

'We certainly are,' says Rosie.

'I would be too, if I was living with a dreamy Frenchman,' says Liz, swooning like a teenager, despite the fact that she must be well into her fifties, if not sixties.

'You've met Alexis, then?' I say, thinking how quickly everyone finds out people's business in this village.

'Oh yes, we met him last night in the pub. We'd gone along to watch the darts, and all of a sudden there he was. He had quite a few of the young girls racing to the loos to top up their make-up, let me tell you.'

'Not just the young-uns either,' says Liz, and the two women laugh a dirty cackle.

I can't help but giggle a little too; their laughter is infectious.

'Such a shame about him and his girlfriend, but I'm sure he'll be back on the horse before he knows it,' says Gerry.

'He can ride me any day,' says Liz.

Their cackling goes up an octave and Rosie gives me a quick wink. It seems I'm not the only one to fall a little for the charms of Alexis.

'Not sure your Graham would be too pleased about that.'

'Pleased? He'd be ecstatic that I wouldn't be bothering him for a change. That's if he even noticed.'

The two women start debating what level of affair Liz could get away with before her husband twigged, and I walk over to the newspapers. I settle on the *Guardian* to see what's happened, and for when I'm truly depressed a copy of *Heat!* magazine to cheer me up with the gossip I'm missing, and *Good Housekeeping*, as, you never know, it might have some design tips for the renovation.

I meet Rosie back at the till where she's picked up another pack of crumpets.

'You know, it's not just that Frenchman you've got to contend with, is it? You've also got Jack and Rodney down that neck of the woods too,' says Liz. 'I bet Rodney's been very attentive to the sheep down by your fields.'

'Is he the older farmer?' asks Rosie as she concentrates on the chocolate bars. 'I haven't spoken to him yet.'

I don't chip in that I have. I'm thinking of popping in on him over lunchtime, well, Jack said he'd be home then, and he did say I could pop over at any time to use the Internet . . .

'I'm sure you soon will. But you've met mysterious Jack, then?' Liz is arching her eyebrow again, as if it's a fishing rod dangling the question into the water.

I pick up a packet of mints as if I'm not interested in the conversation.

'Yes, he's seen a lot of Daisy,' says Rosie, unable to stop herself laughing over her joke about him seeing me naked.

'Oh, has he now? He sees quite a few women, I think,' says Liz knowingly. Gerry's nodding her head and rolling her lips into her mouth as if she doesn't want to say a word, even though she looks like she's itching to. 'I saw him last month, going into that new blonde woman's house in Glassonby.'

I'm not too sure why that bothers me so much. I guess I got the impression that he was a bit of a hermit, and I was somehow special for getting him to write me notes. Knowing that he's some kind of ladies' man makes me feel a bit ordinary.

'She's got two kids who go to the same school as June's grandchildren. But, apparently, she keeps herself to herself.'

Gerry tuts and for once I'm with her, wishing they had more gossip about her.

The bell over the shop goes and a young woman dressed in tight, bright Lycra walks in.

'All right,' she says nodding over as she heads straight for the shelves.

'All right, Trish,' calls Gerry. 'Give us a shout if you need any help.'

'Will do,' calls the voice.

I'm desperate to press them for more information about Jack, but the two ladies appear to be keeping schtum.

'Oh my God, are these aubergines, in May?' we hear Trish shout.

'Oh,' says Liz, clapping her hands over her mouth before releasing them and giving me a big smile. 'I almost forgot.'

She walks round the counter and leads me to the fresh produce aisle. 'Look, aubergines.'

She passes one to me and pats it in my hand. I'm not entirely sure what to do.

'Um,' I say, stammering for words.

'It's an aubergine. We don't usually stock out of season veg, but we got them in specially for you. Not that I read your postcard, but the words jumped out and it seemed as if you were really missing them. I imagine in London you eat them all the time.'

It's been a long time since I've had an aubergine, real or what the Emoji represents.

'Oh, thanks,' I say, nodding encouragingly. I pick up another and smile at her.

Trish takes a couple too, and Liz is practically beaming.

'Told you they'd sell,' she says to Gerry as she walks back round the counter.

'Just these, is it, love?' asks Gerry, obviously not impressed with the new stock.

'Just those,' I say sadly, wishing I could ask for the gossip on Jack too.

'Have you met Trish?' asks Liz as she approaches with her aubergines and bread.

'No, I haven't. Hi, nice to meet you, I'm Rosie and this is my sister, Daisy.'

'Ah, you've moved into Upper Gables, with Alexis. You lucky ladies.'

Is there anyone in the village he hasn't met and charmed?

'Trish here teaches yoga,' says Liz gently nodding.

'I certainly do, at the village hall. Got morning and evening classes. I do personal training too.'

'Oh great,' says Rosie, 'we should definitely look into the yoga – see, Daisy, we were talking about doing yoga on our detox.'

'Detox?' says Trish, raising an eyebrow.

Liz is looking as though her eyes are going to pop out of her head, and I don't want Rosie to explain our digital detox; it'd be around the village before we knew it.

'Uh-huh, but yes, yoga sounds great. Look, we'd better get to the pub as I'm about to eat those crumpets untoasted.'

Rosie winces at the thought.

'Righto, nice to meet you, Trish. See you again, Liz, Gerry.'

As I'm leaving, I raid the leaflet holder, which is rammed full of other accommodation and local attractions, hoping that it will be good market research. Not that I can face looking at any of it in my hungover state.

We cross the road towards the pub, my mind whirring with thoughts of Jack and his lady friends. If only I had access to Facebook, I could have friend requested him and then stalked through his life for the last few years and seen his relationship history.

'You OK?' asks Rosie. 'You've gone really pale.'

'Yeah, I'm fine. Nothing that a pint of coke and a read of these magazines won't fix.'

I'm lying, as right now I'm pining for my old life. I can't bear the thought that there's information out there about a person and that I can't get to it. I've got a digital itch to scratch and a magazine and a newspaper just won't cut it.

Chapter Eighteen

Time since last Internet usage: 5 days, 23 hours, 17 minutes and 15 seconds

'You can just drop me here,' I say to Rosie as we pull into the driveway to our farm.

'Here? Are you sure you want to walk along the drive? It's no bother really.'

'No, it's fine. You might as well go straight off to the builders' merchant. I'm feeling queasy after that big breakfast anyway a walk might do me good.'

I hop out of the car quickly so that she can't read the expression on my face. I'm such a hopeless liar.

'OK, then, I'll see you later on. Don't be out for too long,' she says pointing out towards the village. 'That black cloud doesn't look good.'

'No,' I say shuddering. 'It doesn't.'

I wave her off as she turns out of the drive and heads in the other direction from Lullamby. I wait until her car disappears out of sight and I turn on my heels and head up towards Rodney's farm. I cross the road and start walking quickly, or as quickly as I can on the uneven ground, up towards his house.

I knew it was perched halfway up a hill, and it looked steep, but I feel as if I'm scaling a mountain. Perhaps it's just last night's dancing to S Club 7, but my calves are burning. It seems I'm in desperate need of one of Trish's yoga classes after all.

By the time I make it to Rodney's front door, I'm huffing and puffing like I've scaled Mount Everest and I'm in need of supplementary oxygen.

There's no doorbell, but it doesn't matter as I can hear his sheepdog barking at full volume from inside.

'That's enough from you,' I hear him shout and the dog instantly quietens.

The old wooden door opens and Rodney, who's got a little bit of bread crust in his beard, is standing before me. His scowl instantly lifts as he sees it's me.

'Ah, the young lady of the Gables.'

'Daisy,' I say, realising that I hadn't introduced myself properly. 'You said that if I needed to use the Internet, I could come . . .' I say peering into the dimly lit cottage and, for the first time, considering what I'm about to do. I'm about to go into a dark cottage with a slightly pervy farmer and no one knows I'm here. Hmm. The rational side of my brain that went on a personal-safety training day is trying to tell me that this is a bad idea, but the risk-taking side of my brain is telling me that I'm thirty feet away from Facebook, Twitter, Instagram, Snapchat, my email . . . And besides, he's not giving out any creepy vibes in the slightest.

'Come on in,' he says, holding his arm out in invitation.

I practically leap into his house.

'So, Daisy,' he says, walking around the kitchen, opening cupboards and shutting them again. 'Do you want a cup of tea?'

I don't know why I assumed that, as a farmer who lives on his own, his farmhouse would be a mess, maybe it's because ours is in such a state, but his is ridiculously tidy and not at all what I was expecting.

Finally, he finds what he's looking for and pulls out a china teacup. He blows on it and a spray of dust fills the air. I think he catches my reaction, and he hurries over to the sink to wash it.

I don't really want a cup of tea, I want to check my emails and Twitter, but I'm guessing that he doesn't get many visitors and it would be rude of me to say no.

'Thanks – milk, no sugar.'

'Right you are. Take a seat,' he says, pointing at the sofa in the corner of the kitchen that I'm sure was once red, but it's now hard to tell with the assortment of black and white dog hairs that cover it.

I get nearer and his sheepdog, who's already sitting on one side of it, is looking at me as if I'm trespassing.

I hover awkwardly before Rodney spots what's up. 'Down, Shep,' he says, and the dog jumps off immediately.

As Rodney turns to make the tea, I see Shep give me a scowl before he curls up in front of the Aga.

I look around the kitchen and I realise how homely it is. The Aga's throwing out a welcome amount of heat as, even though it's May, without the sun there's a real chill to the air. The sofa in the kitchen is a nice touch, as I imagine in winter, if you're out in the fields all day, coming to sit here after lunch or in the evening would be nice and cosy.

'There you are,' says Rodney, placing my china cup, which looks like something my nan would have owned, on a small table to the left of me, before he joins me on the sofa. A little too close for my liking.

'So, Daisy, are you and your sister going to be living at the farm? We could do with some more young ladies around here, we could.'

'Um, actually we're only here for a few weeks to do it up. It's going to be a holiday let,' I say a little guiltily, bracing myself for the reaction and tirade that Jack gave me when I told him our plans.

'Ah, right,' he says a little sadly. 'That's all people want to do with the farms these days. Too hard being a farmer. Not that you've got much land at yours anyway. The Johnsons took most of it over after Ned went into hospital the first time.'

It hadn't occurred to me that Rosie has a whopping great barn and farmhouse but only one smallish field. It makes sense that the land was sold.

I pick up my cup of tea and I try to blow on it to cool it down. The quicker I drink it, the quicker I might be able to go on the Internet. I can feel my palms getting clammy and my head feeling dizzy at the thought that any second now I'm going to be logging on. All those messages! Hopefully, the Twittersphere will have forgotten about #priceless. I can't wait to see what I've missed.

'But still,' he says, a twinkle in his eye, 'you're here for a few weeks. We can still make the most of that now, can't we?'

He edges slightly closer to me on the sofa and it makes my teacup clatter on the saucer.

'Oh, um,' I say, not entirely sure what to do.

I'm not certain how old Rodney is; his skin's got that weathered look to it, and with the beard and greyish tint, it's hard to age him. He could be anywhere from early fifties to mid-sixties. Either way, he's out of my maximum Tinder age bracket for sure.

I try and ignore his shuffle and drink my tea, not only scalding my mouth but gagging at the fact that the milk is a little bit sour. The big greasy fry-up didn't settle my stomach enough from the hangover to drink it.

I set the tea on the sideboard instead.

'Where is it you're from, then? I'm guessing you and your sister are from some city, judging by your shoes.'

I look at my New Balance gym trainers, which are caked in a thick layer of crusty mud.

'That's right. We come from Fleet, in Hampshire, but I live in London now and Rosie lives in Manchester.'

Rodney looks pleased that he guessed.

'And what do you think of our neck of the woods?'

'It's pretty,' I say, thinking that I really want to log on now. I can hear the pings of Facebook and the dings of my email calling to me.

'I could never leave this place. Been here all my life. The farm's been in the family for generations. Although that'll stop when I'm gone, you know. Unless I find another wife and have some little ones.'

I'm trying not to look him in the eye, as I get the impression he's looking at me expectantly, as if I'm the one who's going to provide him with an heir.

'Um, so is it OK if I check my emails?' I ask, glancing around for a computer as a lifeline.

'Oh yes, your *emails*,' he says nodding and smiling as if I've told a joke.

I'm beginning to think this was a bad idea. It's funny, as I don't feel in danger with amorous Rodney, but I do feel as if he's got the wrong end of the stick.

'Um, yes,' I say standing up. I plant myself over near the dog and the Aga, which is so lovely and warm. 'Is your computer in the lounge?'

I look over at the nearby door.

'You don't have to be coy with me,' he says sitting forward and leaning his elbows on his knees, a lovesick look on his face. 'I know you city girls are a bit more forward. I watch *Made in Chelsea*. You don't need to pretend, I know you can read your mail on your phone. You came round here to get to know me better. It's the George Clooney-older-man thing, is it?'

Uh-oh. This is not going to plan. All I wanted was to see what I was missing out on on Twitter and now I'm in danger of guest appearing on *Farmer Wants a Wife*.

'I was hoping we'd get to know each other a bit more. It's been a long time since I entertained a woman here, and I might be a bit rusty, but –'

Before I can say anything, Shep the dog begins to bark loudly at the door.

'That's enough,' says Rodney as he walks over and opens it.

There, standing on the other side, are Jack and Buster. I sigh with relief as I watch Shep and Buster have a little sniff of each other's bottoms before they settle side by side at the Aga as if they do this all the time.

'Ah, Jack, cup of tea?' says Rodney. 'Kettle's on, just made a cup for Daisy here.' He points at me hovering awkwardly by the dogs.

'Actually, I'm fine thanks, mate. It's Daisy I came for. Rosie asked me if I'd come and get her to sort out a problem with one of the contractors.'

I look at him and he gives me a look to suggest I should play along.

'Oh right, yeah. Thanks for the tea, Rodney,' I say, heading towards the door as quickly as I can.

He looks a little crestfallen that I'm going. 'Do you have to go? You could use the phone from here,' he says a little hopefully.

'We don't have a phone at our end yet. But thank you again for the tea.'

'You'll have to come back and use that Internet another day.'

I wince as he winks at me. Jack gives me a look as it dawns on him why I'm actually here. We say our goodbyes and Rodney shuts the door behind us.

'How did you know where I was?'

'I was on my way to the village and I saw you walking up. Your red hoodie's a bit like a neon signpost.'

'I thought you'd be pleased – aren't you supposed to be visible when you're hiking?'

'Well, it certainly did you some favours today.'

Jack climbs on the quad bike and he passes me a spare helmet.

'You don't expect me to go on that, do you?'

I look down at the incline of the hill and think I'd rather take my chances sliding all the way down on my bum.

'I can leave you here with Rodney, if you like?'

I turn my head back and see that Rodney is waving out of the window at me, and I wave back quickly, before slipping onto the back of the quad.

'You have to be a bit more careful, Daisy. You could have been stuck there all day if I hadn't come along. Don't get me wrong, Rodney's a lovely man and he wouldn't hurt a fly, but he could talk the hind legs off a donkey.'

'Yeah, I get that now,' I say sheepishly.

'And not to mention, what would Rosie think? You checking your emails . . .'

'You won't tell her, will you? It's not like I actually got to check them.'

'Probably a good job too as I think Rodney keeps his computer in his bedroom.'

'Why is his computer in his . . . I don't want to know,' I say realising that my visit could have got a whole lot more awkward. I'm actually glad that he was chivalrous enough to want to chat before he took me upstairs to see his computer.

'Right, hold on,' says Jack as he starts the engine.

'To what?' I shout, but it's too late, he's off. I grab on to his waist for dear life.

I close my eyes and scream all the way down the hill, which is so steep that it's like I'm lying on top of Jack. I really wish I hadn't eaten that big breakfast as I bet I'm going to squash him. Before long, we even out and we're back on our bumpy drive, and I try to wriggle myself away from being so close to Jack. He pulls up into our courtyard and I take it as my cue to get off.

'Um, thanks,' I say, almost shouting, as Jack cuts the engine. 'I guess I didn't think that through very well.'

I watch Buster as he sniffs his way around the courtyard, probably on the trail of more pigeons.

'As I said, Rodney's harmless, but everyone knows not to visit. Well, not unless you've got nothing better to do with your day. He's just a bit lonely.'

'Is that why you go up?'

'Yeah, I try to go once a week. You know, ever since I arrived in the village he's taken me under his wing. Telling me the best place to get things, checking on me when I've been climbing, translating the local dialect. He couldn't have done more for me.'

I feel bad that I went up there with such selfish intentions. I'd only thought about what I could get out of the trip, not what it would have meant to him.

'I've got to go to the village, so I'll see you.'

'Thanks, Jack.'

'Did you want me to pick you up some sugar – you know, so you don't run out and have to ask a neighbour?' he says, giving me a slight wink.

I feel my cheeks flushing as I try to block out what little I can remember of the note I left him.

'No, I'm quite fine, thank you. We've got plenty.'

I give him a quick wave and I turn to walk away as I hear the sound of his chuckle over the engine noise.

How embarrassing.

I walk over to the house and open the door, the coldness of the kitchen hitting me immediately. What this room needs is a warming Aga like Rodney's. Perhaps it wasn't a wasted visit after all.

I pull the leaflets I picked up from the shop out of my bag and pop them on top of the mountain of paperwork on the table, ready for me to peruse at a later date. I'm just thinking I'll make a cup of tea when I hear a car pull up. I know instantly that it doesn't have the right roar to be Rosie's Land Rover and my jaw drops in shock as I turn and see who's stepping out of a shiny Audi.

Chapter Nineteen

*Time since last Internet usage: 6 days, 48 minutes and
30 seconds*

'Rupert, hi,' I say, opening the door and planting my most
friendly smile on my face.

He does a double take as he clocks me.

'Daisy! I can't believe you're actually here,' he says,
breaking out into a smile and warmly kissing me on both
cheeks.

'I could say the same. Rosie's not here.'

'Ah, well, I couldn't reach her on her phone. Signal
around here's dreadful. How anyone copes with living here is
beyond me,' he says with a hint of a laugh and a shake of the
head.

'Her phone's off. We're on a digital detox. I thought she told
you about it?'

I'm sure I remember her saying she had.

'She said you were up here working on the house with her,
but I don't remember anything about a detox. Maybe I wasn't
listening properly.'

I'm pretty sure he'd remember that. It makes me wonder how much they're actually speaking when she goes to the village phone box.

'Come on in, anyway,' I say ushering him in. 'So you've been here before, right?'

'Briefly. When Rosie ambushed me with the idea. But I'm sure that she told you all about that.' He looks around the kitchen and winces. I get the impression that he wanted to like it more second time around, but it still doesn't seem to be winning him over.

'You know Rosie will be so glad you're here. I think she's really missed you,' I say.

'And I've missed her. I just wish she'd told me about this place before she bought it. I love your sister, but she can be so bloody headstrong at times. She really pushes my buttons. Not that I need to tell you about that,' he says, giving me a knowing look.

Rupert's spent enough Christmases with us to witness our sibling rivalry first-hand.

He walks around the kitchen, knocking at the plastered walls and pulling out old wires that I've avoided touching, fearing electrocution.

'I actually thought she was joking that you were here. I knew she was meeting up with you for lunch in London.'

'Well, it was only supposed to be lunch, but I was going through . . . well, I needed to get away and Rosie suggested . . . here.'

Talk about the edited highlights.

'You voluntarily came, then?' He raises an eyebrow of doubt. 'And you haven't yet killed each other? That's progress. Bet your mum's pleased.'

'The night before we came, I rang her from your flat to tell her and she was pretty surprised.'

'Well, I'm relieved that Rosie hasn't been here on her own. I half imagined that she'd pretended you were with her to stop me worrying. Not that it has done. It's still an isolated place for you two to be, especially with the house being in such a state.'

'Oh, don't worry about us, the two of us are coping just fine.'

I don't tell him that we have our nice, big, burly Frenchman to look after us.

'So, has she roped you into doing work on this place?' he says, still evidently searching for something positive in the room.

'Uh-huh. We've started upstairs in the bathroom. Want to see?'

He stops prodding a wall and looks at me. 'Why not. You know, in the other places Rosie's done up, the work in the bathroom's been pretty good. Did she tell you she tiles them herself?'

'She did. She's full of surprises.'

'Lead on, then.'

I give Rupert the full tour of the bathroom, pointing out where I'd painstakingly stripped all the wallpaper and where the old tiling's been ripped off.

'You two have been busy. How many days have you been here? Four? Five?'

'Five,' I say, feeling relieved as I hear the front door slam. 'That'll be Rosie back.'

We both go back down the rickety stairs, and I'm pleased I'm about to witness a great reunion.

'Look who came to visit,' I say, as I make it down to the kitchen, only to see Alexis standing over the sink and drinking a pint of water.

'Oh, I had to go out for a walk to clear my 'ead,' he says, filling up another glass of water and downing it. 'You are a bad influence.'

I laugh a little coquettishly and I hear Rupert cough behind me. I've realised I've blocked his descent.

'Oh, sorry.' I continue walking into the kitchen allowing Rupert to follow me. 'This is Rosie's husband, Rupert. Rupert, this is Alexis . . .' I know that Rosie had a problem with him knowing we have a male help-ex worker living with us, and things are so rocky between them at the moment, and I don't want to be the one who makes things worse. 'Alexis is my boyfriend.'

I curse myself. Why couldn't I have come up with something better than that?

Alexis narrows his eyes in that way that he does when he can't understand a word we've used.

'That's exciting,' says Rupert, going over and slapping Alexis on the back and shaking his hand. 'So how did you two meet, then?'

He perches up against a sideboard and helps himself to some crisps out of a large packet that's open on the side. He's grinning at us, and waiting for us to elaborate as if he's tuned into his favourite show to watch.

'Well, um . . .'

'I answered the ad,' says Alexis.

'The ad? Oh, online. I guess that's how it's all done these days. Very good, very good.'

'It was very easy,' replies Alexis. 'I fit the criteria of what she wanted.'

'That's brilliant. Criteria, right, that's the key to curing your fussiness.'

Alexis looks momentarily lost.

'I'm not that fussy,' I say through gritted teeth, in a low voice.

'Ha, ha, good one,' he says whispering back.

Mum and Rosie are always saying that the problem with me and my love life is that I'm too picky. Is it so wrong that I want to actually like the person I date? I mean, why would I settle with someone like Dickhead Dominic just to have a boyfriend? I shudder at the thought.

'So you're from France, is it?'

'That's right.'

'Excellent, excellent. So you speak the language of lurve.'

Alexis looks at me, as if he's wondering what Rupert is on about, and I pin an inane grin on my face.

'We certainly do,' I say, slipping my arm around Alexis's back and giving him a squeeze. 'Don't we, *mon chéri*?' I raise an eyebrow, which, in my head, telepathically says play along.

Luckily for me, he seems to speak the international language of eyebrows and responds to my laughing by giving me an enthusiastic slap on the bottom. Easy there, Tiger.

He gives me a cheeky smile and a wink, and for a second he's convinced me, as well as Rupert, that we are actually love's young dream.

'Fantastic. Rosie will be pleased. She worries about you being lonely, you know. I think she thinks you'll end up an old maid.'

'Does she now?' I feel slightly touched that she at least worried about me, even if she did think I was going to die a spinster.

'Yes, but you have Alexis now,' he says in a mock French accent.

Alexis seems to be getting right into this whole boyfriend thing, as he's rubbing my arm for good measure, and it's actually a little too nice for my liking.

'You're looking a bit pale,' I say, turning to my fake boyfriend. 'Did you want to go and lie down for a bit?'

'With you?' he says, a little hopefully.

My brother-in-law gives us a wink. 'Don't let me being here stop you. I can wait for Rosie in the living room.'

'Ha, ha, ha,' I say, a little too enthusiastically, and wanting to get him out of the kitchen before Rupert has us consummating our relationship right here, right now. 'No, no. Alexis looks like he needs to sleep off his hangover. I'll make you a cup of tea.'

'You are sure?' says Alexis, raising an eyebrow of his own.

'Quite. Off you go,' I say dismissing him.

Alexis slinks off upstairs, but he doesn't miss an opportunity to plant a kiss on my lips as he goes.

I can't help blushing, probably adding to the appearance that we're in those early honeymoon days.

'So, by you coming here, does that mean you've forgiven Rosie?' I ask, desperate to steer the conversation away from my fake boyfriend.

'I'm pretty cross at what she did,' he says, sitting down as I put the kettle on. 'Mostly as it feels as if she went behind my back.'

'Wasn't she trying to surprise you?'

'She wanted me to quit my job to move up here. I would have liked a discussion about it first. Can you imagine if I'd have come home one day when she was working and said, "Hi, honey, just to say I've got us a job down South so you'll have to quit your job and come"? I'm pretty sure there'd be outrage.'

When he puts it like that.

'I know she was only doing it for us, but something this big, and this life changing should have been a joint decision.'

I nod.

'I'm sure if you sit down and talk about things you'll get everything out in the open. Rosie shouldn't be too much longer.'

'Where is she anyway?' he asks, picking up some of the leaflets I'd collected from the shop and flicking through them.

The kettle boils and I hunt around the cupboards for the best-looking cups we've got, pulling out one with the least ingrained tea stains to impress our guest.

'She wanted to pop to a builders' merchant on the edge of Penrith to pick up something for the bathroom. I'm sure she won't be too much longer.'

I faff around trying to make the perfect cup of tea, making sure the colour looks just right – not too weak, not too strong, in the hope that the taste makes up for how scrappy it looks.

Happy that my tea could please the most discerning of critics, I turn round to pop it on the table, just as Rupert jumps up.

'Everything, OK?' I ask, as I watch him pick up his car keys and head to the door.

'I've got to go,' he says.

'What? But Rosie will be back any minute and she'd love to see you.'

'I can't stay,' he says, before practically sprinting to his car.

I pop the hot tea on the table and go after him, but he's already pulling out of the drive, albeit very slowly because of the bumps. Maybe I can run and catch up with him and plead with him to stay.

'Wait, wait!' I shout as I run down the drive after him.

But even with the milk-float speed of the Audi, I still can't catch up as he's had too much of a head start.

I watch the car disappear out towards the main road, and I catch my breath as I try to process what happened. One minute he's there, all cheery and looking as if he's going to sweep Rosie off her feet, and the next minute he's gone tearing off in a hurry.

I'm just about to turn back to the farm when I notice a petite woman with long brown hair walking up the drive, and for a minute I'm taken aback.

'Hi there,' shouts the woman, with a friendly wave.

'Ah, hello.'

'Sorry if I startled you.'

'You didn't, not really; it's just that you don't get many people walking up here.'

'That you don't, but I own a crappy Fiesta and it doesn't make the journey well. I park it at the mailboxes and walk down. I'm Jenny. According to Liz and Gerry, you must be either Rosie or Daisy.'

'Daisy,' I say, laughing at the village gossips.

'Ah, pleased to meet you. I'm the village mobile hairdresser, in case you need a trim or anything while you're here.'

'Oh, great to know,' I say smiling.

'I'm just here to see Jack,' she says.

'Oh, right, you'll need thick scissors to tame that mop,' I say laughing, before I look down and realise that Jenny doesn't have anything on her but her car keys in her hand.

'Yes, um.' She smiles and gives a quick laugh.

We stand there awkwardly for a second before I see Rosie's Land Rover coming into view and Jenny sees it as her opportunity to escape.

'I'll see you around the village,' she says. 'It's not very big, so I'm sure we'll bump into each other again.'

She gives me a friendly wave as she bounds off, and I can't help but feel a little sad that Jack really does have other female options.

'Hiya. You haven't got far on your walk,' says Rosie as she rolls down her window and draws up next to me.

'Actually, I've just walked back out. Did you not see Rupert driving out of the village?'

'Ru was here?'

'Uh-huh.'

'Well, why didn't you keep him here? What did he say?'

She's looking round as if she's about to tear off after him.

'He came to talk to you. I thought he was going to sort things out. One minute he was sitting there waiting for me to give him a cup of tea, and the next he was off.'

I walk around the car and get into the passenger seat where Rosie's sitting, looking confused.

'He was here to sort it out and then he left? But why?'

'I'm not sure. He was looking through the leaflets I'd picked up on the table and he took off.'

'But that doesn't make sense,' she says, blinking rapidly as if she's struggling to process everything.

'I know. Maybe he remembered that he had an appointment?'

Rosie starts to drive back to the farm in a hurry, and when we arrive she rushes into the kitchen as if to retrace his steps.

She picks up the top leaflet on the pile, one for a luxury country hotel and spa.

'He was looking at these?'

'Uh-huh. Hey, maybe he thought taking you somewhere like that would be a better place to sort things out. Maybe he's decided to plan something bigger.'

'Maybe,' says Rosie. I can tell she's not convinced.

'If only you could phone him. Why don't you go to the payphone and give him a try?'

'I guess. But now he'll be driving and he never pairs his phone with his car's bluetooth, no matter how many times I tell him to.'

'Well, maybe you should wait, then. Give him a call in a couple of hours when he'll be back at the flat.'

She looks so sad, I just wish I'd been able to keep him here.

'He came once, that shows that he seems willing to work things out.'

'I guess so,' says Rosie.

Alexis walks down the stairs and swoops me up in a big hug.

'Ah, my lover,' he says.

'What the –?' exclaims Rosie. 'I only went to the builders' merchant.'

I push him away firmly. 'Alexis turned up when Rupert was here and he kindly acted as my boyfriend. Thank you for playing along,' I say turning to Alexis.

'Anytime,' he says. 'You know, playing or actual boyfriend, I am available.'

I can't help but snigger as Rosie rolls her eyes.

'Thank you for that, Alexis, but I'm sure Rosie will be the first to tell you that there'll be none of that under her roof.'

He shrugs and makes himself a sandwich from the fridge.

'Right, so are we going to get any work done today?' asks Rosie, sighing and running her fingers through her hands.

I look up at Alexis and he looks as pale as I feel, but I know we've got a schedule to follow.

'Of course we are, but first off, why don't we make a round of crumpets?'

Comfort food is exactly what we need, for the hangover and, in Rosie's case, the heartbreak.

'And then we'll get cracking?' she asks hopefully.

'And then we will, promise, and we'll work our arses off.'

Dear Jack,

Thank you once again for rescuing me. I have got to stop making a habit out of that, or do you have some sort of knight-in-shining-armour complex and you seek out damsels in distress at any opportunity? As much as I'm desperate to use the Internet, I've vowed not to go into the homes of strange men, and I'm also going on a shopping expedition this morning to get kitted out – the next time you see me you won't recognise me, as I'll blend in with the locals in my scruffy fleece and hiking trousers.

That's right, Rosie is letting me off the farm and we're hitting Carlisle – whoop, whoop! The builders are doing something dusty today and we've been told to vacate. Anyway, I'll see you around soon, if I don't get seduced by the bright lights of the city . . .

Daisy

P.S. John Major and The Price is Right – the mind boggles. Don't tell me – he guest presented it once? He was on it for a Christmas special?

DAISY,

I'M SAD THAT I'VE GOT TO HANG UP MY SHIELD AND RETIRE MY STEED. I WAS JUST GETTING INTO THE WHOLE RESCUING THING. I'LL HAVE TO GO BACK TO THE DAY JOB. BUSTER IS ALSO WONDER-ING IF HE HAS FULL SKINNY-DIPPING RIGHTS BACK TO THE STREAM YET? AS AM I, AS HE ROLLED IN DEER POO YESTERDAY AND HE NEEDS A WASH. THE LAST TIME I TRIED TO BATH HIM INSIDE, HE ESCAPED WHEN I WAS TOWEL DRYING HIM AND HE WENT RAMPAGING THROUGH THE HOUSE, ROLL-ING ON ALL THE CARPETS AND RUGS. IT SMELT LIKE WET DOG FOR WEEKS.

HOPE YOU ENJOYED THE GIDDY HEIGHTS OF CARLISLE. I SAW THE LAND ROVER RATTLE DOWN THE ROAD LAST NIGHT, SO I TAKE IT YOU MADE IT BACK OK.

JACK

P.S. NO! GUESS AGAIN. IT INVOLVES JOHN MAJOR'S SON . . .

Chapter Twenty

'And if there are any problems, Rosie, the owner, is going to be back from the builders' merchants in half an hour or so, and she'll be working in the bathroom all day,' I say confidently to one of the carpenters, who have finally come to install the windows and doors.

'Great. Thanks, Daisy. I'll crack on, then.'

The past week, I've gone from never having spoken to a workman, to getting quite good at organising them. Clearly, all the years of watching *Grand Designs* has paid off.

I turn my attention back to my Gantt Chart on the kitchen table, and I highlight carpenters on site. I can't help but smile that, now the project has been whipped into shape, it's coming along nicely. I might not be able to organise my own life, but it seems that I have no problem project managing a major renovation.

I pick up my cup of coffee and curl my hands around it for warmth as I try and work out what I'm going to do next. Rosie and Alexis headed out to look at en-suite options, and I didn't really fancy spending my morning looking at different loos. The carpenters are going to be in and out of the rooms doing the doors and windows, so I can't do any painting. Rosie suggested I look at the leaflets for local B. & B.s and holiday rentals to research the competition, and I'm just trying to motivate myself to pick them up.

There's a tap at the door and I'm instantly relieved of the distraction. I open it, expecting to see a builder, but instead Jack's standing before me.

'Morning,' I say cheerily.

'Morning,' he replies, a slight smile on his face. This is progress from his usual grimace. We stand there for a second and in the end I break the silence.

'Did you want to come in for a cup of tea?' I say, holding the door open further for him to come in.

'Um, no, thanks. I'm just taking Buster for a walk.'

'OK, then,' I say, searching his face for any clue as to why he's standing on our doorstep.

'I was wondering,' he says eventually, 'I mean, I'm sure you're really busy with the renovation, but I saw Rosie and Alexis driving off earlier on so I thought you might be free, and I'm going for a walk with Buster. I thought you might want to come with us. I'm going up to Angel Hill, which is up at the top of the valley. There's a track that leads up on a gradual incline.'

For the first time since I've met him, he seems flustered, and I feel that the tables have turned, as it's usually me who feels out of my comfort zone. It's funny, I feel as if we've got to know each other quite well with our jokey letters, but I sense that today he's nervous.

'I thought you might want to test out your new kit,' he says, pointing at me, before whipping his hand back into his pocket.

Instinctively, I look down at the new hiking trousers and comfy fleece that I'm wearing, and I put a hand on my hip as if I'm doing a catalogue shoot.

'Well,' I say, looking over at the stack of leaflets on the table and then back out the front door where I can see a full blue sky, 'that sounds like a great idea. Come in while I dig out my walking boots.'

Jack comes in as I hunt around the kitchen.

'This looks impressive,' he says, pointing at our workflow plan.

'I'm pretty pleased with it,' I say as I sit down on the stairs to slip my boots on and lace them up. 'Although, to be honest, there's not a lot to it. Just listing the work that needs to be done and getting it in the right order. From then on, it's chasing everyone to make sure they stick to the right timetable. Luckily, it's not like a new build and most of the structural work's been done already, or else there'd be a nightmare juggling contractors and contingency. Not to mention the weather. All our jobs are inside, thank goodness.'

'Yeah, I guess that makes a big difference. Whenever I watch *Grand Designs* they always seem to have torrential rain for weeks when they're trying to get the roof on.'

'I know, they do, don't they?' I say, relieved that we're not at the mercy of the Cumbrian weather, as we'd be massively behind schedule by now.

'I'll just leave Rosie a note to tell her I've gone out,' I say, scribbling something down. I keep straining my ears, listening for the rumble of the Land Rover. I want to get away before she returns as I'm sure she and her meddling would have a field day that I'm going out with Jack on a hike. That, and I don't want Alexis to invite himself along. It's not that I don't enjoy spending time with him, but I've been trying to keep my distance. Ever since our little sketch to Rupert, he's been ever more tactile with me. Of course, I'm flattered by the attention, but, not only is Rosie right – it's not a good idea when we're all under the same roof – I also don't want Jack to see him act that way and presume that something is going on between us.

I poke my head into the lounge and tell the carpenters I'm popping out, before I prop the note for Rosie up against my coffee cup. I then practically bundle Jack out the door.

'Someone's excited about the walk,' he says to me.

'Uh-huh. I can't wait to test these beauties out,' I say shaking my foot, which, with the extra weight, takes a whole lot more effort than usual. They feel like gravity boots.

'I'm sure you'll notice a difference with the Gortex. I might have to get you paddling through a couple of streams just to test them.'

'Um, I think I'll stick to dry land, thanks.' I look down at my feet on the muddy path, 'or what's supposed to be dry land under all these puddles.'

Jack smiles and then opens a gate and we start to walk along the edge of the field. We walk for a while in companionable silence, mainly as I'm trying to avoid stepping in sheep poo while trying to stay vertical. I watch Buster as he zigzags along, investigating each and every smell thoroughly. Every so often he bounds over to us and loops behind us as if to round us up and check we're still following.

'Does he ever get tired?' I ask. I'm exhausted just watching him.

'Believe it or not, he sleeps most of the day. As you open the door and his paws cross the threshold he turns into a puppy, but I guarantee that the minute I light the fire in my cottage this afternoon he'll curl up on his blanket in front of it and he'll not move until I go to bed.'

I watch him dart to the other end of the field, scaring off a pair of magpies, and Jack's right, I don't believe him.

'So, have you got any pets at home? I'm guessing you don't have a dog or else you would have brought it, but a cat, maybe?'

'I'm a single woman therefore I should own a cat?' I say raising an eyebrow.

'I didn't mean it like that. But now that you mention it, I'm sure you could be a crazy cat lady.'

I shoot him a warning look and he smiles.

'I just thought that, with working in London, a cat would be an easier pet to have.'

'To be honest, I can barely feed and look after myself when I'm working. I doubt I'd be able to keep a goldfish alive, let alone something that actually remembers it has an owner.'

'Your job's full on, then?'

I nod. I hesitate for a moment before I realise I've got to correct him. As much as I'd like to pretend I'm still gainfully employed, I've got to come to terms with the fact that I'm not any longer.

'My job *was* full on. That's why I'm here with Rosie. I sort of had to leave my work.'

'Voluntarily or forcibly?'

'Um, I guess forcibly.'

I detect a note of pity in his voice and I cringe. This is exactly why it was a good idea to get away from everything. I can't imagine having to tell everyone what happened.

We're silent for a moment as I take in the scenery. Jack was right about the gentle incline; we've already gone quite far uphill and I'd barely noticed. We get to the end of the field, and we climb over a stile into a small wood. Jack holds his hand out for me to jump down and I gratefully take it as I steady myself.

'So, are you looking for a new job?' asks Jack.

'It's too hard at the moment without the Internet. I should probably start looking soon, though, as I don't want to have too big a gap on my CV.'

I sigh. Without the Internet I can convince myself that it was one tiny tweet and that everyone will have forgotten about it by now. I'm totally fantasising that I'll walk straight into another job, when in reality I won't know until I start trying if I'm going to be able to carry on in marketing. The digital detox and the renovations have been great distractions from the muddle my life is in, but sooner or later I'm going to have to face the real world. I can't hide forever.

'What is it that you do?'

'I'm a marketing account manager, so I oversee the materials that clients send their customers or investors. You know, end-of-year financial reports and shareholder updates.'

It's hard to imagine that something that sounds so simple could take up my whole life.

'And that's what you're going to get another job in?'

'Yes,' I say without even thinking about it. 'I mean, it's the only thing I know how to do, and at my age I can't really be changing careers.'

'At your age,' he says chuckling. 'Aren't you still in your twenties?'

'Actually, I turned thirty-one last month.'

'Right, well, you do realise that you probably still have another thirty-four years left of work? I'm pretty sure that gives you plenty of time for a career change.'

'For a man maybe,' I say rolling my eyes, 'but if I started something new I'd probably have to retrain and then start at the bottom and work my way up. There'd be a drop in salary, which would mean having to live in a shared house as I wouldn't be able to afford to live on my own. And not to mention that I'd want to be in a decent position when I go on maternity leave.'

'Are you . . .?' starts Jack as he looks at me in confusion.

'Of course not, but I am thirty-one, so I'm guessing that if I do meet someone and we want to have kids, then I'm going to have to start in the next ten years.'

Jack's quiet for a minute while he takes it all in. 'You know, you could still do all of that. Maybe you just need to move out of London where things are cheaper and you might not have to give up so much.'

'Oh right, I'll just pack up my life and move somewhere completely random where I know no one,' I say, half laughing.

'That's what I did. I came up here on a walking holiday with some mates, saw the cottage was for sale and bought it. Before that I lived in Islington.'

My eyes almost pop out of my head.

'What?' he says, laughing. 'Do I not look like someone who could come from London? Believe it or not, I used to work in Canary Wharf.'

'You were a trader?' I say in disbelief.

'No, far from it.'

I'm about to quiz him more about what he did, but we've reached the end of the wood and we've found ourselves on top of a ridge.

'Now, this is Angel Hill,' he says, walking along to get out of the tree line.

'Oh wow,' I say, as I spin round on my heels taking in the 360-degree panoramic views of the valley. I can spot the farm nestled in its dip and it looks the size of a piece of Lego from here. The village houses made up of the dark grey slabs seem to merge into one, making it look like one giant building.

'This is incredible,' I say. So much better than the view from the last hill, and as I'm not hanging precariously off a cliff, I'm able to appreciate it too.

'I thought you'd like it. There's a bench up here if you want to sit down for a bit?'

He leads us along the ridge until we get under an oak tree, and there's a small bench carved from a tree underneath it. The brass plaque dedication reads 'In Loving Memory of Angela'.

'I wonder who Angela was,' I say almost in a whisper.

'She was Rodney's wife. She died of breast cancer just before I moved here.'

'I didn't realise he was a widower,' I say, realising just how little I know about him, and, again, making me feel even more guilty for trying to use him for his Internet the other day.

'I can see why he picked this spot for a bench, it's so peaceful here.'

Jack nods. 'And they call it Angel Hill as you feel as if you're looking down on everything from up here.'

'It's beautiful,' I say, as it catches in my throat.

'I know we all joke about him being an amorous farmer, but I think it's only as he misses Angela so much. He still comes up here to be near her.'

I blink back a tear as I imagine Rodney sitting in this very spot.

'So you and Rodney have always been close?'

'Uh-huh, he took me under his wing when I arrived. He needed it as much as I did. He'd had a hard time grieving and when I moved here I gave him someone to look after. I think it was as good for him as it was for me.'

'And now you're taking me under your wing,' I say almost without being able to stop myself.

'Ha,' he says laughing. 'I guess I am. Although it's going to have to be a pretty big wing with all the help you'll need.'

'Oi,' I say poking him in the arm. 'I think I'm doing just fine, thank you. Look, I'm all kitted out. What more do I need?'

'If I'm being honest, a shower . . . I'm guessing that you haven't been for that skinny dip yet.'

My jaw falls open and my eyes go wild. I'm about to give him a right thumping, but he's already jumped up and is walking backwards towards the path we walked up.

'Only kidding,' he says.

I stick my nose under my fleece and wonder if he's got a point, but Rosie promised that the bathroom would be in operation, in some fashion, this evening.

I get up and join him, keeping my distance just in case he does get a whiff of me.

'Thanks for asking me to come on this walk,' I say as we head back into the woods.

'Thanks for coming. I usually like a good walk by myself, but every so often it is nice to have a bit of company.'

'Have you found it easy to make friends since you moved here?'

I can't imagine starting from scratch like that. I took the easy option after university, following Erica, Tess and Amelie when they got jobs in London. I couldn't imagine living somewhere without my ready-made friendship group.

'I've made a few. Of course there's Rodney, but I climb a lot with a couple of guys who live in the next village and I go running sometimes with Trish.'

'Trish the yoga instructor,' I say, hoping it wasn't the super-fit, super-pretty one that I met in the village. I look at my nails to pretend that I'm not interested in what he's saying, cross at myself that I've got prickles of jealousy.

'Yeah, that's the one. She does try and get me to do her yoga class, but it's not quite my scene. I imagine I'd be the person who toppled everyone over like dominoes.'

I smile as I try to picture him attempting to be dainty in a ballerina pose.

'And you're also friends with Jenny the hairdresser, right?'

'Jenny, um, oh yeah, I know Jenny.'

I detect him going a little pink round the cheeks and I start to feel a bit foolish. A part of me had enjoyed feeling special, having Jack's attention, but I think back to what Liz said and it makes me feel as if I'm one of many.

'I also go to the pub once or twice a week. Have you been there yet?' asks Jack.

'Only for lunch yesterday. Rosie doesn't let me out at night,' I say making it sound as if she's my jailor.

'OK . . . well, it's worth a visit as most people are pretty friendly, once they know that you're not tourists. Liz and Gerry are often there with their husbands so I'm sure they'd show you off and introduce you to everyone. That is, if you get let out at night.'

He's smirking at me and I feel the need to explain myself.

'Rosie and I are on a digital detox, remember, which is why she thinks we should stay away from the pub. She has this ridiculous idea that I'll steal someone's phone and hide in the loos using WiFi all night.'

'I wonder why she'd think that. I mean, it's not as if you'd go out of your way to get the Internet, doing something strange, like, I don't know, hiking up a hill in flimsy summer shoes after stealing your housemate's phone.'

'I didn't steal it, I borrowed it,' I say. 'There's a big difference.'

'Oh right, I stand corrected,' he says, holding his hands up, the smirk still planted on his face. I think I preferred him when he scowled all the time. 'I take it the detox isn't going very well, as every time I seem to find you, you're trying to get the Internet.'

'It's going well in the sense that I've stopped twitching and reaching for my phone, so that's progress, right? The problem is I'm worried about getting a job. I felt like I needed a break from the outside world when I agreed to the detox, but that was over a week ago and now I want to get on with my life. Only, Rosie brought me up here and roped me in to the renovation, and I'm now going to be up here for a few more weeks. I'm worried that I'll be out of work too long and that panics me.' I can't face telling Jack about the reason for my sacking. 'I just want to put some feelers out to see if I can get another job.'

'That sounds fair enough. Surely Rosie would understand that if you explained it to her?'

'She doesn't get it. She got made redundant last year and has spent her time renovating and selling houses, so she thinks there's nothing wrong with me having time out before I find something else.'

'Do you think she could be right? Do you have to get a job straight away? Have you got a mortgage or debts?'

I shake my head. 'No, I haven't, but I don't want to eat into my savings too much as I've been saving up for a flat deposit for years.'

We find ourselves out of the wood and in the fields again. Buster runs over to us excitedly before bounding after a rabbit.

'Listen, I know that I don't really know you, so I can't really have an opinion, but from the little I do know it sounds as if you were really stressed out with your job and your lifestyle. I think your sister is probably right that you do need to take some time. You might have some biological clock ticking and you might be worried about CV gaps, but it's not as if you're lying on some beach drinking cocktails. You're project managing a house renovation, surely you can talk about that in an interview and put it on your CV. Didn't you say Rosie was turning it into holiday lets? With the right wording, you could spin it so that people didn't just think you were painting your bathroom.'

I'm silent for a minute as I consider what he's saying.

'I think deep down you know that you need space, as otherwise you'd get on a train back to London. You're a grown woman and Rosie's pretty small; I doubt she'd be able to do anything to stop you if you really wanted to leave. In my humble opinion, you're going along with her and doing this detox, following her rules, because you want a break. So take it.'

'I . . .' I can't help thinking he's right. I'm not imprisoned here; I could walk to the village and get a train. Maybe I'm hiding behind the digital detox because I don't want to face up to the mess my life's in.

'It wasn't supposed to be like this. I always thought I'd have fun in my early twenties, living in London, going out drinking with my friends – working hard, playing harder, that's what you're supposed to do, right? I just assumed that I'd get the big promotions, meet someone and get married, afford to buy my house and have kids. Only, now I'm thirty-one, I have nowhere to live, no job, no boyfriend and no idea if I even want to stay working in marketing. The men I meet are only ever after one thing, and I'm worried I'm never going to find anyone that'll commit to me.'

I can feel tears welling up behind my eyes.

'Instead of focusing on what you haven't got, why don't you focus on what you do have? Your friendships, your relationship with your sister. You've got a roof over your head and you've got a project to work on. And look where you are,' he says waving his arm around.

I stop and take in the view. Under today's blue sky the grass is greener than ever. It's truly beautiful here.

I start walking again, and mull over what he said and what I should be grateful about. It seems funny that he mentioned my relationship with Rosie, as for years I've said how different we are and how we don't get on, but we've lived in the most primitive conditions for the last week and we've got on surprisingly well.

'You're very wise,' I say, finally.

'I have my moments,' he says. 'I'll tell you what, for someone getting space and wanting to find yourself, you couldn't have picked a better place. Now that you're safely kitted out, head out for a walk now and then, and I promise you, without hunting for a mobile signal, it'll give you time to think.'

'Thanks, Jack.'

We climb back over the stile and come to the end of the path.

'Did you want to come back to the farm for a coffee?' I say, not quite wanting the morning to end.

'Actually, I've got a conference call for work, so rain check?'

'OK, thanks for coming to get me today. I think that was just what I needed.'

'Anytime,' he says, waving as he goes.

I walk back through into our courtyard, glancing over at the well, and for the first time since Rosie put my phone down there I don't have the urge to try and recover it. For the first time in a long time, I feel as if it's where it's meant to be for me to really think about where my life is heading.

Chapter Twenty-One

Time since last Internet usage: 1 week, 4 days, 20 hours, 2 minutes and 19 seconds.

'And the grand total is –' says Rosie, as she taps the final figures into her old school calculator. She puts her hand over the screen. 'I can't look.'

'Come on, Rosie, be brave,' I say as I place the final teacup on the draining board and dry my hands. Those builders can certainly drink some amount of tea in a day; I feel as if I've been washing up all morning.

I go over and sit next to my sister, getting ready to help her reveal the project spending.

'OK,' she says, moving her hand and showing me the amount on the calculator.

'Oh,' we both say.

'That's more than I thought,' I say, wincing slightly.

'Actually it's only seven hundred pounds over budget so far,' she says, slightly optimistic sounding.

'And that's a good thing?'

'Well, not a great thing, but considering that the plumber talked us into putting en suites into all the bedrooms and I hadn't originally budgeted for them, that's not too bad. Of course, he's only put the plumbing in for it, so I've still got to buy the suites for them, but with the discount at the plumbers' merchants he's going to organise, hopefully it won't be too bad. Phew. God, I'm so relieved,' she says as she starts copying some figures down, and I'm relieved that she's happy. 'See, with me doing the figures, and you doing the project management, we're making a pretty good team.'

'Yes, we are,' I say nodding, and realising how right Jack was.

The noise in the house is testament to the good job, as there's banging and clanging all over the place as the plumber and the carpenters are finishing off their work. Rosie's given Alexis the day off, and she and I are sorting out the paperwork. I've spent the morning making tea and researching the competition.

'You know, you shouldn't go back to London, you should go into business with me. We could do more projects like this.'

I look around the falling-down kitchen. 'Ha, that's funny.'

'I'm serious. You're good at the project management, and I'm good at the finances; we work well together.'

'That's only because it's not actually work,' I say. It's true, we're getting on pretty well considering we used to be at each other's throats as teenagers.

'But that's the point; it never does feel like work when you're working for yourself. Think about it. At least I wouldn't care about your "priceless" tweet.'

'You're probably the only person who wouldn't,' I say sighing. Perhaps that'll be my only career option. My thoughts turn back to my chat with Jack yesterday, about starting over on a career, but the thought of it turns my stomach. Could I really do it? And do I really want to?

I turn my attention back to the leaflets in front of me, picking up one for another holiday cottage in the area. I read over it and spot the familiar selling points: family friendly, dog friendly, accessible to walks, and it causes me to sigh.

'Still haven't thought of a marketing plan, then?' asks Rosie, wincing as she knows the answer's going to be no.

'Not yet, but give me time,' I say, thinking that it would be almost impossible to stand out from the crowd in this marketplace. All I can hope, for Rosie's sake, is that there's room for one more.

She looks down at the figures again and I can see a slight look of worry. I know she's pleased that she's not too far over budget, but she needs to turn a profit as quickly as she can to show Rupert that she made the right decision doing what she did.

'Oh my God, check out this place,' I say, my eyes popping out of my head.

'Wow, that's like a set from a seventies porno,' says Rosie, laughing.

'It even has pampas grass in the front.'

'Oh, that's too cool.'

At least that's one cottage we probably won't be competing with.

The laughter stops, but Rosie still has a smile on her face, which is nice to see as she's been so down since Rupert's visit.

She's only spoken to him once since then and apparently he was monosyllabic.

'Excuse me, Rosie, can you come and show me where you want the en suite in the attic room?' asks a builder as he leans down the stairs.

'Sure thing,' she says getting up.

'I think I'm going to head out for a walk,' I say, hoping that the fresh air will help, and the sun will actually be shining.

'OK, see you later on.'

I'm wondering if I should leave a note for Jack to say thank you for taking me to Angel Hill yesterday, only I'm not entirely sure what to write. I slip a pen and paper into my pocket in case I think of something on the way.

For once I've got no hidden Internet agenda when going for a walk, mainly because I'm all out of ideas, short of divining for Internet wires.

I walk up the drive, past the crumbling wreck of a building that seems to get entombed by nature more and more each day, and past the sheep in the fields. They have it so easy, being moved from one pretty field to another to eat all day. We'll just gloss over the fact they're out here in all weathers and eventually will end up on a plate, but until then, they have it so easy in comparison to us humans.

There's something so comforting watching them spring around; it's something I'm going to miss when I go back to the real world. I shudder at the thought.

I try to force myself to think about my situation, just as Jack suggested, and I try to contemplate what it is I want from my life.

I'd always thought it would be in London, but ever since Jack put the idea of moving into my head, I can't seem to get it out. Could I really do it? Could I really leave the big smoke? And where would I go?

I look up at the hills and think there are worse places to be than here, and I'd have the added bonus of being able to stay friends with Jack.

I realise I'm at the mailboxes and I'm delighted when I see a letter from Erica waiting for me. I settle down in a nook in the wall at the far side and read it.

Daisy!!!

It sounds amazing up there. If only work wasn't so hectic I'd come and visit. In a way, I'm slightly jealous of your digital detox. Without our conversations I'm pretty much spending my time staring longingly at my phone and trying to work out which bits of Kim Kardashian are still real from her Instagram feed – I'm at a loss to find anything . . .

I want to see Jack and Alexis. If only you could message me a bloody picture! I need to know EVERYTHING about them, please. Sounds a bit like heaven, being stuck in the middle of nowhere with hot men and no phone. Please tell me you are making progress with at least one, if not both of them. If anyone needs a holiday romance it's you.

The estate agent came round and we've put the flat on the market as of today. I woke up this morning in a massive sense of panic, wondering what I'd done. It's ironic that I used to wake up in a blind panic wondering how I was ever going to afford my mammoth mortgage and now that problem's going to disappear with Chris and me taking out a joint mortgage, I'm panicking about sharing it with him. Sometimes I miss the simplicity of our uni days when all we worried about was how drunk we could get on a fiver. Remember when we used to take one five-pound note out of the bank for a night out? LMAO.

BTW: I did as suggested and put your stuff in my loft. Unfortunately, it still looks like a broom cupboard, but at least everything's packed up ready for you - if Rosie ever lets you leave!

Lots of love,

Erica xx

P.S. Please, please, please send photos – of the scenery and Jack and Alexis too!!! Instagram has ruined my imagination :)

P.P.S. an official-looking letter came for you. Do you want me to forward it on to you?

I miss my bestie so much, but it sounds as if she's moving on without me. If only I could get my life as sorted.

I'm about to reach into my pocket to pull out my pen and paper when I see Buster bounding up, and my heart starts to race as I see his owner coming into view. From my vantage point, he can't see me tucked away here, and I feel a flutter in my belly as I spot a letter in his hands.

'For me?' I say as he goes to drop the letter into our box. He practically jumps a mile.

'For God's sake, woman, you scared the life out of me.'

'Sorry, not sorry,' I say grinning. That's the best laugh I've had all day. 'So can I read it?'

'This?' he says examining the letter, and I see a blush of red in his cheeks.

'Uh-huh.'

'Well, you're here now, so I can actually talk to you,' he says shoving it into his pocket.

'Come on, what did it say?' I say, wishing I'd waited until he'd deposited it in the box before scaring the crap out of him.

'It didn't really. Just the normal stuff. You know, *Price is Right* guff, talk about the weather: same old, same old.'

'Right,' I say, doing a slow nod. 'And you walked all the way here just to post a letter about the weather.'

'Well, I guess now we'll never know, will we?'

He sits down on the wall beside me and brushes my leg with his, causing my cheeks to burn a little.

I'm tempted to reach into his trouser pocket to pull out the letter. I'm not too sure what stage it is in a friendship where you can stick your hand down someone's trousers with the potential to accidentally grope them in the process, but I'm pretty sure we're not there yet.

'So what are you doing sitting here – apart from trying to scare the living daylights out of me?'

'Oh, you know. Just thinking about things, and hoping you'd come by with a letter for me. I really do want to read it.'

'Never going to happen,' says Jack, shaking his head. 'It's bad enough that I know you actually read something I've written, let alone that I see you do it. No, I shall take this one with me to the grave. So, thinking more about what we were talking about yesterday?'

'Uh-huh. More about what the hell I'm going to do with my life, and how I've made such a giant mess of it.'

'You've got to stop thinking you've messed it up. You're not on your deathbed, you know. Whatever happened was a small blip.'

'My boss wouldn't agree with that.'

'Well, bosses can be idiots just like anyone else. You know, so many people would envy you at the moment. You're free: no commitments, no strings. You could go wherever you wanted to go.'

I stare at Jack as he's talking, knowing he's right, knowing that I could go travelling or move to Land's End, yet the only place I seem to want to go at the moment is right here.

It's funny, as I've only been here for just over a week, and I know I don't really know anything about him, but at the same time, I want to know everything.

'I know you were saying it's a bad thing that you have no attachments, but use your time wisely as I'm sure you won't stay single forever.'

'I should bloody hope not,' I say, thinking that this pep talk is suddenly taking a depressing turn.

'You do know I was trying to say the opposite of that; it came out all wrong. What I meant to say was, if I'd met you when I was living in London, I wouldn't have been interested in a one-night stand.'

'Oh great, so you wouldn't have wanted to have sex with me – what's wrong with me?' I ask, turning and raising a provocative eyebrow.

Jack looks flustered and he's scratching his head as if wondering how the conversation went so badly wrong.

'I'm just messing with you. Thank you, that's sweet to know,' I say.

It wasn't lost on me that he said if he'd met me in London, which is a nice way of saying nothing's going to happen now.

'You know, if I had my phone, I'd totally take a selfie,' I say, looking behind me. 'I mean, look at the sheep ready to photobomb us in the background. Talk about hashtag squad goals.'

'Hashtag *what* goals? You do realise you talk a different language sometimes, don't you?'

'I'm sorry, Granddad, I forgot you're not down with the cool kids.'

'You know you're over thirty, right? I'm pretty sure we'd tick the same boxes on most marketing surveys.'

I stare into Jack's eyes, trying to get an idea of his age, but that damn beard is a real pain for guessing. I mean, is he mid-thirties, early forties? Who can tell with a disguise like that?

'Go on, then, how old are you?'

'How old do you think I am?'

'Why do you answer every question with a question?'

'Oh, sorry. Habit. I'm thirty-seven.'

'Really? Is that all?' I say, biting my tongue to stop myself from laughing.

He pushes me playfully on the arm. 'It's the beard, right? Rodney's always telling me to get rid of it. It's just, without it, Liz and Gerry kept ID'ing me in the village shop.'

I laugh, 'Got a right baby face under there, have you?'

I can't help stroking his face, and as I look into Jack's eyes, I suddenly want to kiss him. He's smiling back at me and I get the impression that he wants to too. I take a deep breath and I go to lean forward, when the sound of a car horn blasts and I leap up. Now I know exactly how Jack felt when I made him jump.

Rosie winds down her window.

'Ian wants me to grab some more bits for the en suites so I'm off to the plumbers' merchants. You want to come? Thought we could stop off for scones at that little tea shop on the way back.'

I look between Rosie and Jack.

'Go on,' he says. 'Those scones at Mrs Farley's are to die for.'

He stands up and calls Buster over. 'I was going to take Buster up to see Rodney anyway.'

'Are you sure you don't need to post anything first?'

'Quite sure,' he says winking, before he waves at Rosie and crosses the main road.

'That looked cosy,' says Rosie, as I climb onto the passenger seat.

'He was just checking his post,' I say, still not ready to explain my friendship just yet.

'Uh-huh. Very attentive to that mailbox, then, just like you.'

I fold my arms defensively and look out the window, day-dreaming about what was in his letter and gutted that I didn't find out.

Dear Jack,

I know you haven't seen me around for a while, so I thought I'd let you know that I am safe and well now that you've stood down on your rescuing duties. I'm not stuck down a well or anything (I still haven't worked out how I'm going to get my phone out . . .)

Seeing as the weather has been so wet it's been quite easy to throw ourselves into getting the house sorted. It's gone a bit mental this week with contractors everywhere. We've now had new windows installed and I'm no longer shivering, although maybe that's because I'm now dressed in a polar fleece all day. There are also doors on each of the bedrooms, so I can no longer hear Alexis snoring in the night. Someone has come in to plasterboard the ceilings and we've got rid of that awful Artex. It's just like DIY SOS! Unfortunately, Nick Knowles isn't here to lend a hand, so Rosie and I have started to do the painting, but it's coming on in leaps and bounds. I'm sure next time you visit you won't recognise the place.

I hope that Buster is well and isn't attacking too many pigeons, and your day job is keeping you busy now you don't have me to rescue. What exactly is your day job? You've never actually said . . .

Daisy

P.S. Did John Major's son present The Price is Right, or was he a contestant? I can just see him winning a boat, or was that Bullseye where everyone won boats?

DEAR DAISY,

FLIPPING HECK – BULLSEYE ... I SO WANTED ONE OF THOSE MUGS AND A BOAT TOO, OBVIOUSLY. IT WOULD HAVE BEEN QUITE HANDY WITH ALL THE RAIN THIS WEEK. THE ONLY PEOPLE WHO APPRECI-ATE THIS WEATHER ARE BUSTER AND THE FROGS HE'S BEEN CHASING ABOUT.

GLAD YOU ARE COPING OK WITH YOUR SOUL SEARCHING. I WAS WORRIED THAT I HADN'T SEEN YOU AROUND. NEARLY MADE A TRIP TO RODNEY'S HOUSE JUST TO CHECK.

I'M INTRIGUED TO SEE THE HOUSE. I'LL COME AND DO MY BEST KEVIN MCLOUD IMPRESSION WHEN I'M PASSING.

WHAT DO I DO? NOW THAT'S A QUESTION ... I BET IF YOU WERE LOGGED ON, YOU WOULD HAVE LOOKED ME UP ON LINKEDIN ALREADY. WHAT DO YOU THINK I DO??

JACK

Dear Jack,

I saw the sun yesterday. The sun! Did you see it too? I'm guessing you might have blinked and missed it. So just in case, I can confirm that at 2.32 p.m. on Friday, 18 May, the sun was indeed out. I never really got how people talked so much about the weather, but that's clearly because I'd never spent a significant time in

Cumbria before. It's amazing how it changes on a minute-to-minute basis, and it makes London's weather seem pretty dull in comparison.

I've been giving your day job serious thought and have drawn a blank. You clearly aren't a farmer, as you don't appear to have any animals other than Buster, and I think I spot more weeds in your fields than in ours. You spend a lot of time at your house, so you don't appear to keep normal office hours. So what does that make you? Professional stay at homer? You're not an IT genius or you'd have faster Internet than dial-up, so what do you do? The only clues I have are a conference call and that you used to work in Canary Wharf. The mind boggles.

Now, you underestimate me. I may not have LinkedIn, but I do have Gerry and Liz at the post office. I bet they know ;)

Daisy

P.S. I think you can get one of those Bullseye tankards off the Internet on one of those gadget sites.

Chapter Twenty-Two

Time since last Internet usage: 2 weeks, 4 days, 1 hour, 40 minutes and 54 seconds

It's finally stopped raining, and the water seems to have run down the valley, leaving the drive covered in squelchy mud reminiscent of a Seamus Heaney poem. Luckily, my all-singing, all-dancing, super-sturdy Gortex boots are keeping me both dry and upright. They also only need a quick brush off when the mud's crisp and flaky and they live to walk another day, unlike my poor suede espadrilles – RIP.

I've been walking practically at the pace of a snail to get to the mailbox today; I'm that desperate to bump into Jack. Despite our frequent letter writing, it's been almost a week since I've seen him, and after our near kiss . . .

I'm pleased when I open the mailbox to see a folded note that instantly I know is from him, as well as a more official-looking letter. Unable to contain my excitement, I open Jack's note first.

DAISY,

YOU'D NEVER BELIEVE WHAT ARRIVED AT MY DOOR TODAY! THAT'S RIGHT, MY VERY OWN BULL-SEYE MUG!

GLAD ALL IS WELL ON YOUR SIDE OF THE FARM. I CAN CONFIRM THAT I SAW SUNLIGHT TOO, AND, I BETTER WHISPER THIS, IT'S SUPPOSED TO BE SUNNY FOR THE REST OF THIS WEEK AS WELL! I'M HEADING OFF TO NEWCASTLE FOR A COUPLE OF NIGHTS (FOR WORK – STILL NOT TELLING), BUT I'LL PROBABLY SEE YOU OUT AND ABOUT LATER IN THE WEEK, AS I BET YOU'RE DYING TO TEST OUT YOUR NEW OUTDOOR GEAR ON THINGS OTHER THAN TRIPS TO YOUR PORTALOO.

JUST TO LET YOU KNOW, I KEEP A SPARE KEY UNDER THE BOOT CLEANER (THE THING THAT LOOKS LIKE AN UPSIDE DOWN BROOM HEAD) WHICH CAN BE USED FOR EMERGENCIES WHEN I'M AWAY – SUCH AS HAVING A SHOWER.

HOPE THE BUILDING IS GOING WELL.

JACK

P.S. WILL GIVE YOU ANOTHER CLUE ABOUT JOHN MAJOR – IT HAS TO DO WITH HIS SON'S WIFE . . .

As I read the letter, the warm glow that runs over me ebbs away as it dawns on me that I'm not going to see him for another few days. I don't bother to write a reply like I'd planned to do. I don't want him coming back to a full mailbox, as that'll make me look too keen.

I turn my attention to the official-looking letter; the address has been crossed out and the farm's address written next to it, in what looks like Erica's loopy writing. I'm confused for a second, before I remember that she was going to forward me a letter, and I open it, only to find another envelope inside with just my name on it. Hastily, I open it, even more intrigued.

Dear Ms Hobson,

I have asked your previous employer to forward you this letter as we have been trying to contact you without success.

We are a small, recently launched company called E.D.S.M., and we are looking for a forward-thinking marketing manager. From your LinkedIn profile and professional reputation, we think you would be perfect for the role.

Please could you contact us at your earliest convenience to arrange an interview.

Kind regards,

Ben Stone

M.D.

I stare at the typed letter and wonder if it's some sort of joke. Surely no one would go to all that effort to contact me based on my professional reputation, which right about now has to be at laughing-stock level? If I had the Internet, I'd be on it like a rocket to google the company.

I fold the letter up and put it in my pocket as I start walking back to the farm, eager to see what Rosie makes of it. I hurry along, now that I'm not expecting to see Jack, only I freeze as

I pass the turning to his drive. I remember what he wrote in his letter. He's away for a couple of nights and he's left a spare key out for me to have a shower.

I close my eyes for a minute and imagine the hot water rushing over me. Rosie's got the bath working again, yet, with the amount of hot water we have at the moment, we can only fill it a few inches so it's like bathing in the Blitz.

I glance at my watch. I'm sure Rosie won't even notice that I'm not there. She's so busy working on the bathroom.

I practically jog down the path to his house. As it comes into view, it's exactly what I imagined. A small cosy cottage built in dark-grey stone, with ivy creeping over one side. It's got a bright red front door, and despite its austere setting, it looks inviting. I find the boot cleaner – he was right to tell me what it looked like as I would never have guessed that's what its purpose was – and, sure enough, there's a small Yale key. Quickly, I open the door and return the key to its hiding place, not wanting to lose it, before I head inside.

I guess I thought it would be like Rodney's – a bit old fashioned – but instead it's surprisingly modern and everything's white. I slip my shoes off, not wanting to leave a trail of mud, and I head up the stairs, thinking it's the most natural place for a shower. I find a towel resting over the edge of the bath, and there's a note for me:

DAISY,
    GLAD YOU TOOK ME UP ON THE OFFER, NOW YOU'LL SMELL AS FRESH AS YOUR NAME WHEN

I NEXT SEE YOU ;) HERE'S A CLEAN TOWEL, AND
HELP YOURSELF TO SHAMPOO AND SHOWER GEL
(ALTHOUGH THEY'RE PROBABLY A BIT MALE).
  JACK

I don't care that Jack only has Head and Shoulders two-in-one, as right now it's just about the feeling of getting clean. I strip off and walk into the shower cubicle in the corner of the room, and practically groan with delight like the woman out of the Herbal Essences advert. Knowing that Jack won't be home anytime soon, I take the world's longest shower, safe in the knowledge that I'm not using up anyone else's hot water like I would be back at the farm. Never did a shower feel so good.

Finally, I prise myself out of the shower when my hands are fully wrinkled and prune-like, and I dress quickly. I'm just towel-drying my hair, when I realise I've missed a great snooping opportunity. I bet I could find out what Jack does.

I come out of the bathroom and peer into the bedrooms on either side. One is most definitely a guest bedroom, which looks as if it doubles as a laundry room, with all the odd socks and piles of clothes strewn on the bed. The other has a neatly made bed and a bedside cabinet full of books. I'm about to look at what he reads, before I remind myself to be more mission-focused and less Lloyd Grossman nosy.

Padding downstairs, I find a cosy-looking lounge, a modern kitchen and a small office – bingo! That's exactly where I'll find my answers.

I open a drawer and I'm about to start rifling through when I catch the large computer screen out of the corner of my eye. All thoughts of detective work stop as I realise how close I am to the Internet. I hesitate for a second, wondering if I should actually go through with it, before I switch it on. Telling myself that I can be good and that I'll just look up that E.D.S.M. company. I pull the letter out of my jeans pocket, ready to type in the URL.

The computer whirrs into life, the screen begins to load and I feel my stomach churn, as any second now I'm going to be connected to the real world again. I actually feel nervous.

Suddenly, a phone rings behind me and scares the bejesus out of me, forcing me to jump back from the mouse. It only rings three times before the answerphone kicks in.

'You've reached the voicemail for Jack Lowe; I'm not here at the moment, but if you leave your name and your number, I'll get back to you as soon as possible.'

The machine beeps and I half expect his voice to come out of it, as if he's sensed I'm here and knows what I'm doing.

'Jack, it's me, Jenny. I really need to see you. Will you call me as soon as you're back? Thanks, Marra.'

The room goes silent and instinctively I hit play to hear it again it. She's got her own pet name for him? They really must be close. I go to replay the message and realise that it's not flashing anymore, indicating that it's been listened to. Oh crap. I'd not thought of that. If I leave the message on here, then he's going to know I listened to it. And if I delete it, then he'll never know that Jenny wanted to speak to him. I'm torn as I weigh up my options. I guess he could just have a faulty machine . . .? Before I can talk myself out of it, I delete the message, telling myself she'll probably phone again. I mean, who trusts answerphones anyway?

The world's slowest computer is still chugging into life and I idly pick up a card on his desk with a cartoon dinosaur. I know I shouldn't look, but I can't help myself.

I saw this and thought of you! Thanks for being there,
Jenny xxx

That could mean anything, surely? Maybe they're just really good friends. But do really good friends put three kisses on their correspondence?

The computer is finally booted up and I stare at the screen. I'm desperate to connect, but I can't help feeling guilty. I've done so well with this detox over the past two weeks, I don't know if I can go through with breaking it, or even if I really want to. As I wrestle with my conscience, I hear the front door slam. WTF? Desperately, I try to fumble around with the mouse to shut the computer down again. Jack said he wasn't back until later in the week. The footsteps in the house grow louder, as if he's heading straight for his office. What if he's forgotten some important work and now he's going to come back and find me in here using his PC? The screen goes blank as the door swings open. Hastily, I shove my letter from E.D.S.M. into the dinosaur card to hide what I'm up to.

'You,' I shout, relaxing back into the chair in relief when I see it's just Alexis. Though he practically jumps out of his skin at the sight of me.

'Daisy, you scared me,' he says, clutching at his chest. 'I thought I was 'ere alone.'

'Ah, you will be,' I say jumping up. 'I'm heading home. I was just having a shower. Jack said I could,' I add. I start towel drying my damp hair for effect as I shuffle towards the door, before it hits me. 'What are you doing here?'

'Jack told me where the spare key was so I could use his computer. Jack 'as been letting me use it as I organise the next 'elp-exchange placement.'

'Oh, I see,' I say nodding. 'So you're only with us for another couple of weeks, then?'

'I think so. Rosie said that you will be going, and that her 'usband will be coming after. Besides, with you not there – there is no reason to stay.'

I do a double take as I'm sure that was lost in translation, but I feel my cheeks blushing anyway.

'I should head back to the farm,' I say. 'I'm sure Rosie will wonder where I am . . .'

'She went to the village to pick up some food. I like to be alone.'

'Um, OK, I'll go,' I say, taking the hint.

'No, no, I like to be alone, with *you*. I 'ave not spent much time alone with you and I would like to.'

I feel a bit weird being here with Alexis in Jack's house, I really should go.

'Please, I am feeling lonely today and I 'ave been thinking a lot about my dad.'

He raises his eyebrows like a sad puppy dog, and while I'm almost too young to fully remember my dad, I do know about the void a parent dying leaves and I can only imagine the level of grief he has.

'Of course I'll stay.'

He sits down on a leather couch in Jack's office and pats a spot next to him for me to sit on. Reluctantly, I sit down next to him and as I do, I get a whiff of his aftershave which makes me want to lean over and nuzzle his neck. I think being finally clean has heightened my sense of smell, as I'm not just smelling myself anymore.

'So tell me more about yourself.'

'Um, well, you know the main bits. I got fired, I'm living with my sister –'

'Yes, yes, but who is Daisy?'

'Well,' I say, getting a sense of déjà vu about the date with Dickhead Dominic. 'I like to go hiking.' I've never done as much off-road walking as I have in the past two weeks. Surely that has to count for something.

'I like to 'ike too. You must join me on a walk round 'ere. It would make the scenery even more beautiful.'

I almost close my eyes to appreciate his sing-song voice. It's funny as I've been around Alexis a lot over the past few weeks, but this is the first time I've been alone with him where his attention is solely focused on me. And did I mention he smells really good?

What was it Erica was saying about a holiday romance? And what with Jack and Jenny, then perhaps I've been looking in the wrong direction. Especially now we've got doors on our bedrooms – that's a real game changer.

'Stop it,' I say, playfully giggling and hitting his arm.

'It is true. You are the 'ighlight of the area.'

I'm about to protest, but my ego could do with a bit of a boost.

I'm trying to think of a witty reply, better than my goofy thanks, when Alexis leans over to me as if he's going to kiss me. For a second I'm going to let him, before the phone rings, making us jump.

I laugh awkwardly as we wait for it to finish ringing, and the answerphone clicks in.

'Me again,' rings out Jenny's voice. 'Just realised it's the dance on Friday – promise me I'll see you before then. Ring me ASAP.'

'Oh shit,' I say out loud. Now Jack's going to know that someone deleted an earlier message. I jump off the couch and go over to it.

'What are you doing?' asks Alexis coming over with me.

'Oh nothing, just making sure that it's working,' I say, leaning over it, and I'm about to hit the delete key when he grabs my hand and spins me round.

'Where were we?' he says, a smile on his face that could melt my heart and drop my knickers in an instant. Only I have to be strong and delete that message, but every time I turn towards the phone, Alexis spins me round a little more.

In the end, I stop. I can always sneak back later to get rid of it.

'I've got to get back to the farm,' I say to Alexis, who seems to have cheered up no end. 'I'll see you at home later.'

I drop his hands and run out of the room quickly before he can protest. Right now, I need to get away from Alexis and the Lynx effect before I do something silly.

Chapter Twenty-Three

Time since last Internet usage: 2 weeks, 4 days, 19 hours, 48 minutes and 5 seconds

After yesterday's near kiss, I'm not wildly ecstatic about spending the morning painting the lounge with Alexis, but the walls aren't going to paint themselves. At least it's a big room, and hopefully the paint fumes will drown out his aftershave. I've realised that being down in the dumps about my lack of career prospects is not going to get any better by kissing the handsome Frenchman. He's not a frog, after all, who's going to magically turn into a prince and solve all my problems.

'You ready to commence?' says Alexis with a smile. He climbs down a ladder, having masking taped the edges of the newly installed windows.

He goes over to the industrial tin of white paint that we're using to coat most of the farmhouse walls with, and prises off the lid. His arm muscles flex as he does so, and I try not to look. I keep telling myself it would be a bad idea, as how awkward would it be living and working in this small house if we hooked up?

'So, shall I do this one?' I say, picking the wall with the door-frame that leads to the kitchen, as it looks like the one that requires the least amount of attention to detail.

'OK. I start 'ere,' he says, pointing to a section right next to where I'm going to be working. So much for me keeping my distance. He pours the paint into the roller tray for me before doing the same for himself.

There's something very satisfying about painting on a virgin, plastered wall. I roll on a few lines of white and, unlike the stripping, what I've done is immediately visible.

Thanks to yesterday, there's a slight tension in the air and I can't work out if it's frisson or awkwardness. I just wish Rosie were working with us with her endless chatter.

'So, do you like it up here?' I ask, trying to fill the void of silence.

'Up the ladder?'

'Up here, in the Lake District, this part of England,' I say, remembering that I have to be more specific to ease the translation.

'It is a beautiful part of the world. Everyone is very friendly. If you wake early tomorrow, you come with me for a walk.'

'Perhaps I will.'

We go back to our painting and I wonder if I'll wake up alert enough to go with him, as for some reason the Cumbrian air keeps me in a deep sleep.

We roller along in silence again; all small talk seems to have deserted me.

He starts to hum a song and it takes me a few minutes before I realise that it's 'The Sound' by The 1975.

I start to hum it too, and before long he's started tapping away pretending he's on the drums and I'm singing the few lyrics that I know. I start laughing as we peter out, forgetting how the rest of the song goes, and I realise that I've momentarily stopped painting.

'I bloomin' love that song. I saw them last year at a festival; they were amazing. Have you ever seen them live?'

'No,' he says shaking his head. 'I would like to. The last band I went to see was the Foo Fighters.'

'Oh, now *they* are amazing live,' I say, as I'm suddenly transported back to the time when I was sitting on some random man's shoulders as Dave Grohl personally serenaded me with 'Everlong'. Or at least that's what it felt like.

'They were incredible,' he says, looking into my eyes and we both smile.

'If only I had my phone,' I say, realising how much of my life I used it for, 'I could have put on their new album as we paint. I don't think it's as good as the old stuff, but it's still pretty good. Perfect for painting, you know, getting a little bit rocky and angry.'

I start singing 'Best of You' while pounding the walls with paint as if to illustrate my point.

Alexis laughs, and I notice for the first time he has dimples. If only he had longer hair he'd be a dead ringer for Harry Styles, which reminds me that he's far too young for me.

'It's funny, I didn't have you down for someone who liked rock music,' I say.

'Oh yes, I like rock. I love to see bands live.'

'Me too. It's one of my favourite things to do.'

'They 'ave music in the pub sometimes, I think. Not as good as the Foo Fighters, but perhaps you will come?'

It's been a long time since I went to see a garage band in a local pub. Probably not since I was sixteen, when I used to go to the only pubs that weren't picky about having ID. Usually a dive full of underage people, middle-aged grungers and a lot of goths. All I can remember was a sea of black T-shirts and straggly unwashed hair.

I shudder at the thought. The local pub here seemed a bit bigger and brighter than that, so maybe it'll be different.

'Maybe, I will.' I shrug my shoulders as if it's no big deal. I mean, it's just going to watch a band.

I look around at the walls and the room suddenly seems cavernous.

'You know, this paint doesn't seem to be hiding the grey,' I say stepping back. 'We'll be painting this room for days.'

'It won't be so bad, at least we will be painting together,' he says, with a hint of a smile.

I try and hide my blushes, thinking of the silver or, in this case, grey, lining.

'We 'ave a lot in common, you and me, no?'

I think over the question. I guess we do. After bonding about losing our dads, we seem to have more and more in common each time we speak.

'We do,' I say, smiling.

'After this, you will return to London?'

That's the million-dollar question at the moment. When am I going to return back home? Where is home now, with me having been evicted from Erica's? And what will be waiting for me if I do go back?

'I guess.'

'You 'ave a 'ouse there?'

I chortle. 'No, it's very expensive to live there. I've almost saved for a deposit to buy a flat, but it will be small, practically a studio; you know what a studio is?'

He shakes his head.

'Everything's in one room: your bed, kitchen, living room. The whole thing would be in a room smaller than this,' I say laughing.

It feels weird to think about the abundance of space in this house alone, and that's before Rosie tackles the barn. She let slip the other night when we were drinking how much this place cost and I nearly fell off my stool. I'd be lucky if I could buy my studio for that.

I look out of the window at the view over the hills. The lush palette of green striking a contrast to the bright white that Alexis's slapping on next to it. I wonder what my view would be like, or even if I'll have a view. I start to feel claustrophobic thinking of house upon house crammed together in the streets that I'm used to.

Not that I should be worrying about a flat when I have no way of affording a mortgage, which no one would give me anyway without a job.

My breathing starts to get a little shallower and my heart begins to beat faster at the thought of the real world.

'Are you OK?' asks Alexis, coming over and placing his hand on my back.

'Yes, fine,' I say lying, as I try and take deep breaths.

It's funny, as, up until now, I've always loved strolling around London, with its energy and chaos, that feeling that there's always someone awake or something going on. I've always felt like I was part of it. I imagined I'd hate it here – it being almost the polar opposite. It's so quiet and dark, and after I turn in for the night I'm pretty sure that there's nothing going on anywhere. I'd expected to feel lost, but, in fact, I don't, I feel strangely calm.

'What about you? Where do you call home?'

'I was renting an apartment in Toulouse with my girlfriend before we left, but I am from a small town near the mountains, called Foix.'

'Where are you going to go for your next help-ex placement?'

'I am going to Scotland a week on Saturday.'

'Wow, that soon?'

'My month will be up. Unless I have reason to stay.'

That means my month will be up too. I promised Rosie I'd stay as long as he did. I can't imagine being anywhere but here. I've actually got used to the rustic lifestyle. The lack of technology. The letters from Jack . . . I think of the last time I saw him and I hope that he's back soon.

'After Scotland,' says Alexis, snapping me out of my thoughts, 'I might then go to Spain for the summer, before Germany or Austria for the winter, somewhere I can snowboard. Then next year I would like to travel.'

'Ooh, where to?'

I love living vicariously through other people who go travelling. I've never had the itchy feet of wanderlust, but I do have a bit of an obsession with following those who do on Instagram and poring over other people's holiday snaps on Facebook. With the amount that's out there, I often feel like I've seen the major sights without being forced to buy a brightly dyed pair of trousers or having the worst food poisoning imaginable with only squat toilets available.

'I don't know yet – Costa Rica, Panama. Somewhere with ocean and beaches. I'd like to learn to surf.'

Images of turquoise waters with golden sand and lush forest along the shore flood into my mind; the type of beaches that were made for Instagram.

'I had some surfing lessons last year in Newquay. That's in Cornwall, down South,' I say, helpfully giving him a geography lesson. 'It was bloody freezing, but it was a great weekend away.'

SURFING! Why didn't I think of that when I was on the world's worst date with Dickhead Dominic? I'm sure, despite me only doing it for six hours over one weekend, it still counts as a hobby. I bought a new bikini to wear under my wetsuit and everything.

'I think I would like to learn. Was it difficult?'

'Um, I didn't find it easy, but then I'm not naturally very well-balanced. I'm sure you'll find it easier as a snowboarder.'

'Perhaps.'

I look down at my roller tray and realise it's empty so I go to refill it.

'I've never tried snowboarding – or skiing, for that matter. I always wanted to go on the ski trip at university but I could never afford it.' I think back to how cheap it probably was, but back then a couple of hundred pounds would have funded almost an entire term of going out.

'You should try it. I bet you'd like it.'

'Maybe,' I say, thinking that most of my skiing holiday fantasies have me sitting drinking hot chocolate in the lodge waiting for everyone to finish so that we can enjoy the après-ski.

'You can come to my 'ouse in France; it is close to ski stations. I can teach you.'

He's smiling at me again, and there are those bloody dimples.

I nod my head, thinking that this is making my illicit Harry Styles crush a hell of a lot worse. He chooses that exact moment to pick out a clump of paint from my hair, and as we stand there for a second, a wave of lust rolls over me. I almost want him to push me up against the wall and take me right here and right now – although I'm pretty sure it'd ruin my paintwork. By the time I've scanned the room for an alternative – fire hearth, too rough and bumpy; concrete floor, too uncomfortable and far too cold; rocking chair, probably a bit tricky to get the angles right – the moment's gone and he's turned his attention to the paint rollers and we go back to our respective walls.

The rest of the morning passes quickly, with Alexis and I chatting about *Game of Thrones*. A pretty confusing topic, not only because of the complex plots and ridiculous amount of characters in the show itself, but also because of our accents and different pronunciation of names. I'm pretty sure that other than Jon Snow neither of us knew who the other was talking about. Before we know it, we've done our allocated amount of daily hours, and Alexis heads off for another walk. I am far too hungry to go so instead I take up Rosie's offer of lunch, and now she's inspecting our handiwork.

'So you got on OK with the painting, then?' asks Rosie, surveying the lounge.

'Pretty good,' I say, thinking back over it and realising that I've practically been asked out on a date to the pub *and* a skiing holiday.

'The walls are coming along nicely. I reckon they'll take about four coats,' she says.

'Four,' I say, sighing in disbelief, before I remember what Alexis said earlier about spending time together and thinking that might not be all bad.

'So, I was thinking we should probably leave here at about five for the yoga class.'

'I'd completely forgotten about that, but I could do with a good stretch,' I say, demonstrating my difficulty in raising my arms above my head.

'Great. So I'm guessing you're going to do one of your daily pilgrimages to the mailbox, then?' she says, giving me the smug look that she hasn't given me for at least a week.

'I guess I should; you know, to see if Erica has written to me.'

'Erica, of course,' she says, nodding in a way that makes me wonder if she knows what's been going on with Jack.

I'm secretly hoping he's back and has left me a note, but I don't want to show that on my face so I try and look as normal as possible.

With the path being no match for my walking boots, I stride up purposefully and I'm almost there when I hear a woman giggling by the side of the crumbling barn. I recognise that long hair immediately.

'Ooh, stop it,' she says in mock protest, as she leans into a kiss and I see hands creeping over her bum.

It looks as if she got hold of Jack after all, so I spin on my heels, no longer caring what the mailbox holds.

Chapter Twenty-Four

Time since last Internet usage: 2 weeks, 5 days, 5 hours,
58 minutes and 10 seconds

Trish's yoga class is unlike any I ever attended in London. The poses are obviously the same, and Trish's gentle prodding and pulling of my limbs into the right positions is familiar, but the eclectic mix of attendees is certainly very different. It seems every woman, and at least one dog, along with a couple of token males, has come to the village hall. Yet, perhaps more surprising than seeing Liz and Gerry in matching Lycra, is the fact that after the class there's complimentary tea and coffee with Bourbon biscuits. No wheatgrass smoothies or super berries in sight.

'So, how did you enjoy it?' asks Jenny, who, after I'd spotted her earlier, is the last person I want to see.

'I really enjoyed it,' I say stretching my arms around. 'I've had a busy day of decorating. You been working hard all day, have you?' I say, rather more accusatory than I meant.

'Oh, um, I worked this morning.'

'Ah, yes, I thought I saw you up our way this afternoon,' I say as if I'm an amateur sleuth cracking a case.

'Yes, I came to see Jack. Ah, you must be Rosie,' she says, relieved to see my sister, who's joined us.

'I am indeed, nice to meet you . . .'

'Rosie, this is Jenny. She's a mobile hairdresser,' I add helpfully, choosing to leave out that she's also Jack's fancy woman, as I wouldn't be able to keep the bitterness out of my voice.

'Oh great,' says Rosie, 'I'm in desperate need of a cut.'

Jenny looks as if she's studying Rosie's hair, which looks pretty pristine in her neat ponytail. She then looks at mine, which makes me feel self-conscious as I can't remember the last time I had it cut. It probably looks even scruffier than usual now that it's scraped back into a messy bun. I pat it down a little as, thanks to the yoga, it's now half fallen out and sweaty, and I'm pretty sure I've got paint spots in it too.

'Perhaps I can come over next week. I'm over your way a lot.'

I grit my teeth. She sure is.

'Add me as a Facebook friend – I'm Jenny Chops Chapman – I'm the only one.'

'Oh, right,' says Rosie, looking at me. 'We don't have the Internet at the moment . . . You know, because of the renovation.'

'I'll give you my mobile number and you can text me.'

She shakes her head again.

'You don't have a phone? What, neither of you?' she says, looking at us as if we're from the Dark Ages.

'No signal,' I say, lying.

'Of course,' says Jenny. 'Well, how about I leave a list of free appointments with Liz at the post office and you can tell them to let me know if they're any good.'

'Perfect, thank you,' says Rosie.

I make a mental note to go out. As friendly as Jenny is, I don't want to hear her gossiping with Rosie about her boyfriend.

'So, aside from the lack of phone signal and Internet, how are you finding it up here? Everyone friendly enough?'

I'm about to leave Rosie to the conversation, when Gerry yanks her off to the side, and I feel that I can't be rude and leave Jenny on her own.

'It's been really good,' I say. 'I'm going to be sad to leave in a week or so.'

'You're not staying? I thought you'd bought the place.'

'That's Rosie, my sister. I'm just here for a few weeks, taking a break before I head back down to London.'

'Ah, that's a shame. It's nice to have some new blood in the village. Gives us all someone to gossip about.'

I look a little startled.

'Don't worry, most of the village are talking about Alexis, but that's because you girls have been keeping yourselves to yourselves. That is until now. Now we'll be talking about your doggy style.'

I look even more startled.

'You know, your downward-facing dog,' she giggles a little huskily. 'I'm only joking. Besides, I've taken a hairdresser's oath, you know; I don't discuss other people's gossip.'

She winks and I don't believe her for a second.

'So, I must run, I've got a hot date tonight. But hopefully I'll see you at the barn dance.'

'Did someone say barn dance?' says Liz, butting into the conversation.

'I've put a poster up on the noticeboard about it. Have you got your tickets yet, ladies?' she says, eyeballing Jenny and me.

'I've got mine,' says Jenny. 'I found the best little black dress in Newcastle last month, thought it was perfect the moment I laid eyes on it. Think I'll have to dye my hair a dark red to set it off,' she says pulling at her ponytail.

'And you, Daisy. You and Rosie will be coming, won't you?'

I vaguely remember having seen the flyer in the mailbox, but I hadn't paid much attention to it as I'd been looking at Jack's scrawled note on the back.

'When is it?' I ask.

'It's Friday night. There're only a few tickets left, so make sure you hurry,' says Liz waltzing off as quickly as she came.

'You have to come. A barn dance might sound dull, but trust me, there are always fireworks. I've got to run. Date won't wait,' says Jenny giving me a friendly tap on the shoulder as she leaves. If she was going on a date with anyone but Jack I'd probably have marvelled at how lovely and friendly she was, but I can't bring myself to.

'Did you enjoy the class?' asks Gerry as I walk up to her and Rosie, helping myself to a cup of tea as I do so. No one else seems in a hurry to be leaving the yoga, and I get the impression that the social after is as big a draw as the workout.

'Yes, Trish is a great teacher.'

'That she is,' Gerry says nodding.

'Listen, I'm going to get some cash out while we're here as Gerry and Trish have talked me into buying tickets for the barn dance. Sounds like it could be fun. I thought I'd give Rupert a call from the phone box too. Will you be all right here on your own?'

'She won't be on her own, I'll look out for her,' says Gerry.

I'd actually much rather be on my own than grilled by Gerry, but I smile politely.

'So, lovey, how are you getting on at the farm? Seen a lot of Jack around?'

'Not recently, he's been away for work, I think.'

'Ah, his work,' she says leaning in and sidling up a bit closer to me. 'Has he told you what he does, per chance?'

'No,' I say, 'what does he do?' I wouldn't usually indulge in such gossip, but I'm desperate to know.

'I don't know. No one does. He's right secretive that one,' she says tutting. If I weren't so desperate to know, I'd probably admire the fact that he's managed to keep his life so private from nosy Gerry and Liz. That must take some skill.

I look out the window to see how Rosie is getting on. I see her hang up the phone and start to cry. What's going on with Rupert? Despite her calling him every couple of days they haven't talked about what happened; why he came up or why he left so suddenly. If that was my husband, I'd have driven back down to the flat to have it out with him by now, but Rosie seems to have thrown herself into the DIY instead. I've been trying not to get involved, but I don't think I can hold out much longer. If only

I had the bloody Internet I could just drop him an email to get him to come up and see her.

The poster for the barn dance catches my eye, and I suddenly wish he'd come to it. Perhaps getting them together on neutral turf will be just what they need.

'Have you got any extra posters?' I ask Gerry, pointing at the wall.

'We've got stacks of them. Liz always goes overboard. Just take that one, I'll replace it.'

'Thanks, Gerry.'

I unpin it from the noticeboard and, nabbing a pen from a sign-up sheet near the entrance, I scrawl a quick note as close as I can to Rosie's distinctive loopy handwriting.

Ru,
    I miss you. Please come to this so we can talk. I'm sorry for everything.
    xx

'Gerry, I don't suppose I could pop this in the post now, could I?' I say walking back over to her. I pull my purse out of my bag to look for some change for a stamp.

'I can take it and post it first thing tomorrow.'

'Great,' I'm about to hand it over, when I realise a glaring error in my grand plan. 'Bugger, I don't have an envelope.'

She goes over to the small office of the village hall and pulls me one out. 'There you go.'

'Thanks,' I say, smiling.

I quickly address it the best I can. With them living in the penthouse of their building, the address is easy to remember.

'I don't know the postcode.'

'I'll look it up for you,' says Gerry, helpfully.

'Thank you, that's super kind.' OK, so living in a tiny village might mean you don't have any privacy, unless your name is Jack, but they make up for it with helpfulness.

Gerry tucks my envelope in her bag and wanders off.

'You look miles away,' says Trish as she walks up to me.

'I think I was,' I say bringing myself back into the room.

'You and Rosie did well with the yoga. I hope that you'll come back again?'

'Absolutely. I mean, I'm not here for very much longer, but while I'm here I will.'

'That's great. So are you coming to the barn dance on Friday?'

'That seems to be the hot topic of conversation at the moment.'

'Well, there aren't many occasions to get all dressed up. I mean, the Black Horse doesn't really have a dress code.'

'So everyone goes all out?'

'Oh yes,' she says, her eyes sparkling. 'Well, I wear jeans and a shiny top, but I even put make-up on.'

'Wow,' I say, stroking my face and wondering when it was that I stopped putting mine on every morning.

'Hope you've got some glad rags with you.'

'Actually, I do,' I say, thinking through my unsuitable suitcase full of clothes that I brought with me. 'Will a tunic dress and leggings do?'

'Absolutely. To be honest, anything goes, except the usual fleeces and hiking boots. It gets hot and sweaty in here with all those bodies, and the boots aren't conducive for dancing . . .'

'Good tip.'

'Well, I must go and start putting the mats away as the bridge club are in at eight. But I'm so glad you came,' she says rubbing my arm. 'I'll see you on Friday.'

'See you then,' I say, realising that the room has thinned out now and everyone's returning their cups and saucers to the table in the centre of the room.

I hover for a minute wondering if I should help Trish, but she looks like she's got the situation under control and I'd only get in her way. So, instead, I mutter my goodbyes and I go to find Rosie.

She's sitting on the bench outside the village hall. The tears have stopped, but the melancholy look remains.

'Don't worry, sis. It'll all be fine,' I say, hoping that my letter in the post will be enough.

Chapter Twenty-Five

Time since last Internet usage: 2 weeks, 5 days, 20 hours,
11 minutes and 9 seconds

I'm not sure if it's last night's yoga, the Cumbrian air, or the fact
that almost three weeks of physical labour have left me knackered, but I seem to have slept in – again! – this morning. I wake
up in a panic and gulp as I see that it's after 11 a.m.

I know that I'm not being paid to work, and that I'm not on
a help-ex arrangement like Alexis, but I don't want to be a total
slob.

I pull myself out of bed, feeling surprisingly supple, as the
muscle ache I've had over the last few days has gone. Thank you,
Trish's yoga! Hastily, I throw on my old tracksuit bottoms and
old misshapen gym T-shirt, which are destined to be splattered
with paint over the next few hours, and I scrape my hair into a
messy topknot.

Upstairs is eerily quiet, and if Rosie was working in the bathroom, the radio would be booming. I pad downstairs as I can
hear voices from the kitchen, and feel instantly relieved that

they're all sitting around and not hard at work – although the relief is short-lived when I spot Jack at the table.

I freeze like a rabbit in headlights and my heart starts to race quicker than a Formula One car.

I wonder if I could creep back upstairs and maybe brush my hair, or at least my teeth, and put on some clothes that don't look as if I've got my wardrobe mixed up with MC Hammer's.

'Ah, there you are,' says Rosie, sliding a mug towards an empty chair and pointing at the teapot in the centre of the table.

Now that it's too late to escape, I walk slowly towards the table, not wanting to draw any more attention to my baggy trousers than necessary.

'Jack just came round to deliver us our post. The postman had put it in his box by mistake while he was away and he thought he'd bring it round in case we were waiting for it.'

'That's nice of you. When did you get back?' I try and add an air of casualness to my question, despite already knowing that he was back, as I saw him kissing Jenny.

Jenny.

'Oh shit,' I accidentally say out loud. I forgot to go back and delete the other message from her.

'What's wrong?' says Rosie snapping her head round.

'I spilt my tea,' I say, grabbing a tea towel and mopping up the non-existent spill on my trousers.

I chance a look at Jack, and he's giving me a cold stare as if he knows what I did. Even though he doesn't know for certain that I'm the guilty one. Alexis was there too, for all he knows he did it. Besides, I'm the one who should be cross with him. I may have accidentally deleted an answerphone message, an easy mistake to make, but he accidentally forgot to tell me he had a girlfriend when he was leading me on with his letters and near kisses.

'Are you feeling all right this morning?' whispers Rosie, taking back the mug she had passed to me and pouring tea into it.

'I'm fine,' I say, trying to smile and reassure her as she slides the mug towards me.

'I got back yesterday,' Jack replies holding my gaze. 'Something urgent came up.'

And we all know what that was, or should I say, *who* that was.

Rosie picks up a brown envelope that looks suspiciously like it's come from the planning office, and a postcard falls out from under it.

'Ah, here's one for you from Erica,' says Rosie as she turns it over. I snatch it out of her hands before she gets a chance to read it.

Dear Daisy,

Just a quickie to say I miss you! We've got six viewings for the flat lined up for next week, which means I've become obsessed with my Rightmove app. I can't wait to find my dream pad!

Anyway, I want to know about you and your men? How's that search for a holiday fling going? You'd better get some action before you come home, with either handsome Jack or hottie Alexis, or else you'll be in trouble with

me! A fling is just what Dr Erica ordered. I want to hear all
the gossip!

Love and miss you,

Erica xxx

I can't believe she sent a postcard! It would have been
bad enough if Rosie had intercepted it, but for it to have
landed in Jack's mailbox? Man alive. I reread it, and try and
calm myself down, convincing myself that there were worse
things she could have written. At least she only called him
handsome . . .

'So, we're all set for the barn dance on Friday. Are you going?'
Rosie asks Jack.

'I'm not sure. I've got quite a lot on work wise, and it's a bit
complicated.'

Work, my arse; I know exactly why it's complicated.

'Oh, right, work,' I say a little sarcastically.

He looks at me, the scolding still there. 'Yes, actually it is
work. It's very busy at the moment, and recently I didn't get an
important message,' he says raising an eyebrow. I raise mine
back and purse my lips. He's not getting a confession out of me
that easily.

'It's a shame you won't be there,' says Rosie, blowing on her
tea, oblivious to the subtext of the conversation. 'Oh well, Alexis
will have to do lots of dancing with us, then.'

'I'm an excellent dancer,' he says.

'Modest too,' I say.

'*Bien sûr*, of course, and my first dance will be with you,' he says looking at me with his dimpled grin. 'I am happy to be your boyfriend again.'

I notice Rosie looking at us with alarm, but before she can say what she's thinking, Jack stands up, his chair dragging noisily across the floor.

'Right, I'm off. I'm going for a walk with Buster over to Angel Hill. I'll see you around, then.'

'I guess you will,' I say a little frostily. He might be pissed off at me that I rifled through his things and accidentally deleted a message, but that's hardly the same as him concealing a secret girlfriend, is it?

'This 'ill,' says Alexis, 'it's tall?'

'Yeah, it's the biggest around.'

'Can I go with you?' he says quickly, his eyes lighting up.

'Sure,' says Jack, shrugging his shoulders with indifference.

'It's OK?' he says looking at Rosie.

'Fine with me, you've already done more than enough work this morning. Unlike some people.'

I try and hide my shame of waking after eleven.

'I'll get my shoes,' he says hurtling up the stairs.

'Thanks for the tea, Rosie,' Jack says, heading towards the door, and it's then that I realise Buster has been nestled under the table as he starts to jump excitedly around.

'No problem,' she says standing up and glancing out of the window. 'Ah, there's the electrician, I want to grab him before he starts work to talk to him about the barn.'

She hurries out the door to accost the poor electrician while he's unloading his tools from the car.

Great. Now it's just me and Jack while he waits for Alexis. Neither of us says a word to one another, and I'm just waiting for the tumbleweed to roll through.

'It's always a shame when you find out someone's being lying to you,' he says eventually, in almost a whisper.

At first I wonder if I heard him correctly. It's as if he could read my mind.

'I couldn't agree more,' I say, standing up and folding my arms defensively.

'All that stuff you said about it being so hard to find a man who actually wants to commit, and how you're ready to settle down but that men only seem to be after one thing,' he says, shaking his head.

Now I'm confused.

'What does that have to do with anything?'

'The postcard and that article. I know you shouldn't believe everything you read, but . . .'

Rosie comes through the door, chattering away to the electrician as she leads him to the lounge. She briefly looks at us, as if she senses the atmosphere, but she carries on explaining the work that needs doing.

I'm so lost in this conversation. What's Jack talking about? What article?

He opens the door and it looks like he's not even going to elaborate.

'You can't just go,' I say, frustrated that he's started something he's not going to finish.

He hesitates as he steps over the threshold, before turning back and thrusting a piece of paper towards me.

'You left this at my house,' he says, handing me the letter from E.D.S.M.

My heart sinks. That incriminates me. It puts me at the scene of the crime of the answerphone.

I stare at the letter, I'd totally forgotten all about it, what with finding out about him and Jenny.

Jack doesn't wait for a reaction, he simply follows Buster as he bounds off across the courtyard.

'That was a swift exit,' says Rosie as she walks back into the kitchen alone.

I try and laugh it off as I shut the door, but I can't.

'It's a shame that he won't be there for the dance,' she says, not realising the magnitude of what just happened.

'Is it?' I say, walking over to the table and sitting back down.

'Yes, he strikes me as a nice guy, and I got the impression that he quite liked you. He was most inquisitive about where you were this morning. He seemed very disappointed that you were still sleeping. You know, he took an awful long time over his tea,' she says nudging my elbow.

I'm about to protest when Alexis comes bounding down the stairs.

''As he gone?'

'Oh, I think Buster was getting restless. I'm sure he's just up the drive,' I say dismissively.

He gives us a wave and heads off outside.

'What's that?' asks Rosie.

I'm busy thinking about Jack, and processing what just happened, so it takes me a second to realise what she's talking about. I look down at my hands and see the letter from the mysterious company.

'Oh this? It came for me in the post; I think it's probably some type of joke.'

Rosie takes it and reads for herself and I replay this morning's events over in my head.

I can't believe he said I lied to *him*. I've been nothing but honest. He's the one who's been keeping secrets – about what he does, about him dating Jenny. And it's not like I wrote that postcard; it's not my fault Erica's encouraging me to get some.

'Wow. How random. E.D.S.M. – do you think it's some sort of bondage company with a typo?'

I half smile. 'I'm still not sure what to make of it.'

'Are you going to phone them?'

'I don't know. It could be anyone, couldn't it?' I sigh and take it back off Rosie to reread it. 'It does worry me, though, what if this is my only option? I can't imagine that the job offers will be flooding in. You know, if I had the Internet I'd google them.'

'Or look them up on Companies House to see if they're legit,' she says nodding. 'Perhaps you should just ring them to see what they have to say.'

'But what if it's like some fake sheikh sting?'

'You sent one tweet, I don't think you're that famous.'

'Maybe,' I say. The thought of ringing someone work related makes me feel sick. It's been so easy to hide away here with the Internet and to ignore my career meltdown. I don't know if I'm ready to face all that yet.

I look around the kitchen and wonder what I'm doing here. Alexis is due to go next week and acting as a chaperone was the main reason I was staying for so long. I've also managed three weeks on my detox, which I'm sure even Rosie would agree is above and beyond what was expected.

Sooner or later, I'm going to have to face up to the muddle my life is in, and Jack's outburst this morning has made it easier for me to leave.

Chapter Twenty-Six

Time since last Internet usage: 3 weeks, 20 hours, 28 minutes and 18 seconds

For the past forty-eight hours my mind's been in a maelstrom. I keep replaying what Jack said over and over, analysing what I should have said to get to the bottom of it. Then on top of that, I can't stop thinking about the letter from E.D.S.M. and wondering who they are and if I'm brave enough to give them a call?

Rosie must have twigged how distracted I've become as she's summoned me over to the well for an emergency detox meeting.

'So what is it, then? An extra special meditation session, whilst channelling the well's magical healing powers?' I say. 'I was busy working when Alexis gave me the message.'

'Busy working?' she says, raising an eyebrow. 'Is that code for flicking through *Good Housekeeping* again for inspiration?'

'Maybe.' She knows me too well. 'It's important to get ideas for the planning.'

'Uh-huh. Sure. Sorry to have dragged you away, but I thought this was more important. You haven't been yourself since you got that letter.'

. . . And I had that argument with Jack.

'So, I was thinking, I think it's time.'

'Time for what?' First Jack, and now Rosie. Why is everyone talking in bloody riddles?

'Time, my little sister, to end the detox.'

I gasp in shock.

I stare down at the well and then back up at her. I'm wondering if this is some sort of test. Should I pretend not to be bothered? To prove to her that I've curbed my digital addiction once and for all? But she looks really serious.

'You're not joking,' I stutter, as it starts to hit me that I'm going to be reunited with my phone any minute now. 'You're going to give me my phone, just like that.'

I've wanted this moment for weeks, but now that it's about to happen, I can't help feeling a little flat.

'What did you want, some sort of closing ceremony? You are ready, young grasshopper,' she says laughing. 'In all honesty, I can't believe you lasted this long. I kept expecting to find you here trying to get your phone out with a stick or stealing people's phones in desperation.'

'Ha, ha, ha, as if,' I say in a squeaky voice. Has she been tracking my every move? Or is this some kind of sibling telepathy?

'Anyway, the time has come.'

'Has it? Are you sure?'

I'm starting to get so nervous that I'm about to be one step closer to getting connected. The only thing stopping me from totally flipping out is the thought that even when I get the phone in my hand I still won't get any signal here: phone or Internet.

I just hope that I'll be ready when we drive to somewhere with a signal.

In the old days I would have gone nuts if I didn't check my phone every five minutes and now I'm going to be grateful for at least a five-minute respite of the time it'll take us to reach the village.

All this time I've been craving logging on, but, now that I've actually got permission, I'm scared. It's terrifying, not just because I have to think of what I'm going to find, but also because I actually have to figure out a plan for the future.

Receiving the letter from E.D.S.M. has made me remember that I have to go back to the real world, to find a job, and that means finding out what people have been saying about me and that awful tweet.

I turn and look over my shoulder at the ramshackle farmhouse opposite and I feel a pang in my heart. I feel far more at home here than I did in Erica's flat, despite living at the latter for almost four months. The farmhouse has changed so much since I arrived, and I can't believe that I'm not going to see the rest of its transformation.

I already sound as if I'm leaving, when I know I've only been offered an interview, and not a job, but I know that once I open Pandora's box – aka switch my phone back on – I'll have to face up to all I've been running away from.

'Don't look so down,' says Rosie, slipping her arm around me, and I turn back to the well. I'm not sure when we got so tactile around each other as it feels so normal now. 'We both knew you'd have to get back to reality at some point. And I guess you've managed the digital detox for three weeks; I'm sure your fingers have been glad of the rest.'

'They'd be lucky; all that paper stripping has pretty much ruined them. I'm worried that even if they wanted to swipe my phone they wouldn't be able to.'

'See, I told you this type of break would make you a different person.'

I smile. I'm really going to miss my sister. I never really appreciated her when we lived in the same house, but now, in these few weeks, I feel as if I've realised what I missed out on during those teenage years where we spent our time arguing over who'd pinched whose belt or who'd ruined whose Heather Shimmer lipstick.

'I'm going to miss you,' I say, a little sadly.

'You don't have to go right now. I'm just letting you have your phone back. You know you can stay as long as you want.'

I smile, but she knows as well as I do, that as soon as I switch that phone on and my old life comes flooding back to me, I'll have no choice but to go.

'I have to stay, at least until Alexis goes, next week. I did promise.'

'I wouldn't worry about that,' says Rosie shrugging. 'Rupert's barely speaking to me on the phone, so I doubt he'll be rushing up here anytime soon. Besides, he thinks he's your lover anyway, not mine . . .'

I look back at the well. With Rosie's permission to go, all that's keeping me here is my phone.

'So how are you going to get them out, then?' I ask.

'Ah, I have a plan for that.'

She picks up a stick from behind the barn that has a large magnet tied to it.

'Don't tell me that's been there the whole time?'

She shakes her head. 'No, I bought the bits to make it this morning from the builders' merchants. There's a magnet taped to the box that we put the phones in.'

She lowers it down, and there's silence as both of us hold our breath in expectation.

Any second now, and I'm going to get my baby back.

My stomach is well and truly in knots now. I can't decide if I'm excited or terrified. Maybe I'm both. Excited to speak to everyone again, but terrified at what I'm going to find relating to #priceless.

'I think I've got it,' says Rosie. 'Hang on, hang on. *Balls!*'

This time, I don't even react. We've been trying to get the phone for half an hour to no avail. I should have known that she'd have been useless; she was always the one who could never hook a duck at the fair when we were kids.

We hear a splosh in the water at the bottom of the well.

'I'm so sorry, Daisy, I thought it would work. I read about it on the Internet, and I guess the problem is all that rain. This well was supposed to be totally dry. I don't even think a stronger magnet would help as it's too difficult to line up the magnets under all that water. That's if the water hasn't lifted the tape off the box in the first place.'

My nostrils flare as I try to remain calm. *It's only a phone, it's only a phone*, I say to myself. These last few weeks have proved to me that I can survive without it, but it's what's on the phone that's upsetting me.

'Surely there has to be another way. What about getting a rope ladder and climbing down?'

'I think you'd get stuck, it's not the widest of wells.'

'What about a hook? Or a stick? Or a . . .' I'm at a loss.

'I'm sure I can get it out . . . eventually,' says Rosie. 'I can ask one of the builders next week if they've got any ideas. They might be able to help.'

'*Might* be able to? But everything was on that phone: my photos, my contacts, my messages . . .'

'Relax, it'll all be backed up on the iCloud. You'll not have lost anything, and you can get a new SIM from your network provider. Obviously, I'll pay for the iPhone.'

'Too right you will. That was an iPhone 7.'

'Nice try, toots. I know for a fact it was a 5s.'

No harm in trying.

I can't help feeling a little relieved that I can put off connecting to the real world for a little bit longer. 'I guess that's that, then,' I say shrugging. 'I should probably crack on with the painting.'

'Or I could drive you to the station and you could catch the train to Carlisle. There are Internet cafes there.'

'Internet cafes? How retro.'

I was under the illusion that they had died a death along with the traditional phone box. Both, I've discovered on this trip, are still alive and kicking.

Rosie gives her magnetic fishing line one more go, but we both know she's onto a loser. Apparently, she'd taped magnetic metal to the Tupperware boxes, thinking that would work.

'Go grab your wallet and I'll run you to the station.'

I take a deep breath. There's really no getting out of this. Rosie seems to have decided that my detox is over.

I do as I'm told, and go into the house, trying to ignore the sadness that washes over me as I enter the decrepit kitchen. I never imagined when I first walked in that I could possibly get attached to it. But, Rosie's right. I've done what I set out to do and there's a company offering me an interview; I've got to at least go and see what they have to say.

'You know, I'm so proud of you, how you've resisted the Internet for as long as you have. I was sure you'd have cracked,' says Rosie as I climb into the car.

She looks genuinely proud of me and I hang my head in shame as I think of all the times I tried, and failed, to get the Internet. I almost feel guilty for trying.

'Do you want to check the post?' she says, pointing to the box as we approach it.

'Sure,' I say.

I haven't checked it since my run-in with Jack and I'm half expecting him to have written a letter in apology. I unlock the box, and I feel a wave of disappointment wash over me as I see it's empty. Of course it is.

I start to walk over to the car, when I see an old Fiesta drive up to the mailbox. Jenny's waving from behind the wheel.

'Hiya; you guys off out?' she says as she climbs out quickly.

'Uh-huh, I'm going to Carlisle.'

'Oh, you lucky thing.'

'Hmm. And you're going to see Jack, again,' I say, more of a statement than a question. I'm pleased I ran into her, it reminds me that argument or no argument, he's got a girlfriend.

'Yeah, I'll, um, see you later,' she says, a blush spreading over her cheeks.

I sigh as I get into the car.

'Nervous about what you're going to find on the Internet?' asks Rosie.

'Something like that,' I say. I'm more nervous that E.D.S.M. won't lead to anything, as right now I feel as if I want to get as far away from this village, and Jack, as possible.

Chapter Twenty-Seven

Time since last Internet usage: 3 weeks, 22 hours, 5 minutes and 7 seconds

I waste no time when I arrive at Carlisle station, finding an Internet cafe close by. I'm practically shaking as I cross the threshold, like an addict about to get their fix.

At first, I'm so overwhelmed that the person behind the desk has to practically usher me over to a vacant desktop. I've been waiting for this moment for so long that I have no idea what I'm going to check first.

My mind floods with options: Twitter, Facebook, Instagram, Gmail, and in the end I decide to start with my email, as, if there's anything important, that's where it will be.

I almost can't bring myself to do it as I've worked so hard over the last few weeks to teach myself to live offline, but in the end I can't help myself. I'm suddenly desperate to know.

My inbox is loaded – 1,264 unread emails. Holy Moly. This is going to take me ages. I start scanning rapidly through my inbox, ignoring the millions from ASOS and Boohoo, who have clearly missed me. I find one from an HR officer at my old work.

My heart skips a beat as I think that maybe they've realised they'd been too rash in firing me so quickly. Maybe the whole inappropriate tweet had been a godsend with the PR and they're begging to have me back.

Dear Daisy,
　I am writing formally to advise you of your dismissal after gross misconduct. Attached are the terms and conditions of your leave.
　If you have any questions, do not hesitate to contact me.
　Yours,
　Sally Roden

Or maybe not.

That's the only work-related email in a sea of advertising. I scan the rest of my inbox downheartedly, and other than an email from a Nigerian solicitor informing me of a large bequest from a long-lost relative, I seem to have no important correspondence. It takes barely any time at all to realise that I am an advertisers' dream, having signed up to nearly every shop I've ever bought from. When I clear my digital backlog, I'm definitely unsubscribing from everything.

Lack of job offers aside, there was nothing too bad in my emails, and it gives me a little boost in confidence to check my Twitter.

I do a quick scan of what's trending, and I'm pleased to report #priceless is over its fifteen minutes of fame. I sigh with relief, but I still have notifications.

There are over a hundred, and as I scroll through them, I see they're mostly from men saying things that rival my priceless tweet for smut. One of them is a retweet mentioning me, and has an article attached to it from the *Mail Online*. My eyes pop out as I read the headline, 'Hot as Hell Tinder Date slams Big Knicker Disappointment', and there, staring back at me, is a picture – more like a professional head shot – of Dickhead Dominic, next to a picture of me taken at Helen's hen do when I'm pushing my boobs together and pouting at the camera.

My hand shakes as I click onto the link. I already feel sick to my stomach and my eyes can barely focus on the words in the article:

Daisy Hobson, 34, found herself at the centre of a viral twitterstorm, after she accidentally tweeted her thoughts from her company's account, rather than her personal one . . .

I've only read one line and I'm already fuming. I'm thirty-bloody-one, you arseholes!

Daisy was immediately fired after tweeting: Sexy knickers £25, Brazilian £35, New outfit £170. When your Tinder date is hot as hell & you're going to f**k his brains out = #priceless. The apparent party girl's personal feed is already littered with sex tips and risqué musings on life. It seems she's up for anything.

Juxtaposed with the pictures of me from the hen do where I'm dressed in that slutty outfit, doing those ridiculous challenges, are the tweets from the Cards Against Humanity style game:

@DaisyDoesTweet
The Secret to Good Sex is being up for anything!!!

@DaisyDoesTweet
A Woman's Worst enemy is the Missionary Position!!!

Read on Wednesday how the hot-as-hell Tinder date Dominic Cutler, 34, thought that Daisy was a disappointment in our exclusive interview.

I can't bring myself to read any more of the article, which seems to have been stitched together with tweets and Instagram photos. Talk about taking things out of context.

I hastily delete my Twitter account, not wanting any of those vile men to be anywhere near me. It's what I should have done three weeks ago.

I then type my name into Google and brace myself for a deluge of hastily typed articles. I'm almost relieved when there are only a few entries relating to my tweeting disasters: the article I've just read, Dickhead Dominic's exclusive, which I can't bring myself to read, and one in *Marketing Monthly*. I click on that and wince at what the marketing industry are going to say about me.

#Priceless = #Stupidity
Every so often someone commits a heinous social-media faux pas that throws their company into turmoil.

There are examples littered all over the Internet, from the fashion company who tweeted about the #Aurora hashtag, not realising it related to a mass shooting at a cinema, to the beauty company that tweeted about Oprah Winfrey's tattoos, only to find they were looking at a photo of Whoopi Goldberg.

The latest company to find itself in a media storm is marketing company WFM, when one of their account managers, Daisy Robson, tweeted 'Sexy knickers £25, Brazilian £35, New outfit £170. When your Tinder date is hot as hell & you're going to f**k his brains out = #price-less.' It was a tweet meant for her personal account, but she sent it accidentally from the company one. For a company that prides itself on its digital strategies for its clients, it's an embarrassing mistake to have made.

I really have been named and shamed, and that, ladies and gentlemen, is the final nail in my professional coffin. The job offers definitely aren't going to be rolling in now.

It makes me think that the interview from E.D.S.M. might be my last hope. I quickly google the company, and all I find is a holding page with a date next month underneath their logo. No clues as to what their business actually is.

I do a quick check on Companies House, as Rosie suggested, to see whether they are a legit company, and I see the name of the managing director who wrote to me. The company classification of 'Other Software publishing' doesn't really tell me what they do either, but at least they are a bonafide company.

I guess the only way I'm going to find anything else out is to phone them. I can't face it, so I turn to Facebook. My eyes fall on the box at the top: *What's on your mind?*

Thank you for asking, Facebook. *If you must know,* I type, *my life is a f**king disaster.*

I hesitate before I hit the post button. What am I doing? I'm sending one of those awful fishing posts and I can just imagine what will happen if I do that. A number of my good friends will write me messages saying things like: *what's up, hun? xxx* or *Sending hugs, hun xx.*

As if anyone actually cares; they're just being nosey.

I delete the words and shake my head; I'm not going to solve anything by posting it.

I almost can't believe that I used to write things like that without consideration. I think back to the priceless tweet and how its over-sharing nature got me into this mess in the first place.

I turn my attention instead to my messages, only to find that I only have a group message from a friend announcing she's pregnant. But, other than that, no one else has missed me. In *three* weeks. Way to get an ego boost.

I scan through Facebook, reading people's status updates, but it doesn't take me long before I get a bit bored. My friend Ruby has posted umpteen photos of her kitten in cute positions. Simon, who I went to school with, has posted photos of his new Boxster. A number of people have posted about what they had for dinner last night, including my friend Grace, who seems to think that quinoa is the answer to all of life's ills. And this is what I've been missing?

I'm about to log off, when I spot Erica's status, which isn't so much a status as a declaration that she's single. I immediately click on the post to see all the comments, which are flooded with *Are you OK, hun?* and *Call me if you need me.*

WTF? I only got a letter from her a couple of days ago where she was saying how much she loved Chris and that they were on the road to mortgages, marriage and 2.4 children.

I immediately bring up my messages and bang one out to her.

Me:
What's happened? Are you OK?

I'm about to write call me, when I realise I don't have a bloody phone.

Let me know you're all right xxx

I stare at the screen, desperate for the message to go from having a sent tick to the world's tiniest photo, so that I know she's read it. But it doesn't.

I wait for a couple more minutes before deciding that she's not there, and I go back to the main page, still stunned by what I've seen.

I'm barely concentrating as I keep checking to see if Erica's replied. Where could she be? Would she have gone to work? What could have gone wrong?

I have a quick check on Chris's profile, but he hasn't posted an update up for weeks.

After that, I can't concentrate on people's feeds. Looking at their photos with fresh eyes, they all seem so contrived and self-indulgent. Especially when big things are happening in other people's lives. Monumental things. I think of poor Erica.

I click on her profile, hoping that she'll have her number written there, but she's got it hidden and I haven't known anyone's phone number off by heart since I owned my very first Nokia 5110.

I can't just sit here waiting for her to reply. I've got to go to her. I'm sure she'll be holed up in her flat eating carbs and watching her *Cold Feet* box set.

I stand up and pay the guy for my computer time, and as I go back over to the station, I stop at the payphone outside, phone the MD of E.D.S.M. and arrange an interview for Monday. I think about Jack and Jenny – there's nothing keeping me in Cumbria now, and I have every reason to be in London.

I telepathically tell Erica to hold on, that I'll be there soon.

Chapter Twenty-Eight

Time since last Internet usage: 2 hours, 9 minutes, 34 seconds

'But you can't go now. Tonight's the big night,' says Rosie, looking at me as if I've announced I'm emigrating to Australia, rather than attempting to catch the 15.22 to London Euston.

'I know, but Alexis will go with you, and I need to get back to see Erica.'

'I'm sure she's fine,' says Rosie waving her hand. 'She probably just accidentally hit the button.'

'She accidentally hit the button? What, your hand hovers quite regularly over your relationship status in your settings, does it?'

'It would do at the moment, if I was close to Facebook,' she says looking a little bit sad.

There's definitely no sparkle in Rosie's eyes today. Over the past few weeks I've seen embers of that boundless energy and enthusiasm that I remember so vividly from when we were children, but now it's as if they've all been extinguished.

'OK,' I say sighing, and feeling torn between my best friend and my sister. 'I'll stay, just for tonight, and then I'll head back to London tomorrow.'

'You will?' she says, a smile erupting on her face.

'Yeah, I'm sure Erica will understand.'

'I'm sure it'll be one big misunderstanding anyway.'

I wish I shared my sister's optimism.

'So, if we're going to this barn dance tonight, I think it only right that we get properly dolled up. Which means no more painting or manual labour today.'

'Amen to that. I thought you'd put me to work right up until you drive me to the station.'

'I was tempted . . . but I thought that I might as well make the most of having some female company while I still can, as next week it'll just be me and Alexis.'

'Are you sure you don't mind me leaving you two alone? I could stay.'

Rosie sighs. 'No, I barely get more than a grunt out of Rupert on the phone. Even if he did know, I wonder if he'd care. If anything, I'm just thankful I'm not going to be rattling around here on my own.'

She goes over to the sink and starts filling up one of the paint-roller trays.

'I thought you said we weren't going to do any more painting today,' I say, looking at her with confusion.

'I did, but I have other ideas for this. We're going to go all girlie. We can do our nails and each other's hair; it'll be like old times.'

'Um, what old times? When did we ever do things like that?'

'OK, so perhaps I'm getting my childhood confused with the twins in *Sweet Valley High*, but we totally could have done this stuff.'

'Sure, we could. So what does that have to do with the paint tray?'

She comes over and places the tray down in front of me right at my feet. I wish I'd never asked.

'Pedicure,' she says. She hands me a piece of fine sandpaper and smiles.

'You've got to be kidding,' I say, taking it and staring in disbelief.

'I'm improvising,' she says, filling up another tray. 'I'm sure it's no different to the nail files or foot stuff you get. It's either that or the cheese grater.'

I shudder at the thought. I've only just got over those late-night PedEgg adverts.

'Just pretend we're at a spa.'

She places her paint roller down on the floor and sits next to me. She's got her shoes and socks off and shoves her feet straight in.

'I've heard all the best spas use building materials,' I say, as I start taking off my shoes. Well, if you can't beat them, you might as well join them, and after three weeks of punishing building work, my feet could do with a little TLC.

'So what are you going to wear?' asks Rosie.

'I dunno. Probably my leggings and a top.'

'You could make a bit more of an effort. I've got a really nice Reiss top that would suit your hair.'

I shrug. 'It's not like I've got anyone to impress.'

'Oh really? What about Jack?'

I've not told her about the notes we've been passing back and forth, but I guess she's realised something's been going on. She's not stupid.

'I expect he'll be going with his girlfriend.'

'His girlfriend?' she says with almost a gasp.

'That's right, you know Jenny, the hairdresser.'

'Really? Her and Jack. She seems so friendly, and he seems so . . .'

'You know, opposites attract.'

'Oh, but that's a shame,' says Rosie. 'I'd thought something was going on with you two as you kept sneaking off.'

'Ha, no,' I say, pretending she was barking up the wrong tree, but, honestly, I'd thought the same.

I pull my foot out and start to file the crusty skin with sandpaper, which works surprisingly well.

'I'm going back to London anyway, it's not like anything was going to happen on my last night.'

'Does that go for Alexis too? You two seem to have become quite close over the last few days.'

Nothing gets past my sister. Not when I was hiding bottles of Hooch in my underwear drawer or stealing her lipstick as a teen, and evidently not now.

'I have to admit he's been surprising recently. Did you know he's into the Foo Fighters and The 1975?'

'He is? He's always rapping Drake whenever he works with me.'

'Yeah, it's weird as I'd have thought he'd be into rap and R&B, but he's actually seen loads of bands that I have. It turns out that we have tons in common.'

'And he is devilishly handsome.'

'Rosie, you're a married lady.'

'Married, not blind. You could do better than to have a little holiday romance with him on your last night here. I mean he's French and everything. You know what that means,' she says winking.

'I don't know what that means,' I say before I can stop myself. I can't even run an urban dictionary check because I don't have my phone.

'Come on, you know what their reputation is in bed. And, plus, we've got doors now and insulated walls, so I won't be able to hear a thing. Go fill your boots.'

'Rosie, ick.'

My sister and I have never really been ones for discussing boys and things, and now I know why.

'Come on, if I was single, I would.'

'Luckily enough you're not single. Should I be worried about leaving you both here alone?'

'Don't worry, I wouldn't act on it. I'm sure I'm old enough to be his mother.'

'He's only ten years younger than you.'

'I could have been a very forward ten-year-old.'

'I remember you at ten and you still played with your My Little Pony collection.'

'I played with you, and *your* My Little Ponies. I was only being a good older sister.'

'Yeah, yeah,' I say laughing.

The kitchen door swings open and Alexis walks in, bringing a blast of fresh air that makes my wet feet go chilly.

'What are you doing?' he says, looking from our feet to our faces. 'Is this some English tradition?'

Rosie and I get the giggles.

'Yes, yes. It's very normal to bathe your feet in paint trays. We're just getting ready for tonight,' she says, trying to compose herself.

'OK . . .' he says, clearly thinking we're barking. 'It's good, yes?'

He pulls up a chair next to me and unlaces his boots, before slipping them and his socks off and sliding his feet into my tray. I retract mine a little as he makes contact and I can't help my blushes.

'Shall I crack open a bottle of bubbles?' asks Rosie, jumping up. 'Celebrate your last night with us?'

'Your last night?' says Alexis, looking confused.

'Yes, I've got to head back to London tomorrow.' I try and read his facial expression, but I can't tell if he looks sad or if he's struggling to work out my accent.

'The painting won't be the same without you,' he says, and in his sultry French tones he makes it sound so sexy.

'No, it won't be. We might actually get some paint on the walls,' says Rosie.

'Hey, that's not fair,' I say laughing. It's woefully true though. I'm sad about leaving this project, but in reality, Rosie got all the practical genes in the family. I might be the queen of organisation but I'm not a natural when it comes to ticking things off the lists I'm making.

Alexis's foot rubs up against mine and I don't think it is accidental this time. Maybe Rosie's right, I do deserve a little bit of fun on my last night.

'Hark, look at you, lovey, don't you scrub up well,' says Liz as I walk into the village hall. She's sitting behind a trestle table with a cash tin in front of her and a list of names. She looks expectantly at us until we hand her our tickets.

'Go on through and enjoy yourself. And you,' she says pointing her finger determinedly at Alexis, 'you have to save me a dance.'

'Always,' he says with a pout.

It looks like I might have competition for my French fancy. And I don't think it's only from her. We walk into the hall and all eyes are immediately on us. I'm initially flattered before I realise that it's mainly the female eyes of the room, and most of the women are gazing at him. The hall itself and is unrecognisable from the yoga class, with hay bales and bunting and dim lighting.

Rosie and I find the makeshift bar, and Alexis goes off to do his rounds of adoring fans.

'You'd think he's a celebrity,' says Rosie as we watch him have his biceps stroked by one woman, while another leans in close to him and snaps a selfie with him.

I watch him and I bite my lip. I've always wanted to sleep with a celebrity. Maybe now's my chance.

'You both came,' says a woman bounding over to us, and it takes me a minute, as she bundles us into hugs, to work out that it's Jenny.

Now, I thought Rosie and I had made an effort in our jeans and sparkly tops, but Jenny has gone all out with her knicker-grazing, short, lacey black dress, and a fiercely dyed red bob.

'You're just in time for the good stuff. The band'll start in a minute, and I think most people are here.'

I scan the crowd, looking for her date, but I don't see him. I make eye contact with Rodney and he raises a glass in my direction and gives me a wink.

Jack's not here, though. Which I know I should be relieved about; the last thing I wanted to see was him here with Jenny draped over him, but I can't help feeling a little bit sad.

'Drink?' asks Rosie, as Jenny bounds off to give Alexis an even bigger hug than we got.

'Yes, please.'

We get a few odd looks as we get our drinks, not because there's anything wrong with us, but I think because we're outsiders in the village and people have that kind of nosey curiosity.

'You're the ones who have bought Lower Gables farm, aren't you?' chuckles one man. He nods. 'Knew Ned well. It's nice to have a bit of life back in the old place. Good on you.'

He pats Rosie on the arm and walks off.

'I'm so pleased you talked me into coming,' I say to Rosie as we stand up against the wall and try to blend in with the chairs.

The thought of anyone pulling us up into the scary dancing is quite unreal. I do remember doing country dancing once at Guides. The prospect of having to hold hands with sweaty Lucy Rivers, who I always seemed to get partnered with, seems preferable to dancing with most of the men here. Speaking of whom, Rodney has just appeared at our side.

'Ladies,' he says, tipping his imaginary hat.

'Rodney,' I say, feeling awkward. This is the first time I've spoken to him since I left his kitchen. 'Have you met my sister, Rosie?'

'No. It's a pleasure,' he says kissing her hand.

I see him clock her wedding ring and he drops her hand quicker than a hot potato.

'Can I interest you in a dance?' he asks me.

'Um,' I say, wishing that another young man would cut in, but alas Alexis is acting like a maypole with girls dangling off him in all directions, and my usual white knight is nowhere to be seen. 'OK,' I say, at least taking relief in what Jack said about most of his actions just being loneliness.

'Ooh.' I jump as he grabs my bottom, I hope by accident, before his hand finds the small of my back as he leads me across the dance floor.

The band announces the song, and suddenly I find myself being trotted around with my hands latticed with Rodney's.

'Follow my lead,' he says as he proceeds to walk me forwards and backwards.

'Oops,' I say as I step on the woman behind me as we change direction once more. 'I don't think I'm a natural.'

'Stick with me and I'll teach you,' he says winking.

But before I get too freaked out, he's handing me over to a man on the other side of the circle.

Ding dong. He looks just like Colin Firth.

'Hello,' I say, shaking my hair back. 'I'm Daisy, and I have no idea what I'm doing.'

'That's OK, I'm used to dragging my wife around; she's clueless too.'

I sigh in disappointment and as I'm handed back to Rodney I pass by a pretty blonde woman who's presumably Colin's wife, more's the pity.

It's a good job I've not had time to drink too much, as the way I'm being flung backwards and forwards is shaking me right up, and by the end of the dance I'm pretty dizzy.

'Ready for the next one?' Rodney asks eagerly.

'Um, I think I'll sit this one out. How about you ask my sister? I'm sure she's dying to have a dance.'

'OK,' says Rodney, grunting as he goes off in search of Rosie, and I wander over to the entrance to get a bit of fresh air. Jenny was right, it is boiling in here, that and I'm pretty unfit.

I go to walk outside and I walk straight into someone.

'Sorry,' I say, as an automatic reaction. I look up and find myself face to face with Jack.

He looks at me with the same sort of disdain, as if he'd found something unpleasant on his shoe.

'Um, hi,' I say, awkwardly. It's the first time I've seen him since our run in at the farmhouse.

'Hi,' he says, through gritted teeth, more out of politeness than anything,

We stand there for a second in silence, until I can no longer bear it. 'I was just getting some air,' I say, and I go to move past him and we swap places so that he can go off into the hall to find his girlfriend.

To think that I'd almost contemplated staying up here for him. I shake my head. Thank goodness E.D.S.M. wrote and threw me a lifeline back to my old world.

Chapter Twenty-Nine

Time since last Internet usage: 7 hours, 31 minutes, 9 seconds

I shiver a little at the cool breeze coming under the door, and I try to keep myself warm by nodding like a Churchill dog at whatever Liz is talking about. To be honest, I've lost track. I've been edging my feet closer to the main hall for the last ten minutes, hoping she'll take the hint, but she seems too delighted at having an audience.

'And then, she appeared from Russ's house. At 7 a.m. Still in last night's clothes. Now, I'm not one to gossip, but his wife only left a few weeks before.'

If either I knew who she was talking about, or I cared remotely, I might have speculated that perhaps the dirty stop out, as Liz had called her, was the reason the wife left in the first place. But I'm trying to escape from the conversation, not drag myself further into it.

I've got my hand on the door handle, and I'm about to summon the courage to tell her I'm going back in, when the main door opens and a couple walk in. I seize my opportunity and sneak back into the hall. The welcome warmth hits me immediately.

It seems the party is well and truly in full swing now. The dance floor is packed with promenading couples and I spot Rosie holding hands with a young man skipping under the hands of everyone else. She's got a huge smile on her face and seems to be enjoying herself. I'm so pleased that I came with her; this is just what she needed to take her mind off everything going on with her and Rupert. Speaking of whom, it seems that the poster didn't work after all. Perhaps, when I'm back in London, I'll have to give him a ring.

'There you are. I thought you'd exited,' says Alexis as he walks up behind me.

I stifle a giggle at his odd translation, but feel a little flattered that at least he noticed my absence. Which is impressive, given the female admirers he has here tonight. In fact, there are two circling like sharks, waiting for their opportunity to grab him for a dance.

'The next dance is mine,' he says almost purring.

I'm not sure if it's his super sexy French accent, the punch I drank earlier, or the fact that Jenny is giggling with Jack, but whatever it is, I want Alexis, and I want him now.

I lean into him and I find my lips making contact with his, and before I can talk myself out of it, we're kissing. As in proper tongues-and-all kissing. It takes a second before my brain catches up with my lust and we stop before laughing, a little embarrassed at the sudden PDA.

'Sorry,' I say, patting my lip as if to prove to myself that actually happened.

'For what?' he says. He reaches his hand down and grabs mine to take me outside. We find ourselves in the empty vestibule entrance.

We stand there looking at each other, waiting to see who'll make the first move.

'I can't believe you are going tomorrow,' he says stepping forward and stroking my face. 'We are only just getting to know each other.'

'I know,' I say, thinking I should have directed less of my attention to Jack and more to Alexis.

'Don't mind me,' says Liz, winking as she comes out of the toilet and sits back down at her desk. She sits there, not even pretending to disguise the fact that she's watching us.

Alexis grabs my hand to lead me outside when Jenny bursts into the vestibule, arms folded, lips pouting and nostrils flaring.

I look at Alexis's face and he looks a little flustered.

'I don't know what happens where you're from, but here, when you're dating someone, you don't stick your tongue down other people's throats,' she screams at us. I can hear her words echo around the room.

'Um,' I say, suddenly confused. 'I might have written Jack letters, but my tongue has gone nowhere near him.'

'What's this got to do with Jack? I just saw you kissing Alexis. What the hell do you think you're doing?'

Jack walks in and we all stare at him. 'I saw you tear off,' he says to Jenny. 'What's going on?'

He looks at me and scowls as if he's declaring me the trouble-maker.

'Why don't you ask your girlfriend why she's bothered that Alexis and I were kissing?' I snap.

'You've kissed Alexis?' he says at first, before he closes his eyes and furrows his brow. 'And what do you mean "my girlfriend"?'

'Yeah, what are you talking about? Jack's not my boyfriend, I've been dating Alexis for the last two weeks.'

I look between Jack and Alexis, suddenly confused about what I saw.

'But I saw you kissing Jack by the old ruins on our lane.'

'I was kissing Alexis.'

Bloody hell. She's not with Jack? She's dating Alexis – whom I just kissed the hell out of.

Jenny and I both snap our heads round and look at him. I go for the confused look whereas Jenny's going for the downright angry one.

'So you've been dating Jenny?' I say.

'Yes, but that isn't a problem, is it?' says Alexis, squinting a little as if wondering why we've got our knickers in a twist.

'Um, yes, usually it is,' I say, thinking that I really do have the worst luck at the moment. I can't even have a little fling without it going spectacularly wrong. 'And you've not been dating Jenny?' I say, pointing at Jack.

He shakes his head and keeps his scowl fixed on his face.

I'm desperately embarrassed that I've got it all wrong. I turn to go back into the hall and I catch Liz's eye. She's staring agog and mindlessly eating a bag of popcorn as if she's sitting in a multiplex.

'I need some air. Jenny, if you need me I'll be outside,' says Jack.

'I'll just leave you to it, too. You know, I'm going back to London tomorrow anyway. And Jenny here . . .' I say not wanting to finish the sentence as she looks like she wants to stab my eyes with scissors. I want to talk to Jack, to sort things out with him, especially now I know that he's not with Jenny.

'Stay,' says Alexis, holding his hand out as I walk past.

'Really, I'm going to go.'

'What we had, our moments, they were special,' he says catching my hand as I go to walk away.

'Pur-lease,' says Jenny. 'You said the same thing to me last night.'

'And me,' says another voice. We turn and see Trish the yoga teacher coming out of the hall.

'He's been seeing you too?' says Jenny, the tears starting to well up in her eyes.

'Uh-huh,' says Trish. 'We've been on a couple of dates now.'

Liz gasps, and we all glance in her direction. 'Don't mind me,' she says, her eyes almost popping out of her head.

We turn our heads back to Alexis, who seems to have shrugged off the nonchalance and is now looking a little worried.

'But he promised me he was going to take me to France, to go sailing down the Canal-du-Midi, as he loves sailing as much as I do,' says Jenny.

'Hah,' says Trish, 'he was going to take me to Burgundy to do a spirituality retreat because he's into all that.'

The two women turn to me and I feel a bit foolish. 'Skiing holiday in the Pyrenees,' I admit.

All eyes go back to Alexis. 'I wanted to go on all these trips.'

'I thought we had such a connection, you know you loving Beyoncé as much as me,' says Jenny.

'Daft Punk,' says Trish.

'Foo Fighters,' I say.

'I like all these artists,' he says.

'But you told me how much you wanted me to meet your family,' shrieks Jenny. 'You said your dad would love me.'

I freeze. Up until now this whole thing has been a bit comical, but my blood starts to run cold.

'Hold on. Your dad? But he died when you were fifteen,' I say, desperately hoping that Jenny had got her tenses wrong.

'But you said he was coming over to Scotland to see you next month,' clarifies Jenny.

'You lied to me about your dad dying? That's sick,' I say, wondering what other things about him aren't true.

'Why would you pretend your dad was dead?' asks Jenny.

'I ... um ... I ...'

For the first time since first I met him, Alexis isn't his usual confident self. Not even his sexy accent can get him out of this one.

I think back over all our conversations and all those coincidences of things we have in common. The bands we've both seen, the songs we both like.

I take a step back from the situation, as Jenny and Trish start to shout and argue with each other, with Alexis getting in the middle, bravely, may I add, as it's only a matter of time before they turn on him.

But then it hits me.

The 1975.

Foo Fighters.

My dad's death.

I think back to the *Mail Online* and how they'd ravaged my Instagram for photos to put on their website, and it dawns on me that I'd posted photos of those bands and a photo of my dad's grave on my Instagram account. My *unlocked* Instagram account.

It suddenly all makes sense now. His daily walks up the hill. He's being going to where he can get a signal to find out about us.

What an idiot. I can't believe I was almost taken in by him, and if it weren't for the others catching us in the act, I would have been.

'Ladies,' I say. 'Hey, ladies.'

I try and pull them off each other and eventually they stop. I'm slightly worried that they'll gang up on me, but they stroppily fold their arms and listen to what I have to say.

'I think I've figured it out. Are you Facebook friends with Alexis? Or do you have Twitter or Instagram feeds?'

They both nod, rolling their eyes a little as if they couldn't figure out the relevance.

'Think about what you've got on your pages. Is there anything on there that would show Alexis about your love of Beyoncé or Daft Punk? About sailing?'

Trish suddenly starts to nod. 'I'm always sharing what I'm listening to on Spotify.'

'And recently I did a throwback Thursday photo of myself at a Beyoncé concert. And there are loads of photos of me sailing in the Lakes.'

They both turn to look at Alexis, who's started to creep back towards the door, holding his hands up as if to protect his face from the onslaught he fears is to come.

'You cannot blame me. I wanted to get to know you all. I am not here for long, and I thought it would, 'ow do you say . . . *Plus vite.*'

'Speed things up,' I say, guessing his meaning from what little I can remember from my French GCSE.

'Exactly. I do like you all so much. In fact, there is no reason that we cannot, perhaps, *all* go out together sometime.'

'What, after you make up that your family members have died?' I say, shaking my head.

Jenny shrieks. 'Did you make up your sister's abusive relationship, too?' she whispers in a wobbly voice, her shoulders starting to shake through the tears. 'I haven't let anyone get close to me in years,' she says, and Trish wraps an arm protectively around her. 'How did you even know about the abuse?'

Alexis looks at the floor. 'You had liked a number of articles and blogs that follow other victims, and I suspected that was why.'

'Do you want to thump him or shall I?' says Trish to Jenny.

'Oh, no, he's all mine,' she says, suddenly composing herself and walking slowly towards him.

The door swings open and Rosie comes out.

'Hey, hey, hey. What's going on?' asks Rosie, as she pushes between the girls and stands with her back to Alexis to give him protection.

'You should hear what he's being doing,' says Jenny.

'He's been dating us both,' says Trish, her voice all squeaky. It's miles away from the dulcet tones that sent me to sleep at the end of Wednesday's yoga class.

'And he kissed your sister,' says Jenny, pointing the finger at me.

Rosie looks over at me and flashes a quick smile. 'Perhaps dating is a bit more fluid in France. I'm sure he didn't know what he was doing,' she says, turning back to the angry women.

'He was stalking us on Facebook. It's darn right creepy,' says Jenny, folding her arms as if she's a tree standing firm. She's not going anywhere. 'He's taken things that are really personal to me, and used them to get closer to me.'

Rosie flicks her head round and now it's Alexis's turn to get a scolding look.

'I'm sure that he regrets what he did. But perhaps you should be flattered that he liked you enough to go to all that effort. How did he even get onto the Internet anyway?'

'The hill walking,' I say.

'Oh, right,' she says. 'Look, I think it's time everyone calmed down a bit. Maybe Alexis has been playing the field a little, but at least you found out before anyone got hurt, right?'

Looking at Jenny I'm not so sure that's the case.

'Why are you sticking up for him?' asks Trish. 'You're not dating him too, are you?'

'Of course, I'm not. I'm married,' says Rosie.

'Since when has that stopped people in this village? I mean, your husband's not at the house with you, and you're there with him day in and day out.'

'Don't forget Daisy's there with us too.'

'But she's going tomorrow, isn't she? How do we know that you're not just trying to save Alexis all for yourself? It'd be all cosy, just the two of you rattling around on that dilapidated farm, curling up together by the fire.'

The wind flying through the vestibule alerts us to someone having come in, seconds before the door crashes noisily shut. I see the look on Rosie's face and I know before turning round who's walked in, and who's just heard what Trish has said.

'What's she talking about, Rosie? Why would you be living with him at the farm when Daisy's not there?' Rupert's voice is calm and measured, but I recognise the look in his eyes; it's the same look of hurt and anger that's in Jenny's.

'Ru, this isn't what you think,' says Rosie, forgetting she's all that stands between Alexis and two black eyes.

'I don't know what to think anymore, and I don't know what to believe. I mean, you're just going to lie to me again.'

'I didn't lie about the farm, I just wanted to surprise you.'

'It's not about the farm, it's about what I found there when I visited last time. I saw your prescription for your pill. You know, the one that you're supposed to have stopped taking so we can try for a baby.'

'Rosie,' I say in shock. No wonder he left in such a hurry the other day.

'I can explain.'

'Sure you can,' he says, shaking his head. 'I wish you'd never sent the poster.'

'Sent the poster?' she says confused.

'Yeah, you know, the one telling me to come tonight and saying you were sorry for everything. Clearly you aren't.'

Rosie turns her head to me, and for the second time tonight I'm met with a confused and hurt look.

'You pretended to be me?'

'I didn't pretend to be you, I just wanted to nudge Rupert in the right direction.'

'Oh great, so it wasn't even from you. Even better. Your sister is as big a meddler as you are.'

Rupert storms off and Rosie hurries after him.

Alexis, Jenny and Trish are motionless for a moment, as if they're still processing the argument they've just witnessed, but Jenny soon edges closer to him.

'Listen, he's not worth it. Just leave him,' I say to Jenny and Trish before I turn to Alexis and tell him sternly to leave.

'I wait for you at home,' he says as he walks past.

Jenny snarls like a dog and I grab her arm to hold her back.

'The only thing that's going to be waiting for him at home is a taxi to take him to the station,' I say to her. 'I can't imagine that he'll stay on in the village after that.'

'I just feel so stupid,' she says, tears slowly falling down her cheek. 'I thought he really got me, you know? Like he was my soulmate.'

I wrap my arm round her to give her a hug. 'He was very good at convincing people. He had me fooled too.'

'I just wish I hadn't splashed out on this new dress,' she says patting it down.

'Well, there's only one thing for it,' says Trish. 'We should go and get thoroughly wankered and see if there are any decent men from Lazonby who have come along.'

She loops her arm through Jenny's and offers her other to me, but I shake my head. 'I'll be in in a minute.'

I close my eyes, take a deep breath and exhale loudly.

'Well, that was dramatic,' says Liz.

I'd almost forgotten she was there; it's the quietest she's been since I met her.

'I should really see how my sister's getting on.'

'She's having quite the *fratch* out there. Lots of pacing and shouting.'

I peer out the window and they look as if they're having a heated argument. At least they're finally talking; perhaps I should leave them to it.

'Now, I might not know what's been going on, but from what I could tell, Jack didn't seem right pleased that you'd kissed Alexis. And he's just out there,' she says, pointing through a side window at Jack sitting on a bench.

I know I probably should just go back in and try to enjoy the dance, but I can't leave and not talk to him. Especially now that I know he's single.

'Wish me luck,' I say, knowing that the whole town is going to hear of this imminently. I just hope that there's going to be a good ending to her tale.

Chapter Thirty

Time since last Internet usage: 7 hours, 56 minutes and 59 seconds

'So, funny story,' I say as I go and sit down on the bench next to Jack. 'You would not believe the lies Alexis has been telling us.'

The air's got a right chill to it, and I rub my arms, wishing I'd picked up my coat before I came outside.

'I don't want to know,' says Jack, continuing to stare forward.

'You're not even going to hear what I've got to say? You know, nothing really happened with Alexis. I kissed him, but it was only because I thought you were with Jenny.'

'Do you have any idea how ridiculous that sounds?'

'About as ridiculous as you refusing to listen to my explanation. Look, I messed up, Jack. I know I did. I shouldn't have gone snooping in your office, and I really shouldn't have been anywhere near your answerphone. But I thought there was something between us, with the letter writing and our walks.'

I'm searching his face for any hint of the frostiness melting, but his jaw is unmoving, his look as stern as ever.

'I don't care about what you saw in the office, it's not like I'd hidden the thank-you card from Jenny. And she still got hold of me, which means, in the grand scheme of things, that you deleting her message didn't matter.'

'Then why are you so cross with me? I told you, nothing really happened with Alexis . . .'

'You can kiss whoever you want. I mean, it seems that you have had plenty of practice.'

'Excuse me?' I say, feeling as if he's winded me.

'You know, you keep going on about me being so secretive and how you're an open book, but it's all just lies. You and Alexis probably deserve each other.'

'But I've told you all about me; I haven't kept anything hidden. You started saying this the other day before you walked out. I just don't get what you're going on about.'

'I'm going on about you making out that you're looking for the one, and it's the men you meet who are only ever after sex.'

'That's true, that's what it's like Tinder dating –'

'So you'd never say anything like that, then? Funny, I read a pretty interesting article on the *Mail Online* that says otherwise.'

I close my eyes to hold the tears at bay. 'That isn't really me,' I say. 'It was all out of context, and those pictures aren't what they seem.'

'They looked like you to me.'

'Well, it was me, but it was a hen do. The theme was "slutty"; I had to dress like that, and the provocative posts were from a game we were playing. I only posted them for our friend Amelie.'

Jack shakes his head.

'But you could have sent her those pictures or messages rather than posting them for the world to see. No wonder you found it so difficult to go offline, if you were constantly telling everyone what you were doing.'

'But I'm not like that anymore, this detox has changed me. I admit that I used to spend far too much time on social media, and I was probably as addicted as my sister told me I was. But still, those tweets and pictures aren't a reflection of me, not the real me.'

'I don't know what to believe. I mean, the tweet that got you fired . . .'

I can barely look at him.

'You made me think you left because of stress.'

'The tweet was only supposed to be a joke, I didn't even mean it. I mean, the guy was vile, and –'

Jack stands up to walk away.

'Hey,' I shout, calling him back. 'You know, you're the one who told me off for listening to things that other people said. Why didn't you ask me about this? And how did you even find it in the first place, were *you* looking me up online?' I shake my head as he doesn't deny it. 'If you're so into the truth, why don't you tell me what you really do, and why Liz and Gerry are always seeing you with so many women? I'm beginning to think that I should be calling you Jack Bigalow.'

I sound like an American teenager auditioning for a part in *Mean Girls*. But I can't help it.

'Oh right, I'm a male escort, am I? Is that what Gerry and Liz would have you believe?'

'I'm struggling to think of another profession that would have you hanging around so many women. I mean, what other explanation is there?'

'Oh, I don't know,' says Jack, sighing. 'How about because I'm a psychologist, specialising in abusive relationships. And ninety-nine per cent of my clients are women?'

Bugger. That's a much better explanation.

'If that's true,' I say, 'then why don't you tell the villagers?'

'Because I give my clients anonymity. A lot of them are going through extremely sensitive episodes in their lives, and I don't want the villagers to be speculating about what their problems are and gossiping about them. Especially if one of them is from the village.'

'Like Jenny,' I say in a whisper.

He nods and I hang my head in shame. 'Jack, I'm sorry, I jumped to conclusions.'

'It doesn't matter,' he says. 'I don't care at all.'

His words slice through me, how can he not? 'But our letters, I thought we were . . .' I trail off, suddenly feeling stupid. That's twice in one night I've been sucked into thinking that a man is something he's not. He was playing me, just like Alexis.

'Right, then, I see. Obviously I was wrong.'

'You obviously were,' he says snappily. 'You'll just have to make do with Alexis now.'

'I don't want him,' I say shaking my head. 'I never really wanted him.'

Jack shakes his head and it makes me even angrier that he won't listen to how I feel about him and who I really am, and who I've really become.

'I'm going back to London tomorrow.'

For a second, I feel as if his mask drops, as he looks a little shocked. But his expression soon hardens again.

'Of course you are,' he says, with a bitter laugh. 'Going back to your real life, as all this is just fantasy. Oh well, at least I'll be able to go about my business and not find that you've got yourself stuck in some stupid situation you need rescuing from.'

I wish I had some witty retort, but my powers of sarcasm fail me. Short of sticking out my tongue, I've got nothing.

Jack turns to leave as Rosie runs towards us.

'Hey, hey,' I say, instantly jolted by the tears streaming down her face. 'Where's Ru?'

'He took the car,' she says in between hiccups and tears. 'He was so mad. He said he was going home. And now I've got to get back to the farm. I'll pick up the Land Rover and I'll –'

'Woah, woah, woah, you'll do no such thing. You drank as much of that punch as I did.'

'But I've got to get back to the farm, I mean, maybe he regrets what was said and he went back there.'

'I'll drive you,' says Jack.

'Oh, of course, you will,' I snap. 'Anything to play the knight in shining armour. We'll be fine, we'll get a taxi.'

'What are you doing?' says Rosie, looking at me as if I'm suddenly speaking Dothraki. 'Why can't Jack give us a lift? It's practically on his doorstep. Besides, I don't think we'll be able to get a taxi.'

'You'd have a long wait at this time of night, almost pub chucking-out time. Of course, you're welcome to walk, Daisy.'

'Oh, you'd love that. So you could drive back afterwards like a white knight and pick me up? No, I'll come now and save you the gloating.'

We march silently to his four-by-four, Rosie sniffling through the tears as she tries to get them under control, and me silently fuming and replaying the argument with Jack over and over in my mind.

It feels like being back in that tube compartment with Dickhead Dominic, the tension equally as palpable.

Jack doesn't seem any more enamoured with being in the car with me than I am with him, and we seem to make it back to the farm in record time. He barely gives us time to get out before he's pulled off again and gone screeching up the drive.

'Come on, Rosie,' I say tugging at her sleeve. I think she genuinely thought Rupert's car would be here in the courtyard. 'Let's get you a nice cup of tea, yeah? I'm sure he'll come back to speak to you.'

I practically drag Rosie into the kitchen, which is surprisingly difficult as she's digging her heels in like a stubborn mule.

I open the kitchen door and almost break my neck on the large backpack lying on the floor.

'I'm sorry, I was going to move them,' says Alexis. 'I'm getting my stuff together as I'll go at sunrise tomorrow. I was going to see if the pub 'ad a room, but I rang and it is full because of the dance.'

'You're leaving too?' says Rosie, 'I'm going to be all alone.'

'Hey, I can stay if you want, for a bit,' I say, wondering if I could move my interview to later in the week. I'm sure the

MD wouldn't mind, and Rupert's bound to have come to his senses by then.

'You'd stay for me?' she asks looking at me hopefully.

'Of course I would.'

I might want nothing more than to put as many miles between me and Jack right now, but my sister needs me.

'I could stay too,' says Alexis, and as I take Rosie into my arms for a hug, I give him a stare that lets him know he's about as welcome as a case of herpes.

He slopes off upstairs, presumably to pack some more.

'Thanks for staying, Daisy, you have no idea how much it means to me. I know I conned you into coming, and we probably weren't each other's first choices of housemates, but it's been so great having you here. I know you can't stay forever . . .' the word seems to catch in her throat and she stops.

'I'll stay for as long as you need me. I'm sure I could arrange for Erica to come up here. She'll probably want to get away anyway.'

'We could run Heartbroken Hotel,' she says, half snorting a laugh.

I release her from the hug, and go over to fill the kettle from the sink when I start to hear a buzzing sound. I bat my head, thinking that there must be a midge around me, but then I realise it's coming from the cupboard under the sink.

'What's that noise?' I say, straining my ears to hear it better.

'What noise?' says Rosie blowing her nose.

'That one.'

It sounds awfully like a mobile phone, and I bloody hope she can hear it as otherwise I'm going a bit nuts and I'm imagining phone noises again. I thought I'd got over hearing that in the first few days of my detox.

'I don't hear anything,' she says.

Probably because she's still doing that thing when you've been crying and you keep half hiccupping and half sniffing involuntarily.

'It's coming from in here,' I say, opening the cupboard, and the buzzing gets louder.

'Where's my cup of tea? Why don't you make that now?' she says, in the most diva-like way I've ever heard from my sister. 'I'll find the noise.'

'It's OK. I'm here now.'

The yellow bucket at the back appears to be vibrating on its own and I stuff my hand in the dish cloths, trying to find what's causing it.

'It's probably a mouse,' says Rosie coming up behind me and causing me to snap my fingers out immediately.

'It sounds too mechanical to be a mouse,' I say, dubiously.

I put my hand in again and Rosie practically rugby tackles me to the ground, but I've managed to capture the source of the noise in my hand.

A mobile phone.

'What's this?' I say staring at it, even though it's blatantly obvious. 'Do you recognise it, Rosie?'

'No, I've never seen it before in my life. It must be Alexis's phone.'

'No, his is the Samsung one with the big crack on the back of his case . . .' I stop, realising that I'm probably incriminating myself. 'No, I've seen his around and this isn't it.'

'Maybe he's got two phones; he was being secretive dating lots of women and gaining information, maybe he's got multiple phones to keep up with multiple girlfriends.'

I gasp. I knew he was sneaky, but not *that* sneaky. Of course, that makes total sense. Until I turn the phone over and see who the missed call was from: RU

'Um, Rosie, if it's Alexis's phone, why is your husband calling him?'

'Maybe to give him a piece of his mind,' she says, playing with a loose thread on her sleeve.

'And he managed to get the number for Alexis's secret phone, how?'

Rosie's face falls. I've played enough games with her over the years to know I've got her beat.

'I can't believe you've got a phone. But, I saw you put your phone down the well with mine, didn't I? Was it all some illusion, are they both here?'

I hastily put my hand into the bucket looking for mine, but there's nothing there.

'The phones are down the well, I just have another one.'

'What? Rosie, this digital detox was all your idea.'

'I know, I know it was. I thought it would be really good to have a bit of space from Ru, but then, after I put the phones in the well, I wondered what the hell I'd done. So the next day, when I went to the builders' merchants, I bought a new one. I'm sorry, Daisy, I tried, I really did, but it's my marriage on the line.'

'All this time you've had your phone? You've been making me think there was something wrong with me for being so cut up about being without mine, and all the while you've had yours. No wonder you've been so bloody keen to go out to get more cement, and pop out to the shops. You've been sneaking out to use that.'

She pulls a wincing face, before sighing. 'I know I promised I'd do the digital detox with you, but I practically did it. I mean, I've barely looked at it; it's just that now's a bad time for me not to have a phone. My marriage is on the rocks and I had to be in touch with Rupert.'

'I can't believe I listened to you. What if I'd lost a job opportunity from the lack of Internet access?'

'But you didn't. You've got your interview lined up with that company.'

'I do, luckily, but you didn't know that was the case. And what about Erica? She's my best friend and she's going through the biggest life crisis she's ever had to deal with, breaking up with Chris, and she's going through it all by herself.'

Rosie looks sheepish. 'I know; I felt bad when I heard that and I almost offered it to you, but you had to go London anyway to see about the job, so I thought that it wouldn't matter. It was only a day or two.'

'Only a day or two? So it's OK for things in my life to wait for only or day or two, but not yours? You couldn't wait a day or two as your life and your marriage is too important, but I can?' I shake my head.

'I didn't mean it like that, I just mean –' She pauses. I don't think she knows what she meant at all. And I don't want to sit here and wait to find out.

'I can't believe I listened to you. Let's get in touch with our pre-digital selves? What a load of bullshit. You made me feel like such a loser because I was having a tough time being separated from my phone. I couldn't understand how I was the only one twitchy, but now it all makes sense. You fooled me . . . I'm going to pack,' I say huffily. 'I'll leave first thing.'

'Daisy, don't do that. Look, use the phone. Message Erica.'

We both stare at it as it vibrates across the table.

'Rupert's calling, you wouldn't want to miss that,' I say, storming up the stairs.

I take off my sparkly top and replace it with an old T-shirt and a big, comfortable hoodie.

I fling open my case and start throwing in my clothes, which are scattered around my room. I'm furious. First Alexis uses my social media accounts to con me into thinking he's my ideal man, and then I find out my sister's had a phone all along. It's just me who's the mug, me who's been doing this digital detox, and it feels as if everyone's been laughing at me behind my back for taking it seriously.

I wish I could leave now, but I catch a glimpse out the window and it's pitch-black outside and the middle of the night. Even if we weren't on a farm in the absolute middle of nowhere, with no hope of me dragging my suitcase in the dark over the potholed mud track, there'd still be no trains running. I'm going to have to wait for morning. I'll just sit here waiting, as I'm far too angry to sleep.

I don't even bother to take off my clothes and put on my pyjamas. I simply sit on the airbed and fold my arms. The countdown is officially on until I can get back to my normal life and forget all about this hellhole.

Chapter Thirty-One

When I wake the next morning, I'm still fuming. I barely do even the most basic of ablutions before I leave the farm, wanting to escape as quickly as possible. Rosie wasn't in our room when I got up, and I worry that she's done something stupid and driven after Rupert, so I'm relieved to see that the Land Rover is still parked on the drive. I peek into the living room and find her asleep in one of the rocking chairs, using a dustsheet as a blanket. I might be mad as hell, but she's still my sister, and I couldn't leave without making sure she was safe.

Satisfied that she is, I pick up my suitcase and prepare for the long walk to the station. I'm halfway across the courtyard when I hear Alexis call out after me.

'Wait, are you leaving now too?'

I snap my head round. The alcohol has worn off and, where last night it almost seemed comical what he'd done, now in the sober light of day I feel violated.

'I am, but you're not walking with me.'

'Please, let me explain,' he says, jogging to catch up with me.

I try to hurry away, only he's nimble on his feet, thanks to his giant backpack, whereas I might as well be dragging an elephant behind me with the speed I'm going, and he soon catches up with me.

By the time I've made it to the dirt track, my case is flip-flopping all over the place and it's nearly impossible to keep it vertical. Alexis goes to grab it out of my hand.

'Please, let me.'

'No,' I snap. 'You've done quite enough.'

He lets go and holds his hands up. 'You know, I did not mean to –'

'Don't talk to me. I don't want to hear it.'

He shuts up and the two of us walk along in silence. Or near silence, as I'm muttering every swear word in the book under my breath. I'm almost tempted to abandon my case right here on the track, when I hear the putt-putt-putt of an engine.

Oh great. Rosie's come to find us – either that or it's Jack. Neither of whom I want to see.

Luckily, as it passes and stops in front of us, I see that it's Rodney in his pick-up truck.

'Morning!' he says. 'Off somewhere, are we?'

'To the station,' I say. 'Not together though.'

'You want a lift? Obviously, the lift will have to be together,' he says chuckling. 'I've got Shep in the front. So you can either sit with him on your lap or you can sit in the trailer.

Sharing a vehicle with Alexis is the last thing I want to do, but I accept as it's probably the only way I'll make it to the train station before sunset with the speed I'm lugging my case at.

'Yes, please,' I say.

I struggle to lift up my case to put it in the back, and instinctively Alexis goes to help me, but I turn and block his efforts. By the time Rodney's come to help me, my poor arm muscles are practically vibrating in spasm. I stomp round to the passenger door and try to move Shep over, but he's having none of it. I sigh as I walk back round, as Rodney is closing the back flap.

'I'll get in here too,' I say, sounding defeated.

Rodney rather enthusiastically gives me a hand up and I practically leap up as his hands make contact with my bum.

Before I know it, we're bounding along the track, and I cling on to the side for dear life.

I'd half hoped to sneak off to London without anyone knowing I'd gone, but it seems that every man and his dog is out today. The mix of warm, dry weather and gossip from the barn dance means that there are enclaves of chatting villagers dotted along the route. I think only a carnival float with us on would have attracted more attention, not that that's stopping Alexis. He's waving regally like a carnival king as we pass. I try and sink lower in the trailer, but Liz and Gerry still spot me. They'll no doubt be dining on this gossip all day in the shop. Although, with all the drama that unfolded last night, they'll be spoilt for choice.

The only thing that makes it bearable is the thought that soon it won't matter. I'm off today and I'm never going to see the village or these people again. Even if I make it up with Rosie, she'll have finished with the renovations and be back in Manchester in a few weeks, and this little corner of Cumbria will be a distant memory.

The truck pulls up at the station and this time Alexis doesn't even attempt to help me out, he knows the scolding look he'd get. Rodney holds his hand out for me to take as I scrabble down onto the ground.

'I'm sorry to see you go, lass. Will you be back?'

I shake my head. 'I don't think so.'

'Shame. I know Jack'll be sad.'

I laugh out loud. 'I think he'll be pretty glad to see the back of me.'

'He's not as tough as he looks, you know. Did you tell him you were going?'

I try not to think about the argument last night; I've replayed it enough times in my mind since it happened.

'Yes, and said he couldn't care less.'

Rodney nods. 'Did he ever tell you about Catherine?'

'No,' I say, thinking that, in reality, I knew so little about him.

'She was here in the village on holiday, not long after Jack moved up here, and they had a proper holiday romance. Or at least for her it was a holiday romance; he thought it was something more. When she left to go back to Devon where she was from, she ignored all his calls and texts. Eventually, when he went down to see her, as he was so worried that something had happened, he found out that she had a long-term boyfriend. She'd used Jack and it knocked him for six.'

It suddenly makes sense, why he was so upset about my tweets and about Erica's postcard. He thought I was going to do the same thing.

'Of course, that's why he's not fond of the tourists,' he says, trying to laugh a little. 'Anyway, your train will be in soon; you better go and get a ticket. You take care of yourself, OK?'

He reaches over and gives me a hug, and this time he doesn't even try and cop a feel. I watch him get back in the truck and I wonder if I should get a lift back, to sort things out with Jack.

But it wouldn't change anything, not in the grand scheme of things. I'm still going for my job interview in London, I'm going to pick up on my life where I left off and he'll still be here. I'd be no better than the woman who broke his heart the first time.

I wave as Rodney pulls away, deciding that it's better for me just to go; life here was only ever a fantasy.

The first thing I do when I make it back to Dulwich four hours later and one hundred pounds poorer, is to treat myself to a pumpkin spiced latte from my usual coffee shop. I also buy some chocolate brownies, thinking that Erica won't be sticking to her no-chocolate, no-gluten rule while she's going through a break-up. I sip my coffee as I walk along and try to get my head around being back. Initially, the noise is deafening, having been so used to the silence of Cumbria, and it's a good few minutes before I start to tune out the hustle and bustle and noise of the city.

I arrive at the street entrance to Erica's flat and I brace myself as I buzz her, not knowing what I'm going to find.

'Hello?' comes her perky voice. That doesn't marry with the unwashed, unkempt, pyjama-wearing Erica that I had in my head.

'Erica?' I say in disbelief.

She screams so loudly that I have to take a step backwards, and I almost bump into an old lady walking her Yorkshire terrier. I apologise profusely but all she does is tut and shake her head.

'Come on up, I can't believe you're here,' she screeches.

I make my way up the stairs, and I'm genuinely flabbergasted when she opens the door. Her hair is neatly styled into loose waves, her make-up has been flawlessly applied, and she's wearing tailored trousers and a loose shirt. She looks as if she's stepped out of the weekend style supplement that she's holding in her hands, and not out of the pit of heartbroken despair that I imagined.

'Have you finally been released from your detox?'

She guides me into the living room, and I sit down next to her.

'Sort of. I needed to come down for a meeting about a job, and I'd seen your Facebook status about breaking up with Chris. Why aren't you more upset?'

I look around the room and it's completely different from when I left. Clearly, she wasn't kidding about the amount of stuff that Chris brought with him when he moved in. But why is all his stuff still here?

'Oh, *that*,' says Erica, waving her hand as if batting away a fly. 'We broke up for about ten minutes. Do you know he actually refuses to put the dishwasher on until it's absolutely chock-a-block full? We keep running out of spoons and it's driving me crackers. The other morning I was forced to eat my porridge with a teaspoon and I snapped. We had this really stupid argument about all the stuff each other did that wound us up and I told him that there was no way that I was going to start flattening the toothpaste tube every time I brushed my teeth and if he couldn't accept that, we might as well break up.'

Am I hearing this right? They broke up over teaspoons and toothpaste? Erica, the usually level-headed woman, who holds a senior position in an FTSE 100 company let teaspoons and toothpaste bother her?

'So nothing big happened? No affairs? No cheating?'

'No, nothing like that. I was just really mad, and I stormed off to work and on the way I changed my Facebook status. By the time I got to work Chris had already had flowers delivered to me with an apology, and work was so manic that I forgot about my status. Then Chris and I had all the important making up to do, which meant that we didn't get out of bed at all yesterday, so I only changed my status late last night when I remembered.'

'I didn't see that, as my phone's still down a well,' I say through gritted teeth. 'Did you not think that people would be worried about you?'

How could she be so flippant about this?

'I replied to everyone's comments, and I messaged you to say not to worry. I'm sure everyone saw the funny side; it was just a little lovers' tiff.'

'One that you felt the need to broadcast to the whole world.'

'Well, not the *whole* world,' she says, folding her arms to mirror mine. 'Just my friends and family, and, as I said, everyone else knows that it was no big deal. I don't understand why you're making such a big thing out of it. It's not as if you came running when you saw it, is it? I mean, you sent that message to me yesterday morning. You waited a whole twenty-four hours to come to see me.'

She's pouting now.

'I couldn't leave Rosie; she's having *real* relationship problems with her husband.'

We sit there in silence and I begin to think it was a mistake coming here.

'Hello,' says Chris, coming out of the bedroom in jeans and a chunky knitted jumper that makes him look like he's an extra in a Scandi Noir. 'I thought I heard voices. It's lovely to see you, Daisy.'

He leans down and gives me a peck on the cheek, before walking into the kitchen.

'Are you going to join us? We're heading down for a late lunch at the Dog and Whistle.'

I look over at Erica and she's looking away from me, her nose pointing in the air.

'Um, I don't think so,' I say, starting to stand up. 'I think I should be going.'

I'm halfway to the door, when I hear Erica sigh. 'Don't go,' she says. She stands up and comes and gives me a hug. 'I'm sorry. You're right, it was a stupid thing to do and I'm pleased you came all the way here to check on me.'

'Why did you need checking on? Oh, don't tell me, you saw Erica's genius Facebook break-up. Yes, I had my mum on the phone for half an hour on Thursday lamenting about what I'd done, letting her slip through my fingers.'

Erica looks a little sheepish.

'No big deal, huh?' I say, raising an eyebrow.

'How about we just celebrate your return,' she says, tactfully changing the subject. 'You are staying, right?'

'If you'll have me?'

'Of course, now you can come out for a big lunch with us,' she says bossily. 'You must be starving after your journey.'

'Actually, I ate a pretty big breakfast while I waited for my connection at Crewe. You know what I'd love more than anything is to have a shower and probably a nap. I had a bit of a rough night last night.'

'Did you now? Did it involve Jack, or was it that hot Frenchie, what's his name, Alec?'

'Alexis. Yes, it involved both of them.'

'Oh really?' she says in a husky voice.

'Not like that, unfortunately.'

'It sounds as if I've been missing out. I should get the kettle on and –'

'Erica, we'll probably be late, if we don't get going soon. The reservation's at two,' says Chris tapping his watch.

'Of course. Are you sure you won't come with us?'

I look up at the two of them, dressed in their smart-casual attire. I've been for lunch with them numerous times before, but it seems different now, it's as if they've moved on.

'No, you two go ahead. I'll sort myself out with a shower and some sleep and we can have a proper catch-up later.'

'OK,' says Erica giving me another hug. 'I'm so glad you're back. I'm meeting up with the girls after work on Monday night too; you'll have to come. It's not been the same without you. I've really missed you.'

'I've missed you too.'

Chris coughs and breaks up our hug and he takes her hand as they leave. I watch them go, feeling relieved that they are still together. As much as I'm jealous that she's starting a new chapter in her life, and I know it'll mean I'll ultimately get to spend less time with her, I'm pleased that she's happy.

All I need to do now is sort myself out and get back on the road to happiness, and hopefully after Monday's meeting at E.D.S.M., I'll be one step closer to that happening.

Chapter Thirty-Two

Time since last Internet usage: 2 days, 21 hours,
4 minutes and 28 seconds

'Hello, Daisy, is it? I'm Jaz, from Cloud29 Productions,' says a petite brunette with a pixie haircut as she strides across the lobby, clutching a clipboard.

'Um, hi. I'm actually here to meet the managing director from E.D.S.M.,' I say looking over at the building receptionist to see if she's placed a call through to the wrong office.

'Yes, yes,' says the woman nodding. She points for me to sit back down in the waiting room and perches on the sofa next to me. 'We're filming E.D.S.M. for a fly-on-the-wall documentary about start-up companies. It's for Channel 4 daytime, you know the type of thing: an hour-long programme where it jumps around three or four companies per episode, taking a week to tell someone's story. We're following a load of start-ups, of all different types, through their first year trading to see what pitfalls they get into and whether or not they make it.'

'Great to know there's job security here, then,' I say, wondering what I've got myself into.

Jaz gasps. 'Not that this company won't make it. They've actually got loads of investors, and they're bringing in lots of new people. It's expanding pretty fast and it's great for us production-wise as there's always something going on.'

'Like an interview,' I say, trying to smile when really I wish I'd had some advanced warning, as I'd have applied a bit more powder. Any I had on, I sweated off on the train with nerves.

'Exactly. Now we'll just need you to sign the consent forms to say you're happy for us to film you.'

'And what if I'm not?' I say, really not comfortable.

'A marketing manager who's not comfortable being filmed? I'm not sure that that would go down too well.'

Jaz is smiling at me, with the kind of smile that knows I've got no option other than to do exactly what she says.

I scribble the best signature that my nerves will allow.

'Great. Let's get going. Now, when you get upstairs, the cameras are set up to record your initial meet and greet, so just act natural.'

I take a deep breath as she ushers me into the lift and up to the fourteenth floor. I knew I'd have more than the usual interview nerves, due to my lack of confidence after being fired, but being filmed has edged me past nerves into full-on jittery.

'Hi, Daisy,' says a tall wiry man with hipster glasses, before the lift doors have finished opening. 'Welcome to E.D.S.M. I'm Ben, Managing Director.'

I try and steady my hand enough to shake his, all the while attempting to ignore the camera and boom man hanging out to the side. He's not at all who I imagined him to be. I'd imagined a suited and booted middle-aged man, but instead he's dressed in tight jeans and a checked shirt, and his hair is expertly styled to appear like it's not styled at all.

'Nice to meet you,' I stutter.

'You too. Well, here we are in our offices. As you can see we're still fairly small and we're pretty much all in this open-plan area here. Including me and my business partner, as we wanted to make sure that we're accessible for the staff.'

I nod, glancing around and trying to take it in. For starters, it's an assault on the senses with its liberal approach to colour. Neon-green plastic chairs, magenta desks and sunflower-yellow walls. Shrewd move on the boss's part, as you'd never want a night on the tiles before coming to work – this would be the worst place ever to have a hangover.

There are only a dozen desks and only half of those are filled. There's a kitchen area in one corner, surrounded by beanbags and comfy-looking turquoise loungers, and on the opposite side of the office is a glass-panelled conference room.

'We have a Nespresso machine over in the corner, and we provide all the different-flavour capsules. Then we have a small kitchenette, where we also provide bread and different types of spreads. We're also all for creativity, so we've got breakout spaces with the loungers and we've got a skittle alley in the hallway on the way to the loos,' he says rattling on.

I'm nodding, trying to keep up. It's all very well knowing about the free toast, but I'd probably be more interested in knowing what the company did.

'Great, that's very good to know,' I say, as he looks at me as if eager to please.

'OK, so shall we get started?'

'Yes, please.'

I follow him into the conference room and sit down where directed. There's a couple of awkward minutes where the camera crew try to get themselves in the right location, but once they're rolling, Ben gets going again.

'So, we are just waiting for my business partner to arrive, and then we'll get started. Ah, here he is now,' he says, pointing over my shoulder at the door to the conference room. It's not until the door opens that I see who it is and my eyes nearly pop out of my head. I'm fully aware of the camera trained on my face, and I try not to flinch as Dickhead Dominic walks into the room with a beaming smile and takes his place next to Ben.

I want to lean over the table and wring his neck, but I'm guessing that's exactly the type of entertainment Jaz would love to capture. I've already been the butt of Internet jokes once; I'm not making that mistake again by being immortalised as a gif.

'Daisy, this is my partner, Dominic Cutler. I'm the app developer and I deal with all the tech side of things, and Dominic here is the money man who gets the investors onside and oversees the finances.'

'Pleasure to see you again, Daisy,' he says leaning over to shake my hand.

I shake it back, while looking him in the eye as if trying to telepathically tell him how much of a wanker I think he is, all the while keeping a smile on my face for the TV cameras.

'Oh, that's right, you've met before. Dominic suggested we contact you when we decided that we needed a marketing manager. You've clearly got a good reputation,' says Ben, suitably unaware of the looks flying between Dominic and me. If only looks could actually kill.

'Daisy's reputation is well-documented in a number of places,' says Dominic with a smug look on his face. 'Now, I'm sure you're probably wondering what it is we do here, as I doubt you'll have found anything out about us online.'

He raises an eyebrow as if he's fishing.

'Other than your company registration and the fact that you are some sort of software company, no.'

'Well, then,' says Dominic, seemingly pleased. 'We're a dating app.'

'That's what the initials stand for: Evolved Dating Social Media,' says Ben, as he spits out the apparent random words at me. 'We were going to call it Social Media Evolved Dating, but S.M.E.D. sounded a bit naff, and E.D.S.M. is a bit of a play on B.D.S.M.,' he says, rattling away.

'So,' says Dominic, taking back control. 'We have an app you pair with your social media: Facebook, Twitter, Instagram, Snapchat, et cetera, and it matches you with people who have similar online interests. People who watch the same type of viral videos, like similar companies . . .'

'We believe that it gives people more of a match with what they're actually like, rather than just what they want to project on a dating site,' says Ben.

I don't want to point out that, before my digital detox, I used to like things and check in at places just to make me look more intelligent and more cultured; there's always an element of manipulation where social media is involved.

'We're in the product-testing stage at the moment, but we hope to launch in the fourth quarter.'

'That's why we haven't posted anything online up until now, as we don't want any of our competitors hitting on the idea,' says Ben, looking as if it's all a bit clandestine.

'Exactly,' says Dominic. 'So it's essential that we get the marketing and branding right. We want to have an in-house marketing manager, and they can work with a branding agency towards the launch.'

'Which is where you come in. Dominic said you worked as an account manager at an agency, so this would be a bit of a change for you.'

'Yes, it would,' I say, trying to stay professional, despite the fact that I know Dominic has clearly brought me here for a joke, as there's no way in hell we'd work together. 'But I have ten years' experience in different marketing roles, and having managed corporate clients through rebranding and also product launches. I'm more than qualified.'

'Excellent,' says Ben. 'So we'll start asking you questions, then.' He laughs a little nervously, and it comes out as a bit of a honk.

'Daisy,' says Dominic, with a look that lets me know how much he's enjoying this. 'Our business is quite reliant on social media.'

He pauses for effect, and I desperately try to keep my poker face.

'We'll hopefully be looking for something to create a buzz and go viral. Perhaps you could talk us through some good examples of companies that have recently gone viral?'

He raises an eyebrow in his smug way. If I wasn't being filmed, I'd have tipped a glass of water over his head and stormed out, but, instead, I smile politely.

'Well, as I'm sure you are well aware, the problem with relying on things to go viral is that you're at the mercy of other people to do it. A lot of companies spend a lot of money trying to do quirky videos or adverts in the hope that they will be liked and shared, and often what they find is that the things that go viral are unintended things. Misinterpreted tweets,' I say, holding Dominic's eye, 'or letters sent to clients that are exceptional for either the right or wrong reasons. Therefore, I usually advise my clients instead to focus on targeted advertising via social-media platforms. That way, you know who is going to be watching and reacting to it, and you have the control.'

Dominic might not be impressed with how I've answered the question, but Ben certainly is.

It spurs him on to ask another couple of routine interview questions, and I can't help but feel like the smug one as I knock the answers out of the park. Dominic starts fidgeting and looking at his list of interview questions, and when I come to the end of an answer he gives me a look, and I brace myself for what's coming next.

'So, Daisy. What do you think the biggest enemy to a woman in the workplace is?'

I can feel the anger rising up inside me. He's trying to unnerve me by making reference to my tweets during the hen do.

'Dominic,' says Ben in a hushed whisper. He holds up a book in front of the side of his face to shield him from the camera. 'You can't ask that. Not with the camera here. You'll stir up a hornets' nest and everyone will accuse us of not being a feminist-friendly company.'

Dominic flexes his fingers and looks furious at being overruled, but he doesn't argue back.

'So, Daisy,' says Ben, smiling as he puts his book down. 'What's your biggest weakness?'

Dominic perks up again and he raises an eyebrow as if to bait me. Well, if he wants me to talk about social media, maybe I will.

'I think that my greatest weakness is always being switched on. I think it's so easy to do in the modern world, and I'm sure the two of you are just as guilty of answering emails at midnight and interrupting what you're doing to check what's happening online. It's hard sometimes to stay focused when you've got the whole world at your fingertips. Yet, I've recently been on a digital detox and I feel as if I've regained more perspective on my mobile-phone usage, and I believe that this won't be so much of an issue in the future.'

'Ah, a digital detox; that's a bit like what you did, wasn't it, Dominic? In Thailand,' says Ben.

'Mine was more of a spiritual retreat that cut out the trappings of modern life,' he says in his weird accent. Of course his would have to be better than mine.

'Now, our business is based on social-media profiles and seeing what they say about a person. We thought that a good marketing strategy would be to have adverts that made people think about what their social-media accounts say about themselves. So we thought it might be a fun idea to bring up one of your social-media accounts to see if you can analyse your public persona based on it, and see if you could tell us what different interactions say about your personality.'

Dominic's pursing his lips with expectation as Ben taps a few buttons on his iPad and its screen appears on one of the screens on the wall. He opens Twitter and slides it over for me to log in.

I take a deep breath, remembering the film crew sitting there. I don't want to give anyone the satisfaction of seeing me break down.

'I recently deleted my Twitter account after I started to receive obscene messages,' I say, holding Dominic's gaze. 'But, I think it's a very good idea. I'm sure you can tell a lot from someone's Twitter feed.'

I type in Dominic's and bring up his profile. It takes him a good second to realise what I'm doing.

'Now, hang on,' he says, but Ben holds his hand out to stop him.

'Relax, see where it goes,' he says.

Ben clearly wears the trousers in their business relationship, making me think they might not be equal partners.

'Now, most people would probably just look at their tweets on the front page, you know, what they have to say to the Twitter stream, but I always like to click on people's mentions and replies, I say clicking on it. Here, you get a better idea of what makes people tick. Ah, here we go, this is a tweet to a shampoo company that make caffeine shampoo to encourage hair growth. And another to an expensive moisturiser. So what I'd assume from that, is that the man in question is quite vain, perhaps not wanting to show signs of ageing.'

Ben does his honking laugh and I see the camera focus on Dominic. Now he's the one who looks as if he wants to lean over the table and strangle me.

'And take this tweet to KC Husker,' I say, starting to enjoy myself as all eyes in the room read the lewd message he sent the notorious glamour model about peaches. 'He clearly would go for a certain type of woman – clearly he values beauty over brains.'

'Then lastly, this company he's tweeted to, I'm pretty sure it's a haemorrhoid cream, but whatever it is, it shows that he's not got the greatest respect in the world for customer-service reps.'

'Oh my God, this is too funny, huh, Dominic?'

He looks like a volcano about to explode. 'This is such a gross violation. I mean, who I tweet should be private.'

'Well, it could be worse,' I say, trying to keep calm, 'it's not like this is being printed in a national newspaper.'

'I like her, Dom. She's funny. I think she'd be perfect for the role.'

'You can't be serious?' says Dominic. 'Hang on, then. I've got another question. Why did you leave your last employment?'

I take a deep breath and wonder whether enough's enough. I've sat here answering questions for a job I really don't want, all so that I don't humiliate myself on television. But what's to stop me from getting up and walking out silently? It might come across strangely on the telly if it made the edit, but it would probably be preferable to telling the truth.

'Well?' he says, as if he's just performed checkmate.

'I was fired,' I say, surprising myself with my honesty. 'I represented my company badly after a momentary lapse in concentration.'

'You sent a sexually explicit tweet from your work account when you meant to send it from your personal one,' says Dominic.

Ben looks between us as if he's connecting the dots.

'You're the woman behind hashtag priceless? Wow. Just wow,' he says. 'I should be grateful, as it's going to give us some great PR when the company launches. And imagine if you were on board too.'

His eyes light up and I think this is the only interview I'd ever have where they'd be this excited about my major Twitter fuck-up.

'So where do you see yourself in five years' time?' asks Ben, seemingly unfazed with the daggers shooting between Dominic and me.

I close my eyes for a second, as if to conjure up an image of myself sitting in my own office with staff scurrying around me at my every beck and call, only I can't. I can't see myself at a desk, and especially not one that's magenta.

I waffle through the question regardless, giving them the usual spiel of managing teams and wanting more responsibility, but I can't even convince myself that that's what I want for the future.

'Well, thank you for coming to see us,' says Ben, as he concludes the interview. 'We've been very impressed, haven't we, Dominic?'

'Have we?' he replies with a scowl.

'Yes, we have. You're our last candidate for this position, and I have to say that I think you'd be a perfect fit for the company.'

I smile. 'Thank you, Ben. While it would be an absolute pleasure to work with you, and I think the app is a great idea, I could never work with a misogynistic arsehole like Dominic.'

So much for keeping my decorum for the telly.

'I'll see myself out,' I say, shuffling past the camera crew.

Jaz gives me a smile on the way out, which makes me realise I've at least made someone's day. They'll have something exciting for their TV show at least.

I hold my head up high and walk out of the building. This has to be the weirdest interview I've ever had, but probably the only one to make me realise what I *don't* want to do with my life.

Chapter Thirty-Three

Time since last Internet usage: 3 days, 5 hours,
41 minutes and 32 seconds

'I cannot believe that happened. That kind of thing could only have happened to you,' says Erica, giggling as we make our way to the table.

I've just filled her in on the cringey interview with Dickhead Dominic as we made our way through the bar.

'I know, I can't believe it either,' I say sighing. 'Although it means I'm back to square one on the whole not-having-a-job front, and probably not able to get another job.'

'I'm sure something else will come up. Have you contacted any recruitment agencies?'

I shake my head. 'Not yet. I still don't know what I really want. When the MD asked me where I want to be in five years' time, I trotted out my stock answer of wanting to be in a senior marketing role with lots of responsibility, but I don't really know if that's the truth anymore.'

'Interesting,' says Erica, as we arrive at the booth where Tess and Amelie are waiting. We all hug and air-kiss hello.

'So, what are you going to do if you don't stay in marketing?'

'What's this? You're changing careers?' asks Tess, her pencil-thin eyebrow almost lodging itself in her hairline. 'Is this because of that tweet?'

I shake my head. 'I don't know about changing careers. It's more that I don't think I want to work in a big, full-on, corporate company. Maybe I'll look for a job in a smaller one. Something family run, or outside of London.'

All three of them collectively gasp as if I've suggested I'm about to go and live in Antarctica.

'There is life outside of London,' I say, laughing.

'Of course there is,' says Erica, waving her hand dismissively, 'but you don't actually mean it, do you?'

She looks horrified at the thought.

I'm about to reply when the waiter comes over and takes our order. By the time he goes, Tess is leaning over Amelie's phone.

'He's cute, but look at the bags under his eyes. He's either a workaholic or he goes out too much.'

'Good spot,' says Amelia and she swipes her finger left.

'So,' I say, trying to capture their attention again. 'What's been going on with you two since I've been gone?'

'I've been so busy,' says Tess.

'Doing what?' I say, looking her in the eyes, ready to take an interest.

'Um, you know. Work. Going out,' she says shrugging.

Her phone beeps and she picks it up and instantly starts replying.

'Amelie? Has anything happened to you?'

She doesn't even look up; she's still swiping mostly left with the occasional right. 'No, same old. I've got a date on Friday with a super-hot guy though. Want to see a photo?' She taps around on her phone and hands it over for me to see a man posing moodily.

'He looks, um, great.'

She looks pleased with herself and goes back to her Tinder swiping.

'Any more news on the flat sale today?' I ask Erica.

'We had a few more people book in for our open day on Saturday, so that's eighteen. I'm keeping my fingers crossed for some crazy bidding war, as I've seen the most amazing little house in Ealing and it's ever so slightly out of our budget. Hang on, I'll see if I can find it on Rightmove.'

The waiter deposits our cocktails, and I immediately reach up and take a sip.

'Cheers,' I say, raising my glass, only to find the other girls lost in taking photos of their cocktails. Tess is pushing hers round the table, seemingly trying to get the best light, whereas Amelie and Erica don't seem as bothered about the quality of image as long as they get one.

They're tapping away with their thumbs and I can already imagine what hashtags they're using: #NightOutWithTheGirls, #Cocktail, #SchoolNight. I want to add my own – #WhoGivesAFuck. It's a good few minutes before anyone peers over their screens.

'Oh, Daisy. I forgot you haven't got your phone. You must feel so lost. Here,' says Erica, slipping her arm around me. 'Grab your cocktail.'

She holds out her other arm to snap a selfie, and I can barely smile.

Satisfied that she looks OK, she taps away, posting it. I'm left alone to wonder when we stopped really talking to each other when we went out together.

Erica's just moved in with her boyfriend – she should be gushing about him, not browsing identical show-like-homes on the Internet. Tess should be regaling us with tales of being on the frontline of the classroom, with funny anecdotes of her teaching teenagers, like she always used to. And Amelie's spent a week on business in New York.

'So, Amelie, I haven't seen you since you got back from New York,' I say, hoping to get some proper conversation going.

'Oh, it was great. It was really busy with back-to-back meetings, but on the rare bits of time off, I managed to rack up a ginormous credit-card bill. The shopping was insane and the bars were awesome. Expensive, but awesome,' she says sighing, as if wishing herself back there.

'That sounds amazing,' I say, pleased that I've prised her away from her phone for all of a minute.

'It was, but tell us what it was like on the farm. Erica's been keeping us updated, but who were these men, wasn't one of them French?'

'Oh, yes. There's not a whole lot to tell. He was a nice guy, and I thought we had loads in common, but it turned out he'd been looking at my Instagram account to find out what I liked and pretending he liked them too.'

'What!' says Erica. 'What a creep.'

'Yeah, that's what I thought, but the more I've thought about it since, the more I think he was just young and a bit silly. I don't think he was malicious. He probably just thought it was an easy way to get into my pants.'

'And was it?' asks Tess with a cheeky grin on her face.

'Sadly, not.'

'Oh, shame. So there were no other men up there, then?'

'There was Jack . . .' I mutter.

'Did he get in your pants, then?'

'No,' I say, feeling sad that nothing really happened, and for the way we left things. All the suggestion and flirtation in the letters that seemed to bubble away, only to come to an abrupt halt with the argument on Friday night. I didn't even say goodbye to him when he dropped us off, I merely slammed the door and skulked away.

'Well, someone here did let someone into their pants at the weekend,' says Tess, pointing at herself. 'I hooked up with this hot guy at a house party. He's a friend of a friend, so obviously I've been stalking him on Facebook.'

She picks up her phone and scrolls around, before proudly showing us a photo of a blond man grinning wildly at the camera.

'He's cute,' says Amelie, stealing it to have a closer look.

'There are more photos,' says Tess, leaning over and swiping, and the two of them are lost to the phone, critiquing the guy's choice of Facebook photos and imagining what he'd be like.

'So are you going to see him again?' I say, interrupting them talking about his swimming hobby – which they got from one photo of him in a pool on holiday.

'I hope so. I mean, I checked out his profile on LinkedIn and he's a senior accountant at his firm. That's got to be good.'

Amelie's nodding.

'But you haven't actually spoken to him since you slept with him?'

'Well, no, but I know he likes to go drinking at the Florence. He checks in there most Friday nights.'

'You're as bad as Alexis,' I say, as I come to the realisation.

'Alexis?' she says, wrinkling her nose in confusion.

'The French guy who pretended he liked what I did on Instagram. It's the same thing. Manipulating a situation by social media.'

'It's not manipulating,' says Tess, folding her arms. 'I'm sure we'd meet up again anyway as we've got friends in common after all. I'm just helping things along.'

There's a tension in the air, which is only broken when the waiter comes along to see if we want any more drinks, and we almost bite his hand off.

By the time the cocktail reinforcements arrive, Tess and Amelie are back pouring over photos of cheeky blond men; I'm trying to fill Erica in on what went on between me and Jack, as, with Chris around over the weekend, we hadn't had a proper gossip. Trying being the operative word, as every minute or so her phone pings with a message from Chris and she taps a quick reply.

'I am listening,' she says, after I groan at the latest interruption. 'So you talked through letters.'

'Yeah, you know, nothing deep. Just chatty ones. And they had this common theme about *The Price is Right* – remember that TV show in the early nineties? It started because I couldn't remember who presented it, and then he told me there was a link between it and John Major and I couldn't guess what it was.'

Erica looks at me with a look that suggests I've come from Mars. 'Why didn't you google it?'

'Um, hello, digital detox? My phone was down a well.'

'Ah,' she says, picking up her hers and tapping away. 'Here we go. There have been four presenters: Leslie Crowther, Bob Warman, Bruce Forsyth and Joe Pasquale. And the link between John Major – ah-ha, his son was married to Emma Noble, who was one of the models. So what else did your letters talk about?'

My mouth drops open. I didn't want to know the truth about *The Price is Right*, as not knowing somehow preserved the fun of the letters. Imagine if I had just been able to google it, then all that fun and banter wouldn't have existed.

'Oh my God,' says Erica, as her phone beeped for the umpteenth time. 'Look at the photo Helen's just posted on her Instagram. Check out that food.'

Instantly, Tess and Amelie pick up their phones to check it themselves, rather than look at Erica's phone. As the three of them start picking their way through Helen's feed and her unfolding wedding in Vegas, it starts to hit me how much the digital detox affected me. I start to analyse the way they're inter- acting; they might be listening to whoever's talking, but not one of them is looking at each other or really paying attention. They're too busy scrolling on their phones, only half present.

I glance up to my right and there's a cute guy looking over at our table. He seems to be trying to catch Tess's eye. He's way cuter than the pictures of the guy who's on her phone and he's right here. Only she's going to miss him, as she's barely looked around since we've been here.

I feel as if I'm having an out-of-body experience. Now that I don't have my phone to hide behind, I can see everything going on around me with new eyes. I can't believe that if it weren't for my sister's crazy idea of a digital detox I would be sitting here scrolling away too instead of talking and listening to what my friends have to say.

It's ridiculous. We're four intelligent women with interesting lives, and we're wasting our time on looking at fake versions of life on a tiny screen.

If only they could see how much of their lives they're missing. If only I could take them up to Cumbria – they're definitely prime candidates for a digital detox.

In fact, they're not the only ones. I glance around and see that most people have their phones on the table in front of them, or in their hands. There are those who seem to be taking endless amounts of selfies, others who are sitting together on tables not speaking, each tapping away.

'Oh my God,' I say, clapping my hand over my mouth. 'That's it.'

'What's it?' mutters Erica.

'I've got to go,' I say getting up. 'I'm going to head back to your flat. I've got something I need to work on. I have an idea for a new job.'

Chapter Thirty-Four

Time since last Internet usage: I don't know, and I don't really care . . .

I wish I'd had my epiphany a few days ago while I was in still Cumbria, so that I wouldn't have had to buy two extortionate train fares. My dwindling savings took a further hit of eighty pounds this morning buying a ticket back up north.

It feels so strange to be back here at Manchester Piccadilly, almost four weeks on from when I first arrived. Last time, I was a crumbling shell of a person, and now I'm a woman on a mission.

I spot Rupert's shiny silver Audi in the pick-up point and he gives me a wave.

I weave my way through the taxi rank and pedestrians to get to him.

'Hi, thanks for coming to get me,' I say, as I collapse into the passenger seat.

'I'm not sure I entirely had a choice. When you use the words "order" and "demand", it's not really asking.'

'Yeah, sorry about that, but I thought you wouldn't take the afternoon off if I asked politely.'

'No, I probably wouldn't have. Luckily for you, the meeting I had scheduled was cancelled, and I've been working a lot of overtime of late.'

'Well, I'm grateful, anyway.'

'So I take it we're heading to Cumbria?' he says.

'That's right.'

He sighs. 'You're just like your sister – a meddler.'

'Family trait,' I say smiling.

Rupert pulls away into the traffic, and I try to relax but I can't. Getting Rupert to take time off work and drive me there is the easy part of the plan; the hard bit is what's to come.

We make it to Lullamby two hours later, and, thanks to the torrential downpour, there's no one lining the route to the village as we drive through. We soon turn off down the mud track and I can't help but smile at the little mailboxes as we drive by.

'Blimey, it's a bit different driving in this,' I say as I grab on to the handle above the window.

'Yeah, this is exactly what I was talking to Rosie about. This track will need to be paved or smoothed out for guests. It's this kind of stuff she didn't take into consideration when she bought this place.'

I wish I hadn't opened my mouth. I'm trying to bring the two of them back together, not drive them further apart.

We pull into the courtyard and park next to the Land Rover. I get out of the car and notice that Rupert's still clutching the steering wheel.

'Come on,' I say leaning in, my hand resting on my open door. 'I told you that I have something to talk to you and Rosie about.'

Reluctantly, he gets out and I slam my door shut, before walking towards the cottage. I go to barge it open, only to realise it's been replaced, and it glides open with a swishing noise that I notice comes from little brushes underneath to stop the draughts.

I walk into the kitchen, and I'm reassured to see that it's still a complete shambles of broken cupboards and piles of building materials. I've only been gone three days, I couldn't have handled too much change. I hear the radio coming from the lounge and I walk over and poke my head in.

'Hey, Sis.'

She looks up and almost drops her paint roller in surprise. She puts it back on the tray and runs towards me.

'Daisy,' she says, immediately rushing forward, and she's about to give me a big hug before she stops herself. 'I don't want to get you covered in paint.'

I look at her paint-splattered tracksuit and the white flecks all over her face, and I settle with patting her on the shoulder instead.

'I can't believe you came back. I feel so awful about what happened between us. I'm so sorry for tricking you into coming here, hiding that phone and ruining your iPhone,' she says quickly.

I put my hands up to make her stop.

'It's OK, really. In the end, you did me a favour. I couldn't see it while I was here, but I think the digital detox was the best thing that could have happened to me.'

'It was?' she says looking confused. 'I can't believe you're really back. I've missed you so much. So tell me about your interview. What do the company do?'

'You're not going to believe me about the interview, it's a bit of a long story.'

'Something tells me that we need to put the kettle on. How did you get here, by the way?' she asks as she barges past me into the kitchen, 'Did you walk or . . . ?'

She stops dead and I almost bump into her.

There's no need for her to finish her question as she can see exactly how I arrived.

'Ru,' she says quietly. 'You're here.'

'Yep,' he says, putting his hands into his pockets and staying firmly on the doormat.

'I made him come,' I say, causing Rosie's face to fall with disappointment. I guess she'd hoped he'd come back on his own accord to sort things out.

'I asked him to come as I wanted him to hear my idea,' I say.

'Your idea?' she says wrinkling her forehead.

'Yep.'

I had secretly hoped that Rupert and Rosie would have swept each other up in their arms upon seeing each other, leaving me time to work up to my big announcement, but both of them are rooted to their spots on opposite sides of the room.

I had been quite confident when I pitched the idea to Erica over breakfast this morning, but with both of them standing with their arms folded, they are not coming across as being very receptive.

I take a deep breath and hope for the best. 'I know there's obviously been a bit of controversy surrounding the purchase of the property,' I say, trying to downplay it, 'but despite how it happened, I think you both realise that it has an awful lot of potential. I understand, Rupert, that you have concerns about the amount of work involved, and maybe you're right, what with trying to do the barn and everything.'

Rosie shoots me a look as if I'm being disloyal.

'Hear me out,' I say, holding my hands up to try to stop her interrupting. 'Rosie, you told me that when you'd originally bought the place you wanted the cottage as a house for you and Rupert, and the barn to be let out.'

'It's not going to happen,' says Rupert, 'I'm not ready to move this far out, not at the moment.'

'I realise that and I think that Rosie does too, which is why she's started to convert the cottage to be a holiday let. Now, we all know that there are scores of holiday cottages in the area, and what this place needs is a USP, and I think the answer is to run retreats.'

'Retreats,' says Rupert, 'what, like corporate retreats? I'm sure that this area is crawling with hotels and spas that offer just that.'

'Ah, but I thought we could offer a digital detox retreat. I mean those three weeks here have changed me beyond recognition. I couldn't believe how different I was when I went back to my old life in London. It's made me stop and realise what a hold technology had had on me. Just those few weeks here with no phone, no computer, no technology, did wonders for me. It's as if this place was built for it; you know as well as I do how hard it is to get a phone signal around here, and it's impossible to get 3G.'

I risk glancing up to look at Rosie's and Rupert's faces. Rosie's eyes have lit up and a smile has crept over her face, but Rupert's looks as if he's yet to be convinced.

'I've looked it up online,' I say, coughing at the irony, 'and there appears to be a growing market for these types of retreats. It's huge in America but there's barely any in the UK at the moment. I figured that we could use the farmhouse as the accommodation. You were going to put en suites in most of the rooms anyway. You could then do the first fix to the barn. Make it watertight and pigeon proof, with windows and doors, and then convert a small part of it at first to be used as a space for different activities. I was thinking you could get Trish in to do yoga, and maybe talk to that man in the village who does pottery to see if he'd run some workshops. I also thought Jack might be able to come along and do some sessions with his psychologist's hat on.'

'His what?' says Rosie. 'He's a psychologist?'

'Oh yeah, he is,' I say, realising that with all the drama happening on Friday night she didn't hear that nugget of information. 'And I reckon that talking on this subject would be right up his street.'

'Something like that would take an awful lot of management, someone to co-ordinate the sessions. But I don't know if our marriage would survive with you being up here, I've hated being without you for these last few weeks,' Rupert said looking at Rosie.

'You have?' she says, taken a back.

The adrenaline is pumping round my veins and I was so close to the big reveal in my idea, but I don't want to interrupt the reconciliation.

'I have. I've had a lot of time to think since the weekend, and I'm mad as hell that you are still on the pill, but I started to think about what you said on Friday. I was too cross then to fully listen and understand, but the more I've been thinking about it, the more I realise that you're right. If I carry on at work in the same way, you'll be parenting like a single parent and I'll be lucky if I see the kids. Now, I'm not saying that I'm going to give up my job, but I have spoken to my boss to see if I'd be able to do more home-working, and he was open to the idea. I also floated the idea of working four days a week and we decided that we'd review that if and when the time came.'

I'm desperately trying to make myself invisible, and I slowly edge further across the kitchen, out of their way. I sneak a look at Rosie, who's being unusually quiet; she looks as if she's on the verge of tears.

'I also understand that you want to move out of the city, and I'm all for that, but right now I can't be too far away because I still need to commute to work. But, I did think that if you wanted to, we could sell the penthouse and look for somewhere in the Peak District. Not such a grand scale as this, and definitely not a pro-ject,' he stresses, 'but something big enough for us, and our kids.'

I watch a tear escape Rosie's eye and she nods as the tears run down her face.

'I'm so sorry for lying, I just didn't know what to do,' she says, whimpering, as Rupert finally gets off the doormat and goes over and wraps his arms round her.

'Buying a wreck of a farm was pretty extreme. You could just have talked to me, I'm not a monster.'

'I know, I know. It's just that I know how much you love your job; I never thought that you'd change it – for me, or for our family. I thought it would be easier if I made a grand gesture, that you might accept it a lot more easily.'

He nods. 'I just about understood why you did it, even if it was a crazy idea.'

'But, it's not. Not with Daisy's plan,' she says, pulling away from the hug and pointing over at me.

Rupert looks up as if he almost forgot I was here, and I feel my cheeks flush red with embarrassment of having witnessed such a personal reconciliation.

'I still don't understand how it's going to be any better for us,' says Rupert.

'Don't you see? Daisy's going to run it for us,' she says, staring at me for confirmation.

'If you'll let me. I'd essentially live here, do all the marketing and run the courses. I'm guessing it will be a bit of a slow start, so I'll probably pick up some freelance marketing work to tide me over.'

'That's brilliant. You'd be perfect.' The smile on Rosie's face is infectious and I'm grinning too.

'So you'll let me do it?' I ask.

'Of course, isn't it a wonderful idea?' says Rosie to Rupert.

'It's pretty good,' he says, 'but I'd like to see a proper business plan drawn up.'

'Absolutely,' I say nodding, as if I know what would go in one. 'I've got loads of ideas. Especially for generating PR. I'm thinking that the story of the tweet that got me fired would make a great backstory to founding a digital detox company.'

'You're willing to be open about it?' gasps Rosie.

'It's already out there, what with the *Mail Online* article I found online, plus the coverage Dominic is getting about his company. Long story,' I say, seeing the confused looks on their faces. 'It least this way I'd be able to get my side of the story out and get some benefit from it, rather than Dominic.'

'It sounds like you've got it all planned out,' says Rupert, smiling. 'I'm sure you're going to make a great success of it. So are you going to show me the progress you've made since my last visit?'

'Of course,' says Rosie, guiding him into the living room, 'you start here and I'll be in in a sec.'

She turns back to me and squeals as she goes to fling her arms around me, stopping short when she realises she's covered in paint. 'Thank you,' she whispers as she gives me a delicate hug, trying not to get too close. 'For saving me and my marriage.'

'It's me that should be thanking you; you've given me a new life.'

'I can't believe that it's taken me all these years to realise how good a friend my sister is,' she says.

'Ditto. Now, you'd better get back to your tour-guide role. I want you to impress one of the investors.'

Rosie gives my hand a squeeze, and she looks as if she's about to start crying again, which is about to set me off.

'Aren't you going to help me?' she asks.

'I think you've got it under control. I'm going to see if Jack's on board.'

'Oh, right,' she says doing an exaggerated wink, before she practically skips over to Rupert. I watch as she takes his hand and he leans over and snuggles her head with his nose before kissing the top of her earlobe. My heart melts with happiness. This time, I'm not bitter that she's got her happy ever after, as I know how much she deserves it.

I don't think they hear me as I leave, and I suspect that when I return Rupert's clean jeans and jumper will be marked with paint splodges, but with the look in their eyes, I don't think either of them will care.

Thankfully, the rain has stopped, although it's left a quagmire in its wake. I stop off at Rosie's Land Rover, and cupping my hands to look through the window, I see a pair of wellies in the boot. I figure she won't mind if I borrow them, and I set off to Jack's house.

The little cottage comes into view and I immediately hear Buster the dog barking furiously. I wonder if I've got time to run away before he comes, but I take a deep breath and remember to be brave. It's only when I knock and no one answers that I look around and realise that the driveway's empty.

Bugger.

I'd hoped I wouldn't have to go back to Upper Gables so soon. Rosie and Rupert have a lot of making up to do. It was bad enough being caught up in their reconciliation with words, I don't want to be caught up in the middle of anything else.

I slip the handbag off my shoulder and I find a stray receipt and a pen.

Dear Jack,

I am an idiot. I do listen too much to other people. I do rely on the Internet when really I should learn to find out about people in real life. I need to trust my instincts not my Facebook.

This digital detox was the best thing that ever could have happened to me. Not only because I've learnt to be free of my phone, which was controlling my life and stopping me from living it properly, but also because it meant I got to meet you.

I wanted to tell you in person what I've realised, and I wanted to tell you that I'm staying. I'm not going back to London and Rosie's going to let me run digital detox retreats at Upper Gables. With a little help with some people in the village running workshops, and – ahem – you, if you'll do them too. I think it could be a great little business.

Anyway, I'm sort of in limbo as I can't go home because I'm guessing Rosie and Rupert are 'making up' after their big fight, so I'm at a loose end. I thought I'd go up to that hill where I first met you. Last time I was far too distracted looking for a mobile signal to notice the views, which I've been told are incredible. I'm sure I'll not need a knight in shining armour this time, but if you fancy a stroll, I'll be up there for a bit.

Love

Daisy xxx

I start to debate if three kisses is a bit much, but then I get a grip of myself. That's probably the least of my worries, bearing in mind that I practically confessed my undying love for him.

I wedge it into the door handle so that he sees it when he gets home and I start off on my walk, telling myself that he'll catch up any minute as he wouldn't have left Buster at home if he was going far.

I start walking through the muddy field where I fell over all those weeks ago. Good job I've got my wellies on, or else I'd be slipping all over the place. Only, what they make up for in grip, they lack in flexibility, and I have to yank them out as my feet get well and truly stuck. Once free, I attempt to jump over to a grassy patch to the right, only my left boot gets stuck again and instead of landing on the grass, I land in a patch of mud. I desperately try to keep myself upright, as I don't want to put my welly-less foot down. I place my socked foot onto my leg flamingo style and attempt to keep my balance. I'm wobbling about, desperately trying not to fall over headfirst.

I'm starting to ache in flamingo pose, and I'm just about to brave putting my welly-less foot in the mud, when Buster leaps up at me. I windmill my arms, trying my best not to fall, but he keeps jumping up, covering me in muddy paw prints and licks.

'Buster, Buster get down,' I hear Jack yell, but it's too late. Buster gives me one last jump before he goes off in search of his owner, and it's enough to send me tumbling into the mud, bum first.

Jack's laughter carries on the wind, and I can't help but join in.

'Need a hand?' he asks as he gets closer.

'I'm fine here,' I say, looking up at him, my breath catching in my mouth as he's shaved off his beard, and let's just say he's looks hot.

'Right you are. And I guess you were just standing around out here on one leg doing . . .?'

'Yoga. Clearly.'

'Clearly. So what's this? Sitting-down pig pose?'

'Oi,' I say, batting at his legs. 'Who are you calling a pig?'

'Sorry, er, that came out wrong. Here.'

He reaches over and retrieves my lost welly. Not that it matters. I'm caked in mud from the waist down now. He slips it on anyway, in such a gentle way, as if he were Prince Charming slipping on my glass slipper, but then he pulls me up to standing with such a force that my body crashes into him.

'About the other night.'

I shake my head. 'We don't have to –'

'Yes, we do. Or at least, *I* do. I'm sorry for what I said. You were right; I shouldn't have judged you by your Twitter feed. It's just, I started to . . . you know . . .'

He tries to brush a bit of mud off my leg as if to take my attention away from what he's trying to say.

'Actually, I don't know,' I say, finding it amusing how his cheeks are flushed and he can't look me in the eye. 'For a psychologist you're not very good at expressing your own emotions.'

The poor guy must be dying inside, and I'm going to rescue him any second.

'I'm used to listening to other people baring their souls, not the other way round.' He takes a deep breath before exhaling loudly. 'I like you, OK? And then when I saw the article and that postcard about a fling, and I didn't want to be just another holiday romance.'

I think back to what Rodney said about the tourist who broke his heart and I take hold of his hand.

'I want it to be more than that too,' I say. 'And I'm not going anywhere.'

Finally, he looks up at me, and as he looks into my eyes my stomach flips.

And then he kisses me.

It's one of those kisses that makes you weak at the knees, and I'm grateful that the wellies are stuck in the mud again as they're stopping me from collapsing. Although, Jack's doing his best to help with that too; his hand is creeping down my back and grabbing my bum.

'Yuck,' he says, pulling away and looking at his hand, which is now muddy. 'I think it's time we got you home and changed.'

'I might need a hand. Fancy carrying me?' I say, imagining him scooping me up into his arms and carrying me like a true damsel in distress.

'Um, it's a pretty long way to carry you, unless you want a fireman's lift or a piggyback?'

'A piggyback?' I say in disbelief. It's not really worthy of a Hollywood swoon.

'Or you could walk . . .'

I practically leap on his back.

'It looks like I've got you all muddy,' I say, as I wrap my legs around his waist and cling onto his shoulders.

'It does indeed.'

'We'll have to get *you* out of your clothes too . . .' I purr into his ear.

Jack bolts like an untamed horse and practically trots across the field, and I let out a scream.

'You're going to drop me,' I say, laughing uncontrollably as he jumps over tufts of grass and squelches through the mud.

I can't remember a time when I laughed like this or felt happier. And for the first time in a very long time, I feel no desire to share what's going on with anyone. I might be feeling #blessed and #excited, and slightly #NervousThatIHaven'tShavedMyL egs, but I don't need anyone to know or validate it. I know how happy I am, and that's all that matters.

ACKNOWLEDGEMENTS

Blimey, another book written! As always, it's a huge team effort, and I'm so grateful for everyone's help. From readers tweeting me with lovely praise that spurs me on, to my friends and family who act as my loyal fan club trying to peddle my book to anyone that will listen. There are almost too many people to thank, but a few that deserve a special mention.

Thank you firstly to Christie and Simon, for sharing their beautiful part of the world with me (and my readers). Your local knowledge and photos have been super helpful. I only wish we'd all been in better health during the research - but we will be back and we'll make up for it, PIGO!

Thank you to my long suffering agent Hannah, and the rest of the team at Hardman and Swainson, for everything you do behind the scenes. The team at Bonnier Zaffre - Sophie, Bec and (much missed) Joel - as always your editing notes are spot on and my books are all the better for your collective input. Thank you to Alex Allden for my beautiful cover. Also, to my German editor Julia at Droemer - I really do hope we can meet one day in person to talk books, travel and babies.

To my wonderful family and friends: thanks for babysitting, cheerleading and your general enthusiasm and interest in my books. Especially Mum, Jane, Heather and Harold, Laura, Hannah, Kaf, Debs and Julie. Also, to old school and college friends, work colleagues, and friends of friends that read my books - I'm always humbled how many of you support me. And, not forgetting the other Agent Fergie authors, I am so lucky to be part of such a supportive bunch of writers.

A mahousive thank you to all the book bloggers and reviewers who not only take the time to read my book but write lovely reviews too. Thanks especially to Victoria (Victoria Loves Books), Ananda, Becky Gulc, Chloe Spooner, Agi, Simona Elena, Kaisha, Isabelle Broom, Amy Lysette, Natasha Harding, Natasha (The Books Geek wears Pajamas), Aimee and Rachel Gilby.

I definitely couldn't have written this book without my husband feeding me, tidying the house and doing daddy daycare – thank you, Steve for everything you do for us! To Rex the dog, for letting me take him for a walk to iron out those plot holes, and to Evan and Jess for taking those all important strategic naps.

Lastly, thank you to you for reading my book! Do come say hello on Twitter – @annabell_writes, I do love to hear from readers, and do sign up to my reader's club for news and exclusive content.

Read on for a letter from Anna Bell, and an exciting chapter from her hilarious romantic comedy
THE GOOD GIRLFRIEND'S GUIDE
TO GETTING EVEN ...

Dear Reader,

Thank you *so* much for choosing to read IT STARTED WITH A TWEET! I do hope you enjoyed it. It was a lot of fun to write – even if it has made me paranoid that I use my phone too much!

When my family and I moved to rural France a few years ago, I felt a lot like Daisy – *totally* lost without the internet. I too climbed up hills to get that little bit of mobile internet signal. I also used to drive a forty-minute round trip just to go to McDonalds to have a coffee and use their WiFi! When our fixed line was installed a few weeks later, I actually wept at being back in touch with the real world.

I'd love to say that I'm above digital addiction, but scrolling through Twitter and watching Instagram stories are my guilty pleasures! I'm planning to do a digital detox with my little kids – I think it'll be as good for them as it will be for me. I'm a little nervous about how we'll cope with no screens – no Peppa Pig for those 6 a.m. wake-ups! – but I'm actually *really* excited about it. It'll be an adventure . . . famous last words, I'm sure!

At the moment, I'm working on my next novel called THE BACK UP PLAN. It's about two friends who once had one of those '*if we're not married by the time we're 30. . .*' pacts. After a holiday romance, they impulsively decide to put the pact into action. They discover they have to wait twenty-eight days before they can legally wed, but as they begin to get to know each other again, doubt starts to creep in. It's a real will-they-won't-they novel, with a lot of humour and a *lot* of soul searching going on.

If you can't wait for the next book, why not read one of my earlier novels, THE BUCKET LIST TO MEND A BROKEN HEART or THE GOOD GIRLFRIEND'S GUIDE TO GETTING EVEN. Both are – in my opinion! – funny and heartwarming stories.

If you'd like to hear more about my next book, or any future books beyond that, you can visit **www.bit.ly/AnnaBellClub** where you can join the Anna Bell Reader's Club. It only takes a few moments to sign up and there are no catches or costs. Your data will be kept totally private and confidential, and will never be passed on to a third party. I won't spam you with loads of emails, but will get in touch now and again with book news, and you can unsubscribe any time you want.

Also, do stop by and say hello on Twitter (**@annabell_writes**) or find me on Facebook – it's so lovely to hear from readers! I'd also be absolutely thrilled if you'd take the time to review my books too – on Amazon, Goodreads, on your blog or any other e-store. What better way to tell us what you thought of the book!

Thanks once again for reading IT STARTED WITH A TWEET, and I do hope you enjoy reading more of my books in the future!

Best wishes,

Anna

The Good Girlfriend's Guide to Getting Even

When Lexi's sport-mad boyfriend Will skips her friend's wedding
to watch football – after pretending to have food poisoning – it
might just be the final whistle for their relationship.

But fed up of just getting mad, Lexi decides to even the
score. And, when a couple of lost tickets and an 'accidentally'
broken television lead to them spending extra time together,
she's delighted to realise that revenge might be the best thing
that's happened to their relationship.

And if her clever acts of sabotage prove to be a popular
subject for her blog, what harm can that do? It's not as
if he'll ever find out . . .

AVAILABLE NOW IN EBOOK AND PAPERBACK

Read on for an exciting extract . . .

1

'*Ouch!*' I shout as my elbow whacks into the cubicle wall for the zillionth time, and I start muttering swear words like I'm Gordon Ramsay. Hiding in a cubicle in my work toilets and squeezing myself into a tight dress requires the acrobatic skills of a ninja. There seems to be an obstacle at every turn. One wrong hop when I'm putting my tights on and I'll be plunging my foot into somewhere only a bath in Dettol would fix, but hop too far the other way and I risk poking an eye out on the door hook.

It's a tricky minefield, and something I wouldn't be doing if this wasn't a true emergency, but my boyfriend Will and I are meeting my parents for dinner and I'm running late. I'd intended to nip to the gym en route to dinner to have a proper shower and change, but I've been swamped at work and left it too late.

I tried to tell my parents that a six o'clock dinner reservation midweek was a bad idea, but it's my dad's birthday and it was at his insistence. Knowing him, and his frugal ways, there will be some special offer for eating early.

I finally wrestle the zip up my back and make a break for freedom out of the cubicle to pop some make-up on, only to find a woman standing at the sink washing her hands. No need for the extra blusher I'm about to apply; my cheeks automatically pink up in embarrassment at my swearing.

'Going somewhere nice, Lexi?' she asks, clearly trying not to laugh. She's one of the serious women who works in finance and I can never remember her name. She's probably my mum's age, all twin-set and pearls, and I'm guessing she's never had to do a quick change in the toilet. It's practically an impossible task worthy of *The Cube*.

'I'm off to dinner at Le Bistro.'

'Nice. Special occasion?'

'My dad's birthday.'

'Well, have a nice time,' she says, looking at me again and hiding what looks like a smirk.

I quickly glance down at myself, and can't see what she's smirking at. I think I've scrubbed up pretty well. I breathe a sigh of relief that I'm alone once more, and I focus on my face, slapping on my foundation defiantly.

I've discovered on many occasions that the fluorescent lighting in the toilets is not conducive to make-up application. When they designed the 1960s-style council building, with its minimal windows and abundance of strip lighting, they hadn't thought what that would mean for any girl trying to get ready in the windowless toilets. The lights are so bright it's like being on the telly, and it's very easy to overcompensate, which means that when you go back out into the real world, your office colleagues either mistake you for some type of hooker, or you look like your five-year-old niece applied your blusher.

Make-up done, I give myself a quick look in the mirror. I'm wearing a tight-fitting dress with a floaty lace overlay. I bought it in the sale last year and have been dying to find a reason to wear it ever since. I've perhaps put on a couple of pounds since I bought it, and while it might be a little snug, I think it still looks pretty good – no matter what the finance lady thinks.

At least my mum will be impressed that I'm wearing an actual dress and tights. If I'd turned up in what I wore to work this morning (frumpy black palazzo pants and a baggy, misshapen grey cardie), she probably would have sent me back home to change. The last time she met me from work she looked at my outfit and told me that it was no wonder I was thirty-one and unmarried if that's how I dressed.

I put a final coat of lippy on and rush out of the toilets. The only thing worse than having a dressing-down from my mum about my clothes, is her telling me off for being late.

'Oops, sorry,' I say as I turn a corner and bash straight into someone.

'Woah, there,' says Mike, a colleague who I sit next to. 'Where's the fire?'

I'm tempted to stop and talk to him as he's with the fit guy from the top, better known as the guy that works in the executives' department at the top our building. He's all pin-striped suit and perfect hair, and every time I see him he has a strange effect on me.

I've never actually been this close to him, and I try to force myself to keep moving before I fall under the spell of his hypnotic eyes.

'Sorry, Mike. I'm off to dinner at Le Bistro,' I say, fluttering my eyelids at the fit guy from the top while trying to show him how sophisticated I am – like I'm the type of girl who goes to posh restaurants all the time.

'Uh, before you go . . .' he calls.

'Can't stop, I'm running really late.'

I give Mike a quick wave over my shoulder and hot step it out of the council offices. I feel a bit rude not stopping to hear what he's got to say, but I'm sure it was just a question about the audit we're about to have. We're all desperately trying to get all our ducks in a row before an inspector comes in to see what we do as a department, but it's already five past six and if I don't make it to the restaurant soon, not only will my mum tell me off, but she'll be left unchaperoned with Will. Any time she's alone with him she brings up the topic of him proposing.

I dump my work clothes in my car as I pass, before doing a quick jog, or rather totter in these heels, to the restaurant, which is just off the main high street.

I spot my family straight away as I walk past the window – it's hard not to when they're the only people in the restaurant. Will looks relieved as I race through the door and over to the table.

'I'm so sorry I'm late. Work is nuts at the moment,' I say, leaning over to give my dad a quick peck on the cheek and passing him his present. 'Happy Birthday.'

'Thanks, Lexi,' he says, smiling up at me.

I bend down to kiss my mother, too, and as she brushes my cheek with her lips she stops.

'What on earth do you look like?'

'It's a dress,' I say, standing up straight and brushing it down. 'I thought you'd be pleased that I made an effort to wear something that shows off my figure.'

'It might have been nice if perhaps not quite so much of you was on display.'

I'm about to open my mouth to reply that this is the fashion, and lace is in, when Will gets up and stands behind me. Maybe now, after years of nodding along whenever my mother snipes at me, he's decided to stand up for me and defend my wardrobe choice.

'Lex, your skirt's tucked into your tights at the back,' he whispers.

I close my eyes and wish that I could disappear. When I open them a second later and see my mother still staring at me with pursed lips and a raised eyebrow, I realise that it hasn't worked, so instead I try as best I can to pull the dress out from my tights as discreetly as possible. God love my boyfriend for trying to protect what little modesty I had left.

Needless to say my dress must have been in my tights since I came out of the cubicle. Thinking about it, I bet that was what Mike was going to tell me. He's a good egg and I'm sure he wouldn't have let me walk out like that. And while I'm not too embarrassed that he noticed – I'm guessing he saw worse at last year's Christmas party when I drunkenly fell over and flashed our entire department – I am mortified that the fit guy from the top saw. Not to mention everyone on the high street as I walked here. I wonder if the finance lady saw my mistake as well and didn't say anything – that's almost against the code of sisterhood.

She's off my Christmas card list – well, she would be if I could ever remember her name. Thinking about it, maybe that's why she doesn't like me.

I clear my throat and move away from Will to sit down at the table. I place my napkin over my knees and try to act like I've got some dignity.

My parents go back to looking at their menus. 'You look lovely in the dress,' says Will, using his menu as a shield.

'Thanks. It's always a bit awkward doing the quick change in the loo.'

'Ah, well. At least it was empty in here.'

'Too bad the high street wasn't when I was on my way. Do you know, I even had a wolf whistle! I haven't been whistled at for years – I was well chuffed.'

'I'd whistle at you,' he says, winking.

I smile and I'm about to say something cheeky back when my mum coughs. I'd almost forgotten my parents were here.

Will and I lower our menus like naughty schoolchildren that have just been caught passing notes at the back of class.

'So, I bumped into Vanessa's mum yesterday in Sainsbury's. She's all excited about the big day.'

I feel my muscles starting to tense in preparation. It's as if I'm putting up a force field around myself.

'I'm sure she is,' I say, as if it's no big deal.

One of my childhood best friends, Vanessa, is getting married a week on Saturday. While I'm very excited that she's tying the knot, my mother seems to have taken it as a personal insult that she's dared to get married before me.

'I hadn't realised that they'd only been together for *four* years,' she says in a tone as if they'd only met last month.

'That set menu looks good,' I say, pointing at the handwritten chalk board mounted on the walls. 'I adore monkfish.'

My mother chooses to ignore me, and ploughs on like a steam roller.

'Her mum was saying that Vanessa's dress is from that little bridal boutique off Kimberly Lane.'

'Um, yes, I think it is,' I say, trying not fuel the conversation.

'I see it when I'm on the way to Zumba. It looks magical. I always walk past it and hope that one day I'll be going in there,' she says longingly.

I sense Will getting fidgety next to me. If I'm uncomfortable with this topic of conversation, Mr Commitmentphobe is bound to be. You see, Will and I have been together for seven years and, despite us living together, he's yet to produce a small, sparkly ring. Not that I really care *that* much. In my mind, our joint mortgage is probably more binding and difficult to break than a marriage certificate, but it's a different story for my mum. It's not that she objects to us living in sin or anything. As far as I can tell, she needs me to get married so that she has something to write about in her Christmas letter. Last year, she apparently emailed everyone to tell them she was doing a charity donation in lieu of cards, which I think was because she was too embarrassed to write for yet another year that I was neither engaged nor married.

Sure enough, Will's now looking at his watch as if he wants to get home as quickly as possible and away from my interfering mother.

Luckily for both Will and me, the waitress comes over and takes our order. We've all decided to go for a set menu that includes main course and dessert, so at least we've shaved off twenty minutes by not having starters.

'So have you had a nice birthday, Dad?' I ask, well and truly shutting down the Vanessa conversation.

'I have thanks, love. I got an excellent book called *Match of My Life*.'

'Oh, great. From Mum?'

'No, he bought it for himself. I bought him a jumper from M&S.'

Dad gives me a weak smile. Thirty-five years of marriage and every year he gets an M&S jumper for his birthday.

'I've read that one,' says Will. 'It's really good. Have you seen the *Got Not Got* Southampton book? I was reading it thinking you'd like it.'

'Yes, I got that for Christmas. Great book. So many memories.'

I roll my eyes as Will and my dad get lost talking about different football books. The fact that they're both Southampton fans is the only thing they have in common, and therefore the only thing they ever talk to each other about. I always thought it would be nice to have a boyfriend that got on well with my dad, but when they spend hours discussing the percentages of possession in the last game, I realise that I should have been careful what I wished for.

My father thinks Will's the bee's knees, unlike my mother, who disapproves of him, largely for not yet allowing her to become mother of the bride. Of course, my father's impression is based solely on the fact that Will has a Southampton Football Club season ticket. He could be the world's worst boyfriend, but as long as he went dutifully to every home game, then he'd still be OK. Luckily for me, he's actually a pretty good boyfriend, but still . . .

I try and tune out their conversation about the league table, and that of my mother, who's started telling me about her next-door-but-one neighbour whose daughter just had a baby. I'm sure you can imagine how she feels about grandchildren. Instead I use my time to daydream about the novel I'm writing.

We make it through to dessert without me tipping wine over my mum's head, much to my amazement. She was actually quite restrained, having got distracted by telling me all about the scandal of the stolen fridge magnets at her work (it was as riveting as it sounds). My dad and Will are sitting in silence since exhausting their talk about football somewhere between the main course and dessert. All in all, we're on the homeward straight, and bar a cup of coffee we'll be off back home – and it's only 7.30. Gotta love an early dinner.

As another waitress sets down our coffee I notice that Will's hands are shaking as he drops two sugar-lumps into his cup before stirring vigorously. He clatters the spoon so noisily against the china cup that even my dad looks over at him to see if everything's OK.

I know that dinner with my mother would put anyone on edge, but I'm sure he's jumpier than usual.

'Have you got your outfit sorted for the wedding next week, then?' asks my mother.

What was I saying about being on the homeward straight?

I burn my tongue as I try to finish my coffee in a bid to get away more quickly.

'Yes, all sorted. I'll take lots of photos and show you next time I see you.'

Can't wait for that meet-up. I must remember to leave Will at home.

'Ah, perfect. It'll be nice to have some copies of photos of you at a wedding, even if it isn't your own.'

I can feel Will's leg jiggling under the table and I'm just hoping that his coffee is decaf as he's clearly already got way too much nervous energy to add caffeine into the mix.

'Well, thanks for a lovely dinner,' I say, placing my cup down and looking expectantly at my dad for him to summon the bill.

'Yes, thank you,' says Will.

He glances at his wrist and looks in shock at the time, as if he hasn't been checking it every few minutes since we got here.

'The football's just kicked off,' he says, turning to my dad. 'Do you fancy going to the Swan round the corner to watch it?'

'Football? On a Tuesday?' I say, exasperated.

'Champions League,' says Will without missing a beat. 'Real Madrid vs Man City.'

So that's why he's been checking his watch all night. Not because he wanted to get away from my mother, but because he didn't want to miss the game. Honestly, him being that anxious and jumpy about two teams that he doesn't even support is just typical. My boyfriend is so sports-obsessed that he'd watch tiddlywinks if Sky Sports broadcast it.

'Oh, I'd forgotten that was on,' says my dad.

Although he's a big Southampton fan, he's not as addicted to watching sport as Will is.

'We could go to the pub to watch it, and Lexi can take Jean back to ours for a cup of tea until we're finished.'

My mouth drops open.

'Um . . .' I stutter, as the house is definitely not tidy enough to have my mum over. I can't remember the last time I hoovered and I don't even know if I loaded last night's dinner plates into the dishwasher. 'Why can't we come to the pub too?'

I'm not a football fan, and I couldn't think of anything worse than going to the Swan to watch the game, but I feel a bit affronted that we're being farmed off like good little women to drink tea at home while the men go to the pub.

'Because you hate the Swan and you hate football. You'll be much more comfortable at home.'

Really? With my mum turning her nose up at the state of my house? But I can't say that out loud – I wouldn't want her to know how we really live in a pigsty.

'But . . .'

Will is glowering at me with a look so severe that I stop myself from saying anything else.

'Actually, Will, as kind as your offer is,' says my mother, 'I've booked tickets to the cinema for eight o'clock. That's why we're eating so early – it's not just because your dad is tight, Lexi.'

She laughs a little, and my dad even raises a smile.

'Thanks, Will. Some other time, yeah?' he says almost hopefully.

'OK,' says Will, looking crestfallen.

He obviously really wanted company to watch the game. He would usually go with his best mates Aaron and Tom, but they must be busy.

'I'll go with you,' I say, trying to plant an enthusiastic smile on my face.

He narrows his eyes as he looks at me.

'You don't have to.'

'No, I want to. You clearly really want to go and see it.'

'That settles it, then,' says my mother. 'Alan, get the bill, will you?'

My boyfriend smiles, and I see the anxiety fade away. All he wanted was someone to watch football with him. This way at least we can go and have a nice glass of wine together and shake off the dinner with my mother. It's not like I have to watch the football anyway as I've got my trusty Kindle in my bag – one of the many tools I have in my arsenal as a sporting widow. I'm always prepared for being on the sidelines of some sort of sporting activity.

AVAILABLE NOW IN EBOOK AND PAPERBACK